BY C. L. PARKER

Million Dollar Duet
A Million Dirty Secrets
A Million Guilty Pleasures

Monkey Business Trio
Playing Dirty
Getting Rough
Coming Clean

COMING CLEAN

COMING
Clean

Monkey Business Trio

C. L. PARKER

Bantam Books
New York

A Bantam Books Trade Paperback Original

Published in the United States by Bantam Books, an imprint of Random House, a division of Penguin Random House LLC, New York.

BANTAM BOOKS and the HOUSE colophon are registered trademarks of Penguin Random House LLC.

Library of Congress Cataloging-in-Publication Data

Names: Parker, C. L., author.
Title: Coming clean: monkey business trio / C. L. Parker.
Description: New York: Bantam Books, [2016] | Series: Monkey business; 3
Identifiers: LCCN 2016016458 (print) | LCCN 2016021603 (ebook) | ISBN 9781101882986 (paperback) | ISBN 9781101882993 (ebook)
Subjects: LCSH: Man-woman relationships—Fiction. | Competition (Psychology)—Fiction. | BISAC: FICTION / Romance / Contemporary. | FICTION / Contemporary Women. | GSAFD: Erotic fiction. | Love stories.
Classification: LCC PS3616.A74424 C66 2016 (print) | LCC PS3616.A74424 (ebook) | DDC 813/.6—dc23
LC record available at https://lccn.loc.gov/2016016458

Printed in the United States of America on acid-free paper

randomhousebooks.com

2 4 6 8 9 7 5 3 1

This book is dedicated to a mighty man who made me see that the importance of winning is so I'm never beaten again. You are my soulmate, my peace of mind, my Kansas, my home. I love you.

NOTE TO THE READER

Obviously, I took a lot of creative liberty in respect to the therapy, in general, that our characters undergo during this installment of the Monkey Business Trio to serve the purpose intended, which was to give Shaw and Cassidy the kind of finale that best suited their love story. I'm asking you to see it for how it is meant to be: fun . . . and maybe a little sexier than what the real thing might be.

COMING CLEAN

PROLOGUE

Shaw

"Okay, now. I need you to roll over and get on your hands and knees for me."

Cassidy's eyes popped wide. "On my hands and knees? But why?"

"Because it'll give me a better angle to work with," said the British gentleman that Cassidy had insisted we use. Though I was seriously considering how much of a gentleman he truly was at this point.

I could do nothing but watch as Cassidy complied with the soft-spoken command, her movements awkward as she shifted around in the small bed, much like a turtle on its back. When she finally assumed the position, the sheet slipped off her hips, falling to barely dangle from her delicate ankles and exposing her ass for all to see. For the first time in my life, I couldn't get hard at the sight of a naked woman's backside, even though it was attached to the woman I loved.

"Cassidy, I want you to listen very carefully. What I'm about to do might be a bit uncomfortable, but I need you to try to relax as much as possible." The deep timbre of the male's dreamy accent—

dreamy, per my girl—pulled me out of my trance, and I had to stop myself from launching across the bed and knocking the bloke away from her. Especially when he slipped his large hand between her legs and started doing God knows what to her vagina.

My vagina.

I heard Cassidy's slight intake of breath, followed by a string of mumbled curses, and my stomach heaved in protest. The lousy cup of stale coffee I had earlier threatened to make a reappearance on the linoleum and my knees started to give. Before I could kiss the floor, a none-too-gentle shove had me seated in a nearby chair with my head between my legs.

"Is everything okay?" Cassidy's voice came from far away, sounding as weak as I felt.

A cool cloth made its way around my neck and the nausea eased somewhat so I could respond. "I'm fine, sweetness."

"Not you, Shaw. The baby. What's going on?"

"There, I've got a pulse," Dr. Edwards, a.k.a. Dr. McDreamy, said. "Not a bloody good one either. Get the lot of them in here. Now."

I lifted my head as the door opened and what seemed like a swarm of people scurried into the room like ants at a free-for-all buffet. Controlled chaos reigned over the room as IV bags were hung and nurses scuttled around, grabbing supplies and placing them on the bed. Someone wearing blue colored scrubs and a surgical mask around her neck stood at the head, pushing medicine into Cassidy's IV. Words like *emergency C-section* and *prolapsed cord* were singled out of the verbal montage coming from different people in the room. I couldn't tell who was saying what.

All the while, Dr. McDreamy still had his arm up my woman's no-no zone and hadn't even broken out in a sweat. Maybe that was because I was sweating enough for the both of us.

My eyes darted to the fetal monitor beside the bed. The volume had been turned all the way down, though the heart icon continued to flicker. I had no idea what the flashing numbers meant, but the hurried movements of the staff had panic rising up with the force of a tsunami.

I had never felt so fucking helpless in my life. The room seemed to shrink and my vision blurred around the edges until I couldn't catch my breath. I struggled to hold on to my resolve with each passing second. Shit wasn't going right, and there was absolutely nothing I could do about it except be there for her. *With* her.

"Shaw . . . Oh no! Shaw, something's wrong!" Cassidy's voice acted as my lifeline and pulled me back into the moment. I turned to see the woman who had become my reason for breathing looking panicked and afraid as she was rolled off of her knees and onto her back once again. And that scared the shit out of me. Nothing frightened Cassidy Whalen. She was fierce, a force to be reckoned with, unshakeable. But the tears swimming in her green eyes confirmed just how fragile she was and how I needed to man up.

Working the boulder-sized knot down my throat, I feigned a confidence I in no way possessed and pushed between two nurses, ignoring the one giving me the evil eye as I did so. Being careful not to show my own worry, I gave the mother of my soon-to-be-born child's hand a reassuring squeeze. "Everything's going to be okay, sweetness. I promise. I love you."

"I love you, too," she said, and then a tear slipped down her cheek.

Fuck. I'd just made a promise I knew I couldn't keep, seeing as I really had no control over the situation. If anything happened to our child, if anything happened to Cassidy . . . I just couldn't go there. But someone in this room had better damn well make sure I wouldn't have to.

"We need to move, people. The baby is in distress."

"We're going to OR C. Call NICU for standby."

"I'm only thirty-eight weeks. It's too early. Can't you stop it? You were supposed to stop it." Cassidy was frantic, begging for answers from anyone who would give them.

"Shh, sweetie, you need to calm down," one of the nurses with a gentle voice said as she patted Cassidy's arm. "Yes, it's early, but luckily, not too early. Your baby should be fine. You've got the best of the best working for you, but we need to take the little one now."

"Should be? Should be fine?" I repeated, hung up on those two little words. *Should be* was not a guarantee, it was an opinion. It might be worth noting to this particular nurse, however caring she might be, that this child's mother and father preferred fact to opinion. I'd just been unscrambling the words in my jumbled-up brain to do so, but I was too late. The "best of the best" were on the move.

"Shaw, don't leave me." Cassidy's hand slipped from mine as I was jostled to the side as if I were of no importance to the woman carrying the baby they were trying so hard to save. But how do you get mad about something like that when it's your baby?

The hospital staff pulled the bed away from the wall, yanked the cord from the monitor, and proceeded out the door. I went to follow but an iron grip wrapped around my wrist and held me back.

"I need to go with her." I growled the words and tried to yank out of Nurse Evil Eye's hold.

"And you will," she promised. A scowl was etched in her face, accentuating her features into one long line of disapproval. She slapped a plastic-covered package to my chest. "As soon as you put this on. I'll be waiting just outside the door to escort you when you're ready."

"Okay." I ran my fingers through my hair, not really sure where to start, but knowing I needed to get my ass in gear.

"Unless you want to miss the birth of your child, I suggest you get a move on," Nurse Evil Eye said, reading my mind. Or maybe she'd just done this a gazillion times during her career and had already known what to expect.

"Right." Dropping the package at my feet, my fingers went straight to the button of my jeans.

"No, no, no," my escort said, stopping me. "They go over your clothes, genius. Hurry up." And that was all she said before she turned and made a speedy exit, shutting me in the room that had been bustling with activity only moments before and leaving me all alone.

Alone. I definitely felt the weight of that word, but I didn't have to because I wasn't the only one likely freaking out about all of this. Though she was no doubt surrounded by too many people, Cassidy was the one who was alone. The medical staff—adept as they may be—were strangers. Not the father of her soon-to-be-born child. And that wasn't okay with me.

Holy shit, I was about to be a father. I'd had thirty-eight weeks to prepare for this moment—actually, twenty-eight weeks, considering Cassidy had been eight weeks along when she'd first found out but had waited another two weeks before telling me—and I was suddenly aware of how unprepared I really was. From the moment I'd heard those two little words, "I'm pregnant," I'd gone through a whole lifetime of emotions. *My* lifetime.

I'd had the shittiest parents in the world. They couldn't even be called parents, as far as I was concerned. Born the only child to a swindler father who was never around and an alcoholic mother who wished she wasn't, I'd been left to fend for myself on the brutally hard streets of Detroit. I'd seen nightmares happen before my very eyes, survived by any means necessary, and my seed donors never knew or even cared to know how I'd done it. I was a burden, plain and simple, just an extra mouth that they never fed, but the government funding sure was a nice bit of icing on their dysfunctional cake.

I was going to be different. I was going to make my child, gender as yet unknown, the center of my world. Everything I did from here on out would be all about making a better life for him or her. Fuck my hang-ups over my own parents. Fuck the flip-flopping among being terrified, anxious, happy, and then terrified again. Failure had never been an option for me, and it sure as shit wouldn't ever be now.

Besides, I had the most determined partner in life that I'd ever known. Cassidy Whalen.

We'd started out as adversaries, and not one single person I'd ever encountered in my life had been able to give me a run for my money quite the same way Cassidy had. Not even close. We'd gone toe-to-toe for a partnership at the same sports agency where we'd worked, Cassidy winning, though I'd ended up with the title when she'd turned it down. And what had started out as an underhanded evasive maneuver to throw her off her game and into my bed had only managed to catapult her into my heart instead.

The impossible had been made possible by her doing. She'd tamed me.

I loved her. Really fucking loved her. And I'd never thought the emotion was possible for a man like me, who'd done a damn good job of keeping illogical shit like that at bay. If it wasn't driving the bottom line, it didn't deserve my time. Now, because of her presence in my life, I was a regular guy; a domesticated man with a little woman at home and an unofficial family, her family, in Stonington, Maine.

And our family was getting bigger. Christ, moments from now, I'd know if I had a son or a daughter. I'd be someone's daddy . . . provided he or she survived the birth process. My heart hammered hard and fast in my chest with trepidation and anticipation.

Shoving one leg after the other into the scrubs, I grabbed the rest of the blue stuff in the bag and donned it the best I could figure out. I'd just tied the cap on my head when Nurse Evil Eye popped the door open again.

"They're not going to wait on you, sunshine. Let's go." Why couldn't I have gotten the nice one?

Cassidy had a death grip on my hand and it was starting to hurt, but I refused to tell her that. Not after seeing all she had been through over the last few hours. Shortly after 3:00 A.M. this morning, she had woken up with contractions strong enough to take her breath away. Things seemed to move pretty fast after that and there wasn't time to think about how early the baby was coming, how unprepared I felt, and how scared shitless I was at the thought of being a dad. When Cassidy's water had broken in the car, I'd wished to hell I had said yes to those stupid birthing classes. I was starting to feel light-headed as my breathing picked up and matched a laboring Cassidy's erratic pace.

Now sitting on a small swiveling stool in the OR, my fingers were about as numb as the rest of me.

Cassidy tugged at my arm. "Can you see anything? What's happening?"

God, please don't ask me to peek over the blue drape. I don't think my stomach can take it.

"Aren't you, like, supposed to be knocked out or something? Why are you awake?"

Not waiting for a reply, I repeated the question to the doctor beside me, the same one who had given Cassidy medicine through her IV earlier in her room. "Why is she awake?" My leg was doing an imitation of a Mexican jumping bean under the paper scrubs I was given back in the hospital room. Juicy Couture, they were not.

I had since learned that said doctor was the anesthesiologist and would be making sure Cassidy would be comfortable during the C-section. When I came into the OR, I was directed to sit down on this tiny stool and told to stay behind the drape. Panic bubbled and fizzed inside my gut and I was suddenly unprepared for this moment. The constant beeping from machines coming from something that resembled a prop used on a *Dr. Who* episode wasn't helping. And I had yet to figure out if I should be concerned with all those squiggly lines dancing across a monitor, spiking up and down in an erratic pattern.

"She's fine, Mr. Matthews. And she has an epidural for pain relief. She should be fairly comfortable throughout the procedure."

"Fairly?" First *should be* and now *fairly*. I had the sudden urge to ask everyone present in the room for their credentials. Starting with the anesthesiologist, a.k.a. Dr. Feel Good.

"What the hell does that mean?" Cassidy asked as she tried her best to give Dr. Feel Good the stink eye. Which, admittedly, was kind of hard to do when you were strapped down to a table with your insides about to be brought out to play by the medical staff.

Ugh, that visual is so not helping you, Matthews.

"It means you might feel some tugging shortly, Mrs. Matthews, but that's totally normal."

"Ms. Whalen," Cassidy corrected her. "We're not married."

"My apologies," Dr. Feel Good said. With a curt glance in my direction, I might add. "What you shouldn't feel is pain. If you do, let me know."

At that point, Cassidy winced and I leaned in closer, kissing her cheek. Sweat coated her face and neck, her copper hair damp. She looked what she would call a hot mess. But she was my hot mess, and she was about to give birth to my child.

She had never looked more beautiful.

"You okay?" I didn't like the way Cassidy's color seemed to have drained from her face.

"Yes . . . it's just . . . a lot of pressure." She managed a weak smile.

Feeling helpless, I pushed her hair back and away from her face, stroking her scalp with the pads of my fingers. Offering her some sort of comfort in the only way I knew how. My gaze never left hers and a single thought ran through my mind with utter clarity: *This is where I belong.* I had found something essential, something invaluable, and it was mine. Ours. Cassidy and I had created a child, a tiny, living human made up of pieces of ourselves. A connection no one could take away or break. As overwhelming as that was, it also felt so fucking right.

"Get ready to meet your little bundle of joy, folks."

Forgetting how much I didn't want to see Cassidy's insides, I rose from the stool and peered over the drape.

Okay, let's just say what was on the other side was *not* pretty. In fact, I forced my eyes away from things that needed to be unseen and zeroed in on what could only be described as a tiny alien covered in blood and body fluids. I felt a little green behind the gills until I spotted what looked like an impressive package dangling between the smallest legs I have ever seen.

"Holy shit, it's a boy! Look at the size of his cock. . . ." I cleared my throat. "I mean, his penis." Damn, but the little dude took after his dad.

The surgeon quickly cut off my son's dick, and before I could blink, he passed the baby off to someone standing nearby and holding out a blanket. "Whoa, Doc. I didn't know you did the circumcision so soon. Did you have to cut off *that* much?" My poor son, minus part of his junk, was then whisked away to the corner of the room where a shit load of other people had gathered.

"Um, no. That was the umbilical cord," came the subdued reply from the doctor. "But you were right, Mr. Matthews. Congratulations, you have a son."

The most unbelievable wave of pure warmth and joy spread through every fiber of my being. A son. I had a son. The smile that bolted up my cheeks made my face instantly go numb.

I had a son. . . .

But something was wrong. You could sense it with how quiet the room grew as the staff huddled around some sort of contraption where they had placed my little man. I couldn't see anything. There were too many people. And my throat had shrunk down to the size of a grain of sand, allowing only a wheeze to escape as I stood frozen, unable to breathe.

"What's going on?" Cassidy sobbed, trying to lift her head. The anesthesiologist bent down and tried to console her. Something I should have been doing. But I knew if I turned to her—looked at her—I would lose it.

"Shaw, why isn't he crying?"

God, please let everything be all right. Please cry, little man.

I have never been a religious man. But in that moment, I prayed. Hard. I would have begged and bartered my own soul with the devil himself. Every second that passed without a sound from that corner felt like a thousand minutes. A million lifetimes.

Muddled voices giving explanations I couldn't comprehend bounced around my head. I was drowning. Again.

"Shaw . . . stay with me." The feminine, docile tone pulled at me, as I struggled to keep my head above water. Blindly, I reached out and felt Cassidy's cold fingers grasp my own. Her touch grounded me and gave me the strength I needed.

Finally, after what seemed like an eternity, the most wonderful earsplitting wail filled the operating room.

I collapsed back on the stool like a stone and let loose a long, shaky breath. "He's okay." I squeezed her hand and tried to squelch the lingering fear under my skin. "I mean, he's truly okay? Right?" I asked for confirmation from the doctor, who I couldn't see behind the drape. My palm was sweaty but I refused to let Cassidy's hand go.

"Sounds like he has a strong set of lungs, Mr. Matthews. He just needed a minute to clear out his airway and it didn't help that the umbilical cord had been wrapped around his neck. That's what was causing all the trouble in the labor room."

Really, I heard nothing past *"strong set of lungs."* All the rest was gibberish, medical mumbo jumbo that meant nothing to me. The little bugger hadn't stopped bawling and a niggling of doubt resurfaced. "All that crying is good, right? He's not in any pain, is he?"

One of the nurses—hell, it was hard to tell with all the blue scrubs, masks, and awful head covers in the place—approached the bed. In her arms was a tiny blanket-wrapped bundle. She arranged the squirming wad of cotton on Cassidy's chest. "Why don't you take a look for yourself," she murmured behind the mask.

I lost the ability to move. I had no words.

Peeking out from his warm cocoon, his pink face scrunched up in mid-cry, he was the most amazing thing I had ever seen.

When I remained frozen and didn't respond, the nurse chuckled and placed my arm behind my son in a protective hold before stepping away.

"You have your legacy, Shaw. He's beautiful." Cassidy's soft-spoken words had the effect of a battering ram, right in the solar plexus.

Shaw Matthews, a rehabilitated selfish asshole extraordinaire, had a legacy. It was hard to tell which of us he looked like in his current state, but there was no denying he had his mommy's ginger curls. A lot of them, too, which I'd been told would explain all the heartburn she'd had. And then he took a chance and slowly opened his eyes to take a glimpse at the world. Baby-blue peepers. Just like his daddy, who, incidentally, was the first sight he beheld.

"No, he's more than beautiful," I told her, falling in love with the way he blinked his eyes. "He's perfect." My voice cracked, my face hurt from smiling nonstop, and my vision may have blurred a little with unshed tears, but I was too damn happy to give a shit.

I reached out and stroked his cheek with my thumb. *Incredible*. He was soft and warm. And when he turned his head toward my touch, his tiny mouth working in a sucking motion, I was a goner.

"So?" Cassidy said around a dazzling, brilliant smile of her own. "Have you decided which name we're going with?"

We'd opted to wait until the birth of our baby to know the sex, but Cassidy had picked two names for each. Although I'd liked both of the names she'd come up with for a boy, I'd wanted to wait until I met him to decide. One look at him, and I knew.

With a nod, I said my first words to our son. "Welcome to the world, Abe. It can be a cold, cruel bitch, but we've got your back." The words felt thick on my tongue but were no less true. I would not fail my son like my parents had failed me. I would be there, for everything.

"Always." I swore.

And I fucking meant it.

"Abraham Whalen Matthews." Cassidy's voice caressed each syllable as if embracing them in that motherly tone would cement them in time. I think it did. "We're going to love you forever. You'll see."

As Cassidy leaned forward to kiss his forehead, I did the same to her. She shivered as if an invisible yet unbreakable bond among the three of us had formed with our dual action. Real or not, it didn't matter. It was there, and I was going to protect it at all costs.

This was my family.

CHAPTER 1

Cassidy

"Come on, we talked about this, little man. Mr. Binks needs to get under way so he can find the next little boy or girl who needs him. You can't be selfish." Shaw was doing his best to re-convince Abe to give up his pacifier, for the millionth time.

Abe crossed his arms over his chest, his chunky fist still holding tight to his best friend, and then he stomped his little foot in defiance. "I not a shellfish, Daddy. I da baby."

"No, you're not. You're a big boy now."

While it was true that Abe had been knocking down milestone after milestone—giving up the bottle, walking, and getting the potty training down with ease and in record time—like he'd been born to conquer, he was only three. And he was still a baby. He was *my* baby. My gorgeous baby.

Though Abe was only a toddler, it was clear to see he'd be a heartbreaker when he got older. The child was Shaw's mini-me, with his father's bone structure, crystal blue eyes, and long lashes that brushed his cherub cheeks. He had my pale skin and ginger hair, but those thick locks were a tousled mess atop his head . . . just like Shaw's. Abe even dressed like Shaw in blue jeans and button-down shirts—sometimes with a tie, sometimes without.

And he was being so brave to give up Mr. Binks, even if he'd had to be bribed to do so. Shaw had managed it with a promise to take him to Dixon Lake, a beautiful park just outside San Diego that Abe had really grown to love. And in addition to that, Mr. Binks was captaining one of the many toy sailboats Casey and Mia—my best friend and his wife—had gotten him for his third birthday. Mr. Binks was to set out on a voyage to find his next grand adventure. But Abe was having second thoughts about that.

Right on cue, Shaw looked down at his wrist . . . and the watch my father had given to him as a gift when Abe was born. It had been a family heirloom, one passed down through the Whalen generations when each male had become a father. Since I'd been Duff Whalen's only child, a daughter, Shaw was the lucky inheritor. Originally a pewter pocket watch that showcased its inner workings in the center of a Celtic knot in the twelve o'clock position, it had since been altered to be worn on the wrist and had seen a fair turnover of leather bands. Engraved on the back was a reminder to all the Whalen men, a note that read: *Time makes men of men who make time.*

I gave an annoyed sigh that I didn't bother trying to hide. Knowing the glimpse at his favorite trinket meant the father of my son was about to cut things very short—again—agitated me to no end. Shaw noticed. He knew I hated that watch. Not so much the watch but his obsession with it. An obsession that might have been okay if it had centered on the sentimentality that should've been attached to it, but that wasn't at all what it was about. No, Shaw's obsession was with his schedule and how late he was running. Always.

Business was good for Shaw, though hectic. Since becoming a partner at Striker Sports Entertainment, the partnership we'd gone head-to-head to win, he'd been slammed with not only the corporate part of the business but also his own clients. Clients he'd refused to give up. Superstar clients who demanded a lot of attention.

I knew exactly what that was like. Or at least I used to.

Was I jealous? You bet your sweet ass I was. For several reasons. Several good reasons. For one, I'd technically won that partnership but had defaulted it to Shaw when a family emergency back home in Stonington, Maine, had left me with no choice. For two, though it would have been acceptable for a partner and an agent to date, I'd become pregnant and my duty was to stay at home to raise our child. Not because Shaw had insisted, but because I had.

Antifeminist as it might have seemed, I was the daughter of an Irishman from a small fishing village in Maine; it was in my blood to put family first, to be a mother first, to put my son's care before my own career. No matter how hard I'd worked to become successful as a sports agent—and that had been pretty darn hard, considering it was a male-dominated industry—Abe was so much more important. And considering an agent's grueling schedule— cue another glance from Shaw to his watch—would have me away from home more often than not, Abe would practically be raised by a total stranger. I wasn't okay with that. Honestly, though he'd never voiced it, I knew Shaw wasn't either. His very effed-up absentee parents had really done a number on him, and he was hellbent on making sure Abe would never have to suffer the same fate.

So Shaw got to live the glorious life of a sports agent, yukking it up with the rich and famous while furthering his career, and I was living the glorious life of a mother. An unwed mother. That's right, Shaw had yet to marry me. He hadn't even proposed and had zero intention of doing so. Which was another side effect of the number his effed-up absentee parents had done on him. Shaw didn't believe in the institution of marriage, citing it was nothing more than a piece of paper, a legal document that had no bearing on how he felt about me. I was of the mind-set that if it was nothing more than a piece of paper, one that didn't determine whether we would be together or not, what was the big deal about having it?

Of course, I'd never pushed the issue. Traditional as I might have been, my living together with Shaw as a family unit without having said the "I do's" had become commonplace over the last decade or so. I was still a "wifey," I just wasn't wearing a ring to prove it.

I squatted down to Abe's level, a feat made easy by the soccer mom outfit I'd donned this morning. I'd gone from pencil skirts, high heels, jackets, Wayfarer glasses, and my hair in a no-nonsense bun to khaki shorts, deck shoes, contacts, polo shirts, and a ponytail. And I even had the hybrid SUV with smashed Cheerios in the seats, tiny arms and legs from broken superhero dolls in the floorboards, and the Kidz Bop station queued up on the satellite radio. Hey, it was better than listening to a grown man dressed in a giant purple dinosaur costume singing a love song to my three-year-old . . . because that was just plain creepy.

"Abey Baby," I started, using my pet name for him, "Daddy doesn't have a very long lunch break, so the sooner we bid a bon voyage to Mr. Binks, the sooner you can play with Daddy. Yeah?"

Abe tilted his head to the side, the breeze blowing a wavy lock over an eye. He was past due for a haircut, but that was Daddy's duty. One he'd kept putting off because of his many meetings.

"What's a bon voy-osh, Mommy?"

"It's something people say to someone going on a trip. It means goodbye and safe travels."

Looking down at the silicone and plastic pacifier in his hand, Abe ran a thumb over the smooth grooves etched into the blue shell. "Mr. Binks is going bye-bye? When will he be back?"

My heart broke for him. The sting of tears prickled the tip of my nose and made my eyes water. Much the same way as Abe's did now. Not until Abe had I ever known how much a child's pain hurt a mother. I was so close to calling off the whole thing and telling him he could keep Mr. Binks forever.

Shaw must have sensed my wavering because he chose that moment to step in, also squatting down to our baby boy's level. "He's not coming back, little man."

Abe sniffled. "Never?" he pressed, hoping for a different answer.

Shaw and I both shook our heads.

Taking his hand, I changed the tone of my voice, hoping like crazy that the cheerfulness might help my son over the hump of letting go of something that had become a source of security for him. "Hey, do you remember what you packed in your bag?"

Abe's eyebrows furrowed in contemplation and then shot up to his hairline the moment he remembered. His eyes were wide with excitement, a smile finally lighting up his face. God, he was such a little heartbreaker.

"Let's put Mr. Binks at the helm, and then you can show Daddy. Okay?"

The vigorous nod of his head and the slight bounce of his toes said so much more than words ever could. Without hesitation, he handed off Mr. Binks to Shaw, and then watched studiously as his father secured the pacifier in place behind the helm. Taking Abe's other hand, Shaw stood and we walked Abe and the boat over to the water's edge.

"Is there anything you'd like to say, little man?"

The breeze off the lake ruffled Abe's wayward hair and he was still bouncing up and down with excitement. "Put him in, Daddy! Put him in! I gots some'sing in my bag!"

Shaw chuckled when the ants in Abe's pants seemed to be getting the better of him before we'd even finished. His smile still devastated me to this day. Though stress had added years to his features, they'd been distinguished years. His dark brown hair had started to gray a bit at the temples and the laugh lines at the corners of his crystal blue eyes had become more pronounced. He'd also been wearing a stubble on his strong jaw that made me weak in the knees. I'd never get tired of looking at him, though I sure wished I could touch him more.

With a ceremonious salute, Shaw steadied the toy boat atop the water and then said, "Fare thee well, Mr. Binks. May you have calm waters and smooth sailing. Because trust me, drowning sucks."

And Shaw knew that all too well, having fallen overboard while helping my da during hurricane weather. He'd nearly died. Would have, if it hadn't been for Casey diving into the churning, dark ocean to pull him out. The near-death experience had changed Shaw somehow, making him a more caring, less selfish man. For a split second, I entertained the thought of pushing him into the lake to see if it might jog his memory a bit, but that would be cruel. And illegal. And damaging to Abe's mental well-being.

"Bye-bye, Mr. Binks!" Abe gave a quick wave to his friend and then took off.

Shaw gave me a shrug. "Well, guess he's not much for long goodbyes."

Abe ran over to his bag, unzipping it to pull out his most prized possession. When he came back, he was wearing his Superman cape around his neck. Stopping to stand in that classic superhero pose with his fists at his hips and the cape flapping in the wind, he looked up at Shaw and said, "I ready, Daddy!" Then he raised his hands into the air, waiting for his father to pick him up.

Again, Shaw looked at his watch, rubbing his chin with his other hand. "Uh, I don't have time to play Superman right now, son. I have to get to a meeting."

"Another meeting?" I asked, exasperated with him. "Shaw, you promised Abe you'd take him to the park if he agreed to give up Mr. Binks. He kept up his end of the deal."

"So did I." He threw out his arms, turning to gesture toward our surroundings. "We're at the park, aren't we?"

Closing my eyes, I reined in my anger. "Don't do this to him. Please?" Opening them again, I tried with all my might not to break into a fit of tears. The same way Abe had just started to. "He packed his backpack all by himself. He even put the last of his chocolate chip cookies into a Baggie for you." They were broken into pieces, but bless him, he'd done the best he could, adamant to do it all on his own. He'd even helped me bake the cookies from Abby's—the "adopted" mother Shaw shared with my ex, Casey—recipe because they were Shaw's favorite.

Guilt sat heavy on Shaw's features when he looked down at our son. Good. He should feel guilty. Reaching down to scoop up his legacy, he kissed the tip of his nose and said, "Sorry, man. Sometimes Daddy's job really sucks. But I've got time to help you leap at least one tall building in a single bound. What do ya say?"

The smile that spread across Abe's face as he gave another one of his excited nods was infectious.

"Yeah? Well then," Shaw said, splaying his hand across Abe's chest so that his fingertips and thumb cupped him under the arms while placing his other hand at Abe's waist so that his little body was horizontal to the ground. Lifting him over his head, Shaw yelled, "Up, up, and away!"

Abe giggled as Shaw flew him through the air, his tiny fingers wrapped around Shaw's large hand on his chest. I used to be so apprehensive when Shaw first started doing this, afraid he'd accidentally drop him, but I knew he loved Abe more than life itself, and he'd never let anything happen to his baby boy.

"Look up in the sky," Shaw started, and then Abe and I joined him for the "It's a bird! It's a plane! No, it's Super Abe!"

Abe let go of his father's hands then, making one arm straight with a fist at the end and putting the other at his hip. Just like his favorite superhero. His cape fluttered in the breeze with each swooshing sound effect his daddy made, dipping him low and then high again until Shaw finally set him upright on his feet and back onto the ground.

"Again! Again!" Abe squealed, bouncing up on his tiptoes and reaching for Shaw.

"No, no, little man. That's enough for right now. Daddy's gotta go."

Abe's bottom lip poked out into a pout and the fat tears started to well in his eyes. "No, Daddy! Don't weave. Have a pic-a-nic with me and Mommy," he said, wrapping his hand around Shaw's finger and trying with all his might to pull his father toward his bag under the tree.

To Abe, Shaw was larger than life. He adored his father,

wanted to be just like him in every way. I often thought he loved Shaw more than he loved me, but maybe that was because he was with me all day, every day, and he knew his time with his father was nothing short of . . . limited.

"Abe, stop. I can't. I'm sorry, but I *have* to go." Shaw bent over and picked up Abe again. "How about if I fly you to the car?"

Abe still cried, even as he nodded in agreement. As Shaw headed toward the parking lot where his company car sat reflecting the sun's glare off its sleek black paint, flawless wax, and chrome wheels, I grabbed Abe's backpack and followed behind. He stopped at my dull brown hybrid, which was seriously in need of a bath, and waited for me to unlock the doors.

"What's the attitude about?" he asked when I wouldn't look at him.

"I don't have an attitude, Shaw. I just can't understand why you'd schedule a meeting that would interfere with a promise you made to our son, but I'm not really surprised."

"Seriously? I'm out here busting my ass for us, and you're pissed?"

I could've predicted his response. The fact that he was the breadwinner in our family was something he threw in my face every time I got my panties in a wad over his broken promises. It wasn't like I didn't have my own savings. "Nope. Worse. I'm disappointed, but then I always am lately, so maybe it's my problem, not yours."

"Cass, don't start. I'm so close to signing Ingram, and I'm still drowning in Denver's newest endorsement contracts, not to mention headhunter recommendations for the agent opening—"

Before he could go any further on his tangent, one filled with all the excuses I'd heard a thousand times, I cut him off. "Don't forget we have that appointment at four o'clock this afternoon," I reminded him. "Might want to set an alarm on that watch so you're not late for that either."

I knew the watch didn't have the capability of setting an alarm, but it was a pop shot I couldn't resist getting in.

Shaw's shoulders slumped with a roll of his eyes and an annoyed sigh. "Do we really have to go through with that?"

Hoisting Abe's bag of essential toys, snacks, and a change of clothes onto my shoulder, I arched a brow at him and that was enough to make him concede the unspoken argument. Actually, it had just been spoken so many times that he was likely as exhausted by it as I was, but there'd be no budging on this subject, and he knew it.

"Fine," he huffed. "But I still think it's a giant waste of time . . . and money."

Giant waste of time? His precious, *precious* time. As I lifted a crying Abe from his arms and situated him on the hip opposite his bag, I huffed right back at my baby daddy. "Shaw, we need this."

"Respectfully, I disagree, but I don't have time to have this conversation again. I'm already going to be late." He kissed me so fast it was over before I'd realized he'd even leaned in. "Love you," he said. "You, too, little man. Promise, I'll make it up to you." With a kiss to Abe's forehead and a ruffle of his hair, Shaw was gone.

As I watched him walk away, he pulled his ringing cellphone out of his pocket, giving a boisterous greeting to whoever was on the other end with a hardy laugh. Staring after him, I said, "Yet another promise you'll break." But he hadn't heard me. Shaw heard very little I ever had to say, and he listened even less.

My frustration got the better of me and I resorted to a very childish side of myself, flipping him the bird.

Abe sniffled, his voice thick with tears when he said, "What's that mean, Mommy?"

Crap! "Oh, nothing, sweetie. It's just sign language. And you are to never do it." Dropping the subject, and hoping it wouldn't come back to bite me in the ass, I did my mommy duty and put a very disgruntled little boy into the SUV. Abe's tears were back in full force, and he kicked and screamed, making it incredibly difficult for me to fasten him into his car seat with any kind of ease. But I'd become practiced at working around his mini-tantrums since he'd hit the dreaded terrible twos.

"I wanna play with Daddy!" Abe wailed over and over again, his face flaming red with big, fat tears streaming down his cheeks.

"I know, baby. Daddy wants to play with you, too, but he has to work." I was so sick and tired of making excuses for his father. It was one thing when Abe was smaller, quite another now that he understood his emotions a little better.

Snapping the last buckle of his car seat into place and making sure he was snug as a bug in a rug, I kissed him on the forehead, wishing for all the world that I could take away his disappointment and sadness. I knew the feeling, but as an adult, I could process those emotions better.

"Daddy promised! Daddy promised, 'n' I want Mr. Binks!" He stretched his hand toward the lake, but Mr. Binks was already out of sight.

There was nothing I could do to quell this episode, so I decided to ride it out. My baby boy was perfectly within his right to be upset, after all. "I'm going to kill Daddy," I mumbled under my breath through clenched teeth as I closed his door. Getting into the driver's seat, I shut mine as well. As I clicked my own seatbelt into place, Abe continued his tantrum, and a very nasty headache started to develop at the front lobe of my brain. My nerves were absolutely shot.

After starting the motor, I took a moment to gather myself, flipping down the visor and finding the reflection of a woman I didn't know staring back at me in the mirror. God, I looked exactly like I felt. Exhausted. Where Shaw had gotten better-looking over the time we'd been together, I'd become haggard. Not wanting to dwell on all the ways my outward appearance had changed over the last four years, I flipped the thing shut and put the vehicle into gear.

"Let's go have a playdate with Uncle Quinn, Abey Baby. Huh? Doesn't that sound like fun?" I looked up at him through the rearview mirror as I pulled away from the curb.

Abe's crying quieted, though he still sniffled. "And Uncle Denver?"

"Maybe," I answered him, not wanting to make promises I might not be able to keep.

He loved his uncle Denver, and Uncle Denver was a master at getting Abe to take a nap. Judging by the heavy droop of his eyelids, I'd say he was due for one. And I was due for some adult time. I loved every second of every day that I got to have with Abe, but that didn't mean I didn't need a break from time to time. Lord knows Shaw wasn't going to be the one to give it to me, so I had to get it where I could for my own sanity.

Yet another valid reason for Shaw to make sure he showed up for our appointment this afternoon. If he didn't, I wasn't sure there'd be much hope for our future.

Shaw

"Is he here yet?" I asked Ben the second I stepped into my office suite. He'd know whom I was talking about.

Ben was already on his feet, taking my jacket and handing me the most important messages that had come in while I'd been at the park with my family. "Yep! He's waiting for you in your office. I didn't think you'd mind."

I might have, if I hadn't already been running late myself, thanks to the hour drive from Lake Dixon. My next meeting deserved the respect of punctuality, but I didn't want to come off as being too eager, nor did I want him to turn diva on me before he'd actually made the big time, so it worked out just as well. I'd seen plenty of good kids turned into spoiled brats with an obnoxious sense of entitlement to last a lifetime, and I didn't want that for my latest conquest. I wasn't sure what it was about him, but I had a feeling he would be my greatest contribution to the industry yet.

Marcel Ingram was a Kentucky native who'd made big plays for Alabama as a running back, rushing for a school record of 291 yards as a redshirt freshman. And he just kept racking up the records after that, holding fifteen by the end of his senior year, as well as the Heisman Trophy. He could've gone pro much earlier, but he'd kept his cool and hadn't let the fame and endless ego boosting go to his head. He'd stayed in school to earn his degree . . . and the respect of every lover of the game—coaches, players, and fans alike. Clever kid. As such, it was a gimme that he'd be drafted in the number one slot on Draft Day. That number one slot would earn him a payout of somewhere around twenty-two million dollars, including a hefty signing bonus and a guaranteed four-year contract with a team option for a fifth season.

Three percent of twenty-two million dollars was great money and all for an agent, but not the thing that drew me to him the most. Although it was against the rules for agents to even speak to a player before the end of his last college game, they were notorious for doing so, to not risk losing that player to another rule-breaking agent. Young rookies were dazzled by the gifts and promises a smooth-talking agent could give, whether they could follow through on them or not, and often fell for them, signing representation agreements pre-dated and then stored in a safety deposit box until they could legally be revealed.

But not Marcel Ingram.

Marcel had refused to speak to an agent until after his last bowl game, and even then, he simply entertained the suckasses. I know because I was there. Only, I hadn't stood in line behind a single one of them, and I hadn't fought my way through the horde to get to Marcel. Alabama's head coach—a very good friend of mine—had given me a personal escort into the locker room and had taken me straight to Marcel without my even having to utter a word. That is, until I found myself standing in front of the golden boy himself. But I didn't fawn all over him and I hadn't been starstruck. Why should I be? I was Shaw Matthews, after all.

Marcel's eyes had been big as saucers when I'd stood before him. He'd even stopped talking right in the middle of an interview with a major sports television station, the reporter all but disappearing when he'd caught sight of me.

"Good game," I'd said, offering my handshake.

Marcel had taken my handshake with a "Thank you, Mr. Matthews." Because yeah, my reputation had preceded me, and no introduction was necessary.

And then I'd handed him my business card before turning and walking away, leaving the swarm of reporters buzzing with speculation for Marcel to deal with. "Marcel! Marcel! Will Shaw Matthews be your representation?" I'd heard at least half a dozen different voices ask him. I hadn't stuck around to hear his response. They'd all know soon enough anyway. As would I.

See, most athletes choose an agent because they have family members in the industry who use that agent, or the agent represents players from the same school they attended, or, most likely, the agent has a close relationship with the coach the rookie knows and trusts. But sometimes . . . sometimes an athlete makes up his own mind about what is important to him.

Marcel, as it had turned out, was one of those athletes.

I'd gone about my business after our first meeting and waited for him to make the next move. I'd really had no idea if he'd call. Truthfully, he could take his pick of which agent he wanted to go with, or he could follow the Elam model and choose none at all. It would be one way to pocket as much cash as possible, and I certainly wouldn't blame him. Though it would be stupid. The money for his contract was guaranteed, but the added perks were not. He needed someone to weed through all the legal bullshit, someone to negotiate extras like his signing-bonus payment terms and off-season injury protection, to name a couple. Most important, he needed a confidant he could trust, someone who knew the ins and outs of our world and how to work them.

He needed me.

It had taken Marcel a few days, but he did contact me. The first call had been all about the introduction—where he'd been in his career and where he wanted to go. The second call had been the generic questions about fees, services, financial and injury strategies, and how I planned to divide my time with all the other clients I represented. I had a damn good answer for that one. In the three years since I'd become co-partner of Striker Sports Entertainment, I'd handed off all but my major athletes to some of the other agents. And although those major clients could be quite demanding of my time, they were all settled in their contract negotiations, so I could give Marcel my full attention.

He liked that. Or so I'd assumed, since the third call had been all about setting up a face-to-face, not at his home in Kentucky but right here in San Diego at my office with SSE. He was coming to me, and that spelled all kinds of "in the bag."

Which was exactly the reason I felt comfortable enough to make him wait in there right now. Not that I had anywhere else to be at the moment.

Leaning back against Ben's desk, I checked my watch—shit, I didn't have much time—and then crossed my legs at the ankles and my arms over my chest. I was already fifteen minutes late for this meeting. Another five should just about do it.

My assistant perked up, his brows asking the question his mouth didn't need to, but that didn't stop him from getting verbal with it anyway. "You're making him wait?"

I shushed him, not wanting Marcel to overhear our conversation. "Have you learned nothing from me over the last five years that I've graciously kept you in my employment?"

Graciously wasn't exactly accurate. Ben had more than earned his position, though just as I couldn't let Marcel get a big head, I couldn't let Ben do the same. Without a doubt, he knew how invaluable he was to me, but that didn't mean I had to clue him in to the fact. He'd likely demand an even bigger pay raise than he'd gotten once I'd taken the partnership role, and it had been a pretty hefty one.

Taking care to lower his voice to match my volume, he said, "You want to represent him, and he obviously wants you to do the representing. So what's the point of playing head games?"

"Three percent. That's the point," I told him.

Marcel could choose any agent he wanted, and in return, any of those agents would use a sizable cut in their commission as a negotiation tactic. In the past, I would've done the same, might have even come out of my pocket for a full-service training center before the Combine. Simply put, the Combine was like a job interview, except an interview with the professional football league involved athletes showing off their physical and mental capabilities. No matter how good an athlete, he still needed to prepare. And despite the predictions that Marcel Ingram would be the first draft pick, if he looked like shit at the Combine, he'd be lucky to go in the first round at all.

Another check of my watch found that all systems were a go, so I gave Ben a wink, straightened my tie, and got my strut on toward my office.

When I cracked the door open, I found Marcel sitting in one of the chairs in front of my desk, hunched over with his elbows on his knees. He turned at the sound and straightened immediately when he saw me.

"Marcel! I apologize, but I had an urgent matter to attend," I lied, still going with my plan of not letting him know just how important this deal was to me.

And then I pulled up short, my confident swagger missing a beat when the door opened fully and I saw we had company. Sitting on my sofa was a woman with long, dark hair and Latin features. Jumping up and down with a giggle on the same sofa beside her was a little girl with similar features. Only her hair was curly.

"Vale, stop," the woman said with a tone of chastisement. The little girl did as she was told, quickly plopping down onto her bottom and ducking her head, suddenly becoming shy.

"Well, hello there, angel," I said, hoping to put her at ease. "That's not the first time that couch has been jumped on, you know, and I'm sure it won't be the last."

Closing the door behind me, I crossed the floor to greet the man who was about to make the Shaw Matthews brand even bigger. "How you doing, man?" I asked, shaking his hand.

"Good, good," he answered. "This is my wife, Camille, and our daughter, Vale." He smiled as he looked at them, a real sense of pride lighting up his features.

"Beautiful family you got there, Marcel. How'd you get that lucky?"

"I ask myself the same question every day. Still don't know the answer." He laughed. "Are you a family man, Mr. Matthews?"

"Please, just Shaw," I told him, waving off the formality. "And yes, I have a son of my own. Abe. He's three." Then I turned to Vale. "And how old are you, angel?"

She held up four fingers and said, "I'm this many."

"No, you're not, baby," Camille said while lifting Vale's thumb to open her hand wide. "You're this many. Five. Remember? You just had another birthday."

"Oh, yeah." The little girl beamed. "I'm five. I get to go to school this time."

"And I bet you're excited, too," I said, smiling along with her as she nodded. She was beyond sweet.

Though I wouldn't show it, I was surprised, caught unaware. I had no idea Marcel was married, much less a father. Cassidy would have. The woman had been unparalleled as an agent, a super-sleuth when it came to knowing everything there was to know about a potential client.

"Well, it's very nice to finally meet you, Vale. And you, too, Camille," I covered, acting as if I'd known about them all along.

Ben and I would be having a talk about his not having forewarned me of the additional presence, in addition to not having fact-checked behind me. What was I paying him for, anyway?

Taking the seat behind my desk, I got comfortable and turned my attention back to Marcel to get our meeting under way. "I've got to say I'm a little surprised that you decided to come all the way to San Diego to talk to me, Marcel. I'm sure you have agents camped out on your front lawn. Am I right?"

Marcel rubbed the back of his neck as he nodded. "Annoying as hell, too. My family and I needed the break. Camille and I have never been west of Louisville, and Vale has never seen the ocean, so we thought we'd kill two birds with one stone: a family vacation and a meet-'n'-greet with the one man *not* beating down my door and stalking me around every corner." He laughed. "I wanted to see what you're all about."

"Did you?" I asked, swiveling back and forth in my chair. "And what would you like to know about me?"

"Obviously, I have a few questions, but I suppose my first should be . . . Are you even interested in representing me?"

Like I'd said, "in the bag." But I wanted to let it play out a bit more to see where his head was.

"Well, that depends on how you'd like to be represented, Marcel." I leaned forward and propped my elbows on my desk. "I don't normally take on rookies because they're too much of a risk. You're a good player and all—"

"I'm a winner," he interrupted. "Losing is not an option. And every GM out there knows it. My game is flawless."

"Your game might be, but can you say the same about your attitude? Because I'm not hearing a whole lot of modesty right now. GMs want a team player."

"They want someone who can make the plays."

"Yes, but that involves *play*ing well with others," I corrected him. "I've yet to meet a man who can hike the ball to himself, block himself while he throws the ball to himself, and then run it all the way down the field for a touchdown."

"I've always been a team player. You can ask any one of my teammates and they won't disagree."

"I've no doubt of that," I assured him. "Still, there's the risk factor."

"What risk?"

"Nothing is guaranteed until you're actually drafted, and if you don't show up and show out at the Combine . . ." I let the rest dangle in the air.

"I can run the forty in four point two six," he said.

Impressive. Really impressive. Top-five-of-all-time impressive. But it could've been a fluke.

"That doesn't mean you will when the real test comes. You have to work hard, Marcel. You can't get too comfortable and think everything is just going to be handed to you. I've seen stars rise and fall in this business, and the landing is never pretty." One bad injury, one slip from grace, and his whole career would be over. I knew I was being hypercritical. After all, I represented a whole gang of superstar athletes, none of whom could fit into my office at the same time due to their big heads. But they'd come to me that way. This kid . . . this kid wasn't tainted. Yet. I liked Marcel and didn't want him to forget what was most important: the family sitting in my office with him today.

Shit! I looked down at my watch, noticing the time was getting really close to four o'clock. "Goddammit, I'm late," I said, adding a mental thank-you to Cassidy for making me do the Lake Dixon thing today of all days.

I gave an apologetic look to Camille when she cleared her throat, reminding me little ears were present. "Oops," I said, blushing. And then I also apologized to Marcel. "Hey, man, I'm really sorry, but I'm late for another meeting. I'd blow it off, but it's with the little missus, and she can get ten kinds of crazy when I piss . . . um, tick her off," I said, catching myself too late. "How long are you going to be in town? Can we schedule a follow-up?"

"Sure," Marcel said, standing along with Camille and Vale. "We'll be in town for a bit longer. I can give you my number."

"I already have it," I told him, revealing a card in my hand. Having his number meant I was definitely interested.

"Okay, fine," he said, thankfully, not catching the reveal. "Just give me a call when you're free. Hey, maybe we can even set up a playdate with your wife and son."

"Oh, we're not married, but I'm sure a playdate can be arranged. Sounds like fun," I said, clapping him on the shoulder as I escorted him to the door.

Once he and his family were gone, Ben came over to me. "Well, that didn't last long."

"Cassidy's going to kill me," I said. "I'm late again for that stupid appointment she insists on dragging me to."

"Ah! Couples therapy . . . what fun," he said sarcastically.

"Yeah, no kidding." Going back to my office, I gathered my things for the day. I really fucking hated the idea of someone else prying into our relationship, and I was almost one hundred percent sure these quacks always sided with the woman anyway. But Cassidy was adamant about this one, so I'd begrudgingly agreed to the damn thing.

Ben sniggered and started back toward his desk. And since he delighted a little too much in my misery, I decided to give him some work to make sure he didn't get to leave early just because I was. "Get in touch with API and get Marcel a spot in their training program. I want him in prime shape for the Combine."

"So you signed him?"

"Not officially, but it's as good as done," I answered with a smug grin. "I'm going to keep him hanging for a little bit more, though."

"As good as done? If he chooses you, you mean." Ben still hadn't learned to stop doubting me.

I clapped him on the back. "He wouldn't be here if he hadn't already chosen to sign with me, Ben." Heading toward the exit, I called over my shoulder, "Make sure you answer your phone if it rings in case I'm calling from jail to get you to bail me out."

Yes, I was going into this appointment already on the defensive. And if this asshole started running off at the mouth and putting me down because, in his opinion, I wasn't a good partner to Cassidy, I was going to put my hands on him in a very brutal way.

At exactly four o'clock, I was stuck in standstill traffic, thanks to a three-car pileup on the I-5.

"Shit!" I hit the steering wheel of my Lincoln Continental once, twice, three times before laying on the horn and yelling a string of profanities no one would pay the slightest attention to.

I'd never hear the end of it from Cassidy. Actually, I probably wouldn't hear anything at all from her, earning the silent treatment instead. I fucking hated it when she got quiet. I needed her to yell at me, to say something smart-mouthed, something I could argue with.

My cell rang then and I pushed the Bluetooth control to answer it. "Matthews," I damn near shouted.

I expected Cassidy's subdued voice to be on the other end, asking me where I was, but it wasn't her. "Ewwweee! Where you at? Where you at? Where you *at*, my man?" Denver "Rocket Man" Rockford was one giant party. It didn't matter where he was or whom he was with, he'd turn every situation into an epically good time. He was also the biggest client on my roster and the reason I held the title of partner at Striker Sports Entertainment.

"Rocket! How's it going, man?" I asked, my spirits instantly lifted. His raucous personality was infectious.

"Ah, you *know* my life is good," he said. Bragging, as usual. He had every right to. He was the highest-paid quarterback in the league, with nearly thirteen million dollars in endorsements for this year alone. Plus, he was happy and in love with one of my closest friends, Quinn. His coming-out announcement had actually increased his popularity instead of decreasing it, as he'd feared.

"Hey, I'm in town, hanging out with your boys over here at Monkey Business, wondering when your pussy ass is going to show up to throw back a few with us."

Monkey Business was the favorite hangout spot for both Cassidy and me, as well as our mutual group of friends. A pub where my best buddy, Chaz, was the bartender. And after checking the time, I was positive Landon would be posted up on a barstool next to Denver.

Fuck it. I could really use a drink. I'd already missed the scheduled appointment time with the shrink, anyway, and though I'd had Ben clear my schedule for the rest of the day, Denver was still my highest-paid client. Ergo, I could technically count this as a business meeting. So after checking the mirrors for any ticket-writing types, I gave the recently battered steering wheel before me a hard turn to the right and veered into the emergency lane to take the exit a quarter of a mile ahead.

"Line 'em up and keep a stool warm for me," I told Denver.

He gave a bellow of "Woohoo!" before disconnecting the call.

Cassidy would already be pissed, so I might as well make it worth the bitching.

CHAPTER 2

Cassidy

Shaw had missed our appointment. Again. Though I'd suspected it before, I was convinced now that he was doing it on purpose. I wanted to be mad, should've been, but I wasn't. I was hurt. Hurt because I wanted to mean more to him. I wanted us, his family, to mean more to him.

As usual, our order of importance fell behind Shaw's own agenda of furthering his career. He could use whatever excuse he wanted to for why that was, and it was usually all about how he was busting his ass for us, but I wasn't buying it. Since the day I'd met him, Shaw had been hell-bent on making a name for himself. I'd thought he'd changed after the time we'd spent in Stonington with my family, after he'd professed his love for me and told me it was him and me against the world, and even more so after Abe had been born. But actions speak louder than words, and I was reading him loud and clear.

It made me no less desperate to cling to him, no less hopeful that he'd see what was right in front of his face, no less hopeful that he'd realize that the unnecessary risks he was taking left the future of the family he claimed to love so much hanging in the balance.

To make matters worse, he hadn't come home after work. Instead, I'd gotten a phone call from Quinn, offering to come sit with Abe so I could take a time-out to hang with some adults for once. Apparently, Shaw had shown up at Monkey Business, where he was keeping a bar stool warm while I was trying to keep his dinner from getting cold.

And the butthead hadn't even bothered to call.

"Thanks, but no thanks," I'd told Quinn. "You and Denver won't be in town for long, and I know Demi and Sasha have been dying to see you. So you guys have fun."

I was used to being left home alone with Abe, except for the few occasions Uncle Chaz kept him for me. Finding a sitter was always left to me if I wanted some time for myself. Shaw, on the other hand, came and went as he pleased as if his world hadn't changed the moment *we'd* decided to bring a life into it. We might not have been married, but we were supposed to be partners, equal partners, in this whole parenting thing. It takes two to tango, you play, you pay, and all that jazz. He wasn't single, and it was high time he stopped acting like he was.

"Fun? We aren't doing anything but huddling around the tiny screen of Sasha's cellphone since she's forcing us to look at every damn picture she took on her honeymoon. If you've seen one palm tree, you've seen 'em all," he said.

I'd been so lost in my own life that I hadn't even noticed that a month had passed since Sasha and Landon's wedding. I'd been a bridesmaid, Shaw a groomsman, and Abe the ring bearer. Afterward, they'd taken an extended honeymoon to Hawaii, thanks to the insane generosity of Sasha's parents, who had more money than they knew what to do with. Of course *they* were married. It was the natural progression of a relationship, after all—something two people who were in love and planned to spend the rest of their lives together did.

"He's here alone." Quinn's hushed voice pulled me back to the here and now. "I just didn't want you to think he was creeping around on you. Three sheets to the wind, maybe, but not with so much as a wandering gaze."

It had never crossed my mind that Shaw would cheat on me. Despite all the rumors that had circulated about him before we'd gotten together, I knew he was loyal to me. Though in a sense, I supposed he had been cheating. He might not have been sharing his body with anyone else, but he sure as hell was sharing his time with everyone other than Abe and me. And when you had a family, time was the most valuable thing you had to share. So sayeth the watch on my baby daddy's wrist.

Not to mention, it was just plain disrespectful of him to not even pick up the phone to let me know what he was doing. It wasn't that I wanted him to ask my permission to do whatever he wanted, but should some emergency break out—like, say, an earthquake that caused half of California to break off and sink into the ocean, or hell, even the start of a zombie apocalypse—it would've been nice to know where to begin to look for his body— alive, mutilated, or wandering undead.

So I'd hung up with Quinn, asking him to give Sasha and Demi my love, and then snuggled into bed with Abe.

I woke with a start at the sound of Shaw finally finding his way home. Not just the sound of the door closing, but of his keys noisily finding the countertop and his shoes being kicked off across the floor and hitting the wall.

Taking care not to wake Abe, I slipped from the bed and out of his room, closing the door quietly behind me. I found Shaw stumbling into the kitchen, using the wall as a prop to keep his inebriated body upright. It wasn't until he opened the refrigerator door to grab the bottle of orange juice and began to chug it that I let my presence be known.

"Your dinner is on the second shelf," I told him, pleased that I'd startled him into a choking fit that left juice dribbling down his chin and onto his expensive silk tie.

"Jesus, Cass! You scared the shit out of me," he said, using the back of his hand to wipe his mouth. Classy.

"Did I? Funny that my presence scares you where your MIA routine is what worries me," I said in a calm, even, matter-of-fact tone. Shaw and I never yelled at each other anymore; fighting was yet another area of our life together that had lost its passion.

"I'm sorry. I got caught in traffic and was already too late for the appointment. Then Denver called to ask me to meet him at Monkey's, and I've had some things I needed to go over with him so—"

"So you decided to go get drunk," I finished for him. "Nice. Please tell me you didn't get behind the wheel of a car like that."

"I had a couple of drinks with the fellas, Cassidy. God knows I deserve to blow off a little steam every now and then. Don't start."

Oh, like I didn't have any steam to blow off? But I let it go.

"I'm not starting anything, Shaw. I'm too tired to start anything." I waved him off and then headed toward the bathroom off our bedroom.

Shaw followed. Somehow, I knew he would. Maybe because I was aware of the pattern—the same old, predictable routine we'd found ourselves in. I could practically spell it all out before the order of events happened. But because I was a creature of habit, I went along with it.

Picking up my toothbrush and toothpaste, I got busy with the brusha-brusha-brusha. Right on cue, Shaw slipped in behind me, wrapping his arms around my waist and nuzzling my neck while he pressed his hard-on to my ass. For a second, I thought about turning my toothbrush on him to get rid of the strong smell of whiskey coming from his breath—a couple of drinks, huh?—but got distracted by his next two cues. One hand reached up to cup my braless breast, tweaking the nipple through my nightshirt while his other hand snaked its way underneath and into my panties.

"Spit," he ordered. Then, "Rinse."

I did because I knew what was next. I'd never been immune to Shaw's exploration of my body, despite how much he infuriated me to no end. Well, my body had never been immune to his explorations. My mind, sadly, had become another matter.

The moment his fingertips made contact with my clit, I went Niagara Falls down south. Shaw hummed in appreciation, taking no care in roughly palming my breast while biting my shoulder and then shoving my panties down to fall at my feet.

Within seconds, his belt was undone, his cock freed, and one of my knees was lifted to the counter to open me up for him. One splayed hand positioned just so on my back forced me to lean forward, right where he wanted me.

Again, I found myself studying my own reflection in the mirror, curious as to my stoic expression when he pushed the broad tip of his cock inside me. It wasn't that I was immune to that feeling of being completely filled, I just knew what the outcome would be, and *not* because I was psychic.

With Shaw's grip on my hips, I watched as my body lunged forward and back with each of his frantic thrusts. Deep and hard, he penetrated me, working toward his endgame. Two players on the field, only one was a ball hog, stealing all the glory for himself. But I knew what he expected of me, so I gave it to him.

"Oh, Shaw . . . Oh, Shaw . . . Right there. Yes, right . . . *there*," I said, egging him on until I Kegel'ed it, squeezing his rigid shaft inside me in pulsing intervals to mock an orgasm. And then I gave a final, languid moan. That stoic expression I'd been sporting had not changed.

Following that cue, Shaw bucked harder, grunting with his forehead pressed to my shoulder and never once looking up at me in the mirror. And then he came. Lucky him.

He took but a moment to collect himself, pressing three chaste kisses to my shoulder before he pulled his cock free of my sheath and said, "Thank you, sweetness. I promise I won't be late again." An empty promise.

And just like that, our makeup sex was complete. I tried not to take it too personally that he always felt the need to shower afterward when I was the one dripping semen from my vagina, but how could I not? Yet another selfish act of Shaw—a Shawism, as I'd come to dub these frequent actions of "all Shaw, all the time."

God, I miss foreplay, I thought as I grabbed a wash towel to clean myself up. I also missed the way we were. The couples therapy had been my idea, my insistence, and Shaw had been fighting me tooth and nail on it. But something was wrong with us. How could he not see it? There was no real intimacy between us. We'd been living like roommates with a child in common, nothing more, just going through the motions like a couple of drones. I wanted to feel something again, to feel him again. The one thing I didn't want to feel was helpless.

So I made my mind up. Shaw and I were going to need to

settle this thing once and for all. Because I didn't know how much longer I could go on living this way. I had to know if his feelings for me had changed, and I knew if I wanted an answer that was genuine, I'd have to see his words, not hear them.

The next morning, I left Abe sleeping in his room to be sure I caught Shaw before he could leave for work. Usually, I never heard him in the mornings because I hadn't been spending the nights in our bedroom for quite some time. What had seemed comforting to both Abe and me when he was a baby, allowing him to fall asleep in my arms, had turned out to be a big mistake. Now that he was used to sleeping with me, it was hard to break the habit. Since Shaw and I had been less than intimate, I figured it didn't matter. But I missed snuggling into the crook of Shaw's arm and nuzzling his chest as I slept. I missed falling asleep to his steady breathing and the sound of his heartbeat, and I missed waking to his manly scent. I missed a lot of things about Shaw.

And I hated having conversations like the one I felt forced to have with him first thing in the morning. It would just make the rest of the day as crappy as crappy could be. I had no choice, though. This had to be done.

Just as I walked into our bedroom, I caught the sight of Shaw's back as he closed the bathroom door behind him. So I sat on the edge of the bed and waited for him to finish up his morning business.

The covers were still a mess, though only on one side. His side. I took comfort in the fact my pillow was out of place and at an angle to Shaw's side, squished in the middle as if he'd been snuggling it all night. I wondered if he had. If he'd held it as close as he would've liked to have held me, if he ever drew deep breaths with it to his nose to find some faint remembrance of my scent.

Drawn by that thought, I reached over and grabbed up his pillow, hugging it to my chest and doing the same. It smelled like him, and memories bombarded me. Memories of the way we used to be, of lying in bed with each other until the last possible second. Memories of Shaw resting his head on my chest while talking to our unborn child through my very round belly, his horrendous singing voice quietly crooning lullabies he didn't quite know all the words to. I smiled to myself, nearly transported back to that time and feeling the warm and fuzzies all over again.

When the toilet flushed, I quickly put his pillow back in place and collected myself. Or attempted to. My palms were too sweaty, my body too tense for any sort of confidence to be believable. Why was I so apprehensive about talking to the man I loved?

Shifting into a more comfortable position on the bed, I did my best to not let any nervousness show on my face. Jesus, this shouldn't be this hard to do. I supposed somewhere in my subconscious mind, I knew things might not go the way I was hoping.

Red flag, red flag, red flag!

And then the shower started up. *Oh, come on!* He'd just showered last night before bed. A glance at the alarm clock kicked my determination into overdrive. Shaw would be leaving soon if he had any chance of making a punctual appearance at Striker. Though actually, he was the boss now and on a salary income, so it wasn't like he was punching the time clock. I'd used that argument on many occasions, but he'd always countered it with the whole "leading by example" stance. Excuses: he always had a slew of them.

Not this morning.

Steeling my nerves, I walked into the bathroom, determined to get some things off my chest before he could shut me down.

"Shaw?" I called to him through the shower door.

"Cassidy? What are you doing up so early?" Though the design of the shower door skewed the details of his body, I could still make out that he was washing up.

"I need to talk to you, so I left Abe sleeping—"

"What?" he asked, still not pausing in his bathing routine. "I can't hear you over the shower."

Taking care not to be too loud as to wake Abe, I raised the volume of my voice a bit and tried again. "I said, I need to talk to you, so—"

"Can it wait until I get out, sweetness? I really can't hear you."

"Sure." I hadn't even tried to be heard that time. Something told me even if I'd yelled it, the word would've fallen on deaf ears. I wasn't ready to give up, though.

Back out in the bedroom, I made the most of my time by making the bed, and then I took a seat again, waiting for him to emerge from the bathroom. Once the water shut off, I knew it would be only moments before he came out. I was wrong. By the time Shaw made an appearance, his teeth were brushed, his hair was styled, his face was clean-shaven, and his cologne had been applied. But he was still naked. With the exception of the towel he wore around his waist, that is.

My body had changed markedly over the last three years. Having a baby never affected the father's physique, only the mother's. Where there used to be a flat belly, I now had a pooch with faint stretch marks marring my skin. Proof that I was a tigress who'd earned her stripes, they said. And the gravitational pull of the entire freaking universe had inevitably found what used to be perky breasts. My hips were wider, my ass a little flatter, and all my muscle tone was now solely in my arms, and only then thanks to packing Abe around so much. But Shaw?

Shaw's body hadn't changed in the least. Strong shoulders sloped into arms corded by taut muscles. His chest was toned to perfection, decorated by a smattering of curly hair in the center. The way his abs rippled seemed like a trip to the gym was part of his regular schedule, though it wasn't. And then there was that V cut to his waist. He was definitely still drool worthy. In that moment, I wished with all my might that he'd stalk over to where I sat and push me back onto the bed to have his very wicked way with me. Just like he used to do. Though that wasn't going to happen.

"What's up?" he asked as he went to his dresser and pulled out a pair of underwear.

I wanted to answer him, I really did, but my brain went all wonky when the towel dropped to the floor and his glorious ass was bared. And that wasn't the only thing that had been bared. Apparently, his wet body exposed to the cool air of the room had no effect on Shaw's other rather endowed assets. His cock and balls hung heavy amid a patch of dark hair, the size most men probably wanted to be. And he was *limp,* for goodness' sake.

"Hello? Earth to Cassidy," he said, snapping the boxer briefs in place and removing the distraction.

"Sorry," I said, closing my eyes to gather my wits about me, though all I could think about was the time in Stonington when I'd begged to suck his cock and he had denied me over and over again until he'd been ready to *feed* it to me. "Um, I need . . . I need to talk to you."

Crossing the room to his closet, he pulled out his attire for the day and began to dress. "About?"

Good question. Perhaps if I hadn't seen him nude, I would've known the answer. Just as I was about to attempt verbal communication, his cellphone rang.

"Hold on," he said, grabbing it to check the caller ID. "Shit. I have to take this. Matthews," he answered the phone without waiting for any further argument from me.

Defeated, I huffed out of the room, closing the door none too quietly behind me. Once I'd stomped my way into the kitchen, I started a pot of coffee and planted myself on one of the stools at the counter bar. I'd be the first thing Shaw would see when he came out of the room, an obstacle on his way out the door. It dawned on me that there was something wholly wrong about thinking of myself as an obstacle in the first place, but that was what I'd become.

When Shaw came out, he was completely dressed with briefcase in one hand and his cellphone still in the other, just wrapping up a conversation. "Okay, I'll be there within a few minutes."

Ending the call, he put the phone into his pocket, leaning down as he did so to give me a chaste kiss on the cheek. "Have a good day. I'll see you when I get home."

A chaste kiss. That was all I was going to get? I remembered a time when Shaw's farewells included bending me over the counter for a quickie because he couldn't stand the thought of being away from me all day. Those were the sorts of quickies I didn't mind, feverish and passionate, so unlike the one from last night.

My trip down Memory Lane nearly sidetracked me from my mission as Shaw was two steps away from disappearing for the day. I stood and rushed for the front door, throwing myself against it to block him from leaving.

Shaw pulled up short, drawing his head back in confusion. "What are you doing?"

I had to admit even I was a little shocked by my behavior. I guess desperate times call for desperate measures. "I've been waiting all morning, Shaw. Patiently. Can I have a minute, please?"

His brow furrowed, the first sign of concern I'd seen from him in what seemed like forever. And then he looked down at his watch again. "Yeah, sure," he said. "But a minute is about *all* I have. What's going on? Is Abe okay?"

"He's fine, but we need to talk."

He waved his free hand in the air for me to continue with every indication that I should make it quick. "You said that earlier. Should I guess at the topic, or would you like for me to read your mind?"

"Us," I said simply. "We need to talk about us."

Right on cue, he rolled his eyes in annoyance. "Cass, Wade apparently has some epic announcement he wants to make to the rest of the staff today, but not before discussing it with me. As I speak, he's sitting in my office, waiting for me to haul my ass in there. I'm sorry, but I can't do this right now."

"Well, I *have* to do this right now. I can't go through another second without doing it. Wade will get over it."

Shaw dropped his briefcase onto the couch, undoubtedly aggravated by my insistence. "Fine. What is it? I already apologized for yesterday, so what could I possibly have done wrong between last night and this morning?"

"Are you serious right now?" I was flabbergasted by his annoyance. "You make me feel like I can't talk to you about things that are bothering me, Shaw. Don't you see that as a problem? This is exactly why I wanted to see a counselor. Because you refuse to talk to me about our issues."

His stare was blank, though the way he looked down at that

stupid watch was a clear indication that the clock was running on how much time he'd allow me to get out what I had to say.

"I *love* you." Hearing my own voice, I wondered if people were supposed to sound so desperate when they said those three words. Like I was willing him to love me back. To say it and convince me that he meant it. "Look at me."

He did.

I needed to hold his attention without any distraction so I could see with my own eyes what I knew with my heart. And oh, God, but I hoped my heart was wrong. "Tell me."

"Really? You want to do this right now?" When I didn't answer, he closed his eyes and let his head fall back in aggravation. Then he put a hand on his hip, took a deep breath, and faced off with me again. But he looked nothing like the Shaw I once knew. The way he regarded me was like he was looking right through me. "I love you, Cass."

I shook my head, knowing in an instant that what he said wasn't true.

Shaw jumped on my reaction, quick to come to his own defense. "Yes, I do. I tell you I love you *every single day*. Multiple times a day."

I nodded because it was true. He did. "You *tell* me. But it's the way you look at me."

Another one of those exasperated sighs. "That doesn't even make any sense. What are you talking about?"

"It's not the same, Shaw."

He threw exasperated hands into the air and spun around in a circle. "Oh. My. God! How? How is it not the same?"

"Your eyes don't match the sentiment anymore. It's like you're on autopilot." I closed my eyes to gather my thoughts and find the words that would make him understand. Once I had them, I opened my eyes again. "You used to look at me like I hung the moon."

He saw me then, those piercing blue eyes conveying the potent truth of his next words. "That's because once upon a time, you did."

Finally. Truth.

There was a moment of stillness then. A moment that held the same eerie awkwardness one might feel during a ceremonial silence at a funeral. I think we both realized it at the same time. Shaw picked up his briefcase, turned his back to me, and walked away. All I could do was stare after him. So I did. I stared until the tears flooding my eyes rendered me blind and I could see him no more. Though maybe I hadn't seen him in quite a long time.

I'd like to say my heart was broken, but it wasn't. I was feeling something much more devastating than that. I felt empty and cold, like that place inside me that held the core of everything I believed in was suddenly vacant.

Vacant. That was the word. Like the room built for three, once filled to capacity with love, now only held a lonely woman clinging tightly to the hand of a small child, and there was way too much space on her other side. I wondered if that was how a war widow felt when she received the news that the love of her life had suddenly been erased from existence. I decided it wasn't. It wasn't, because those men had not chosen to be eradicated. Shaw had. He had and there was nothing I could do about it.

There was nothing left of what we once were to hold on to anymore.

Wiping the tears from my eyes, I gathered myself to do what needed to be done. There was no time for a breakdown because I had a child I needed to take care of, plans to make for our future.

So with a shaky hand, I fished my cellphone out of my purse and dialed the number that had been my lifeline for as many years as I'd been living. By the second ring, a warm, loving voice answered.

"Cassidy? Is everything okay?"

"No, Ma. Everything is not okay. I'm coming home."

CHAPTER 3

Shaw

I didn't mean it. I swear, I didn't. Cassidy's insistence that something was wrong between us, that I felt any differently about her now than I did when I'd first realized I was in love with her damn near four years ago, had finally pushed me to my limit. So I'd told her what I'd thought she wanted to hear.

I still loved her. I still thought she hung the moon. Though I was concerned that the lie had fallen so easily from my lips.

Goddammit! Why did she have to push me so much? She knew I was in a hurry, so why did we *have* to have that conversation right then and there instead of waiting until I got home from work? I was stressed the fuck out, juggling clients while being a partner at SSE and doing my absolute best to take care of my family, to be different from my own parents. I didn't sleep well at nights, my brain constantly spinning out of control with everything I had to do, who I had to please, moves I needed to forecast . . . everything. And Cassidy was just piling the bullshit on top.

No, I didn't spend much time at home, but that was because I couldn't. I was only one man; there was only so much I could do, and I'd been stretched pretty damn thin as it was. You'd think the woman who was supposed to love me would try to understand that.

I thought Cassidy and I were supposed to be partners in this whole parenting thing. It had been working well, by my assessment. She was the nurturer. I was the provider. Abe had the best of both worlds, and that was a million miles away from Planet Don't Give a Shit, where my parents had apparently hailed from.

Abe had it made. So had Cassidy. She got to be at home with Abe, for Christ's sake! If either of us had a reason to feel resentment toward the other, it was me, not her. I'd give anything to be able to spend a day playing with him. But I had to provide for my little man, make sure he'd never want for anything, that he'd get the best education money could buy and every opportunity that may come his way until he could make his own name in life. I was making sacrifices so he wouldn't have to, so Cassidy wouldn't have to. And what thanks did I get for that? Reminders that my best just wasn't good enough, and probably never would be.

This was the exact reason I never did the relationship thing in the past!

When the car in front of me moved ahead, I gave a roar of frustration and punched the gas pedal, only to have to stomp on the brake because morning traffic in San Diego was stop-and-go, at best. I might have stood a chance with it if I'd left on time, but Cassidy's need to talk had landed me smack dab in the middle of it. My day could only keep getting better from here. Yeah, right. How was I supposed to concentrate on anything else when all I could hear was the sheer desperation in my woman's voice, when all I could see in her eyes was some sort of plea for me to make things right? Jesus, I'd made her cry, broken her fucking heart.

And then I'd walked out on her. I was an ass of the highest degree.

I thought about turning around and going back to her . . . to apologize, to let her beat the shit out of me, to hold her tight and make sweet love to her the way we used to. Thought about it and then thought better of it. We both needed some time, a breather to let things cool down. Plus my business partner, Wade, was waiting for me at the office to discuss a pertinent matter, or so I assumed, considering the urgency surrounding the phone call I'd received from him earlier.

Great. Something else to pile on top of my plate.

By the time I made it to the office—late—I'd already convinced myself of half a dozen things that could be wrong. Things like Striker Sports Entertainment going bankrupt or that every client we represented was currently breaking contracts and jumping ship. Not that they'd have cause to; we treated all of our clients with the utmost respect and made sure we were available to them whenever and wherever they needed us.

I'd been overreacting, though, stressing myself out for no reason. I really needed to stop doing that before I developed an ulcer. Or worse, had a stroke.

"Sorry I'm late. Rush-hour traffic," I told Wade as I put my briefcase on the floor and took the seat behind my desk.

He was sitting legs crossed in front of me with a piping hot cup of coffee in hand. Thank God, Ben had been seeing to his needs.

My partner grimaced with a shake of his head. "Goddamn traffic. At some point, California really should try to put a cap on the amount of people they allow to relocate here from other countries—hell, even other states. It's getting more and more crowded every day. They say an earthquake is going to make the state fall off into the sea, but I say the weight of all the goddamn people living here will be the cause."

"I relocated from out of state," I reminded him. "So did Cassidy."

"Yeah, but at least you two are contributing something. Too many numbnuts out there dreaming of being *discovered* for the silver screen or *making it big* in the music industry," he said with a shake of his head.

Wade was grouchy before, but he'd gotten surlier over the last couple of years. He reminded me more and more every day of Max from *Grumpy Old Men*. His hair was more gray than black now, balding just at the crown. His skin had started to show deeper wrinkles, and age spots had popped up all over his face and hands, the appearance of which had probably been accelerated courtesy of too much time spent out under the California sun.

I chuckled at his prediction, not entirely sure how I managed it when my mood was every bit as cantankerous as his, thanks to the morning I'd had thus far. "Maybe you need a break, Wade. Take a timeout and go enjoy the tranquillity of Lake Tahoe for a while."

"Funny you should mention that," he said, shifting in his seat. "That's what I wanted to talk to you about."

Wade going on vacation was hardly a serious enough matter to warrant my rush into the office this morning. There had to be something more to it. Maybe he was going to force me to take a vacation? Or worse . . . a permanent vacation. Could he do that?

I started mentally poring through my contract while trying to think of any offenses I might have made and whether it was possible that there'd been a secret board meeting to discuss my removal.

"Matthews, are you okay?" Wade's brow was furrowed with concern. "Christ, man, you're sweating bullets over there. If you're sick and need to take some time off—"

"I'm fine," I told him. "Just not entirely sure what all of this is about. Don't leave me hanging. What's going on?"

For the first time since I'd met Wade, he slouched in his chair, looking worse for the wear. "I'm done, son. Ready to hang it up, kick back, and enjoy the rest of my life."

I was still confused. "What does that mean?"

"It means I've decided to retire. Done deal. I've been thinking about it for a long time now and don't need to think about it anymore," he said with a note of finality, one meant to shut down any argument I might try to throw his way to dissuade him. "Obviously, I wanted to tell you before I announce it to the rest of the staff this afternoon."

I was stunned silent. The retirement of SSE's co-founder, Monty Prather, was what had spurred the competition between Cassidy and me, which had landed me the partnership in the first place. But Wade? Striker was his baby. He'd been the one to bring Monty onboard before the doors had ever opened for business. I'd felt sure he'd never let it go, that he'd hold on to it with a death grip until death finally gripped him.

And then an even heavier weight circled my neck like a horseshoe around a stake to bear down on my shoulders. "Of course. Thank you for the heads-up. But I have to ask what this will mean for Striker. For me?"

"Striker is still going to be here. Don't you worry about that," he assured me. "I'm not selling, and neither is Monty. But I'm turning over the reins of the day-to-day business to you. Monty and I have discussed it, and we feel given the added stress of keeping us out of the poor house, a larger percentage of the shares would be in order."

"That's, um . . . that's a relief." At least I didn't have to worry

about being unemployed. "But it's also a whole lot of responsibility to take on by myself."

"Oh, sorry." Wade laughed. "Forgot the last part. I'm going
to see to it that you're not doing it all on your own. I know you
like to take the hands-on approach, keeping your skills sharp with
your own clients, and I respect that. Always have. Gotta lead by
example, after all."

"I'm glad you can appreciate that, Wade. So I can expect a
replacement for you, then?"

"Well, no one can replace me." He laughed, metaphorically
patting himself on the back. "But I'm not going to burden you
with trying to find someone who can come close. I know you
have your plate full enough. So before I make my grand exit—and
I *am* hoping for an elaborate retirement party," he not so subtly
hinted, "I'll make sure the most qualified candidate I can find is in
place and ready to stand by your side at the helm."

I wasn't really sure how I felt about that. Wade was more than
capable of choosing his replacement, but I would've liked to have
a say in the final decision. Still, he was right. I did have a full plate.
Dealing with headhunters and conducting interviews would only
tie up even more of my time. Time I needed to devote to Marcel
and, more important, to my family. So I supposed I should've
been grateful for the assistance. Besides, contrary to what Cassidy
had always believed about me—and had no doubt relayed to her
mentor, Wade—I *could* play well with others. I'd adjust. Period.

"One more thing," I said. "Will this person you find also be a
partner? If so, how will the share split go then?"

When I had become a partner, I wasn't an equal partner. Wade
held controlling interest with 51 percent, Monty (a silent partner)
still held 24 percent, and I had the remaining 25 percent. If Wade

and Monty planned to sell off their shares, I could be in a whole lot of trouble. So could SSE, its employees, and its clients.

He chuckled. "That's my boy. I would have been disappointed if you hadn't asked." He re-crossed his legs. "The replacement will be auditioning, so to speak, for a role as partner. We want to make sure the person we find will be a viable contribution to the future of SSE. Once you, Monty, and I are convinced the new person has proven himself, we'll make it official. The share split will be Monty and me at ten percent each, the new partner at thirty, and you with fifty. As Monty and I, inevitably, die off, our shares will go to the new partner to balance things out. Until then, you'll be making more than the rest of us." He laughed. "You've more than earned it, and Monty and I will feel safe knowing SSE is in your hands."

"Wow. That's quite an honor. I don't know what to say," I admitted.

"Just say yes, my boy."

It was a lot to take in, an even bigger responsibility. Though wasn't this exactly what I'd worked so hard for? Wasn't this the dream I'd had as a practically orphaned child with no prospect of a promising future? I'd have a real legacy, half of a more than prosperous company. Abe could follow in his father's footsteps and be proud to stand where I once stood. Generations after him could do the same. I could start a *true* legacy. Right here. Right now. I could really be worthy of a woman like Cassidy.

Smacking my hand on the desk, much like a judge's gavel at a final verdict, I answered, "Yes!" and then I sat back with a sigh of relief. A very major decision had just been made, but it was one that I felt good about.

"Excellent!" Wade said. "Monty will be so proud of his protégé's enthusiasm. You've never disappointed, Matthews. I wouldn't be able to make this leap if I didn't have the utmost confidence in you."

"Thank you for saying so, Wade. I sure am sorry to see you go, and admittedly, maybe even a little jealous of all the free time you're about to get, but I can't think of many other people who deserve it more." It was true. Wade had built SSE from the ground up, now boasting a clientele roster of the most well-known athletes in every sport imaginable. "Thank you for taking care of finding our next partner. Though I know he'll never be a match to you, I'll try not to hold it against him."

"Good man," he said, standing. "I'm sure I never did the same with you." He winked playfully before coming over to shake my hand. As he made his exit to get on with his day and leave me to mine, he stopped and looked back over his shoulder. "Oh, and *he* could very well turn out to be a *she*. You might want to be prepared for that, just in case."

I had absolutely no problem with that. I was just glad I didn't have to make the decision one way or the other.

The rest of my day had been hectic, as usual. Though I was still bothered by the exchange I'd had with Cassidy that morning, I hadn't had the time to dwell on it. Between going over my strategy concerning Marcel, handling a contract crisis for one of my top clients, reviewing contracts Ben had drawn up for a couple others, I'd had enough to stay distracted—to say the very least.

And then came the staff meeting.

Wade had made the announcement about his retirement, inviting anyone who felt qualified to submit his or her résumé for consideration. Though everyone at SSE was sad for Wade to go, the excited chatter over the prospect of having a shot at the partnership had become like white noise in the background. There was no guarantee the next partner would be someone internal, but Wade liked to keep things close to home, so it was possible. If one of our agents got it, I was going to make sure my assistant, Ben, got a promotion to fill the vacancy. I'd miss him, but I couldn't hold him back for selfish reasons.

Ally, Cassidy's old assistant, seemed less than interested in the partnership. Of course, she'd only been an agent for around three and a half years, taking over Cassidy's clients when she'd gone on a maternity leave that had turned into her resignation. I was proud of the work Ally had done. She was like a carbon copy of Cassidy in the way she approached and landed a client. The roster she'd inherited from her former boss had been free to choose another agent, but they'd all declined after private meetings with Cassidy to discuss Ally's capabilities.

After the staff meeting, I didn't dally. I didn't even make a stop off at Monkey Business. I had one goal in mind: calling a cease-fire with the woman I loved, who had felt less-than as of late, and spending some quality time with my family. I had a lot of groveling to do. Groveling that would hopefully lead to the best makeup sex we'd ever had. I'd sort of missed throwing her against the wall to bury my cock balls deep in her delectable pussy. Hell, I sort of even felt like having her juices for dessert before that.

Once we made up with the nicey-nice and were each perfectly sated, I was going to tell Cassidy the big news Wade had shared, how our lives were going to change for the better. I was going to own Striker with the majority share. God, I couldn't wait to see her look at me with pride when she realized all my hard work had finally paid off, that my absenteeism hadn't been for nothing. I finally had *something*. And it was pretty damn big.

But all of my excitement, my feeling of accomplishment, flew right out the window the moment I stepped over the threshold and into the home we shared. Cassidy was in our bedroom, zipping up a suitcase while Abe played on the floor.

Weird.

"Daddy!" Abe squealed when he saw me and then ran over to hug my leg. I really fucking loved it when he did that.

"Hey, little man! Did you have big fun today?" I sat my briefcase on the floor and bent over to kiss his forehead before straightening to discern the scene before me more closely.

"Mommy and I pwayed pack-it-or-weave-it today," he told me with an adorable smile that showed all his baby teeth.

"You did, did you? I bet that *was* big fun." I turned my attention to Cassidy then, more than concerned, but unwilling to jump to conclusions. "Was that a game or are you actually going somewhere?"

"Both." Though it was only one syllable, I could hear the disdain in her voice. Uh-oh, I was still in the doghouse.

"Really? And where might you be going?"

"Stonington." Her answer was short. Clipped.

And surprising. Shit. Had we had a conversation about this? No, I was sure we hadn't. Though if I were wrong, she was definitely going to jump all over it, once again telling me how much I don't pay attention to her when she talks. It wasn't true. Most of the time. Okay, it was true more than it should be, but this was not one of those times.

"Huh. Okay, then. I mean, a little warning would've been nice, but I think a visit to see Pop-Pop and Mimi would do my boy some good." I lifted Abe off the floor and tossed him into the air, earning a giggle in turn. After the day I'd had, I really needed it. Tucking my arm under his little tush to hold him, I kissed his forehead and then ruffled his hair. "And I'm sure Mommy could use a bit of fresh air, too."

Cassidy yanked the suitcase from the bed and onto the floor. The thing nearly pulled her arm out of the socket, clueing me in to just how heavy it was. Blowing her crimson locks out of her face with a huff, she stood and put those damn hands of hers on those damn hips. Jesus, what had I done this time?

"Fresh? Because things have gotten so stale around here, you mean."

With a sigh, I sat Abe down so his squirmy butt could get back to playing with his Superman and Batman action figures while Mommy and I had yet another strained discussion. "Stop putting words into my mouth, Cass. I was only trying to say a short vacation might do you some good. Maybe for both of us."

"My thoughts exactly. Only, it won't be a short vacation." She went over to her dresser, rifling through her jewelry box.

"Oh, okay. An extended vacation. When will you be back?" I started toward the closet to get out of my suit and put on something more comfortable.

"We're not coming back, Shaw."

Stopping in my tracks, I turned to face her, sure I hadn't heard her right. "I'm sorry, what?"

"For once, you actually did hear me. Bully for you, Matthews," she said sarcastically without looking up. Matthews was what she'd called me when we were at odds with each other.

"Is this about what I said this morning? Because I didn't mean it. I was frustrated and running late, and *shit* . . . I just said what I thought you wanted to hear."

"You thought I wanted to hear that you don't feel the same way about me as you used to?"

I rubbed my hand over my face, frustrated that nothing was coming out quite the way I wanted it to. "No. I'm sorry, okay? It was eating at me all day. I was going to call to apologize, but—"

"Something came up. Right?" she finished for me. I'd never seen her so fed up. It unnerved me to the bone. "Something always comes up, Shaw. Always. You have an excuse for not being here. You have an excuse for not showing up on time for our appointments. You have an excuse for breaking promises to our son. You have an excuse for saying hurtful things that you can't take back. You always have an excuse. And when you don't, I'm making them for you. Not anymore. I'm done with the excuses. I'm done trying to be the glue that holds all of this together without any assistance from you. I'm done being taken for granted, and I'm done with being unappreciated." Closing her jewelry box, she stuffed the little travel bag into her purse, zipping it up and hoisting it over her shoulder, and then she turned to face off with me. "I'm just plain done. Clearly, you are, too. So I'm taking Abe back home to Stonington to raise him. At least there, neither of us will be in the way of your rise to superstardom any longer. Enjoy your career. Come on, Abey Baby."

The moment Cassidy took Abe's hand and grabbed the suitcase in her other, my whole world came crashing down around me. She wasn't bluffing; she was serious. And she had my undivided attention.

"Stop," I said, blocking her way. "Where do you think you're going?"

"I already told you, Shaw. I'll call you once we've both had time to process this to discuss custody and visitation, but not right now. Move." She made to go around me, but I stepped in the way again.

"No," I said, shaking my head. I was near panic, unable to say or do much more than repeat the same word and action. "No, no, no." Not my son. Not her. I couldn't stomach either of them walking out that door. I was going to be sick. Or maybe I was about to have a heart attack because there was this unbearable pressure building in my chest, and shit all over my body was going numb and cold as if the circulation of blood had simply decided it was as done as Cassidy was.

"You can't go," I choked out.

"I have to go, Shaw. Because I can't stay. Not like this. I just can't do it anymore." She closed her eyes, her shoulders sagging. "I'm *tired*."

She did look tired. Not only tired, defeated. There was an empty sort of sadness to eyes that were once as vibrant and green as new leaves in the spring. They were puffy and red now, and the tip of her nose was tinged pink. She'd been crying. I'd done that, hadn't I? How had I missed it before?

"I'm sorry," I told her, meaning every single syllable.

She shook her head. "I wish that fixed things, but it doesn't."

"What will? Tell me. I'll do anything. Just don't leave me. *Please*." I'd never begged for anything, had never felt the need to because there wasn't anything I'd wanted bad enough.

The room went quiet except for the whooshing sounds Abe made as he flew Superman through the air. I turned to look at him, unable to fight the grin that tugged at my lips when Superman swooped down to punch Batman with a loud "Pow!" from my baby boy.

Cassidy stooped down to Abe's level, stilling his play as she gave him a forced smile with tears swimming in her eyes. "Sweetie, I want you to go play in your room for a little bit while Mommy and Daddy have a talk. Okay?"

"We're not going bye-bye, Mommy?"

"You're not going anywhere, little man. You're staying right here," I told him.

Cassidy gave me a disapproving look, then turned back to Abe. "Not just yet, baby. Be my sweet boy and go play for now."

"Okay!"

Cassidy kissed our son's forehead before he grabbed up his toys and ran off to his room. When she stood, she used the back of her hand to wipe a tear from her cheek and then faced me again.

I wanted to wrap my arms around her and thank God for the near miss of losing the woman I loved, but I knew I couldn't. Not yet. For one, the vibes were all kinds of "keep your distance" and for two, though I was relieved she hadn't left, I was also pissed that walking out on me and taking my son had been the plan.

"Cassidy, you're my everything," I told her because I meant it.

She nodded with a sniffle. "You say I'm you're everything and then treat me like I'm nothing. Actions speak louder than words. And if that saying is true, I also have to believe that your job is more important than your family."

Well, damn. "That's not true." When she just looked at me, I became more determined, taking her face in my hands and making her look at me. "It isn't. You and Abe . . . I can't. I can't lose you. You're all I have, all I ever want."

"Things haven't been right between us for quite some time now, Shaw. You know I'm right."

She was. No matter how hard I tried to remain in denial about it, to go about my day as if everything was hunky-dory, it wasn't. We'd become distant, in large part, thanks to my determination to not fail my family. But all couples went through that, didn't they? That was why there was such a thing as a honeymoon phase in the first place.

"Then tell me how to make it right, sweetness." I brushed her cheek, but she wouldn't look at me.

Instead, she pulled back, putting distance between us. Too much distance. "I shouldn't have to tell you how to make it right, Shaw. That's something that comes naturally, instinct or something."

"Naturally? For someone like me?" I wanted to touch her again, but I knew she didn't want me to, so I raked my anxious fingers through my hair instead and walked toward the window.

The glass pane was cool when I put my forearm against it and rested my forehead on it. Looking down at all the passersby from the window of our apartment on the twentieth floor, I thought about how easy it would be to wish I could trade places with any one of them in that moment. But I couldn't. I couldn't because none of them had my Cassidy or my Abe in their life. And despite the shit we were wading through right now, I'd rather be with them than with anyone else. It was entirely possible that all of this was my fault. Likely, even. Not that I knew how to fix it.

"You have to remember that I'd never been in a relationship before you," I told her. "I don't know how this shit is supposed to work. Hell, I didn't even have decent parents to give me something to go by. It's a wonder *I'm* functional at all. And that's not me making excuses again. That's a cold, hard fact of my life. Maybe I just don't know *how* to love you."

"You either love me or you don't. It's that simple."

I chuckled, though not because I was amused. "No, it isn't. I do love you. But I don't know how to fix this. I'm man enough to admit that much. So help me. Tell me what I need to do. Give me another chance, Cassidy. Please. For Abe. For us."

"Look at me." She was all business, so I did as she ordered. When I turned to face her, she tilted her head to the side and regarded me with steadfast determination. "Tell me," she said.

I crossed the room to where she stood, no longer okay with

the distance between us, literally and figuratively. Taking her hand in both of mine, I placed it flat against my chest, right over my heart. And then I looked her in the eye, seeing there the mother of my child, my greatest rival, and my fated love . . . all wrapped up in one amazing and incredible woman. She was all I'd ever want. "I love you," I told her, never more sure of the words I'd spoken.

It felt like a lifetime passed before she answered, though I knew it was only seconds. With a nod, she caved. "Okay. We'll give this one more chance."

"Oh, thank God," I said, breathing a sigh of relief and stepping in closer.

Cassidy pushed back against my chest, stopping me before I could seal the deal with a hug. "On one condition," she warned.

I didn't care what the condition was; she'd have whatever she wanted. "Anything."

"Counseling, Shaw."

Fuck me.

"We don't need counseling, sweetness. We can do this on our own. Just you and me working together . . . we're the Dynamic Duo, baby." I gave her a smile I knew would charm the pants off her, as it had done on *many* occasions before.

She shook her head, dead set on her path and as unrelenting in this as a pit bull with a meaty bone. "The truth of the matter is that I don't have a clue what I'm doing either, Shaw. We need help—a neutral party who can coach us into becoming better partners to each other and better parents for Abe. You have to agree to the counseling or I'm leaving."

An ultimatum. Jesus, I hated ultimatums. There was something about them that made me want to do the opposite, if for no other reason than just for the sake of maintaining control. But I loved Cassidy, and if this was what she needed . . . Like I'd said, she'd have whatever she wanted.

"Okay," I conceded.

"Okay?" she asked. Apparently, she hadn't expected an easy victory on the matter.

"Okay," I repeated.

She closed her eyes and sighed in relief as her shoulders dropped with the tension that evacuated her muscles. Damn. I'd done that to her.

Cupping her face, I kissed her lips softly and then pressed my forehead to hers as I released a relieved sigh of my own. "Thank you, sweetness."

I'd almost lost everything.

CHAPTER 4

Shaw

Jesus! I was late. Again. And no doubt, about to be crucified for it.

Though I'd agreed to the counseling, it didn't mean I had to like it. I was still convinced it would do more harm than good and was nothing short of a big, fat waste of time. The only reason I'd made a halfway-decent attempt was because I'd promised Cassidy I would. Ultimatums had a way of forcing one's hand, after all.

Still, I wasn't made up of the stuff that would allow me to roll over and play dead while some quack put me down and told me all the ways I didn't deserve Cassidy and Abe. I'd play nice, but not too nice.

Once I'd parked in the garage, I took the elevator to the floor the directory listed for Cassidy's chosen cohort. I knew I had the right place when I got to the office at the end of a long hallway, a trek that felt like walking death row, I might add. *Dr. Jeremy Sparling, PhD, LMFT* was stamped in sparkly gold lettering on the tinted glass door. Sparkly, just like his personality, I'd bet. Eager to get this over with, I pulled the heavy door open and walked in.

A girl in her early twenties sat behind the receptionist desk, beaming up at me with a bright smile when she saw me. "Hi! How can I help you?"

"I have an appointment," I told her. "I'm late."

"Oh! You must be Mr. Matthews?"

"In the flesh," I said, not hiding my annoyance. Not that this young lady had ever done anything to deserve my bucket-of-shit fest. Guilt by association, I supposed, was my subconscious reasoning for my rude behavior.

"Dr. Sparling and Ms. Whalen are waiting for you," Ashley—per her nameplate—told me, bubbly smile still in place and undeterred by my attitude. Though I could tell it was fake. I assumed she'd had a lot of practice with her perma-grin while working with the public. I'd mastered the same smile, but years of practice had rendered mine flawless. "Just through there," Ashley said, pointing to another door around the corner.

I nodded a thanks and then forced myself to drag heavy feet to the final destination. This door wasn't glass, likely, to keep busybodies from seeing the sessions inside. Right in line with the whole doctor/patient confidentiality agreement, I supposed.

Jesus . . . Was I really going to go through with this?

"Don't be shy," Ashley called after me. "You can walk on in."

Big breath in and then out, I turned the knob and pushed the door open.

A thin man stood on my arrival, wearing the same sort of smile as Ashley's, more polished and genuine and all "Let's be friends!" As he walked over with his hand outstretched to greet me, I surmised he couldn't have been any more than five feet six inches tall. "And finally, we meet. Yaayyy!" he said, laughing at himself. He apparently thought he was funny. I didn't. "I'm Dr. Sparling, but I absolutely insist that you call me Jeremy."

Of course he would.

"Shaw Matthews." I took his hand, instantly wanting to draw it back when I felt how warm it was. Too warm. Creepy, like maybe he'd just had it shoved down his pants.

I wasn't sure what I expected of our shrink, but Dr. Jeremy Sparling was not the least bit intimidating in the physical sense. His hair was dark and cropped short, heavily applied hair product forcing an unnatural part for a greaser style. His skin was pale, though rosy at the cheeks, like a ripe jolly old elf's. Black-rimmed glasses sat on the bridge of his long nose. A dense pornstache nearly covered the top lip of his full mouth, and he wore a "fun" sweater vest over a button-down shirt with khaki pants. Dude had to be hot in that getup. And then it occurred to me . . . I was looking at the doppelgänger of *Ghostbusters*'s Louis Tully. It gave me the heebie-jeebies, and I mentally swore that if he invited us to some hip party at his pad, I was going to call in an exorcist.

Though he looked harmless enough, the dark brown eyes that sat behind those thick lenses made me throw up all kinds of security walls. The scrutiny there unnerved me to the core. I'd lay odds there wasn't much he ever missed.

"Hey," Cassidy said, drawing my attention. She smiled up at me. "You made it."

Why did she seem so surprised? She was the one who'd issued the ultimatum, giving me no other choice. Did she really think I'd risk losing her and Abe over some stupid counseling sessions? Not a chance.

Dr. Sparling took his seat in the only chair, waving for me to get comfortable as well. Cassidy was sitting on the couch across from him, so I took a seat on the other end with a huff, ready to get this whole thing over with already.

"Okay, let's get started," he said. Turning to me, he crossed his legs. "What brings you here?"

He was asking me? "Who," I corrected him. "And the answer is Cassidy. She thinks we need this."

"And why do you think that is?"

"You'll have to ask her."

"I already have. I'd like to know why *you* think you're here."

"Why does any couple come to see you? Because they have issues, right?"

"Yes, but you've avoided addressing those issues, missing every other appointment. Why are you here now?"

I was becoming increasingly frustrated by the shame game my new pal, *Jeremy*, was playing. "Because Cassidy said she'd leave me if I didn't agree to this."

"I see. And why were you refusing to show for all the other appointments we've scheduled?"

"Obviously, it's because I didn't want to see you. Not you, personally, but any shrink."

"Relationship coach," he corrected me, with a polite smile. "You don't think the two of you can benefit from outside help?"

"Not entirely," I admitted. "Mostly, my reluctance is because I'm a little uncomfortable about dishing all of my personal business to a total stranger."

"Ah. Rest assured, you aren't the first and likely won't be the last client to have that concern." He sat back in his Chesterfield armchair—the brown leather groaning with his movement—and then uncrossed and re-crossed his legs. Propping a little white notepad on his knee to begin writing something down, he continued, "How might I set you at ease with this new adventure we're about to embark upon?"

"I don't know. How about you start with your qualifications?"

"Shaw—" Cassidy started, but was cut off by our *relationship coach*.

"It's quite all right, Ms. Whalen—"

"Just Cassidy. Please," she insisted with as genuine a smile as I'd seen from her in a long time. Except when it came to Abe, that is.

Dr. Sparling looked up, returning the smile. "Cassidy, then. Do you mind if I use your first name, Mr. Matthews?"

"Sure. Knock yourself out," I told him with a roll of my eyes and a subdued huff of annoyance.

"Great!" Redirecting to Cassidy, he said, "If your partner needs reassurances as to my qualifications, I'm more than happy to list them."

My "partner" turned to me with a narrowing of her eyes only I would've perceived. A silent warning for me to behave, or else. I wasn't afraid of her "or else," so I did nothing to stop our coach from continuing with his list of credentials.

"I have been a registered and licensed marriage and family therapist for over fifteen years. As for my educational background, as it applies to our current situation, I hold a doctorate in psychology with a specialization in marriage and family therapy. I also earned a master's in marriage and family therapy. You're free to do some fact-checking on me if you'd like, though I would've thought you'd have done that before you called my office to schedule an appointment."

"*I* didn't call. She did," I said with a nod in Cassidy's direction.

"And I did the research, Shaw. You know I don't do anything halfway."

"No, you don't, do you? I'm sure you probably even conducted phone interviews with a dozen or more therapists and psychiatrists before you chose this one."

"Does it bother you that she's so thorough, Shaw?"

Was that an air of condescension I detected?

"I'm sorry, have we already begun the judgmental thing without my realizing it?"

"I'm not here to judge you. I do not own a black robe or a gavel. But to answer your question, your session began the moment you walked through the door. The clock for the bill, however, began at the time you were *scheduled* to walk through the door." He said all this without looking at me and while scribbling more notes on his pad. It irked me.

"Is that what you're writing, that I was late?"

He stopped and peered up at me over the rim of his glasses. "Would that bother you?"

"It bothers me that you answer every question with a question asking me if it bothers me."

"I see," he said, again returning to the notepad. Just when I thought I might launch across the space between the "therapy couch" and his comfy chair, he stopped, crossing his forearms over the pad as he leaned toward us. "How about this? Since you seem to be distracted so much by what I may or may not be writing, and I do need to keep notes, would you be more comfortable if I record our sessions to play back later so that I can note your file accordingly?"

I suddenly saw this guy's appeal to Cassidy. He was as meticulous as she was about keeping an accurate account of everything there was to know about a subject of interest. It was his job, I got it, and it would make me feel less scrutinized if I didn't have to watch him write down every body gesture or interesting choice of word I'd used.

"That would be preferable, yes." Though I wasn't completely onboard with this whole thing, I relaxed a little at his willingness to compromise. I even sat back and draped my arm over the back of the couch as the doc moved to his desk to pull out a small black recorder. He did some shit to make sure it was good to go, and then sat it on the table between us with a little red light seeming to point the blame finger right at me like a laser centering on the kill shot.

"Does that bother you?" he asked, chuckling at his own attempt to be funny. "I'm sorry. Just a little therapist humor."

Even Cassidy's laugh was forced. I shot her a sideways glance with a humorless chuckle of my own. I couldn't believe she was torturing me like this.

Before returning to his cushy chair, Dr. Sparling grabbed a file folder off his desk. I thought he wasn't going to be taking notes?

"So," he continued, "as Cassidy is aware, I'm a little unconventional in my coaching methods. I prefer to keep things fun, shake it up a bit, and make it less like therapy and more like talking to an old friend who happens to be a pretty good referee, if you will.

"As I said before, I am not a judge and promise not to be judgmental, but I need you to trust that I know what I'm talking about and will do my utter best to help the two of you through any issues you might have in your relationship, obvious or buried. I can't simply fix the problem areas for you. I can only act as a neutral party, a guide to help you resolve them together.

"Now, let's jump right in, shall we?" Dr. Sparling opened the file on his lap, perusing the contents as he spoke. "When Cassidy and I first planned to meet, I'd emailed a questionnaire that each of you completed for me to get a snapshot of you individually and as a couple. The questionnaire, as you may recall—or not, since it was so long ago," he said, giving me a pointed glance—I supposed to shame me for all the appointments that had had to be rescheduled on my account—"was to help me determine what the two of you feel, separately, are the issues in your relationship so that we might find a common focus point.

"Unfortunately, only one of you took it seriously," he concluded. He was about to rat me out.

"What do you mean?" Cassidy asked, shocked. Not sure why.

Sometimes I believed she asked questions she already knew the answers to just to prove an already obvious point. No, I hadn't taken the questionnaire seriously. Mostly because I'd had no intention of showing up to these sessions in the first place and saw no sense in divulging personal information to a stranger I'd never meet anyway.

"Well, here's one example. . . . For the question asking what his childhood was like, Shaw wrote that he was the illegitimate son of Santa Claus, who'd had an illicit affair with his mother, the Tooth Fairy, and that she'd abandoned him to be raised by a pack of chupacabras until he was eventually abducted by aliens at the age of six and sold off to a succubus that had . . ." Dr. Sparling pulled at the collar of his shirt, uncomfortable with his next reveal, "sucked him off so much, his cock was permanently swollen to the size of a baby's arm."

I did my best to stifle my laughter, but no way could I hide my amused grin from Cassidy.

"Shaw!"

"What?" I asked, defensively, and then turned the tables on our therapist. "I thought those questionnaires were supposed to be confidential. Don't you have some sort of hypocritical oath you have to uphold or something?"

"It's a *Hippocratic* Oath, Shaw—"

I knew that.

"—and this is couple's therapy. Which means I won't disclose details about our sessions to anyone outside this office, but the two of you count as one client, and there will be no secrets held in this room. The contract you signed detailed that information."

It did? That would've been useful information to have before filling out that form.

"You didn't even read the contract, did you?" Cassidy asked me. Again, not sure why she was shocked.

"Yes, I read the agreement. . . . Okay, I didn't," I admitted when she opened her mouth to call bullshit. Damned if I could ever lie to her.

"Would you like to take a moment to look over it now before we continue?" Dr. Sparling handed a copy toward me. "I don't want to move forward until you know exactly what you can expect of me and what I expect of you in return."

"Fine." Reaching across the way, I took the sheet of paper from him with a huff, while secretly hoping he'd gotten a paper cut when I ripped it from his hand.

Scanning through the document, I realized it hadn't been as basic as I'd thought it would be. Dr. Sparling's expectations were pretty specific. By signing the document, I'd agreed to take our sessions seriously and follow the advice he gave regarding the future of my relationship with Cassidy. No matter. It wasn't like he could dictate what we ultimately decided to do. On the other hand, what *Cassidy* ultimately decided, based on his recommendation, would be another story.

"Got it." I handed the agreement back to him.

"And you still agree?"

One glance at Cassidy, at the pleading in every detail of her expression, and I knew the answer. "I do." I shuddered when I realized how much that had sounded like a wedding vow.

"Excellent! Moving on," he said, all Mr. Rogers–like. And then finally, he turned the spotlight off me and onto Cassidy.

"Cassidy, since it seems you were earnest with your questionnaire, let's start with you."

Oh, I couldn't wait to hear what she'd put on her form. . . .

Cassidy

Jeremy seemed like an okay guy. Sort of like he was having an identity crisis that he should maybe seek counseling for himself, but okay, nonetheless. Maybe his outward appearance was simply an attempt to set his clients at ease with the illusion that he had something in common with just about anyone from any walk of life. I liked that about him.

I also liked the way he effortlessly put Shaw in his place. Reminded me a lot of myself, or at least the way I used to be with him. Over time, I'd lost my spunk, my sass, my competitive edge.

Filling out the questionnaire had been a "come to Jesus" moment for me, so to speak. Maybe I'd been in defensive mode while studying it, looking for all the ways my answers might make me look like a villain. In the end, though, I'd answered honestly, viewing this as an opportunity to tell the story of Shaw and me. If there were issues, they weren't mine alone. They weren't even Shaw's alone. They were ours. And if Jeremy could offer advice on how I might approach our relationship differently, I was all ears. Unlike Shaw, I had no chip on my shoulder. I knew I wasn't perfect.

"It says here that the two of you met at work."

Feeling like I'd just taken the witness stand, I squared my shoulders, prepared to defend my actions. "That's right."

"Workplace romances can be quite complicated."

I snorted. "You don't know the half of it."

"Then by all means, fill me in." He smiled and sat back, making a show of getting comfortable.

Shaw sighed his agitation, but I didn't spare him a glance.

Crossing my legs, I entwined my fingers and hooked my hands around my knee. Bracing, maybe? "Shaw and I worked for the same company, but there was no love lost between the two of us right from the beginning. I thought he was a pompous ass who expected everything to be handed to him—"

"And I thought she was the biggest bitch I'd ever met," Shaw tacked on, making me narrow my eyes at him.

"You didn't at first," I taunted him with a knowing smirk.

"Nope," he admitted. "I thought you were sexy as hell until you opened that smart-ass mouth of yours."

"I thought my smart mouth turned you on?" What I didn't add was the rather intimate story Shaw had recounted to me about a certain shower where he'd masturbated to visions of shutting me up with his fat cock in my mouth. The thought heated my skin and made me wish for all the world that he'd do it for real. God, I missed that part of Shaw so much.

"It did. Still wanted to wring your neck, though."

And now I was thinking about a little flirtation with danger, about what it would be like to have Shaw's fingers around my neck while plunging deep inside me, his eyes daring me to make a sound.

"Oh, my . . ." Jeremy pulled at his collar. If I didn't know better, I'd swear he'd been reading my mind. Clearly, his reaction was aimed at Shaw's statement, though the teasing grin on his lips meant he hadn't taken it literally to mean we had an abusive relationship. A little sick and twisted in the beginning with a whole lot of physicality, maybe, but not in the abusive sense.

"Anyway," I said, continuing, "we were both agents going

after the same client to win a partnership. Neither of us played fair. In fact, we used everything at our disposal to gain the upper hand. And I do mean *everything*."

"Such as?" Jeremy was going to make me spell it out.

"Sex," I said in a matter-of-fact way.

"Really? So you were rivals who didn't much like each other, but you still had sex?"

"Oh, yeah," Shaw said, egotistical smirk in place. It was sexy as hell. "And lots of it."

"It's interesting that you were able to disconnect yourselves from your feelings about each other to engage in something so intimate."

"Tactics," Shaw said simply. "Fuck or be fucked."

"Shaw!" I gasped. "There's no need to be so crude."

"Did you feel the same way, Cassidy?"

As much as I didn't want to look to be less of a lady, honesty was in the driver's seat.

I shrugged. "Yes." But then I realized a stronger truth. "Though I suppose that wasn't my only reason. You see, even when I hated Shaw, I still wanted him. It was a very physical, carnal attraction for me."

Shaw's brows drew together. "Wait . . . You *hated* me?"

"Oh, get off it, Shaw. We hated each other. We *loved* to hate each other, in fact."

"Well, they do say there's a very thin line between love and hate." Jeremy chuckled. "Was it the same for you, Shaw? Did you hate Cassidy, as well?"

I could tell he struggled to admit the truth, but with a single nod, he did. "It was a turn-on."

"And then your relationship grew into something more?"

"Yes."

"So is it fair to say that sex was the foundation of your relationship?"

"Yeah, I suppose so."

"Great! That's our starting point, then. Sometimes, to figure out how to move forward, we have to go back to the beginning." Jeremy kicked off his shoes and tucked his feet under him, criss-cross applesauce–style. It was quite odd, but I had a feeling not a lot about our relationship coach was normal.

Eyes widening, he leaned forward in the chair, engrossed and apparently excited by this revelation. It was like he'd just found a pivotal puzzle piece. "I'm not saying your sexual attraction is the foundation of your entire relationship, but it certainly is a very large component. Desire plus provocation is the elemental compound driving the formula of your base chemistry. Again, not the entire formula, as I'm sure you care for each other on many different levels, which is likely the reason you're here in my office today.

"But let's change gears for a moment. Sexual attraction usually begins with a physical attraction. A person's physical appearance can change over time, so I have to ask the hard question." Jeremy turned his attention to me. "Are you still physically attracted to Shaw, Cassidy?"

I faced Shaw, almost scrutinizing everything about his appearance, though I hadn't needed to. I already knew the answer. "Without a doubt."

"And you, Shaw?"

Shaw gave me the same once-over, the corner of his mouth turning up into that gorgeous half grin/half smirk of his I could never resist. "She's just as sexy now as she was that night we got it on like a couple of teenagers in a seedy alley during the pouring rain."

The memory of that night caused a stir in my nether region. I had to fight the urge to scissor my thighs for friction. Shaw had given me a reverse shoulder ride in the rain, right before he'd fucked me while I was forced to keep quiet or else the lady standing on the balcony directly above would have busted us in all our naughtiness.

I could hear the sadness in my own voice as I ducked my head and said, "We don't have sex like that anymore."

"We don't have time to have sex like that anymore," Shaw said, again defensive. Then he gave me another reminder. "Plus there's Abe."

"Where there's a will, there's a way." I didn't need to look at him to see his reaction.

Jeremy perked up at that. "The will is gone?"

Before Shaw could answer with what I was sure he thought our coach wanted to hear, I did it for him. "For both of us."

"Well then." Jeremy sighed. "It would seem you've simply lost your passion for each other. Does that seem like a fair assessment?"

Why did that hit me like a ton of bricks? Our relationship coach's diagnosis screamed all kinds of right answer. Even our arguments had become tame compared to the ones we'd had before Abe had come along. It stood to reason that if heated arguments had turned into scorching sex in the past, tame arguments would turn into lame sex now.

"Yes, that's fair," I answered. "I just don't feel like he wants me the same as he used to."

Shaw looked taken aback by my statement. "What are you talking about? Of course I want you."

"I can't tell," I told him. "It's like you're just going through the motions."

Jeremy resumed control of the conversation, steering us in a different direction. "How often do you have sex?"

I snorted. "Ha! After arguments and whenever Shaw wants it, which is rare."

Shaw rose to his own defense. "That's not true! We have sex. Pretty regularly, I might add."

He wasn't even being honest with himself, let alone our therapist. And was he really trying to tell *me* how often we had sex? If I were a participant in said sex, wouldn't I be aware of how often it was? Or maybe it was just that Shaw had been that oblivious to the decline in our sex life.

Fine, it was up to me to inform him. *If I must, I must.* "No, *you* have sex. My only purpose during it is to serve as your own personal pocket pussy."

Jeremy nearly choked on his startled gasp. I wasn't usually so blunt, but what did I have to lose? Besides, we were in a couples therapist's office, so I'd say there wasn't much he hadn't heard.

Shaw didn't fare much better from the outburst that surprised even me. He shifted on the couch with his hands fisted at his sides, gone white at the knuckles even as his teeth clenched. "What the hell is *that* supposed to mean?"

With an indignant lift of my chin, I spelled it out for him. "It means you work very well toward your endgame without a single thought of mine. It must be nice to be able to release all the tension and stress you claim to have."

"All the tension and stress I *claim* to have?" He raked his fingers through his hair in a way that seemed almost painful. It was nothing short of an attempt to regain some semblance of control over his emotions. And the first time I'd seen him do it in a very long time. "You get off, too. So I don't know where all of this is coming from."

I'd had it. Simply had it. While I was already dishing out the cold, hard truth, I decided now was as good a time as any to reveal another. One that would send us past the point of no return on the subject at hand. "I fake it."

The veins in Shaw's forehead and neck threatened to break the skin. "You *do not* fake it! I would know!"

Calmly lifting a brow in challenge, I faced off with him. "Would you?"

"Yes! Jesus, where is all of this coming from?"

There was only one way to prove my point, and having embraced my newfound bluntness, I went with it once again. Grabbing onto the armrest at my side and the couch cushion on the other, I dropped my head back and closed my eyes as I allowed my body, coiled tight with unrelieved tension, to relax. "Oh, Shaw . . . Oh, Shaw . . . Right there. Yes, right . . . *there!*" I moaned, giving him and the good doctor a sampling of my incredible acting skills.

Shaw gaped. Jeremy resituated himself in his chair, glasses practically fogging.

Point. Proven. I was tempted to take a bow but decided to save it for the end of my acceptance speech when I won an Emmy.

Since the room had grown deathly quiet, enough so that I could practically hear the echoing of my performance, I decided to punctuate it with a conversation ender. "Once upon a time, you would've known I was faking it. All you had to do was listen and observe, but you haven't done that in a very long time, which should tell you just how long I've gone without an orgasm for myself. At least from you."

He looked like he was still trying to process this new information, like he was trying to find fault in my claim.

"Think about it, Shaw. Since when have I ever made that much noise while coming?"

Jesus, I'd have thought he'd gone into shock if not for the churning turbulence in his eyes. Something there had changed, an emotional mix of confusion and clarity, and then back to confusion again that one might attribute to a madman. Ah, he'd found the truth in my words and was venturing into that space of denial.

Jeremy cleared his throat, but it did nothing to clear the tension in the room. "I don't often do this, but I believe you two to be a special case. I'd like to refer you to a colleague of mine, Dr. Katya Minkov. She happens to be in town for a bit, and I can see if she's available."

"Another therapist? In addition to you?" Shaw asked, already gearing up to shoot the idea down. "I don't have the time or the patience—"

"Need I remind you that you said you'd do anything to keep Abe and me here?"

Shaw stopped talking, which, judging by the way he tensed, was a hard thing for him to do.

"Just tell me if I need to book a flight, Shaw," I told him with a shake of my head. "That's all I want to know."

"No," he grated between clenched teeth.

Turning to Jeremy, I waved for him to continue. "You were saying?"

But he wasn't really answering me so much as he was reassuring Shaw. "What I'm proposing is something I think you'll find . . . interesting, Shaw. I almost wish I had a reason to book a session or two with Katya."

"Is that so? Would you like to switch places?"

Jeremy looked at me, blushing for some unknown reason, and then pulled at his collar. "I, um—I don't think so. That would be quite unethical since, as I said, Dr. Minkov is a colleague. Though I'm not sure if she can really be called a therapist. Of sorts, maybe," he concluded with a sideways bob of his head.

"What does that mean?"

With a professional smile in place, he eased into the explanation. "Nothing about what Katya does is *clinical*. She's very hands-on, unorthodox in her methods, and extremely effective with her techniques."

"I'm still not following, Doc. What makes her better than you?"

The chuckle that came from Jeremy when he pulled at his collar was downright mischievous. "Not better. We simply have a different field of study. Katya's expertise, you see, is in *sex*. The kind of sex that, um," he shifted in his seat, "let's just say it's an adventure you'll want to embark upon time and time again."

Shaw perked up at that, his back and shoulders a little straighter. "Really?"

My question, exactly. *Really, Shaw?* I crossed my arms over my chest and eyeballed him. He noticed and visibly swallowed, but I could tell my disapproval hadn't done much to subdue his curiosity.

"Indeed," Jeremy said, reaching for his notepad and beginning to jot something down. "I must warn you that should you agree to see her, and she you, it will be an experience like none you've ever had before. To say Katya is unconventional would be an understatement. She's a professional, of course, but she's also the most . . ." He shook his head with a very deep breath and long exhalation. Were his glasses fogging up again? "Let's just say you'll thank me for this."

Ripping off a sheet of paper, Jeremy passed it over to us. He hadn't been writing notes. He'd been scribbling Dr. Minkov's contact information.

"Is this really necessary?" I asked, not entirely sure how we'd gotten to this place. A sex therapist who isn't really a therapist at all? I had some serious research to do on this Dr. Katya Minkov.

Jeremy's eyebrows lifted. "I can't see how it could possibly hurt. Think of it as an adventure of sorts. After all, sex was the foundation of your relationship. You said so yourself. So let's fix the cracks in that foundation before we look at the rest of your house."

Though I was apprehensive about making an even bigger deal out of our issues, I supposed he did have a point. Besides, I could use a little adventure. Peering over at Shaw, I knew we both could. Maybe he'd make more time for his family if we could find our passion for each other again.

"Of course," Jeremy added, "confidentiality runs both ways with Dr. Minkov. The agreement you signed with me safeguards the contact information I just gave you for Katya as well. Whether you choose to use her or not, you must not share it with anyone."

"Sounds secretive, very *Mission Impossible*–ish," I told him, suspicious of the hush-hush behavior. "Is this Dr. Minkov even on the up-and-up? Because if we end up in the Nevada desert at a brothel . . ."

"Cassidy, I assure you that I would not recommend you see her if she were not. Katya is simply *very* good at what she does. So good that her clients have to go through an intense application process and she handpicks each and every one. Referrals get to skip the application process, but she will take them on only if *she* chooses to."

"What do you think, Shaw?"

Relaxed back into his seat with an elbow propped up on the armrest, his thumb cradling his jaw, and a finger lying across his full lips, Shaw gave a lackadaisical shrug. "You're calling the shots here. I'm just along for the ride."

Great. He was pouting. No doubt because I'd bruised his delicate ego. Fine. If he wanted to behave like a child resorting to dropping into deadweight mode, I'd drag his butt to yet another therapist's office and see how much he liked that.

CHAPTER 5

Shaw

I fake it. . . . Cassidy's admission kept replaying through my mind on a loop, each syllable pounding my ego like the clapper of a ten-ton bell and the reverberation drowning out any other thought. She'd been faking it? Could there be a worse blow to an alpha male's self-esteem?

I was Shaw Matthews. Never had a woman ever had to fake it with me. Least of all, Cassidy. And worse, I'd never so much as thought it a possibility. I mean, I had some mad skills.

"You're angry about what I told Dr. Sparling about faking it, aren't you?" Everything about Cassidy's demeanor screamed apprehensive and nervous as hell as I escorted her to the parking garage.

Nervous? After she'd given me an ultimatum to see that damn therapist in the first place or she'd leave and take our son with her? Apprehensive? After devastating my pride the way she had in front of a total fucking stranger?

Yeah, served her right.

So I didn't answer.

"Say something, Shaw. I need to know how that made you feel."

I gave her an incredulous grunt. We'd seen a shrink all of one time and now she wanted to fit the cliché and talk about feelings. Right.

I wanted to continue to ignore her, but there was one question still plaguing me. Stopping by the hybrid I bought for her—highly rated for the safety of our son with a price tag to match—I turned on her. "How long, Cassidy? How long have you been faking it?"

She kicked her hip out and crossed her arms over her chest with an irritated huff. Like she had any right to be annoyed. "I don't know. A while. Why? What does it matter?"

It really didn't. A day, a month, a year . . . no matter how long, it wasn't acceptable.

Instinct and pride urged me to rip off all of Cassidy's clothes and take her against some stranger's car right there in the parking garage, giving not a single damn if anyone saw us. All to prove I didn't need a fucking sex therapist, who wasn't really a therapist, to show me how to pleasure my girl. But I didn't. I didn't because I wasn't much in the mood to pleasure her at the moment, a mood that was very much warring with my alpha nature at the same time.

She'd stripped me of something with those three little words. Something essential to my core. My dominance. My manhood.

"Shaw?"

I was back to not answering her again. It wasn't like I knew what to say even if I could get my teeth to stop grinding long enough to get any words out. No, I wasn't angry. I was pissed. At her, yes, but mostly at myself.

My woman had gone without getting off for God only knew how long. She'd been walking around our place, taking care of our child, feeling like I didn't want her, like I no longer found her sexy. But that wasn't true. Even now, as mad as she'd made me, my cock was straining against my zipper, wanting nothing more than to answer her body's call for release, for the pleasure it had been deprived of.

Emotionally, I couldn't deny my anger. Physically, I couldn't deny the pull to satisfy her sexual need. Mentally, it was all fucking with my head in a very messed-up way that demanded I restore some semblance of balance immediately.

"Shaw," Cassidy prodded.

"What?" Even I could hear the warning in my voice for her to drop it.

It did nothing to keep Cassidy from poking the bear, though. "You haven't said anything."

"Goddammit, Cassidy!" I snapped at her persistence and then unloaded without a care for who might overhear. "A whole lot of shit was said back there! Shit I didn't know! And now we have to go see a sex therapist on top of it all? I've just been blindsided, and you want to know how I feel? I don't *know* how I feel! Is it too much to ask for a fucking moment to organize my thoughts so I can figure it out for myself?"

Cassidy's astonished eyes blinked up at me. "Oh . . . Okay. Sorry. You're right."

"Jesus!" I said with an incredulous shake of my head that did nothing for the stabbing ache beginning to ice-pick my brain. I rubbed my forehead, not that it did anything to relieve the throbbing, and then took a deep, calming breath. "Look, I told you I'd do whatever you need to make things right between us, to fix things for my family, and I will. But you . . . You've gotta give me some time to process all of this."

She nodded, her gaze fixating on the ground. Dammit, I couldn't do anything right.

She turned to open the door to her vehicle, saying, "Abe's having a sleepover with Quinn and Denver tonight, so I'll just see you whenever you get home."

I stopped her before she got inside and closed me out. "Hey." Cassidy froze in place but didn't turn around. Instead, she faced forward with her back to me and her shoulders bowed. "Tell me."

I don't know why, but I needed to hear her say it.

"I love you." Her voice sounded small and unemotional, like an automated response. She'd done what was expected of her but still hadn't looked at me. With that, she got into the car as if she couldn't do so fast enough and shut the door.

I just stood there as she started the damn thing, putting it into gear and checking the rearview mirror before backing out of her parking space and pulling away. Not a glance was spared in my direction.

"Love you, too," I said to her taillights.

Even when she was out of sight, I remained where I was, still staring after her with an overwhelming sense of shame, anger, and frustration. She'd wanted me to discuss my feelings, and I couldn't. Instead, I'd bitten her head off and then let her drive away. Once again, I'd left her unsatisfied.

What *the fuck* was wrong with me? And why did I feel justified despite my guilt?

Cassidy

Well, *that* had gone in no way, shape, or form the way I'd thought it would.

Dr. Sparling, Jeremy, had scheduled our next appointment, and I was already apprehensive about what might come out during it. Good Lord, one appointment had already revealed so much.

He'd also given us a heads-up on what we'd be discussing. Since it had been determined that the foundation of our relationship revolved around sex, Jeremy wanted to see how much Shaw and I actually knew about each other. I was nervous. Really nervous. Though I'd just outed Shaw in front of Dr. Sparling for not paying enough attention to me to know I'd been faking, I'd started to question exactly how well I knew the man I'd built a life with.

Most of my and Shaw's conversations were usually about Abe or work, or my family and what had been going on with them. We never really discussed Shaw's family. I didn't even know if he had any relatives other than his mother and father. I'd only seen his mother the one time, and his father not at all. He had no pictures of them, there'd been no greeting cards on special occasions, no trips home for Christmas, no anything. They hadn't even met their grandson, and probably didn't even know he existed, for that matter.

And I'd never questioned any of it. Hadn't really given it a second thought.

Holy crap! Talk about having your head in the sand! And I'd been on Shaw's case about a freaking orgasm fake?

"Cassidy Rose, you're a clueless moron," I said aloud to myself.

Suddenly, all sorts of questions about Shaw started bombarding me. What was his favorite color? His favorite meal? His favorite song? Favorite book?

My mind was blank on every single one. I had nothing, not a single answer.

But I knew how to fix that, didn't I? I'd just have to switch gears, dust the cobwebs from my good ol' trusty agent hat and don it once more to use my impeccable research skills to our advantage. This was a test, and I was not lacking the tools by which to ace it. Though I was a total ass for not knowing so much as the basics about the man I claimed to love.

Sex was the basis of our relationship, true enough. But was that all it had ever been? No, I refused to believe that. And I refused to lose Shaw on a technicality. I knew what my heart wanted, who my heart wanted. Shaw, plain and simple.

But I'd signed Dr. Sparling's contract, fully prepared to abide by his recommendation as it pertained to the future of my and Shaw's relationship. Since I wasn't okay with throwing in the towel—never had been—I was going to buckle in and get back on my game. My ma and da hadn't raised a quitter, though I wasn't exactly doing them proud with all my double-standard behavior either.

Shaw needed a moment? Yeah, well, I needed a drink. So I pulled into the parking lot of our building, locked things up tight, and walked the couple of blocks to Monkey Business.

Monkey Business was the neighborhood pub where all my friends and I hung out, or at least used to. They still did. Me? Not as much now that I was a mom. It had an old-world Irish feel with the traditional emerald green and gold trim, dark wood everything, and a few mounted televisions tuned in to different sporting events and news. Walking through the doors, I breathed in deep, letting the smell of ale and history, the quiet hum of various conversations, and the soft glow of painted glass chandeliers and neon signs begin to work their magic. For years, this was where I'd gone after so many long hours at the office to unwind and ease the stress of the day. Now, that seemed like a lifetime ago.

I'd missed it.

I tried not to be disappointed when I didn't find what I was looking for. On the far side of the room and to the left corner of the bar was a table of rich, dark wood with a glossy top. Four unmatched chairs sat empty, which meant Demi and Sasha weren't here.

"Holy shit, ladies and gentlemen," a boisterous baritone voice shouted in my direction, "Monkey's misplaced daughter has finally returned home!"

I'd know that voice anywhere.

The grin that pushed my cheeks to a nearly painful split was unavoidable as I headed toward the stretch of lacquered wood that lined the west end of the room with matching stools along its front. Chaz Michaels, one of my nearest and dearest friends, was the barkeep with the big mouth. He was a chiseled mountain of a man with spiky blond hair, soft baby blues, and a pristine smile. For someone who didn't know him, the body ink and piercings, not to mention his build, might be intimidating. But I knew him to be nothing more than a giant teddy bear. He was also Demi's adoring beau.

"What's up, handsome?" I said, stepping up on the brass foot rail and meeting him half the distance to kiss his cheek. I couldn't help but notice the picture taped to the mirror behind him. It was one Demi had taken of Chaz and Abe when they'd kept him so I could go to a doctor's appointment I'd had while Shaw was out of town. Abe mirrored his "uncle" Chaz, dressed in identical blue jeans and white T-shirt with a Harley-Davidson hat turned backward on his head. The fist bump pose they were in was cute times a gazillion.

"Hey, I know that handsome devil," I said, pulling back and nodding toward the picture.

Chaz looked over his shoulder, a proud grin on his face. "Aww, thanks, Cass! I think I'm pretty cute, too."

"Not you!" I laughed. "Abe!"

Chaz laughed, too. "Yeah, that's my little dude," he told me. "Man, I love that kid. You need to stop being so stingy with him and let us hang out more often."

"Yeah, yeah, yeah." I waved him off, though I knew I'd make it happen as soon as possible. "Where are my girls?"

Chaz's fitted black T-shirt was stretched taut across his broad chest, the short sleeves threatening a tear around his biceps as he worked a bar towel inside a tall mug he'd been drying. "Demi's got a class and Sasha is still honeymooning."

Demi I got—she taught self-defense with various class times to accommodate different schedules—but Sasha?

"Wait, I just talked to Quinn the other night and he was here with Demi and Sasha, so I assumed she and Landon were already home."

He put the mug away and started on the next. "Oh, yeah, they're back in town, but that doesn't mean the honeymoon is over," he said with a suggestive waggle of his brows and a mischievous laugh. "They want a baby right away, and, well, practice makes perfect."

Wow! I hadn't even known they were trying. Which only proved how out of touch with the world, my world, I'd become.

"I so didn't need that visual." I laughed. "Okay, then. Super-bummed about finally having the chance to have a drink with my girls and them not being here, so I guess I'll just head home."

"Oh, so you're too good to have a drink with me? Ouch, my feelings, Cass." In dramatic fashion, he rubbed the spot on his chest that was just over his heart.

"Stop it!" I swatted at him and missed. "You're working."

He shrugged and dropped the towel onto the counter below the bar. "It's my break time anyway. Come on. I'll get some beers and meet you at the table. And yeah, even though you haven't shown your face around here for like a million years, I still remember what you like," the smart-ass tacked on.

"Okay! Sure!"

I got a little pep in my step as I went over to the table that he'd reserved for the girls, Quinn, and me when our visits had been more predictable. I was out of the house, among adults, and about to have a drink with a cooler-than-cool friend who'd always had a knack for making me laugh.

"Everyone in here is going to think we're on a date." I laughed before taking the first sip of beer I'd had since I couldn't remember when. The moan at the flavors exploding on my tongue was nearly X-rated. "Oh, that is *so* good!"

"No, everyone is going to think you and that mug are here on a date." Chaz looked around, presumably to see if anyone else had heard me, though his chuckle was deep and hardy. "Damn . . . Keep it in your pants, Cass. You pervs and your weird fetishes, jeez!"

"Speaking of pervs . . . ," I said, arching a brow at him. "You and Demi getting it on behind the bar with everyone watching?"

"She told you about that?"

"Nope! Quinn did." I took another swig of my beer.

"Yeah, well, it seems the details have been skewed. First of all, it was *on top* of the bar, not behind it," he corrected. "Second, it was after hours, so she and I were here alone and the only one getting a free show was Demi. She wanted to use the mirror to watch me go down on her. Was I supposed to say no to that? I mean, because, come on, what man in his right mind would? Besides, you know your girl as well as I do; what Demi wants . . ."

"Demi sure as hell is going to get," I finished for him.

Chaz raised his bottle, tilting the neck toward me for a toast before taking a long pull from it. "Your friend is corrupting me," he said with another chuckle.

I shook my head, swallowing my own gulp. "She's not corrupting you. She's encouraging you to be more adventurous. And judging by the *billion years* it took you to get up the nerve to ask her out in the first place, I'd say you need all the encouragement she's willing to give."

"Ah, shit. Can we not go there?" He sat back, his very large body sagging in the chair.

I loved riding him about dragging his feet in the beginning where she was concerned. It wasn't that he hadn't been attracted to Demi; it was just that he hadn't thought he was good enough for her. Forget about their opposite-side-of-the-tracks upbringing. His hang-up had largely been due to the significant difference in their pay grades. Probably still was.

"So when are you two going to tie the knot?" I asked.

Chaz choked on his beer. It took him a moment to recover, and when he did, he shook his head. "Not until I can be the man she deserves."

"But you're already the man she wants," I pointed out. "And if you're willing to act out her fantasies, you're also what she needs."

"Are we back to the bar top thing again?" he asked with another laugh. "You women always complain about us men having a one-track mind, but you're even worse than we are. Moving on . . ."

"Yeah, this conversation is all kinds of TMI, isn't it?"

"No such thing as TMI between good friends," he said with a genuine smile. And then he changed the subject. Or rather, redirected the spotlight. "So what's up with you and my boy? How's the counseling going?"

I shrugged, not really sure if I wanted to ruin my drastically improved mood. "It's going. We've only had one so far, but, man, was it a doozy."

"Want to talk about it?"

Not really, but I supposed it couldn't make matters worse. I was actually glad to have a neutral party to talk to. Like every good bartender, Chaz was an excellent listener who gave pretty sound advice. Besides that, he had always claimed he was Switzerland when it came to Shaw and me back when we were at each other's throat all the time, so I knew he wouldn't take sides. The fact that he was a man meant I could get a solid male point of view on things.

"He's bucking it, of course," I told him with a roll of my eyes.

"You get why, though, right?"

"Yeah, he told our therapist he wasn't crazy about discussing personal issues with a stranger. I think it's more than that, though."

"Like what?"

"I don't know. Like maybe he simply doesn't want to hear that he's wrong. You know Shaw. He thinks he's perfect and has the right answer for everything."

"Hi, pot! Meet kettle," he said sarcastically.

My eyes widened at his insinuation. "I do not think I have the right answer to everything! And I might be a perfectionist, but I don't think I'm perfect in the least bit. I'm full of doubts! Constantly questioning everything I do as a partner to him, a mother to Abe . . ."

"And you don't think Shaw has any doubts?"

"Not before today, but I'm pretty sure he does now," I mumbled, taking a swig.

"Yeah? Why's that?"

Before I knew it, I'd blurted out the words. "I told him and the therapist that I fake my orgasms."

And we were right back to the TMI stuff.

Chaz sputtered, all wide-eyed with brows reaching for his hairline. "You *what*?"

"Oh, God. Please don't make me say it again," I half-whined with a slump of my shoulders. I'd talked about it enough, thought about it enough, and knew all of that was only the beginning because Shaw and I had yet to really discuss it, what with his needing a *fucking moment*.

"Damn, Cass! I joke all the time about Demi carrying my balls around in her purse, but that? You castrated the man, for real." His hand disappeared beneath the table like he was making sure his own junk was still there, and then he made a show of checking out my neck. "You wearing 'em around your neck now? Because *duuude* . . . ," he said, exaggerating a shiver down his back.

Propping my elbows on the table, I put my head in my hands, feeling like absolute doo-doo that I'd revealed something so embarrassing to Shaw's best friend. In fact, Chaz was the only one of our friends who even knew we were going to counseling in the first place.

"It wasn't like I intentionally set out to do that. I was just being honest." I forced myself to look up at him, though I really wanted to get my ostrich on and hide my head in the sand again.

Chaz's head bobbed as he sat forward to rest his forearms on the table. "See, I can dig the whole honesty bit, but what's harder to understand is why you chose to come clean in front of someone else. Shit like that's way personal, you know? Why didn't you just talk to him about it?"

"Because I didn't feel like I could. I'd tried to talk to him about other things and he'd only blow me off, saying he didn't have the time."

"And you accepted that?"

I cocked my head in confusion. "What do you mean?"

"I mean that's not the Cassidy Whalen I know. See, *my* good friend Cassidy is fierce. Fierce enough to put a bunch of spoiled athletes in their place. Fierce enough to schmooze a whole room full of I-know-better-than-everyone-else suits. Fierce enough to be a top player in a male-dominated field. . . . Fierce enough to bring a man like Shaw Matthews to his fucking knees." He shook his head. "Maybe this whole motherhood thing has made you go soft. *Maybe* you need to get off the goddamn bench and get your ass back in the game, make some plays, score some points . . . and bring home the win. Though maybe you've forgotten how to win. Or is it that you just don't want it bad enough?"

My teddy bear image of Chaz Michaels had just taken up a clipboard and whistle while wearing too-short shorts, a polo shirt with pit stains, and a ball cap with some any-team logo all over the place. He might as well have been in my grill with a red face and spittle flying everywhere, and I half-expected him to order me to take a lap in full, padded uniform.

"Of course I want it. That's why I insisted on the counseling in the first place." I was well aware of how frustrated I sounded, though it was more at the situation than my friend. "And, um," I started fiddling with my fingers, "now we have to go see a sex therapist."

I squeezed my eyes shut, my body going tense and bracing for another WTF moment.

"Hey, hey, now!" I heard Chaz say, his voice full of approval. When I opened my eyes, I found him with a shit-eating grin on his face. "Now, that sounds like it might be aaalll riiight."

Funny, Shaw had had the same sort of reaction.

"Really?"

"Oh, hell yeah! That's guaranteed sex, girl! Prescribed by a professional, even! That lucky bastard!" Chaz sat his beer bottle down a little harder than I was sure he meant to. Not because he was angry but because he seemed to be genuinely envious of Shaw.

"But you," he said, wagging a finger at me. "You gotta take some control or lose it altogether."

"What do you mean?"

"I mean . . . you want something, so go get it."

I guffawed. "I can't rape him."

"Trust me, honey, you can't rape the willing. And men are *always* willing," he said with a wink as he took another drink of beer.

"I seriously doubt he's going to be willing after what I said today."

"Again, he's a man. Believe me, his little buddy is going to show up and out, whether he's in the mood or not. And maybe he won't get off, but then again, how long has it been since you have?"

"Chaz, I can't believe you're suggesting I take advantage of your best friend!"

"That's right! He *is* my best friend, so I know him better than you think I do. He'd give you anything you wanted, and you wouldn't even need to ask because it's there for the taking. Trust me on this." He looked across at the bar filling with customers, then down at his watch. "Oh, shit! Sorry, Cass, but I gotta get back to work."

"Oh, no, yeah. Go ahead," I said, shooing him away.

Chaz stood, grabbing his empty bottle and nodding toward my mug. "You want another one?"

I shook my head. "I think I'm going to head home now."

"Sure thing," he said. "I'm really glad you came in today, Cass. We've missed you around here."

"Yeah, I've missed you, too," I said, smiling up at him. "Oh, hey, look," I added, keeping him from leaving. "If Shaw knew I'd told you about any of this . . ."

The rest was understood. "Nah, don't worry about it, kid. I'm Switzerland, remember? This conversation never happened."

"Thank you."

"Not a problem, chica. Now go home and take a page out of my woman's book," he said with a wink. As he turned toward the bar, he shouted a "Hey, yo! Who needs what?"

I really loved the big lug. And maybe, just maybe, I should follow his advice.

By the time I got home, I found Shaw's sedan in his assigned parking spot. Though I was nervous about facing him, I was even more relieved that he'd decided to come home at all. He'd been pretty mad when I'd left him in the garage. No doubt, he was wondering where I'd been. Not that he'd called to check up on me or anything. He was probably just glad to have had his "fuck-ing moment," per his earlier request. Before, I might have been worried I was about to interrupt said moment, thereby exacerbating his mood even more, but I had a little liquid courage working through my system and had therefore decided his moment was up. So I squared my shoulders and made the trek inside and up to our apartment.

The door was unlocked when I got there, which was always dangerous, in my book, but . . . He Shaw. He man. He big and bad and bulletproof. Apparently.

Wow, that one beer really had given me a buzz.

However, I sobered almost immediately the moment I opened the door and saw what was playing out on the other side.

Shaw was sitting on the couch with his pants pushed down to his calves while fisting his cock.

"What are you doing?" I squeaked, hurriedly shutting the door behind me before a neighbor strolled by and got an eyeful. And believe me, it would have been an eye *very* full.

"You want to fuck, right?" Shaw stroked his cock with exaggerated movements, his thumb sweeping over the head on the upstroke before pushing all the way back down to the base to repeat the action with a tight squeeze.

Christ Almighty. All I could do was stand there, stunned. Or was I mesmerized?

"Here's your chance. Come here," he said, insistently waving me over. "If I'm not doing a good enough job of getting you off, then you're going to use my body to do it yourself."

When I said nothing and just continued to stare wide-eyed at him, he leveled me with a look that was every bit as menacing as the tone in his voice. His next words abruptly shook me from my stupor. "Take your fucking pants off and ride my fucking dick, Cassidy." It was a direct order.

Like that was a turn-on?

And then something occurred to me. It was definitely a turn-on. But I wondered, if he was so angry at me, how was this situation even possible? "You're hard?"

I'd figured if anything would throw the ice bucket on a man's sex drive, his girl admitting she was faking her orgasms would be it. Again, that hadn't at all been my intention.

"Of course, I am. Your smart mouth has that effect on me. Always has." He stopped masturbating, putting his hands on his hips, all business. Though it got zero assistance from Shaw, his cock still jutted proudly from his crotch like the flag being raised at Iwo Jima. "So are we doing this or what?"

Yes, we were definitely doing this. Shaw had a very important lesson to learn, and I was just the person to teach it to him. Plus, my panties were positively drenched at the thought of him being so hard for me, *seeing* him so hard for me.

In a matter of seconds, I'd gotten my inner Demi on, had stepped free of my leggings—the ones that used to turn him on—and had straddled his lap. I'd left my shirt in place because Shaw wasn't going to do anything about my breasts anyway. And then I took his thick cock in my hand, guiding it to my entrance, not needing any help in the least from my very surly assistant.

This wasn't about making love. This was about me finally getting what I wanted, for a change. Even if I had to do it myself. So I did.

Sinking down onto his cock, I took him all the way. Every . . . single . . . inch. It didn't matter how many times he'd been inside me, it had never stopped being a tight fit, one that had always made me feel powerful just for being able to accomplish the task. With no care at all as to how he might want me to ride him, I found my own stroke and was on the way toward Happy-Happy, Joy-Joy Land.

Sure, I could've closed my eyes and fantasized about any other man—Jensen Ackles, Scott Eastwood, or Adam Levine would've done nicely—but I didn't. I didn't because the thing that was shoving me toward what was shaping up to be the most intense orgasm I'd had lately was looking down at this man who had been denying me and taking it from him anyway.

Mine.

I rocked back and forth with deliberate motions and an exaggerated roll of my hips. Again, not for his pleasure, but mine. And you bet your sweet ass, I knew what I was doing was driving him insane, knew everything this man liked and didn't, and I used it all to my advantage. Not only would I have my pleasure, but I'd also make damn sure he'd remember who could give him his.

Digging my nails into his shoulders, I met his challenging glare and rode him harder, quickening my pace and letting the mental and physical sensations of the moment carry me away. I caught the furrow of his brow, the tell that he was nearing an orgasm, too. Nope. Not going to happen. He knew it. I could see it in his eyes. He knew I had no intention of letting him get his rocks off. And that pissed him off, good and proper.

Thank you, Shaw, for making this even more interesting for me. Giving him a knowing smirk—made famous by my fierce competitor—I acknowledged my intent. The race was on, both of us sprinting toward the finish line.

Reaching between us, I spread the folds of my pussy to expose my clit more fully and to take advantage of the friction my grinding against his groin was serving up. That was the edge I'd needed. Bearing down, I came hard, pinning him in my sights for the kill.

As my orgasm surged, Shaw tried to take over, but I swatted his hands away, denying the mutiny. Once the pleasure began to ebb, I didn't risk the chance Shaw would follow suit, quickly dismounting on wobbly knees and doing my best to get my breathing under control.

"What are you doing?" Shaw's cock was still raging hard, bobbing and slick with my orgasm. "I'm not done."

"But I am," I told him, going for my leggings. "And now you know how it feels to be left hanging."

"Fuck that," he said, the words rough and grated. I'd only managed to stab one leg into my leggings before Shaw reached out and grabbed me, his big hands lifting me up by the waist and hoisting me into the air. I landed with a thud back on the couch, the air whooshing out of my lungs and nearly vacating them entirely.

Shaw was between my thighs, his face buried against my neck and his shoulders taking the assist in pinning me down. With both hands full of my ass, he'd effectively secured me in place. And then he pushed into me. Entirely. His hips pistoned, thrusting into me with hard, fast, shallow pumps while he grunted against my skin.

Shaw was fucking me, and by God, there was *finally* some show of emotion while he was doing so. Anger, frustration, determination—not the emotions I truly wanted, but he was animated, and that made me feel alive.

With four hard thrusts, he came, growling in my ear as his final feral roar vibrated against my chest. I wanted to come all over again, but the tool attached to my partner was spent. Our labored breaths were the only sounds left after that.

Shaw didn't hold me to him. He didn't pepper my skin with light kisses, and he didn't whisper terms of endearment or promises of change. He didn't do any of that. In fact, he didn't linger at all.

Quickly climbing off me, he stood, yanking his pants up, and then working the zipper and button without a single word.

This was the man I'd chosen to spend the rest of my life with, the man who'd fathered my only child, the man I'd allowed to bask in the career I'd always wanted for myself while raising said child. I'd thought he was absent before, but now? Now he was standing right in front of me, but I couldn't sense his presence at all.

Mad that he'd taken something I'd tried to deny, I narrowed my eyes at him. "Do you feel better now?"

"I'm sure *you* do," he grated out.

"I absolutely do." Sitting upright, I finished the job of putting on my leggings that I'd started earlier. "But you didn't answer my question. How do you feel now?"

Working his belt through its buckle and then securing the leftover with the loop on his pants, he stopped and put his hands on his hips. Still without sparing me a glance, he said, "A real man *always* tends to his woman's needs before his own. Mere moments ago, I found out that, apparently, I haven't *been* much of a man lately." He paused with an incredulous shake of his head as his eyes finally met mine. "You emasculated me in front of a total fucking stranger, Cassidy. How the *fuck* do you think I feel?"

God, he looked so disconnected, lost. No, not lost. Abandoned.

I could empathize. But I couldn't make all of that go away even if I'd wanted to. Why should I when he'd never deigned to do the same for me? Maybe he hadn't known how he'd made me feel, but ignorance was no excuse when it came to matters of the heart.

With tears filling my eyes, I dealt another blow on the day.

"The same way I feel when you look at me like the only purpose I serve is to be a mother to your child. The same way I feel when every time you touch me, it's out of habit, like some sense of duty or a simple chore that has to be done. The same way I feel," I choked back a sob, "when you feel nothing at all."

His head fell back and he gazed at the ceiling. "If you really believe that . . . if you really think I feel nothing at all for you, then why are you still here?"

I stood, going up to him and putting my hands on either side of his face to force him to see me. "For all my life, I've only ever had one weakness: you, Shaw. I'm still here because I can't *be* anywhere without you."

Releasing him, I took a step back, surprised by my own confession. Once upon a time, I'd thought this man had made me stronger, pushed me harder, and challenged me to be so much more than what I was. And now? Now he was no longer my motivator but had instead become that by which I defined myself.

That was what Chaz had meant. I'd lost *me*, not Shaw.

Suddenly, I felt sick to my stomach. Sick and in desperate need to be anywhere but here. "I'm . . . I'm going to go get Abe," I said, grabbing my keys off the counter and making a beeline for the door.

Shaw grabbed me around my waist and pulled me back against his bare chest. Gone was the harsh tone, replaced by something gentler. "No, you're not. You've been drinking. I can smell it on your breath." He slowly took the keys from my hand.

"Shit." I'd forgotten. "It was just one beer, but I wouldn't have . . . Oh, God, I swear I wouldn't ever do that!"

"I know," he said with a comforting squeeze and a kiss to the hair over my ear. There was no tone of disappointment about either his words or his actions.

The roiling in my stomach increased tenfold, and I knew it was only a matter of seconds before I lost its contents all over the place. Pulling away from him, I ran for the bathroom, not only because I was about to be sick but also because I was so tired of letting him see the tears in my eyes. For once, he hadn't been the one to cause them. Maybe he never had.

CHAPTER 6

Shaw

Last night, for the first time in a really long time, Cassidy had slept in our bed. So close, yet still so very far away. I'd wanted to reach out and hold her, I really had, but there was just so much *distance* between us.

When I'd gone to bed, she'd been situated all the way on the edge of her side with the blankets pulled up to her cheek, her face barely visible. And that was where she'd stayed. I'd tried to pretend I hadn't heard her tears, as much as she'd tried to hide the fact that she was crying. But I'd heard her. And with every sniffle, my heart had broken a little more.

She was right. Something was very wrong between us. The problem was that, though I'd always been able to find a solution when glitches happened in business, some way around the hiccup, matters of the heart weren't as easily solved. Whatever the issue between us, it certainly was not a glitch or hiccup, and no amount of fast talking or kissing ass was going to make this go away.

It was time for me to admit defeat, stop fighting her perceived solution, and just do things her way as a willing participant. That was the conclusion I'd drawn by the time my alarm clock had gone off and I'd rolled over to find her side of the bed empty once more.

With a weighted sigh, I pulled the covers back and stood, clad in nothing but pajama bottoms, which was more than I normally ever wore to bed. Of course I'd done that out of respect to Cassidy. I was sure the last thing she'd want to wake to was me, now a virtual stranger, naked and sporting a woody next to her. Especially not after what had happened between us the night before.

I knew where she'd be, so I made the short walk through the living area and stopped, looking down at my bare feet as I stood before the door to Abe's room. Not entirely sure what I should do, I raised a knuckle to knock, then decided that was silly. This was my son's bedroom, in my home, and my woman was on the other side of that door.

So I quietly cracked it open and stepped inside, not at all surprised to find Cassidy curled up in Abe's bed while snuggling his favorite Superman blanket, which matched the superhero décor of the rest of his room. For whatever reason, the sight was like being slapped in the face with a cold, dead fish.

The only two people who believed me to be a superhero, who wished with all their might for me to live up to the image, had lost faith in me. Hell, I had lost faith in myself.

How could I let them down? And more to the point, how was I going to find a way around my kryptonite when the kryptonite was me? Me and my pride. Me and my ambitions. Me and my inability to see the fucked-up choices I was making before said choices had been made.

Creeping across the room, careful not to make a sound, I looked down at my Cassidy and smiled when I saw the tiniest bit of drool at the corner of her full, pink mouth. Her hair was a mess of tangles the color of a Southern Californian sunset, and her long lashes rested gently upon flawless ivory skin, tinged a natural flush of color at the cheeks. Her breasts were fuller, her hips more rounded, her belly a little pooched, and her ass supple rather than toned. No doubt she saw all those physical characteristics as flaws. But not me. I saw her as a stunning woman made even more magnificent by the effects of motherhood.

I'd never want another as much as I wanted her.

Brushing a strand of hair away from her face, I grinned when her forehead crinkled and her lips did that pouty thing that reminded me so much of Abe. God, there was so much of her in him. His willfulness, his determination, his ability to always see the positive in every situation—that was all Cassidy.

Peering down at her I wondered if she realized *she* was the superhero. Not me.

But I could be her sidekick. Which meant I needed to follow her lead while sharing the load. And I knew just where to start.

Leaving Cassidy undisturbed, I backed out of Abe's room and made my way back to our bedroom, where my cellphone was charging. Then I went over to the pants I'd worn the day before and pulled the little black card out of the back pocket where I'd tucked it away with every intention of discarding it later. Dialing the number, I paced as the line began to ring. I was shocked when a voice answered on the other end of the line. Mostly because it was before seven o'clock in the morning, and I'd only thought to leave a message for a return call.

"Hello, is anyone there?" the voice—a distinctly rich and smooth female voice, accented—asked when I didn't respond to her initial greeting.

"I . . . I'm sorry, I must have dialed the wrong number."

Surely I had. There was no rambling of the customary office name and "How may I help/direct your call?" that I'd expect from a receptionist of a business.

But before I could disconnect the line, the woman on the other end said, "No one ever dials this number by mistake, darling. You are looking for Katya?"

"Uh, yes. Dr. Katya Minkov," I told her. "I was given this number by a colleague of hers, and—"

"Not hers, yours," she interrupted.

"Excuse me?"

"I am Katya. And you are Shaw Matthews, are you not?"

Holy shit. How could she possibly know that? Duh. Caller ID.

"Jeremy, my precious secret agent, has already phoned ahead with his recommendation for you and your lover. I will meet with you tonight at eight P.M., sharp."

"Wait, wait, wait," I said, anticipating an abrupt dial tone. "I don't know if we can do that."

Eight o'clock? Who keeps those kinds of office hours? Plus, that was Abe's bedtime, and if the way Cassidy was hugging his blanket had been any indication, I highly doubted she'd want to be separated from him for another night.

"Come, don't come. Makes no difference to me. The opportunity will not be presented again." She quickly recited an address, and I had to scramble to find a pen to jot it down on the back of the card, hoping I'd gotten it right before the line went dead.

I pulled back the phone and looked at it as if there were going to be some kind of explanation for my confusing encounter on the screen. What a very weird way to start the day, and I had a feeling that phone call would not be the weirdest thing about Dr. Katya Minkov.

After I'd showered and dressed—hurriedly, since I was already running late for work—I went out to the main room and found Cassidy sitting at the bar counter with a cup of coffee and bowl of Apple Jacks, Abe's favorite, in front of her. She'd pulled her tangled hair into a haphazard ponytail and draped a robe over her boxer shorts and cami pajamas. Her shoulders were slumped and her socked feet propped up on the rungs of the stool as she pushed the little green and orange circles through the milk in a lazy manner. I couldn't tell if she was still half asleep or maybe just didn't know what to do with herself since Abe wasn't running around and using our living room furniture as a jungle gym while she begged him to sit and eat his breakfast. Either way, she simply looked . . . sad and lonely.

But I had news that would cheer her up, and even though I didn't have the time to, I went to the cabinet and got a bowl, determined that she wouldn't eat alone.

"Good morning," I said, pouring my own cereal.

Cassidy looked at me, then to the clock on the wall, and back to me again, clearly confused. "Um, good morning. You're not working today?"

Putting the milk back into the refrigerator, I closed the door and looked down at myself and the business attire I wore every day. Arching a brow at the clear indication, I gave her an amused grin. "Yep," I said, and then took the seat on the stool next to her.

"But you're going to be late." Her statement sounded more like a question.

"Yep," I repeated. "I think they can survive for a little bit without me while I have breakfast with my woman."

"Oh. Okay." She was clearly still confused, but resumed eating all the same.

We ate in silence for a time, neither of us quite sure what to say. I supposed it had been longer than I'd thought since it had just been the two of us alone like this. Maybe Abe had always filled the quiet before.

"So I made an appointment with Dr. Minkov this morning," I told her, hoping to ease the awkwardness. "Or at least I think I made an appointment."

"What do you mean?"

"Well, I didn't so much schedule an appointment as I was issued a directive that we should show up at eight o'clock tonight or not at all."

"What?"

"Weird, right? Still," I shrugged, "it's done."

"But what about Abe? I don't like not having him here."

"I know. Me neither. But like I said, it has to be tonight or not at all."

Cassidy sighed. "This is too much, isn't it? Maybe we just shouldn't go."

"What are you talking about? I want to go!"

"Really?"

"Yeah! Come on, where's your sense of adventure?" My hand found her knee and I gave her a playful nudge. "I think it's going to be a lot of fun."

She drew her head back, suspicious. "You do?"

"Are you kidding me? Sex," I told her. "Prescribed sex, even. How could that *not* be fun?" I laughed, hoping she would, too.

She didn't, but she did smile. "I have no idea what to expect, to be honest, but if you're so gung ho about it, I guess we should at least give it a try."

"That's the spirit!" I said, giving her knee a squeeze before finishing off my cereal.

"So what should we do about Abe, then?"

I shrugged, mostly because Cassidy was usually the one who took care of that sort of thing. That was my bad. Yet another example of the ways I'd failed at being a father. "Well, obviously he can't go with us. Do you think maybe Quinn will keep him again?"

Cassidy shook her head. "I'm sure he and Denver don't want to play house two nights in a row, though they'd never say it. They love spending time with him and all, but they also like sending him back home." She nibbled her lip in contemplation as she stirred her cereal. "Oh, I know! Chaz and Demi have wanted some time with him. I'll call them."

"Sounds like a plan," I said, rinsing my bowl and putting it in the sink. "Sorry, but I've gotta run. Meet you at Monkey's for dinner before we head out to our next shrink?"

At the slight narrowing of her eyes, I laughed. "Kidding, kidding! I'll see you later." Kissing the top of her head, I grabbed my briefcase and headed for the door.

"Shaw?"

I pulled up short and turned on my heel to face her. "Yeah?"

Cassidy set her spoon down and pushed the bowl away. "Why are you suddenly willing to do all of this? I mean, I'm glad"—her brow creased—"but why?"

I should've expected her suspicion, and I didn't blame her for asking about my intentions. I'd been tugging pretty damn hard in the opposite direction on this whole therapist thing, and I hadn't exactly been forthright about my feelings other than to tell her all the negatives. Call it a man thing or whatever, but it was time I came clean, time for me to show her a side of Shaw Matthews she rarely got a glimpse of, others not at all. "Because I can't *be* anywhere without you, either, Cassidy. Nor do I want to. So I'm all in. Just don't . . . don't give up on me."

Cassidy looked contemplative but still nodded her acceptance of my answer, even though I could tell she was trying to make sense of my one-eighty. I set my briefcase down by the door and crossed the space between us. Cassidy twisted around on her stool toward me, eyes wide as she drew back, not quite sure what I was about to do.

The backs of my fingers caressed her cheek down to her chin and then I swept my thumb over her worried lip. Cassidy closed her eyes and slowly exhaled a breath I hadn't realized she'd been holding. Leaning down, I pressed my lips to hers with a firm yet gentle kiss. After a moment, she kissed me back, her mouth pliant and giving. I could taste the faint sugary sweetness from the cereal she'd just had, and I licked at her bottom lip for more of it. My tongue swept inside her mouth, coaxing hers into submission so I could show her. Show her that this was where I wanted to be, that she was the only woman I'd ever need, that I might not know how to convey my feelings for her sometimes, but that they were there and they were real.

We were breathing for each other by the time I broke the kiss, my forehead resting against hers as I tried to get my thoughts in line because the woman had a way of making me disoriented just from a single kiss.

Cassidy's eyes were still closed, almost as if she were saying a silent prayer, though I'd never known her to be a particularly religious person. I could feel the warmth of her breath as it fanned out against my lips, my cheeks, cooling as it spread over my neck. I saw it so clearly then, the resemblance of that one action, so intimate and vital, to our relationship. Like a breath, we were warm, red-hot, the closer to each other we remained, but if we let the distance come between us . . . that was when the coldness crept in.

I wasn't going to let that happen.

Cupping her face in both hands, I told her, "We're going to get through this. I need you to know we will, Cassidy, because I'm going to do the right thing by you. I'm not saying I'll be perfect along the way or that some asshole part of me won't come out when I get frustrated, but I'm going to *try*. Okay?"

Her nod was barely perceptible, but I felt it against my forehead.

Leaving the cocoon of our embrace, I pulled back and looked down at her. Cassidy's eyes were open but cast down toward her lap, where she was fidgeting with her fingers.

"Hey," I said, and then waited for her to look up. She did, orbs the color of sprouting tufts of grass in the spring peering back at me with so much hope. "I love you."

Her resulting grin was about as unexpected, yet finally genuine, as could be. Though I knew it didn't seem like a very masculine response, my heart fluttered in my chest and then filled with that "feel good" sort of warmth when her voice, ever so soft and sweet, said, "I love you, too."

That morning when I left our home to face the drudging day ahead, I did it with a little extra pep in my step. Even if I was anxious as hell about the mysterious appointment with our *sex therapist*.

Cassidy

Today had been one of the better days I'd had over the last couple of years. Thanks in large part to Shaw's tiniest bit of submission this morning. Abe and I spent the day together, doing everything he wanted to do and eating whatever junk food his little heart desired. I might have been overcompensating a bit because of my guilt over sending him off again to spend the night somewhere other than his own bed.

Though I felt like the crappiest mother of all time, my Abey Baby was thrilled to go see his uncle Chaz and aunt Demi. In fact, he'd jumped up and down clapping when Demi had asked him if he wanted to play "Wrestlemania" again. Apparently, Demi and Abe team up against Chaz, who lets Abe win until Uncle Chaz deploys the tickle-claw maneuver, and then Abe tags Demi in. Abe laughed and said it was "big fun" to see Aunt Demi beat up Uncle Chaz. Since Demi was a self-defense instructor, I knew her winning had nothing to do with Chaz letting her. I almost felt sorry for Chaz, to be honest. More so when he groaned and cupped his balls.

Shaw was even on time for dinner at Monkey's. Sasha and Landon had joined us and I'd actually felt like an adult for once. We'd laughed and done the catching-up thing until Shaw looked down at his watch and cleared his throat to get my attention, tapping on the face of the thing to tell me we needed to get going or we'd be late. Neither of us wanted that since this whole ordeal felt like we were agents going undercover to expose some deeply concealed secret society of sexaholics plotting to take over the world or whatever.

But when we got to the address Dr. Minkov had given to Shaw, it quickly became clear that my amusing wonderings might not have been far off the mark.

"Are you sure this is the right address?" I leaned forward in my seat as if the windshield would behave as a pair of glasses and allow me to see things more clearly.

I saw things clearly enough, all right. We were in an empty lot, the painted lines of the parking spaces on the cracked asphalt faded, obviously not having been maintained for quite some time.

Thanks to the illumination of Shaw's headlights, I could see there was one building, giant and looming and dark—an abandoned industrial warehouse, complete with broken windows, rain-rusted stains down the corrugated aluminum siding, and graffiti spray painted on every surface.

Shaw checked and double-checked the address against his GPS. "This is what I wrote down. She said it so fast, I must have gotten it wrong."

If I hadn't known beyond a shadow of a doubt that Shaw had been genuine when he'd said he was all in on this therapy thing, I would've thought he'd gotten the address wrong on purpose. Further proving my belief that "it had been an accident" was his explanation for the intentional error. He raked his fingers through his hair, his jaw ticking and leg bouncing. "Fuck, I'm sorry."

I knew he really was. Putting a hand on his arm, I took a deep breath. "It's okay." I shrugged and forced a smile. "Guess it wasn't meant to be. Let's just go get Abe and head home."

With another curse at himself, Shaw put the car in reverse and started to back out, only to have to stomp on the brake. I jerked forward, caught by the seatbelt and pushed back into an upright position.

"What the hell?" Shaw shouted, looking into the rearview mirror. I turned the top half of my body to see what the holdup was and saw a pair of headlights from another car getting closer and closer until the thing was practically on top of our rear bumper. Shoving the gear into park, Shaw cut the engine and ripped off his seatbelt as he flung open the door.

"Shaw, don't!" I tugged on his arm, trying to make him stay put, but he yanked away. Dark parking lot, plus abandoned building, plus strange vehicle with high-beam lights equaled all kinds of *Dateline* murder mystery.

"I'm just going to see what this asshole's problem is. I'll be okay," he told me. Not at all convincingly, I might add.

My heart was racing with fear. This was the industrial district of San Diego, California, for Christ's sake. Abandoned warehouses were ideal for drug deals and murders. I gasped, suddenly thinking about Abe being orphaned after both of his parents were killed in cold blood, *if* our bodies were ever found. "Shaw, get back in the car! They could have a gun!"

He *pfft*'d me. Actually drew his head back and looked at me like I was being overly dramatic with a "*Pfft!* They don't have a gun. It's probably a couple of teenagers coming here to make out. Stop worrying. I'm just going to scare them a little and then I'll be back."

Really, it wasn't necessary to even do that much. But I stayed in the car, watching him through the back window the whole time. Not that I could see much with the headlights glaring like that. A minute or two passed, though it seemed like way more, before Shaw came back, opening the door and bending down to poke his head inside.

"Come on, let's go."

"Go? Go where?" My voice was ten octaves higher than normal. Or at least it seemed that way to me.

"That's our ride," he told me, nodding back toward the bright lights.

I shook my head vehemently. "Uh-uh. Get back in the car and let's get out of here."

"Cassidy, I called Dr. Minkov myself to confirm what the driver told me. Apparently, she's taking extra precautions to make sure her location remains a secret. I'm not sure what the big deal is, but you really wanted to do this, so let's do it."

"Let me get this straight," I began, still astounded that he was being so nonchalant about the scary weirdness of our current situation. "We're given an address to an empty parking lot where a strange vehicle closes us in, and then we're instructed to leave the safety of our car to get into said strange vehicle to be taken to an unknown secret location to meet up with some sex doctor, and none of our family or friends know our whereabouts . . . and you don't see a problem with that?"

"Oh, this has *probable homicide* written all over it," he admitted. "In fact, I think you just described the plot of like a thousand horror flicks, but . . ."

"But what?"

"Where's your sense of adventure?" He chuckled at my disapproving scowl. "Cass, you trust Dr. Sparling, right?"

I nodded. At least I thought I trusted him. It was entirely possible he could be a member of a cult, in charge of sending unsuspecting innocents into a trap so they could be strapped to a sacrificial altar to pay homage to some gruesome deity with a thirst for blood.

"He's the one who gave us the referral, and he did say Dr. Minkov's methods were unusual."

"Unusual? That's an understatement." I worried my bottom lip as my brain went haywire, recalling all the reviews I'd found for Dr. Sparling online. Not only that, but his credentials had checked out. I'd done the research myself, and I trusted my own findings far better than anything Google could throw out there. On the other hand, I hadn't found anything on Dr. Minkov at all.

"Cass, you know I'd never let anything happen to you."

Men and their machismo. Almost every one of them I knew thought they were bulletproof.

"Are we going or not?" Shaw prodded. "I have a feeling

Dr. Minkov doesn't like to be kept waiting, so it's sort of a now-or-never kind of deal."

Feeling the urgency of the moment, I made a quick decision that I hoped I wouldn't live to regret, *if* I came out of this alive at all. "Okay, fine. But if we die, I'm so going to kill you," I said, grabbing my purse and getting out of the car.

I heard the distinctive two-tone beeps of Shaw locking the car and setting the alarm, and then he joined me at the rear. Placing a hand at the small of my back, he escorted me toward the back door of the black sedan. I tried to get a look at the driver in case I'd need details for a sketch artist later, but the front windshield was completely blacked out. As were the rest of the windows.

The driver stepped around the car and met us at the back passenger door, opening it for us. I hadn't even seen him get out. What, was he made of shadows? At least I was able to get a good look at him. He was much taller than Shaw with broad shoulders and thick arms that he kept at his sides as he waited for us to get inside. I couldn't see the color of his eyes or hair since he wore sunglasses—at night—and his hair was cropped short beneath a driver's hat, but I did get a good look at the tattoo on his right hand. It was the side profile of a lion's head with long, sharp canines and a serpent's tongue. It could have been something artistic, but it seemed more like something found in a crest of some sort. Maybe even for that fictional secret society that was becoming more real by the minute.

Leery as I was about the whole situation, I got into the back, sliding along the smooth, soft black leather. Shaw got in behind me, relaxing into the cushiony seat as if he hadn't a care in the world. The driver did nothing but nod when Shaw thanked him and then the door was closed.

"Um . . . so this is odd," I said, realizing that not only could no one see into the car, but we also couldn't see out. Except for the front windshield. Until the driver got inside and a blacked-out partition lifted into place, and then we were essentially blindfolded with nothing more than the muted illumination of a floor light.

I was reminded of a wet dream I'd had so very long ago. A dream I still believe had been an implanted suggestion when my friends had recommended I sleep with Shaw in order to knock him off his game, when we'd been competing for the partnership. I crossed my legs, the memory of it so naughty a sudden need began to blossom at my core. I'd never told Shaw about that dream. Looking at him now, I wondered whether he would have tried to reenact it if I had. We were so far away from that place now. I'd do anything to get back there, though.

Even get into a strange car with a scary driver to be taken to an unknown location.

Shaw reached over and took my hand, giving me a reassuring smile. I gaped down at where he held me, the act such a small thing, but it had been so long since he'd done even that much, I hadn't realized I'd been missing it. Until now.

We rode in awkward silence for a while, having no clue where we were or where we'd end up. After a bit, I heard the distinct sound of gravel under tires, the car's weight shifting ever so slightly, as if traversing uneven ground. We had to have been climbing because gravity pushed me back into my seat ever so slightly. And then we came to a stop.

Shaw squeezed my hand. "Well, guess we're here."

"Wherever here is," I mumbled.

The car door opened and our chauffeur took up the same stance as before, giving us enough room to exit. Shaw offered me his hand again, and I took it, following his line of sight once I got out.

I don't know what I'd been expecting—an office building, for sure—but instead it was a house. Splendid, but still just a house. And we were on top of a hill that looked out over the ocean in the distance from an A-frame log cabin with solid glass that made up the entire front. The giant trees that encased the house on both sides swayed back and forth in the ocean breeze, the sound of waves crashing on the shore in the distance a comforting cadence during an otherwise anxious moment.

The driver uttered his first words as he closed the car door behind us. "Dr. Minkov is waiting for you inside." His voice was a deep baritone, almost Lurch-like in its cadence.

Again, Shaw thanked him. And again, the driver only nodded in response as he went around to get back into the car and pull away.

Shaw again put his hand at the small of my back. "Ready?"

"Not really, but I guess there's no backing out now," I said, letting him guide me toward the porch.

By the time we'd climbed the steps, I saw movement inside the house. A well-dressed man in a suit greeted us at the front door, opening it wide before we'd had a chance to knock. "Shaw and Cassidy, I presume?"

"That would be us," Shaw answered.

"Welcome to the home of Dr. Katya Minkov. Please, come inside. Dr. Minkov is expecting you." He stepped to the side with a courteous smile to allow us passage before shutting us in.

"If you'll follow me, I'll take you to her office," he said, taking up a comfortable pace forward as we fell in line behind him.

I couldn't help but look around in awe of Dr. Minkov's home. Though the floors and walls were made of a polished red cedar, the fixtures had a contrasting elegance of gold and crystal. The huge chandelier of teardrop crystals that hung above the main living space gave off prisms of rainbow light that reflected off the front floor-to-ceiling window, which provided a picturesque view of the moonlit ocean. A warm fire of driftwood crackled in the fireplace, scenting the air with a natural fragrance. Large area rugs and runners of deep red and cream to match the leather furniture covered the expanse of the flooring, giving the place a cozy sort of feel.

Down the corridor and to the left, we followed another hallway toward the back of the house, where our guide stepped inside the open door to a room.

"Please, make yourselves comfortable. Dr. Minkov will be with you shortly." He bowed slightly, motioning for us to enter the room, and then he crossed back over the threshold to take his leave.

We were in an office, decorated much like the rest of the house, but with two chairs before a large ornate desk. There were no pictures on the desk or the walls, nothing that would hint at the personal life of this woman to whom we were expected to divulge the intimate details of our life.

Shaw walked over to the small couch in the center of the room, turning with his brow lifted in expectation for me to follow. I had no idea what we'd gotten ourselves into, but at this point, it was a little too late to back out.

"You okay?" he asked.

"Yeah, I guess," I said, joining him. "I hope she doesn't keep us waiting long."

"Ah, but anticipation is the catalyst of everything worth waiting for, darling," a silky-smooth, accented voice said from the doorway.

CHAPTER 7

Cassidy

I jumped, startled by the new presence I hadn't heard approaching. With my pulse still racing, I turned in my chair just in time to see the door close as the woman who'd joined us tilted the corner of her mouth up into a sultry smile.

Standing at nearly six feet tall, she was dressed in a black leather pantsuit that hugged her generous curves so tightly it must have taken her hours to get into it. Creamy skin covered a regal neck and collarbone, while the deep cut of her jacket boasted a plentiful bosom. I'd wager she wasn't wearing anything more than a matching bra under that suit, if that. Black peep-toe heels of no less than five inches were on her feet, accounting for her height, with bold red nail polish adorning her toes, which complemented her fingernails. Platinum blond hair was stacked in a complicated up-do of curls, braids, and more curls, each strand threatening to fall lose from the weight of it, yet it looked carefully controlled. Much like her demeanor.

She crossed the room to the wingback chair at my right, her walk something like a Pied Piper for grown men that commanded a following.

"My name is Dr. Minkov, but considering the personal topic we'll be discussing, in depth," she said with a not-so-subtle meaning as she took a seat, "I prefer to be as informal as possible. So please, call me Katya. And you are?"

"You don't know who you scheduled a meeting with?" Shaw wasn't nearly as tongue-tied as I'd become in this woman's presence.

"I find that an introduction of one's self can be an icebreaker of sorts. Like an alcoholic finally breaking his silence and deciding to discuss a problem he hasn't seen as a problem until he says it out loud."

Shaw set his shoulders. "We're not alcoholics. Or sexaholics, for that matter." He'd gone from more relaxed than I'd seen him in a long time to defensive again.

"Ah, but there is a problem, is there not?"

"I'm Cassidy," I told her, hoping to ease the mounting tension.

Katya leaned forward, the movement sending a waft of her perfume to caress my senses. I'd had no idea *forbidden* was a scent, but she was wearing it as if it were a designer fragrance of her own making. I was still caught in the spell of it when I registered her hand on my knee and the flagrant squeeze that followed before she looked directly at me and said, "I look forward to becoming very intimate with you, Cassidy. You've pleased me well already."

I swallowed hard, clearly affected by her words. This woman had to have been a dominatrix in her off time because, though I didn't know how I'd pleased her, I found I was eager to do it again.

Katya's eyes were stunning. Catlike in color—golden brown with a jade green burst that fanned out into a darker outer ring—

and framed by dramatic lashes and dark eyebrows with a definitively perfect arch. Her lips were lush, stained the same color red as her fingernails, so plump one bite promised to yield the sweetest juice. I nibbled my own lip, not realizing it until Katya's gaze went to my mouth and she smiled before pulling my imprisoned lip free with her thumb.

"I'm Shaw."

I sobered at the sound of Shaw's voice, having forgotten for a moment that he was in the room. No idea what had come over me. I wasn't into women, but Katya exuded sex. Male, female, it didn't matter.

Katya turned her attention to Shaw, but it was a distinctly different sort of attention. No hands-on greeting like I'd just received. And he seemed unaffected by her obvious charms. In fact, I think I detected a low growl of warning from him. Was he jealous of a woman?

"Shaw." She inclined her head in acknowledgment before she sat back, her posture perfect, chest proud, legs crossed, and arms regal on the armrests of the chair. "Before we continue, I must first determine whether the two of you can benefit from the sort of coaching I provide. I'm quite unorthodox in my methods, and, as such, I need to be sure you qualify for my services."

"You're interviewing us?" Shaw asked, surprised by the role reversal.

"Yes." Her answer was simple, confident. "What do you hope to accomplish during our sessions?"

My palms had begun to sweat. Why was I suddenly so nervous? "I'm not really sure what to expect from our time with you."

"Sex," she said, matter-of-factly. Bulgarian. Her accent was definitely Bulgarian, and it carried an alluring undertone of sensuality. "My purpose is to help coax that spark you once had back into a raging inferno. I want you to burn for each other, for your desire to devour the very oxygen in the air until you're breathing fire into your lungs, pumping molten lava through your veins, and feeling the threat of self-combustion with your every orgasm."

"Sounds . . . dangerous." Judging by Shaw's mocking tone, he was not impressed.

But I was. "I think it sounds exciting."

Katya's grin was mischievous. "Danger and excitement should be the foundation of every sexual encounter. If your heart isn't racing, your pulse pounding, how else will you know you're alive?"

As if commanded by her words, my body reacted in the same manner she'd described, and I understood what she meant about feeling alive. I'd felt the same way when Shaw and I had first started our clandestine relationship, back when being trapped in an elevator or the back of a limousine or the bathroom on a private jet meant we were about to embark upon a sexual adventure like none I'd ever known before him.

"When do we start?" I sat forward with unabashed eagerness.

Katya gave me another one of those approving grins. "You are willing. I like it. But when one learns to swim, he or she does not simply jump into the deepest part of the sea. You must first get your feet wet on the beach, feel the sand caress your toes as the surf beckons you forward, and then wade into the shallow water until you've become accustomed to the pull of the ocean and learn to simply let go and allow it to set you adrift."

How had she managed to make swimming so devastatingly sexy? As the daughter of a fisherman, practically born and raised on the ocean, I could appreciate the analogy.

"We already know how to swim," Shaw interjected. "What

you're describing sounds an awful lot like you want us to get lost at sea."

"Are you not already lost? Is that not why you are sitting here with me at this moment, seeking my help?" Point well made. "Splashing around in the water will only make waves and create a lot of noise, an invitation for a predator to have a sampling of your dinghy if you are not careful." Katya grinned at her own double entendre. So did I.

"Consider me a lifeguard, Shaw," Katya told him. She certainly had the whole *Baywatch* look down. "My guidance and the methods I use will only act as a flotation device until your lessons are complete. Are you agreeable to that, or are you such a master of the sea that you do not need my help?"

I turned toward Shaw, placing my hand high on his thigh and giving it a squeeze. "I want to feel the pull of the ocean." Making a show of letting my eyes rake over his body to settle on his crotch, I licked my bottom lip and then pulled it between my teeth. "Please?"

He crooked a finger under my chin, lifting my gaze to his. Startling blue eyes stared back at me, a measure of lust present there that I hadn't seen in quite some time. When the pad of his thumb swept over my lip, I pressed a kiss to it. And there went that sexy half grin/half smirk of his that made me weak in the knees. "You have no idea what it does to me to hear you beg."

Oh, I had an idea, all right. Even though I was sure it had pained him to do so, I remembered a time when he'd kept his cock away from me when I'd wanted it in my mouth so bad I couldn't stand it. Shaw had only given me my way after I'd begged and pleaded on my knees.

Dear God, we hadn't even begun our session yet, and I was

already aching for a release. Maybe I'd take another from him once we returned home tonight.

"She will be doing a great deal of begging . . . if I decide the three of us are a good fit." Katya's reminder that she hadn't yet agreed to take us on as clients was like a douse of cold water to the smoldering hot coals Shaw had just stoked.

Keeping my hand right where it was on Shaw's thigh, I shifted to face her. "When will you know?"

"Before you leave here this evening." Katya stood, doing the Pied Piper thing again as she went to her desk and took a seat. She opened the folder that sat atop the cherry-red leather blotter and picked up a pen. "Let's get to it, shall we? I'm going to ask some personal questions of the both of you to help me get an idea of where the issue may lie and whether I can help you. And if you feel these questions are too personal"—she gave Shaw a pointed look—"we will not be a good fit as things are going to become much, much more personal than that, I assure you."

Shaw covered my hand with his as he readjusted his position the slightest bit. A semi-quiet gasp of surprise fell from my lips when I felt something rigid graze my palm and I looked directly at the spot of contact. It wasn't just something rigid. It was his cock. Clearly he was so onboard with all of this now. When I met his eyes, I was rewarded with a pantie-melting wink.

"Shoot, Doc," he told her, redirecting his attention.

Katya had just looked up from the folder, having missed the exchange. "Do either of you have any issues preparing for sex?"

Shaw's brow furrowed. "What do you mean?"

Katya leaned forward, enunciating each of her next words. "Does your cock get hard for her?"

I looked between Katya and Shaw, markedly turned on by the

topic at hand. Though I already knew the answer to her question, I wanted to hear how Shaw would respond. If the rest of our discussions with Katya were going to be anything remotely close to this, I'd do anything to make sure we passed her test.

"I don't have a problem getting it up, Doc. In fact, I'm hard for her right this very second."

Any other woman would've looked to see the truth for herself, but not Katya. She merely grinned, a muted "touché" adorning her expression.

"And how about you, Cassidy?"

Oh. How to answer this? "My body reacts to his," I told her. "I just don't, um, orgasm during sex like I used to."

Shaw went rigid beside me, obviously still ego-struck by the truth. But we were here to fix it, so I had to be honest.

Katya tilted her head. "Is that so? And why do you think that is?"

I shrugged. "I guess because it doesn't feel good."

On cue, an exaggerated, insulted *pfft!* from Shaw. He pushed my hand from his lap. "Sex with me doesn't feel good? So I suck in bed now?"

Of course he would take offense.

"It's not that. It's . . . I don't know, a mental thing, maybe? Mentally, I'm not engaged." I drew my head back, not liking that he was making me out to be the bad guy here when it took two to tango. "Neither are you. It's like . . . like something we do out of habit now. And not very often, at that."

Before Shaw could respond, Katya did some refereeing. "It's quality, not quantity, that matters," she told me.

"Yeah, well, nothing but quickies doesn't exactly allow for much quality," I mumbled under my breath, though I knew they could both hear me.

Shaw bristled, proving me right. "Oh, so let's just bash Shaw, right? It's all my fault? We don't have a lot of time for sex because of the hours I work. That's what you're driving at, right?"

Oh, my God! I was so exasperated by the hot-and-cold volleying we'd become so good at. He was just hard, I was just wet, and now we were back at each other's throat. My hands slapped down on my thighs and my head whipped toward him. "I'm home all day and all night, so I'm really not sure how it can be my fault."

Shaw got that look in his eye that said he was about to put me in my place. "We'd have plenty of chances to not only *have* sex more often, but more *thoroughly* if you actually slept in our bed."

Ouch.

Katya arched a disapproving brow at me. "You don't sleep together in the same bed?"

"Okay, fine. No. I sleep with our son a lot of the time," I admitted, sounding very much like the accused on the stand confessing to a crime before the judge.

"I can help you," Katya said, abruptly ending the discussion on the matter.

"What?" I asked, confused.

"I said, I can help you. But you will need to do everything I say and trust that I know what I'm doing. Will you agree?"

I knew that I should be leery of allowing a stranger to have complete control over my life, but I trusted Dr. Minkov, though it made no sense for me to. Maybe I was just desperate to get things back to the way they used to be between Shaw and me. Maybe I was just desperate to know that passion again. Or maybe I was just riding that competitive high of having won a prize. Because, yeah, we'd just aced Dr. Minkov's test and she looked well pleased!

I looked at Shaw. While it was true that we argued a lot, that was simply who we were, who we'd always been. Still, I knew with every fiber of my being that I wanted no one but him, that I'd never find with another the passion he and I had shared once upon a time. We could get it back. I knew we could. We could go back to the way we were.

"Yes," I told her without turning away from Shaw.

All that turbulence turned into determination. The Shaw I knew and loved had made an appearance once more and I felt the first flicker of confidence that we could come back from this faraway place where we'd found ourselves.

Shaw took my hand and placed it back on his lap. "We'll do whatever it takes," he said.

"I'd hoped you'd agree." Katya returned her attention to the folder on her desk, pulling out some forms and handing the stack over to Shaw and me. "The first document is our contract. You'll each need to sign it before we can begin. The second is a questionnaire designed to help me get to know your desires better. I only need you to sign the contract today. Take a moment to look it over so that you understand everything that will be expected of you and what you can expect from me."

I read over the document, noting a lot of the same expectations as Dr. Sparling had had. The confidentiality section was ironclad, on both sides, and we'd be agreeing to follow the plan Katya would design for us.

Admittedly, I was a little anxious about signing an agreement promising to do whatever someone else told me to regarding a topic as intimate as my sexual relationship, but if I hadn't been willing, I wouldn't have been there to begin with. So I took a leap of faith and scribbled my signature on the dotted line. Shaw did the same, taking mine from me and rising out of the chair to hand the contracts back across the desk.

Katya took them, signing the witness section of each before returning them to the folder and filing it away in a drawer. "Marvelous! Now, the first thing I need you to do is to send your son to stay with a relative for a bit."

I drew my head back, eyes wide. I don't know what I'd expected, but that certainly hadn't been it. "Whoa! Is that really necessary?" I laughed.

Katya put her palms on the desk, linking her fingers. "I don't like to have my time wasted, so I won't do the same with yours."

Um, okay. That really wasn't such a big deal. We could totally do that. I shrugged at Shaw. "I guess we can ask Chaz and Demi if they'd mind having more time with him. I'm sure they'd love another sleepover."

"Oh, no. You misunderstand, darling," Katya told me. "It will need to be for the duration of our sessions. *All* of our sessions."

I was confused at first until I started doing the math and put two and two together.

"You want us to send our child away?" This airy sort of discombobulated panic rushed to my fingertips and toes and then retraced the path back to my heart before it ping-ponged up to my brain and then crash-landed into my heart again. Though likely it had found its final resting place in my throat because I was having a hell of a time getting any words to come out. "I—I can't—I can't do that!"

"You came to me for help, and I'm offering it. Did you not just say you trusted me?"

"Well, yeah, but I'm not going to send my child away!"

Katya frowned, disappointment settling into her features. "That is a shame. I am sorry we could not work together. Nevertheless, I wish you the best of luck. Do see yourselves out."

"Hold on just a minute," Shaw said, standing.

But Katya cut him off before he could protest further. "As I've already said, I do not like to have my time wasted. Nor do I like to repeat myself."

"Can't you just tell us why it's necessary to send our son away?"

Katya sighed, though softened. "It would only be a temporary situation. Your relationship is lacking intimacy, and a great deal of that comes when a couple actually sleeps together. Cassidy sleeps with your child, and will likely continue to do so as long as he is there. It is a habit that develops not only for the young one but for the parent as well.

"Aside from that," she continued, "I will be giving you assignments to complete. Assignments that will be detailed and vary in timing and setting. Having to make arrangements for the child will alter the mood I'm trying to create for these missions. I cannot help if you insist on working against me."

Shaw and I looked to each other for an answer, neither of us seeming to have the right one. I could see the apprehension etched into his expression. Abe had never been away from us for more than an overnight visit. If the separation anxiety was already beginning to set in for me, I couldn't imagine what that might be like for Abe.

"I don't want to be separated from him any more than you do," Shaw told me. "It's just temporary?" he asked Katya.

"Of course, darlings." She laughed, the playful sound oozing with sensuality. "I only desire to stoke your passions once more, not to have you abandon your child."

Shaw turned to me. "Do you think you can be okay with this?"

I knew he expected me to say I wouldn't, which would have been an honest answer, but I nodded instead. I didn't like it, not one bit, but we were doing this for Abe as much as we were doing it for us. Shaw and I were the catalyst of our family. Without a healthy relationship, Abe would be another statistic from a broken home.

"Yeah, it's temporary." I managed a weak smile, one I knew Shaw wasn't buying. "I could use a break, right? I mean, *we* need a break, some time to sort things out and get back to the way we used to be. So yeah . . . We need to do this for us. We can send him to Stonington to spend some time with Da and Ma. Besides, he'll just think of it as a grand adventure."

Shaw smiled, leaning over to kiss my forehead. "Okay, we'll do it," he told Katya.

"Excellent." Katya purred her approval. "The three of us are going to have so much naughty fun together. You will see.

"Now that we have that settled, you will need to answer your questionnaires, leaving no blanks, and get them back to me this evening. You can email the scanned copies to the address included in the header. It is very important that I receive them before your next visit. Those forms will help me develop a plan that is right for you. Do you understand?"

"Absolutely." I'd make sure Shaw sat his butt down tonight and filled this form out without making a mockery of it like he did with Jeremy's.

"Wonderful. And no peeking at each other's answers." She stood and walked around her desk to center herself in front of it. Long, lean legs with curvy calf muscles, the definition of which could be seen even through all of that tight leather, crossed at the ankles above her sensual feet. "And now for my number one rule: no orgasms by any method not directed by me. Which means . . . no sex, no heavy petting, and no masturbating for either of you. No exceptions."

"What?" both Shaw and I squeaked at the same time.

"Doesn't that sort of defeat the purpose?" Shaw asked.

"The purpose is to find your passion again, is it not?"

"Well, yeah, but . . ."

"But, but, but," Katya said, waving him off. "Katya knows best, sweetling. Do not ask questions. Simply do as I say."

For whatever reason, I suddenly got an image of Mr. Miyagi saying, *We make sacred pact. I promise teach karate to you, you promise learn. I say, you do, no questions.*

Shaw leaned over and whispered, "Wax on, wax off, Danielson."

"Oh, my God, get out of my head." I laughed, suddenly straightening when Katya cleared her throat.

I could feel embarrassment warming my cheeks as I apologized, elbowing Shaw to do the same. I hadn't been called out by the teacher since the third grade when I'd giggled at the fart noises my best friend—and ex-lover—Casey, had been making with his armpit.

"If you do not want my help, we can destroy the contracts now," she threatened.

"No! We do, we do!" I was surprised by how much I really meant it. "We'll do whatever you say. Won't we, Shaw?"

Holy Jesus! When I turned to look at him, expecting his agreement—however forced—I saw a version of Shaw that I hadn't seen in a very long time. His mouth was turned up in a teasing smirk, a sexy confidence smoldered in his eyes, and he sat back as if opening himself up, like he was daring another to try her hand at attempting to handle all that his body had to offer. That was the Shaw Matthews I'd hated, lusted after, and then ultimately come to love. And he was back in the game.

"I'm dying to see what's in store," he told Katya.

Excitement coursed through my veins and my heart thundered in my chest. I'd lost me and he'd lost him, but we were on the right track to finding each other again. And we had a gorgeous instructor that oozed all things hot and bothered to help us along the way. I could hardly wait to see what our first assignment would be!

CHAPTER 8

Shaw

"Shaw, you must find a way to bring Cassidy to orgasm without touching her."

That had been the very first assignment Dr. Minkov had given to us. Well, to me.

"And to be clear," she'd continued, "you may not use dildos, vibrators, wands, whips, or any other fun little toys you might have on hand." And then she'd leaned in to whisper something into Cassidy's ear, her bosom pressing suggestively close to my woman's. Cassidy still hadn't told me what all that was about, saying she was permitted to tell me only if I figured out how to accomplish the task.

It was more a riddle than a task. How the hell was I supposed to get her off if I couldn't touch her? I would've pulled a Cassidy and run an Internet search on it, but if anyone had felt the need to check my search history, that shit would've been embarrassing as hell.

No matter. Where there was a will, there was a way. Despite my already aching balls—a suggestion I was sure had been planted by Dr. Minkov herself, thanks to the "no getting off without her permission" rule, which Cassidy was damn sure going to stick to—I was determined to figure out the puzzle. It was just going to take a little thought. Thankfully, I had some time.

Katya had given us a week before our next session to get things with Abe settled. Cassidy was milking every second of our time with him, though she'd already made the arrangements to get him to Stonington and into her family's care by the end of the week. Abby, my "adopted" mother, was taking the primary role since Anna, Cassidy's ma, had the bed-and-breakfast to tend to with the beginning of the tourism season, which happened to co-incide with the busiest time of year for Duff, as well as Abby's husband and son, Thomas and Casey, as they refreshed all of their lobstering gear and reset the traps. I knew firsthand how grueling that work could be.

In the meantime, I had more pressing matters to tend to. Like the matter of Wade's replacement in our partnership and getting Marcel Ingram signed.

I'd gone to see Wade and had asked him how the search for his substitute was going. The secretive bastard had only given me a dubious grin and said, "I've got it covered."

"What the hell does that mean?" I'd asked.

He'd stood, come over to me to put his hand on my shoulder, and then said, "It means, I've got it covered." He'd escorted me toward the exit after that, nudging me over the threshold and then closing me out, to leave me standing there looking like an idiot with a solid slab of wood touching the tip of my nose. Rude, much?

The office rumor, according to my assistant, Ben—who was absolutely on top of any gossip circulating the office and its valid-ity, worse than any teenage girl—was that Wade already had a good idea who his replacement would be. In fact, many of our own agents had dropped out of the running because they were sure the decision had already been made. It would've been nice if Wade had filled me in, but it seemed he wasn't even willing to give me a clue. Whatever. He knew what he was doing. I hoped.

So that had left me with only the Marcel thing to deal with, and he wasn't going to be in town for much longer, so I had Ben get him on the line for me.

"Hey, man! You got any plans for today?" I asked Marcel once I'd picked up the line. "I thought maybe we could spend some time together."

"Sorry, man, but the fam and I are going to head to the beach for a bit," he told me. "Vale has never seen the ocean, and I'd like to try my hand at surfing."

"Wow, surfing?"

"Yeah. When in Rome, right?" He laughed. "It's something I've always wanted to do, and Kentucky isn't exactly known for its bitchin' waves."

I laughed when I heard Camille in the background, scolding him for the language usage in front of their daughter.

And then an idea hit me. A wonderfully brilliant idea. If it didn't backfire and blow up in my face, that is. "That sounds like a lot of fun," I lied, having no desire to teeter precariously on a slim piece of wood—or whatever surfboards were made of—in the middle of a shark-infested ocean, the sister of which, the Atlantic, had once attempted to steal the life from me. Nevertheless, I made sacrifices where necessary when it came to business and the bottom line, and signing Marcel was a very lucrative bottom line. "Camille and Vale are going?"

"Yep!"

"Mind if my family and I tag along? My boy, Abe, loves the beach, and he doesn't get many playdates with kids his age. I bet he and Vale would have a blast. Plus, it'll give Cassidy and Camille a chance to get to know each other."

"Actually, that sounds like a great idea. Camille has asked about meeting your woman. Cassidy Whalen, right?"

"Yeah. How'd she know?"

Marcel laughed. "Because where I'm the brawn, she's the brains in this family. She's done her research, and Cassidy Whalen is a pretty big name in the industry."

"That she is." I barely kept my competitive nature at bay, trying not to let the memory of Cassidy's past victory over me with the whole Denver Rockford thing rear its ugly head. She wasn't my competition on this one, but it seemed she might be in the plus category of my current endeavor. "Sounds like your girl and mine have a lot in common already," I said with a forced chuckle of my own. "So let's do this, man."

Marcel was on board. Score one for Shaw Matthews. I offered to arrange for a surfing instructor to meet us at a beach that I'd heard had decent waves without being overly crowded. Though he was game for the beach suggestion, Marcel was confident he could figure out the how-to's of the surfing on his own. I wasn't so sure of that for myself, so I'd have to YouTube it. We'd decided I would get a spot ready for us on the beach, complete with boards, a sun umbrella, and some refreshments. Ben would handle that shit, grumbling the whole time, but, hey, at least he'd get out of the office for a while.

After agreeing to meet at the beach in an hour, I disconnected the call, gave Ben his assignment, and then made another call.

Cassidy answered, sounding slightly out of breath, having been chasing Abe around the house. "Get him ready and pack a bag," I told her. "We're going to the beach. All three of us."

Once we pulled into the parking lot off the shore, I got out and looked down toward the beach. Marcel was next to Camille as she lathered sunblock onto every inch of Vale's exposed skin. I tapped the horn twice, getting his attention and returning his wave.

When I closed the car door, Cassidy was standing beside me, hands on her hips. Hips that held a sarong skirt knotted on one side, which matched the sea-green one-piece she wore. The bathing suit showed off every voluptuous curve and swell of her body. The color, however, contrasted with the angry shade of her accusing glare. "I can't believe you, Matthews."

"What?"

She gestured toward the beach. "That's Marcel Ingram! And I assume that's his wife and kid, right? Please tell me you're not seriously using Abe and me to get the contract."

Not entirely, but admitting even a minuscule amount was not going to bode well for me. "Look, the biggest complaint I ever hear from you is that I don't give you and Abe more time because of my work. But I *do* still have to work, Cass. I figured this way, two birds, one stone. Besides, Abe's about to leave for who knows how long, and I'd like to have a little fun with my family if that's okay with you. What's so bad about that?"

She crossed her arms over her chest and narrowed suspicious eyes. Uh-oh. "Why do I get the feeling there's more to it than that?"

There was no use in lying. The woman could read me like a book, and lying would only make things worse. "Fine. I was kind of hoping you could work on Camille while I work on Marcel."

"I knew it!" she shrieked. A vicious Cassidy Whalen tirade was about to commence at any second, so I had to get her calmed down.

"Wait a minute, Cass. Just hear me out on this," I demanded. "Marcel and Camille are here on vacation and want to have a good time. And I know you miss this."

Her eyes narrowed further. "Miss what?"

"Schmoozing clients."

Her mouth dropped open. "I have not *ever* schmoozed clients." Great, I'd insulted her delicate pride again.

"Fine. I schmooze; you show off how incredibly smart, talented, and sincerely invested you are in an athlete's future." I crossed my fingers behind my back.

"I know what you're doing, Shaw. You don't actually think I'm stupid enough to fall for this line of bullcrap, do you?"

"No. You've always seen right through my *bullcrap*," I admitted, and then stooped to eye level with her. Cassidy stared off, the crease in her brow that was always present when she was mad at me made an appearance, but I kept going. "I'm trying to spend time with you and Abe while showing Marcel we have the whole loving-family thing in common. Plus, it's a prime opportunity for me to give to you that which I know you miss so very much. I promise, my intentions are not purely selfish on this one. You miss it, and I miss seeing you in your element. I miss the vitality and snap you embody when you're doing your thing."

I took her hips, pulling her closer and incredibly tempted to work that damn sarong knot loose. Dr. Minkov was a master of suggestion, indeed. "It makes me so fucking hard, Cassidy. Do it for me. Please?"

She finally looked at me; her lips parted and the crease

smoothed. My words had affected her. "Okay, fine," she said, succumbing to my charm.

"Yes! You're the best!" I said triumphantly with a loud "Muah!" kiss to her lips.

"But," she poked me in the chest with her finger and then continued, "you've got bath duty with Abe tonight."

"Totally cool," I relented, following it up with a suckass, "*You're* totally cool. Like, the coolest baby-mama on the face of the planet. In the whole universe!"

She laughed at my antics. "You're such a suck-up. Get your son. I'll grab the beach bag."

The introductions between Marcel's family and mine went swimmingly. Vale hid behind her daddy's leg, giving Abe a blushing grin. My boy, so much like his daddy, unabashedly stepped forward and asked her if she wanted to be friends. Vale nodded, that grin becoming more flirtatious as Abe gathered his sand pail and shovel in one hand and took hers in the other to run to the beach less than ten yards away.

Camille's excitement over meeting Cassidy wasn't anything like her daughter's shyness. She hadn't smiled like that even when meeting me. I knew right then that I was lucky Cassidy and I weren't competing over Marcel like we had over Denver. If we had been, I'd have been forced to throw in the towel early on.

Leaving the ladies to get to know each other better—or do their nails, braid each other's hair, gossip, or whatever it was women did—a very eager Marcel and I headed for the deep blue abyss. My onetime nemesis. Our relationship had been fragile. Scratch *fragile;* it had been downright death-defying.

"Shaw!" Cassidy called out to me. I turned to see what she wanted, noting the silent vote of confidence written in her expression. She must have noticed the hesitation in my steps. She wagged a finger at me. "No showboating." Well, would you look at that? My woman was laying down cover before I even needed it.

"No worries. I'll let Marcel have all the fun," I said, going with it. I hated that she knew I had a weakness, but I loved that she read me well enough to bail me out before shit got too real. "Women, right?" I laughed it off to Marcel.

"Right. Let's go, man." Marcel grabbed one of the boards, nothing more than an unassuming rental, and ran toward the water with me following suit.

Luckily, I did have the time to review a short tutorial on surfing before I'd left the office, so I repeated the steps over and over in my head. Stringer, rails, nose, tail, fins, leg strap, check. Those were the important parts. The actual surfing basics had seemed simple enough. Paddle out, duck-dive under the crashing waves, paddle out farther, sit and wait for a swell, and then manage to pop up and keep my balance on the board to ride the wave in without falling off and sucking gulps of salty water into my lungs. Or hitting my head on a jagged reef. Or being mistaken for a seal and becoming a meaty morsel for a shark snack. Right. Simple.

Or not. The board and I fought for dominance as I tried to mount the damn thing to get started in the first place. I looked like a flailing fledgling, I was sure, but it was cool because so did Marcel. Finally remembering the video instructions, I found the middle of the board and was off and running, er, paddling. Marcel was no more than a half beat behind me on that one. Amazingly, we both managed to make it out to the swells without incident, and there we sat, waiting for the waves to kick up again.

"Sorry, man. I heard this was normally a good spot for surfing. Guess that explains why we're the only two out here." I laughed.

"It's all good." Marcel centered himself on his board and

damn near teetered off. "I'm cool just being out here, you know? Reminds me of how small I am. And it's quiet . . ."

The way he trailed off like he was lost in thought made me take notice.

"Opposed to the screaming fans?"

He chuckled. "And the constant ringing of the phone, the doorbell, the clicks and flashes of cameramen, the whispering in my ear by every person I've ever known in the industry who has considered themselves to be my mentor. It's a lot."

"That's because you're a superstar."

He sighed. "So they tell me." A plane flew overhead, dragging an aerial advertising banner behind it, and Marcel looked up, following its path. "Out here, I'm just an imperceptible speck of dust."

"Is the fame too much for you to handle?" I had to ask because a client with spotlight issues and an MIA tendency was a risk to take on. If he thought the attention was bad now, what would come down the line once I was done blowing him up even further would hit him like a nuclear explosion.

"Nah, I can handle it. Just need some peace and quiet every now and then to reflect on all of my blessings and not lose sight of what's important."

I kicked my feet back and forth, marveling at the stray cool current that passed by and hoping like hell Jaws wouldn't torpedo up and out of the water from beneath me. "And what's important?"

He nodded toward the shore. "My ladies. I'm nothing without them."

I looked, too, thoroughly amused when Abe accidentally dumped a bucket of sand onto Vale's leg and then started wiping it away. He was every bit as gallant as those superheroes he looked up to, and I was a proud papa. Guilt sat heavy on my shoulders since I couldn't say he'd learned that chivalry from his father. Fictional characters were raising my boy because I hadn't been around enough to do it myself. Yet somehow, Marcel had managed to play a huge role in his daughter's upbringing.

"How do you do it, man? How do you persevere despite the odds against you? Don't take it the wrong way, but being a kid with a kid and a wife while trying to go to school and play ball at the same time can't be easy."

"It wasn't, but Cam and Vale give me reason."

"Reason?" I asked.

"Yeah, reason." Marcel shrugged. "A reason to endure, a reason to play, a reason to keep going, and a reason to never give up. They're my motivation for not getting twisted up in the game, both on the field and off. I don't do this for fame or notoriety. I love the game, man. Not only that, but football is a means to an end. I play to support my family because it's what I'm good at, but they will always come first. The pressures of this job aren't easy to deal with. The only way I come out of it okay is if I have a family to go home to at the end of the day. Besides, they're my biggest fans."

I laughed with him, making light of the very heavy conversation. Especially since my next question could be taken the wrong way. "But why get married at such a young age? That's an epic commitment. I'm sure Camille still would've supported you without the legal tie."

"You're right, it is. I didn't have to marry her. Even after we'd found out she was pregnant Cam never pressured me to make an honest woman out of her. But I wanted to. I mean, I don't want to be with anyone else, so why not give my last name and everything I have to the woman who helped make me who I am today?

In my opinion, a man who refuses to take that last step is still unsure, isn't one hundred percent committed. He's holding out for an escape route in case he wants to make a speedy exit."

Was that what I'd been doing? I'd avoided relationships all my life, and then once I'd found myself smack-dab in the middle of one, I'd been adamant that I'd never marry. Looking back on it now, I recalled hating the way my parents had made a mockery of it, and that had been my reasoning. But Cassidy and I were not Clarice and Jerry Matthews. We genuinely loved each other, loved our child, and we were a family. And that was some real-deal shit. Had I shut down the idea of marriage in lieu of keeping the door open for an escape should said real-deal shit get too deep for me to handle?

"Here comes one, man," Marcel said, nodding behind us at a building swell. "I'm going for it."

Stretching out on his board, he began to paddle, staying ahead of a quickly gaining mound of water. At just the right time, he put his palms beneath his shoulders and then popped up onto both feet in a sideways stance. He even had the whole Elvis Presley arm thing going on as he bent at the knee and floated his board along the whitecap of the wave until he eventually wiped out.

Whistles and cheers abounded from the shore, Cassidy, Camille, and both kids congratulating Marcel for a bitchin' ride. I laughed to myself, at myself. I so was not cut out to be a surfer dude.

It took no time at all for Marcel to make his way back to me with a blindingly white smile that stretched from ear to ear. "Dude, that was awesome!"

"Dude? One wave and you're already talking like the locals?" I laughed.

"Man, whatever. Don't harsh on my buzz," he said, purposely getting his slang on while flashing the shaka sign.

"By the way, you're full of shit! You have, too, done this before."

Marcel shook his head and made a cross over his heart. "Swear, man. That was my first time. Guess I'm a natural-born athlete or whatever. It never takes me long to pick up on a sport."

"Yeah, well, I choose not to let you make me look like a fool in front of my boy, so how about we head back in for a bit?"

Marcel chuckled at my admission of defeat. If he'd known I'd nearly taken a permanent nap with the fishies, I bet he'd have cut me some slack. I wasn't offended, though. I'd have laughed, too.

"Just one more," he said. "The adrenaline rush is off the charts. I can totally understand how people get addicted to this."

"Do your thing, Marcel," I said, waving to the vast expanse of ocean. "But don't break anything. We don't need any injuries going into the Combine."

Cassidy

I'd decided if given the option, I might actually consider committing murder to look like Camille Ingram. I wondered what it must be like to have hair that straight and shiny, skin that golden brown, and a stomach that flat after giving birth to a child. A two-piece . . . she was wearing a two-piece. And well, too, I might add. With her long legs stretched out elegantly before her and that lustrous hair blowing in the breeze, she was soaking up the sun while I sat under the shade of the beach umbrella to avoid scorching my pale, blotchy skin. Her eyes were an interesting hazel mix of both blue and green with long lashes and thick brows that were expertly groomed into a high arch. She wore no makeup, though she didn't need to because her natural Latina features made her unfairly beautiful.

I adjusted my sarong, trying my best to hide the kangaroo-style pooch still left over from when my little joey had called my belly home.

"I hope this doesn't sound rude of me," I began, "but I just have to know where Vale got her blond hair and green eyes from." Her hair was more golden than blond with dark roots at the core of a puffy mane that looked soft to the touch, and her eyes were a light green that looked even brighter against her butterscotch complexion.

A sweet laugh carried over to me on the breeze, setting me at ease regarding my level of rudeness. "Marcel. His mother was African American, but his father was white."

"Ah," I said, my agent persona fitting pieces of the puzzle together. "You said *was*. Past tense. Are they still living?"

She shrugged. "No clue."

I perceived her short answer as an indication that she had no desire to discuss the matter further. Sore subject, check. But having dealt with my own baby-daddy with parental issues, I knew that was the sort of thing that could and usually did shape a man. I'd have to dig deeper if I was going to be able to report back to Shaw with a solid opinion on his quest to sign this athlete.

Camille nodded toward the water where her husband was attempting to shred a wave he'd caught, shaking her head when he wiped out. "I bet he gets back on and tries it again."

Sure enough, Marcel grabbed the board, mounted it, and paddled hard back to where Shaw still bobbed up and down on the swells. Marcel was no quitter, and though I knew Shaw wasn't either, the memory of the time I'd nearly lost him to the sea made me mentally plead with him not to be as daring.

"Tell me about him," I said, trying to take my mind off the close call with Mother Nature that had almost ripped the man I love from my grasp. Shaw apparently wanted to hang out with Marcel and get to know him better in order to further his agenda of signing him, but what he failed to realize was that the best way to get to know a man was through his woman.

Camille shrugged. "Most everything there is to know about Marcel has already been plastered all over the media. I'm not sure there's much else I can add to it."

Au contraire. "I find the media to be superficial and subjective when it comes to athletes. Typically, they're more concerned with statistical facts rather than really getting to know the person behind them. I'm more curious about the secret behind his winning career. What drives him?"

Camille regarded me with an expression of respect. "Do you know you're the first person who's ever asked that?"

"Really? I'm surprised," I said, though I really wasn't. "An agent should know what an athlete's motivation is just in case he needs a reminder. And trust me, they definitely need a good shove from time to time."

"You're not an agent anymore." It was a statement, not a question. Maybe Camille had done a little homework of her own on me.

"No, not anymore. But I guess old habits die hard." I laughed.

"We'd wanted to sign with you," she said, taking me unaware. "When we'd found out you'd left the business, we thought Shaw would be the next best thing."

Though I knew it shouldn't have, her reveal appealed to the

competitive side of me that I thought had become dormant over the last couple of years. I hadn't realized how much I'd missed it.

"Oh, God, please don't tell him that," I told her, knowing it would be another hit to Shaw's ego that he wouldn't be able to take. "And I didn't leave for good," I added, needing her to know that I wasn't a quitter. "I'm just on hiatus until Abe gets a little older and starts school."

"Determination," Camille said simply. At my questioning glance, she continued, "You asked what drives Marcel. It's his determination."

She took her bottled water and drank from it before replacing the cap. "The reason we don't know whether his parents are still living is because when Marcel was a kid, he'd been abused by them—mentally, emotionally, and physically. They did horrible things to him. Left him alone for days at a time, tried to sell him for drug money, and beat him nearly within an inch of his life." She cringed, the thought of someone torturing the man she loved like that no doubt affecting her, but she shook it off. "Luckily for Marcel, someone tipped off Child Protective Services and he was finally rescued. They removed him from the home and put him in the system."

My chest tightened with the visual that had embedded itself in my mind. As a mother, I couldn't fathom bringing any sort of harm to Abe. Intentional or not.

"Though the foster homes he was in weren't much better. He suffered more beatings and emotional detachment from some who were only taking in kids to collect the state funds," she said with a disgust I completely understood. "I think he was somewhere around eight before he was eventually placed with Allen and Lynn.

"They were my neighbors, and some of the sweetest, most God-fearing people I've ever met. Lynn couldn't have any children of her own, and Marcel can be quite the charmer, so they eventually adopted him. They knew about everything Marcel had been through, but they were devoted to making sure he'd never feel like a victim again. They gave Marcel something he hadn't ever had before . . . a home where he could feel safe with a family who genuinely loved him. But they didn't try to erase his past. Instead, they encouraged him to use it as a tool, to take all the bad and turn it into something good." She paused, watching her husband with a pride that was palpable. "And he did. So to answer your question, Marcel wins because he's been beaten so much that he refuses to be beaten again."

Suddenly, the issues I thought I'd had with Shaw didn't seem all that important. "Wow. If anything is going to make someone put their own life and problems into perspective, that'll do it."

"Maybe one day they'll make a Lifetime movie about him," she said, making light of what had to be a hard thing to talk about. "There aren't too many people who know his story."

"I'm sorry. I shouldn't have pried."

"No, no, no," she said, attempting to make me feel better. "Marcel isn't ashamed of where he came from. Not many people know the story because not many have cared enough to ask."

"Oh. And what about you?" I asked, shifting gears. "It's got to be hard being the wife of a superstar athlete. Do you worry about what his fame will do to your marriage?"

Camille's laugh was confident. "Not in the least. I've watched girls throw themselves at him time after time. Girls who I know are much prettier than me. Marcel has never even given them a second glance. That doesn't mean I wouldn't love anything more than to rip their fake lashes, fake hair, fake nails, and fake tits off their bodies, though."

I nearly choked on the gulp of water I'd just taken. "Oh, wow!" I laughed, knowing exactly how she felt.

"Hey, I might be a God-fearing woman, but that doesn't mean I don't get tested from time to time. And believe me, these women *test me* . . . ," she trailed off in a singsong voice.

"Oh, I feel ya," I said, remembering all the times I'd witnessed complete strangers bat their lashes a little too hard at Shaw when we'd been out and about. "So you're not worried he'll cheat on you. How about the time it'll take from you and Vale? Have you thought about that?"

Camille sat up, straightening her arms behind her. The breeze off the ocean blew her straight locks, one strand stubbornly sticking to her glossy lip before she pulled it away. She looked out over the water, eyes squinting against the sun. "I've thought about that, and I've come to the conclusion that I have to let Marcel do his thing, find his own way. He's done a pretty good job of it on his own so far, so I have no reason to believe it won't all work out in the end. He has to become the man he's supposed to be, and there's nothing I can say or do that will alter the course he's meant to follow. Given his start in life, it might take him a little more time to get there, but I'm prepared to wait. Because I know he's worth it—I know our family is worth it. That's what you're supposed to do when you love someone, right?"

"I'm sorry, how old are you again?" I asked, drawing a laugh from her. I couldn't believe how incredibly strong and mature this young wife and mother was. I could definitely take a cue or two from her.

While I was caught up in my awe of this fledgling couple who had defeated the odds stacked so high against them, Shaw and Marcel waded through the surf washing onto the beach. I watched as they each stabbed their boards into the sand, Shaw reaching down to unclasp the ankle strap and then sweep up his baby boy as he'd barreled toward him. Marcel did the same with his sweet baby girl. Dual giggles abounded as the fathers tossed their little ones into the air, and then Marcel swung Vale around in a circle to bring her back to his chest and carry her bridal-style. Shaw lifted Abe and ducked his head to perch our son on his shoulders. Abe's chunky little hands fisted his father's wet hair as Shaw clamped a hold on his legs to secure him in place.

My cheeks hurt from the smile pushing at them, and I allowed myself a moment to absorb the view before me. From Shaw's golden tanned legs with muscular calves bulging, up to those delectable obliques that disappeared beneath the band of his trunks and the rippling abdominals with that glorious trail of dark hair, and higher still to those flat, dusky nipples haloed by a smattering of curly fuzz. He was God's gift to women. No, not to women. To me. But his sexiest asset of all was the pristine white of his teeth that showed through the smile he wore from ear to ear while looking up at his son. *Our* son.

"Down you go, little man," he said despite the groaning protest from Abe as he lifted him once again and put his shoe–clad feet back onto the sand.

"Hey, you want a snack?" I asked my baby boy, wiping the sand from his chunky legs as best I could. He nodded, excited for his apples and caramel dip, I was sure. "How about you, Vale? Abe packed the snack all by himself. Didn't you, Abe?"

Abe's little chest swelled with pride. "Uh-huh. A'cause we're boyfwiend girlfwiend like my mommy and daddy."

He was so his father's son. As cute as it was, I felt a pang of embarrassment that he couldn't say *husband and wife*. Because his daddy and mommy weren't and probably never would be.

"Yeah? She's your girlfriend?" Marcel hiked a fatherly brow. "You don't think she's a little too old for you?"

Abe shook his head, his beige bucket hat flapping in the breeze as he handed the Baggie of green apple slices to a giggling Vale.

Shaw clapped Marcel on the back. "What can I say, man? My boy's into older women."

"He's not allowed to be into any women," I said pointedly, handing the opened container of caramel dipping sauce to Abe. Abe smiled slyly and then he and Vale ran, hand in hand, back toward their sand castle in progress, which looked more like a village of ant mounds.

"Hey!" Marcel called toward them. "I'm keeping my eye on you, boy! That's my little girl!"

Shaw, Camille, and I had a laugh at his expense. He ignored us, taking the spot before Camille with his back to the rest of us and bending his knees toward his chest so he could watch the kids play.

"Marcel, they're not playing doctor. They're playing princess." Camille tilted her head back and closed her eyes, letting the sun warm her face.

"Got my little man whipped already." Shaw shook his head in disbelief and then took a bottle of water from the cooler before claiming the corner of blanket in front of me. Easing back on his right forearm, he stretched one long leg out and raised the knee of the other. "So Marcel, how'd you like to meet Denver Rockford while you're in town?"

Marcel's eyes lit up as he turned away from the kids. I guessed that was one way of getting his attention. "Ah, man! Are you kidding me? I'd love to!" And then suddenly, that light was extinguished. "Damn, I can't."

Swallowing his gulp and then recapping the bottle, Shaw said, "What are you talking about? Of course you can."

"Actually, we can't," Camille added.

Marcel's shoulders sagged. "We're heading back home tomorrow."

"So stay longer," Shaw said as if it were a simple answer.

Camille snorted. "Right. Because hanging out in California is so inexpensive."

I knew what Shaw was going to say and do before he ever got it out. "If it's a question of money, I've got it covered." And cue winning smile . . .

Marcel shook his head. "Nah, man. I can't let you do that. I pay my own way."

"Marcel, buddy . . . Really, it's no big deal. My company sets money aside for just such an occasion. It's not going to cost me a thing."

Shaw wasn't feeding him a line of crap. One of the very first things he'd done when he'd stepped in as a partner at Striker was increase the expense account for wining and dining the major players. I supposed he figured no one else should have to sacrifice the way he had in the name of the company.

Marcel raised a questioning brow at his wife.

"I don't know, Papi," she said, her gaze wandering toward Vale. "I've got work and Vale's got to get ready for school. . . ."

"What are you talking about? School doesn't start for months. We have the whole summer to get her ready."

"Well, I've still got work."

Marcel's head drew back. "Babe, if all goes well, you'll never have to work again. Come on. A little longer?"

Camille gave a resigned sigh. "Okay, fine. We'll stay a *little* longer," she said.

I wanted to be happy for them, and I wanted to be happy for Shaw, but I couldn't help but wonder what that meant for the momentum he and I had started to gain toward rebuilding our relationship. I supposed as Camille had said, I had to let Shaw do his thing and hope it all worked out in the end.

Marcel cupped her neck and pulled her in for a loud smack on the lips, much the same way Shaw had done with me earlier. Maybe these two men had more in common than either of them realized.

"Hey, can we do a group selfie?" Marcel asked, that excitement lighting his eyes again. "Your family and mine. I won't post it on social media or anything. I'd just like to have it for myself."

Shaw grinned victoriously, and I already knew what he was thinking. "You should definitely post it. It'll give the media something to speculate and gossip about, and that's always a good thing for your career."

CHAPTER 9

Cassidy

Letting my baby, my three-year-old baby, leave my side to go a million miles away for an undetermined amount of time was not an easy thing to do, but I'd done it. With the help of Abby, anyway. Shaw and I had paid for her to fly in so she could fly right back out with Abe in tow because no way was I going to trust a total stranger with my unaccompanied minor. I'd felt bad about the long trip for Abby, knowing she had to have been exhausted, but she'd looked fresh as a dew-drenched daisy on a spring morning once we'd finally met up with her. We'd only been able to spend half a day and one night with her before she and Abe left for the return trip this morning.

Abe hadn't even shed a tear over leaving his mommy. Mommy had cried buckets.

So there Shaw and I were, sitting at a private booth in a quaint little bistro. We had two nights before our next session with Katya, and I was very anxious to see if Shaw would be able to find out the trick to her assignment. I already had, of course, and not because I'd cheated. I'd known because, quite frankly, it had been a fantasy of mine, something I'd gotten myself off to on more than a few occasions.

"Are you thinking about Abe?" Shaw asked.

I shook my head, pushing the salad around on my plate. "I've come to terms with that, somewhat."

"Then where were you just now? You seemed a million miles away."

"Actually, I was just thinking about Katya's assignment. Have you figured it out yet?"

The corner of Shaw's mouth lifted into that signature smirk that always made me want to rip my panties off. Directing his attention to the steak before him, he plunged a fork into it and began to carve away a bite-sized piece. "Maybe. Anxious to find out?" The morsel disappeared into his mouth with a purposeful chew.

I met his smirk with one of my own. Hopefully, it was at least half as sexy. "Maybe."

Shaw's eyes did a slow perusal of my face, drifting down the line of my neck to hover over my exposed cleavage. He licked the juice from his lips, nearly accomplishing the feat Katya had given him on the spot.

"Katya. What did she whisper to you before we left?" Ah, so he'd been thinking about the same thing. I'd bet it was torture for the man who'd always found a way to get what he wanted to not be able to throw money at this one.

"I already told you the only part I could disclose."

"Tell me again."

Nice try. "The only thing I can tell you is that she told me I can't tell you anything at all . . . until after you've succeeded."

Shaw arched a brow. "Have you forgotten how persuasive I can be?"

"Not as persuasive as you used to be. Hence the reason we're seeing Katya to begin with." The words were out before I'd thought out the repercussions. Reminding Shaw of his shortcomings in our sexual relationship as of late wasn't exactly conducive to getting him to play along.

Removing the napkin from his lap, he placed it on the table and then took the wallet from his back pocket to pull out some cash and tossed it on top of the napkin. "Let's go," he said, standing and holding out his hand for me.

"Shaw, I didn't mean to—"

"I have a point to prove, and I don't think either you or Katya mean for me to do it right here, so let's go."

I took his hand, also standing before tucking my clutch under my arm. "You're not mad?"

Shaw pulled my body flush to his and I gasped when I felt the hard line of his thick cock pressed against my hip. "Does it feel like I'm mad?"

Actually, it did. Anger and frustration toward me had always acted as a sort of aphrodisiac for Shaw. If he was hard now—and he most certainly was—that only meant one thing: I was about to be punished in the most sinfully delightful way.

Seeing a devastating orgasm in my future, I took the lead, yanking on his arm to drag him along behind me as I made a beeline for the door. And yes, I ignored his knowing chuckle.

Dear God, please don't let there be any traffic.

Shaw

For the whole drive home, I'd become increasingly frustrated about the insinuation that I didn't know how to bring my woman pleasure. Even more so about the fact that it seemed to be true because I hadn't in a very long time. I still didn't know the key to unlocking Katya's riddle, and my balls were aching in need of release even as the strained cock in my pants taunted me like it knew the answer my stupid brain couldn't come up with. Which only proved the saying about a man thinking with the head inside his pants instead of the one on his shoulders wasn't true. I'd have given anything to let my little buddy take over since he had been faster on the draw than me on this one.

Once inside our bedroom, I closed the door and turned to find Cassidy confronting me with all that goddamn challenge and expectation in every nuance of her posture and countenance.

"What now?" she asked me with a smug air about her.

She already knew the answer. That much was clear. And she was still clothed, which would never do if I was going to get her off. But I couldn't touch her either, so . . .

It came to me then, the resolution to the brainteaser having apparently traveled from my crotch to my brain via the supercharged blood pumping through my veins.

Oh, Dr. Minkov, you are a wonderfully genius bit of minxy trickery, but I've figured out your game.

"Get undressed," was my direct order.

Cassidy's movements stuttered with confusion. "You want me to—"

"I want you to take off your fucking clothes. Do it. Now." There was nothing nice about my demeanor. By design.

Trembling fingers worked the top buttons of her blouse, slowly revealing the tempting bit of cleavage created by those mounds of flesh that pushed up from the white lace bra she wore beneath. My palm shoved down the length of the anxious appendage throbbing beneath the jeans I wore.

Cassidy noticed and stilled all movement. "Did you forget Katya's rule, Shaw? You're not allowed to make yourself come."

Wrenching my hand away at the reminder, I growled low. This was about her, not me. Damn, but I was going to be in some serious blue ball discomfort by morning, and that wasn't going to bode well for the agreement we'd made with Katya.

"Hurry up." It occurred to me that this little exercise might not have been so much about my being able to pleasure Cassidy as it was about torturing me because I'd been so selfish as of late.

Cassidy looked around the room, stalling and testing my very fragile patience. "Um, will you turn off the light?"

"No. I want to see you." I couldn't remember the last time she'd been fully naked in front of me. Christ, no wonder she thought I wasn't attracted to her anymore.

"Fine." She kicked off her sensible shoes and then her pants were the next to go.

When her fingers got back to work on her shirt, I stopped her. "Slow down."

Cassidy's shoulders slumped in frustration. "Which is it, Shaw? Do you want me to hurry up or slow down?"

"I want you to shut up and do what I tell you to do."

She leveled me with a narrow glare as she continued, but I could see the smooth alabaster of her skin warm to a luscious pink. She was turned on. So was I. This was how it had been for us in the beginning, back when pissing each other off had been every bit a form of foreplay as oral sex or hand jobs.

The memory of the way we once were, coupled with the sight of all those curves being revealed before me, heated my own blood. As if my body had become a stand-in for that which I was forbidden to touch, I pulled my own shirt over my head and threw it to the floor, kicking my shoes off afterward. Fearing I wouldn't be able to resist taking her, I left my pants on.

Cassidy had finished undressing, standing among a pile of her own clothes with her panties still covering her bare feet. Her body had filled out more since birthing Abe, but those curves were in all the right places, a voluptuous smorgasbord of "touch me here, taste me there."

"Turn around. Slowly."

She did as I said, and I was nearly brought to my knees at the sight of her backside. It had always been one of her sexiest assets, but now . . . my God, now more than ever I wanted to grab two handfuls of those juicy cheeks and spread her wide while fucking her ass.

"You're so goddamn tempting," I told her.

She faced me once more. "Am I? Is that why you're touching yourself again?"

I looked down, the bulge protruding from my groin almost capping the waistband of my pants to give the object of its lust a not so proper greeting. And, yeah, I'd been palming it again.

"Get on the bed."

Cassidy went over to her side and lifted the corner of the duvet to climb under.

"Stop." She froze in place at my command. "On top of the covers, not under them. I want you laid out before me."

She did as I said, stretching her length down the center of the bed, though she crossed her arms over her gently marred stomach. Those faded stretch marks had been the result of carrying my son in her womb. She had nothing to be ashamed of.

"Don't hide yourself from me, Cassidy. Your body is mine, and I crave all of it. Now put your arms at your sides and don't move until I tell you to."

With a protesting huff, her arms found their place as directed. I stood at the foot of the bed, taking my time looking her over and letting the anticipation build. The thin patch of strawberry blond curls at her mound would be soft to the touch—if I'd been allowed to feel them—but the plump folds glistening with her wetness would be like silk on my fingers, like honeysuckle on my tongue. Lifting one knee, I placed my hands flat on either side of Cassidy to crawl over her.

Cassidy's eyes shot wide as the mattress sank with my weight. "What are you doing? You're not allowed to touch me."

"I'm not touching you." I stopped with my face inches from her pussy, letting her feel the warmth of my breath on all that sensitive flesh. Tempted. I was so tempted to taste her, but I refrained, leisurely edging farther up her body. "What did she say to you, Cassidy? What did Katya whisper into your ear? Did she say anything at all, or was it merely an excuse to put her breasts on you?"

Her breaths were coming quicker now. Ah, yes, she'd been affected. "I . . . I can't tell you."

"Can't?" I stopped to hover over one very pert nipple, the same peachy pink as her mouth, and let my warm breath tease it. "Or won't?"

"Both." Cassidy arched her back, nearly causing my lips to brush the bud surrounded by the puckered flesh that screamed for my attention.

I drew back to a safe distance and then gave her a chastising *tsk*. "Careful. If we break the rules, we'll have to stop. You don't want to stop, do you, Cassidy?"

She rubbed her thighs together, her fists clenching the duvet as she shook her head back and forth.

"Good girl." I ducked my head, careful not to graze her with so much as a hair when I peered down to see what the fuss was about. Cassidy was positively drenched, slick, and, if I had to guess, silky soft to the touch with all the self-lubing going on.

Inhaling the scent of her arousal, I let a long, audible exhale release through my nose. I knew she felt it on her stomach, and, with any luck, it had traveled down to provide a cooling sensation to the wetness at the center of her mound. "Jesus, I bet that little clit of yours is every bit as swollen and hard as my cock is right now. Isn't it?"

She moaned and rubbed her thighs together again. I looked up, finding her eyes hooded and her teeth scraping the meaty morsel of her lip.

"Do you need to be touched?"

"Y-you can't touch me," she reminded me once more.

"That's not what I asked you. Do you need to be touched?"

"Yes." Her answer was a breathy whisper.

I could hear my own voice, low and husky. "Then do it. Let me watch as you touch yourself."

"I don't know how."

"You're lying. You've been taking care of your own needs all this time that I've failed to do so for you. So show me."

"Shaw—"

"If you don't sully our sheets with your come, I'm going to break the goddamn rules and fuck you with a vengeance. Either way, you *will* come. Now, show me."

She lifted her hand, timidly moving it across her abdomen before making the detour to the intended destination. My own anticipation began to build as her fingers pushed through the soft and curlies and the pad of her middle digit made first contact with that tiny bundle of nerves.

I moaned. Me. I was the one that fucking moaned. "More," I rasped.

That middle digit's two neighbors joined in the fun as she pushed farther south, finally coating her fingers in the wet and wild before starting a circular motion.

"That should be my tongue on you, Cassidy," I told her, drawing a moan that had not belonged to me this time. "Have you ever wondered why I chose sweetness as my pet name for you?"

She said nothing, just kept moving those fingers round and round. I was so captivated I couldn't peer up to see if she'd heard me.

"It's because of the way you taste," I divulged. "So sweet my mouth waters thinking about it. Coat your fingers in all that honey for me, sweetness. It's gathering *inside* you."

Still she said nothing, but she did as I asked, dipping her fingers low. I scooted down her body and off the mattress, deciding to get a better vantage point to watch as my woman masturbated for me. Standing at the foot of the bed, I issued another directive. "Spread your legs for me, Cassidy. Let me see you."

Fucking A, but she did. Not only did she spread her legs, but she also raised her knees to let them fall open even farther to the glorious view. The lips of her pussy were already tinged a glorious pink, her bud begging me to have a suckle, and her opening now filled to the knuckle by her own finger.

I inched back onto the bed, the lower half of my body remaining on the floor as I propped myself up by my elbows and watched Cassidy work herself.

"Add another," I told her, only then realizing that I was grinding my jean-clad cock against the mattress. Fuck it. I'd stop myself before coming, but easing a little bit of the pressure couldn't hurt.

Cassidy pushed a second finger inside herself, slowly pumping them back and forth as the heel of her palm rubbed at her clit.

"That's my good girl." Goddamn, those should have been my fingers fucking her while I sucked on that pearl.

"Do you remember the first time I touched you there, sweetness?" Her breath stuttered and she plunged deeper into that tight recess. "I do. I couldn't believe how warm and wet you were for me, how snug the walls of your pussy felt as they clenched *my* fingers."

She moaned and I chanced a glance up to see those crimson locks spread out like a halo on the pillow beneath her thrashing head. Her eyes were closed, denying me the green depths of them. "Yeah . . . you remember. Pull your fingers free. Let me see."

Cassidy did as I said, and the light of the room reflected off the slick glistening of those two lucky bits that had felt what I craved.

"I want to taste them," I told her. "Wrap my tongue around them and suck them into my mouth to lick them clean."

Her moan was louder this time, her knees drawing up further as she remained spread and lifted her ass, instinctively searching for friction.

"Put them back inside you. Deeper this time. Faster."

It wasn't often that Cassidy ever followed my orders. In fact, she usually did the opposite, adamant about maintaining control. But she was at my mercy in this weakened state, more susceptible to my manipulations when the promise of release awaited her at the end.

Harder and faster she pumped her fingers, abandoning the in-and-out to seat them deep, all the way to the knuckles. Her hand moved back and forth and I knew she'd found what she'd been looking for. She arched her back, bringing her palm closer to her clit to double the sensation.

"You found your G-spot, didn't you? Stroke it harder, Cassidy. You're on the brink. I can smell it." I inhaled sharply to punctuate my point and couldn't help but lick my lips, too, as if I could taste her scent in the air. God, why did the mattress feel so good rubbing against my cock?

"Katya is going to be well pleased," I reminded her, grunting with a little back-and-forth action of my own below the waist. "She thought we couldn't do this, but she was wrong, and she'll be very happy to know you found pleasure while touching yourself, not only at my directive, but at hers."

It must have been exactly the right thing to say at exactly the right time because all that work she'd been doing on her clit intensified along with the thrusting going on inside her fucking gorgeous pussy. A pussy that would've felt glorious wrapped around my cock at the moment.

"Shaw," she moaned my name, a desperate sort of plea.

"Do it for me, sweetness. Let me watch your come spill out of that pussy with your orgasm. Do it. Do it now!"

She lifted her head, and her abdomen contracted as she partially rose off the bed to look down at the center attraction. When her mouth dropped open and her wrist adamantly sprung forward for a deeper reach, I knew what was coming next. Her.

Cassidy clenched her teeth on the moan that filled the room as she retracted her fingers and the milky proof of her orgasm spilled forth.

"Holy fuck," I growled, my hips slamming against the mattress as if that were going to beat away the seed trying to make its way up my shaft to join her.

When she'd finished coming, Cassidy looked down at the mess and began to laugh even through all that heavy breathing. "Oh, my God . . . I . . . I can't believe we just . . . did that." She fell back onto the mattress with an exhausted huff, throwing her arm over her head.

Yeah, we just fucking did that. I smiled victoriously to myself, but there was still one bit of business left on the table. A prize I'd say I'd earned. The final piece of the puzzle.

Mentally issuing an "at ease" to the soldier boy in my pants, not that he was as good at following orders as the lady of the hour was, I climbed farther onto the bed to lie beside a very satisfied Cassidy. "I believe there was a part two to our assignment?"

She turned her face to look at me past her limp arm. "You want to know what Katya said?"

I reached up and took her wrist, pulling her arm free and stopping with her hand before me. With deliberate motion, I sucked those two orgasm-soaked fingers into my mouth and took my consolation prize. "Tell me."

Cassidy sat up and twisted around to lean into me, her naked breasts pressing against my chest. It was the first physical contact I'd had with her body since we'd begun and it put my entire nervous system on high alert. Turning the tables of my own teasing technique against me, her warm breath caressed my neck as she whispered into my ear, " 'Once Shaw has brought you to orgasm, you will gift him the same. I want you to *suck . . . his . . . cock.*' " She mocked Katya's accent, putting direct emphasis on the last three words before continuing, " 'Swallow his cum and take it into yourself. Do not be a wasteful girl.' "

My fucking dick was hard enough to plow through concrete like a jackhammer. I closed my eyes, listening to the words while recalling the sight of another woman pressing herself so seductively against Cassidy. Though I in no way desired Katya for my own, it was clear she would love nothing more than to touch my girl the same way Cassidy had just touched herself. And that was definitely a turn-on. Cassidy might not ever admit to it, but I suspected it was true for her as well.

Cassidy's hand inched down my stomach. "That's what she said to me, Shaw. And that's what I'm going to do."

There is a God. There is a God. There is a God!

Scrambling toward the foot of the bed with explicit purpose, she tugged my belt loose and popped the button of my jeans before releasing the zipper. I was forced to lift my ass when she grabbed the waistband of my pants and gave them a hard yank to pull them free of my legs.

My cock sprung to attention, slowly rising of its own accord as if to show off for her. Cassidy's gaze locked on to it, and then she licked her goddamn lips. In response, the head leaked precum, weeping a salty tear of joy for what was about to come. And come. And come.

Thinking back on it—though I wasn't sure how I was able to form a coherent thought about anything at the moment—I realized she hadn't blown me since Valentine's Day. Before that, it had been our anniversary. Incidentally, it had been those same two occasions that I'd gone down on her. Yeah, I'd really dropped the ball.

Cassidy wasted no time getting down to it with a long lap from base to tip, a swirl of her tongue, followed by some deep throat action with some hellafied suction. My eyes rolled to the back of my head and I forced the fuckers to face front and center because no way did I want to miss seeing a second of this.

It wasn't going to take long. Fuck me, but it wouldn't. Cassidy's mouth was hot, her plump lips sealed around my cock as her cheeks hollowed out with an intense draw. Cupping my balls, she massaged them with a skilled precision that worked in tandem with the rhythmic bobbing of her head. Her mouth was spread wide to accommodate my size, but still she was able to take me all the way to the back of her throat, swallowing around the head and then pulling back to let her flattened tongue do wicked things to my ultrasensitive skin.

"Oh, God, sweetness," I groaned, my hands finding their way into her hair for no other reason than because I wanted to feel the up-and-down motion on my palms. I didn't push, I didn't pull; I just let her do the damn thing. She certainly didn't need any help from me.

Pressure began to build higher and higher in my sac, and then Cassidy gripped the base of my cock, giving it a not so gentle squeeze while her mouth took on the head. Her lips curled tight around the place just below the pronounced ridge of the tip, and she manipulated the hell out of that spot, sparing no mercy because there was none to give.

"Fuck, Cass . . . Are you sure you want me to come in your mouth?" The words were strained as every muscle in my body went taut. I gripped her hair, making sure she didn't venture into "let's switch it up" land. Because I was about to come. Hard.

She didn't say anything—couldn't, what with her mouth being full and all—but she did look up at me with an unequivocal determination in her eyes that was synonymous with the name Cassidy Whalen. I fucking loved it.

A ferocious growl that I could feel building in my chest before it clawed its way out preceded the rocketing sensation of my seed. I shoved Cassidy's head all the way down until my cock touched the back of her throat, and then I let it go, coming hard in my girl's mouth.

I watched in awe as Cassidy continued to suck me. Her eyes closed and she moaned around each demanding draw and swallow.

When it became too much for me to handle and I had nothing more to give her, I eased my grip on Cassidy's hair and lifted her chin so she'd release me. With a self-satisfied air about her, she wiped the corner of her mouth with her middle finger, and then her tongue made one more appearance to lick it clean.

When I arched a brow in question, she shrugged and said, "Katya told me not to be wasteful."

Katya was my new best friend. I laughed, pulling her up my body to nestle in the crook of my arm. We stayed like that for some time before we both decided we had the munchies and got dressed to hit the fridge.

I was damn proud of us. For the good of our relationship, we'd sacrificed time with Abe and we'd successfully managed our very naughty assignment. Next on the list was our meeting with Dr. Sparling. And yeah, he'd given us a sort of assignment as well, food for thought. He was going to quiz us on how well we really knew each other, and Cassidy was now freaking out because she'd forgotten about it.

Sitting in the corner of the couch, her legs were curled up to her chest. "What if he tells us we have no business being together? What then?"

"That's not going to happen, Cass."

"But it *could* happen."

"Not likely. And even if it does, so what? It doesn't change anything. We're two grown adults. We don't have to do what he says."

"Yes, we do. We signed a contract."

Ah, yes. The contract. Ms. By-the-Book wouldn't dare go against a document she'd signed. Not under duress.

"Come on, Shaw. If a total stranger, a professional in the field, says we've got no business being together, maybe we'd better listen. And oh, my God"—she gripped her own fingers, twisting them this way and that—"what's that going to mean for Abe? He's going to be so confused. That sort of thing could really damage a kid his age. He'll hate us both. And then he'll probably grow up to be a serial killer or something."

"Cassidy, stop!" I might have raised my voice a little bit on that one, but she was pseudo-hyperventilating, eyes wild with panic as her frantic mind started drumming up all sorts of fictional scenarios. It was best I put the brakes on before she mentally had our son living out the rest of his days in a straitjacket and a muzzle before going to the electric chair. "Nothing like that is going to happen because I won't let it."

She didn't look convinced, just started rocking back and forth with her arms hugged tight around her torso. No doubt, she was putting herself in Abe's crazy suit, feeling his abandonment issues and trying to see the world through his eyes.

I took a seat next to her so I could unwrap her arms and replace them with my own. "Look, sweetness, if it'll make you feel better, and I know it will, we can stay up all night drilling each other and making sure we know everything there is to know about each other."

"Really? You'd do that?"

"Of course I would. I told you I'd do whatever it takes, didn't I?"

Her panicked eyes softened and her shoulders relaxed as she tilted her head to the side and smiled adoringly at me. "You did. I'm sorry I'm such a basket case when it comes to stuff like this. I just want to be prepared."

"I know," I told her. "And I understand. I really do. It's one of the things I love most about you."

She leaned up and kissed me sweetly. "I love you, too," she said when she pulled back. "Thank you."

"No need to thank me, sweets. That scorching-hot blow job you just gave me was gratitude enough." I gave her a wink, which earned me a light slap on the shoulder, but she laughed, and that was so much better than watching her freak out. "Now, what would you like to know about me?"

CHAPTER 10

Cassidy

Shaw and I had stayed up well into the morning, quizzing each other on likes, dislikes, and our favorite everything. Strange that you could be with someone for as long as Shaw and I had been together, even conceiving and raising a child together, and still not know the basic facts about them. But we did now, and I was confident going into our appointment with our relationship coach, Dr. Jeremy Sparling. Or as Shaw liked to refer to him, the Keymaster. I totally saw the resemblance.

Still riding the high of the unbelievable orgasm I'd given myself via Shaw's provocation, there was a little bounce in my step, which was a miracle considering the limited number of hours I'd slept. Not to mention I was missing my Abey Baby like crazy. I'd talked to him first thing this morning, and had completely melted at the sound of his cheery voice on the other end of the phone line. His uncle Casey was going to take him out on the boat tomorrow, and he was ten kinds of excited about it. Most overprotective mothers would be worried, but that was the way of life in Stonington, and I wanted Abe to have as much exposure to it as possible because it was what shaped boys into men.

"So . . . how have things been since our last session?" Today, Dr. Sparling was wearing a vintage *We Are the World* T-shirt under a sports jacket and blue jeans with deck shoes. His hair was dry this time, less greaser and more seventies feather bang.

"Good," I told him, and Shaw grunted his agreement.

"And did you go see Dr. Minkov?" The way he asked the question gave away his eagerness for the response, much like a dirty boy propositioning a hooker in the seedy part of town, not wanting to get caught but unable to resist the urge at the same time.

Shaw gave a short snicker. "We absolutely did. You know, if you had told us to expect an unmarked car, an abandoned warehouse parking lot, and a secluded getaway, we might not have been so afraid for our lives."

Jeremy nodded his head with a chortle. "Katya does have a flair for the dramatic, doesn't she?" He pulled opened the notebook on his lap and flipped a few pages over the top. "Did she agree to . . . um, counsel you?"

"Yes," I told him, wondering just how much he knew of her tactics.

Again with the nod, though he still hadn't looked up. I, too, had a knack for reading body language and could tell he wanted to ask more, but was afraid doing so might give something away. He cleared his throat and pulled a pen from his front pocket before finally lifting his head with a plastered smile. "Shaw, if it's okay with you, I'll need to not only record this meeting but also take notes. Will that be a problem?"

Shaw threw his hand up dismissively. "Nah, go ahead, Doc."

Pressing a button on the recorder, he got things under way. "Okay, let's get started. No worries; this little game is always so much fun, probably the least intimidating of all the sessions we'll have."

I wished I'd had even a fraction of Jeremy's excitement over what was about to go down, but I was nervous despite my confidence that we'd studied as much as we could about each other.

"First question goes to Shaw. What is Cassidy's favorite color?"

"Blue," he answered confidently.

"Yep, that's right!" I beamed, wanting to high-five my teammate.

"Great! Cassidy, what's Shaw's favorite color?"

"Green." Two points on the board to our favor. I moved to the edge of the couch, anxious for the next question. Dr. Sparling noticed and looked at me like I was a weirdo, which I might have been, but we were going to win this.

Pen met paper. Darn it. "It's interesting that you both chose the color of your partner's eyes."

Not that I needed to, but I turned to examine Shaw's, which seemed to be a brighter blue today for whatever reason. "I've always loved his eyes. That shade of blue reminds me of the sky and sea, two things my hometown has plenty of. The sky, the ocean . . . You know, they're both so vast, their reach so far and deep, that I think of endless possibilities. That's the reason the color has always been my favorite."

"Do you think maybe you've subconsciously seen the same in Shaw? Endless possibilities? Home?"

I'd never considered it, hadn't ever read that much into it. "Yeah, I suppose it's possible."

"And Shaw, what does the color green represent for you?"

"Damn, Doc. You're getting deep on this color thing, aren't you?"

Jeremy just grinned victoriously, nodding for Shaw to answer the question. I already knew what he'd say. Green was the color of money, after all. And Shaw loved to make lots of it.

Shaw sighed as if he was being forced to admit something he hadn't wanted to. "Green reminds me of the spring. I guess maybe I like it because that's a time when everything is refreshed, sort of reborn with new life. Does that make sense?"

My jaw fell open and I turned to gawk at him, astonished by this deeper side of Shaw Matthews that I'd never seen before.

The sound Jeremy made was almost like a pat on the back, as if a theory had been proven. "Yes, that makes perfect sense. Now, I'll ask you the same question as I did with Cassidy. Do you think maybe you've subconsciously seen the same fresh start in her?"

Shaw turned to me. "My life certainly has changed since I met her. She's my first relationship, the mother of my firstborn, and the first person I've ever had any real feelings for. So yeah, I can see the correlation."

Scribble, scribble, scribble, and then a push of his glasses up the bridge of his nose. "Excellent! Let's move on. Tell me about the best vacation you've ever taken together."

Shaw tilted his head in thought. "Huh. You know, I don't think we've ever been on a vacation. Not a real one, anyway." He looked to me as if asking whether I'd realized that. I hadn't, but it was no big deal, so I shrugged indifferently. "After the draft," Shaw said. "We'll take one after the draft."

I nodded in agreement.

"Oh, you definitely should. Couples need a timeout every now and then to regroup." Jeremy wrote something and then scanned the pad in front of him for his next question. "Where was your first date?"

Shaw and I looked to each other. I was sure my expression was just as dumbfounded as his in my perplexity. "We've never," I stopped to clear my throat. "We haven't ever really been on a date," I admitted. It was the truth. Sure, we'd eaten together, but that was more out of necessity than a date-type situation.

"Really? That's interesting." Jeremy crossed his legs at the knee and then sat forward with his forearms crossed over the lower part of his top thigh. "Tell me why that is."

I shifted under his scrutiny, aware that Shaw and I had never been what was considered a normal couple. "Well, as you know, our relationship started as coworkers and advanced into something a little more competitive, which naturally put us at odds with each other."

"Yes, we discussed that there was no love lost between the two of you in the beginning." He steepled his index fingers and touched them to his lips. "But what about afterward, as your feelings grew?"

Shaw tagged in on that one, sitting forward as if to drive home the point he was about to make. "We went from being '*enemies with benefits*,' I suppose you'd say—you know, always at each other's throats even when we were trying to get down each other's pants—" he explained, "to being in love, then finding out Cassidy was pregnant, and straight to moving in with each other after that. There was never any time for dating, and it didn't seem necessary by that point."

"So you went from zero to a hundred with no buildup in between? You were never friends?"

"I don't think that's true. I mean, I think we always had a mutual respect for each other." Shaw sat back, a retreat I'd have said was barely noticeable, but nothing about body posture seemed to ever get by Jeremy.

As expected, he made a note on his pad. "Respect is not the same thing as friendship, though, is it?"

"No, I suppose not. But, hey, look." Shaw got animated. "A

friend puts your ass in check when you need it, right? Cassidy did that to me all the time. Still does."

He pitched a good point, so I caught the ball and ran with it. "Yeah. And they support each other, as well. When I had to go back to my hometown in Stonington, and Shaw followed . . . well, let's just say I was going through some things, and Shaw was sort of my savior during all of that. Even when my town got destroyed by a hurricane, Shaw stayed to help with the cleanup."

Jeremy nodded, making even more notes. "You're certainly defensive of each other, as friends tend to be."

Shaw reached over and took my hand, linking our fingers together in a show of solidarity. "No one knows me like Cassidy does. Maybe that's because no one else really knows me at all. She's the only person I've ever let see the real me, and maybe that wasn't by choice—she's as nosy as they come—" he added with a teasing tone, "but she was the only person who ever cared to pry. She isn't just my friend; she's my best friend."

"I'm a firm believer that friendship is crucially important to the success of any relationship, so I'm really glad to hear you say that." Jeremy looked down at his notepad and read from it. "Tell me, Shaw. Which do you think Cassidy is likely to say was the one day of your relationship she would *least* like to experience again?"

Shaw didn't even hesitate. "Oh, that's easy. The day I almost drowned."

I could see why he'd think that, but he was wrong. "That's not true, actually," I told him. "You know, as scared as I was about your near-death experience, that was also the day I really knew that I loved you. I'd relive that feeling over and over again, even though that, too, scared the crap out of me."

Shaw's voice was tender. "Really? You never told me that, sweetness."

I nodded, the moment coming back to me with perfect clarity, how terrified I was that I'd teetered over the thin line between lust and love. "I remember the exact moment. It was while you were making love to me that night. Maybe it was even before then and I'd just suppressed it because that wasn't how things were supposed to have been between us."

"Yeah, my feelings for you had caught me unaware, too." Shaw lifted my hand to give it an affectionate kiss. His lips were warm and soft, lingering for as long as his gaze did on my face. That was my Shaw, the man I'd fallen head over heels for.

"That's how it usually works," Jeremy interjected. I'd been so caught up in the moment with Shaw that I'd almost forgotten he was there. "When we're not looking for love, it usually finds us." He looked down at his watch and then back up with a smile. "Ready for the next question?"

"Shoot," Shaw said as I nodded.

"Okeydokey! Shaw, when Cassidy says, 'Honey, they're playing our song,' what song are they playing?"

"Um . . ." Shaw's brow furrowed, and he turned to me with all sorts of "help me out here" in his expression. "I don't think we have a song."

We didn't. How in the world did we not have a song? Didn't every couple?

My eyes shot wide, panic over two, back-to-back failed answers making me desperate to pull out a win. "Shaw's favorite genre of music is R-and-B from the eighties and nineties," I blurted out, holding out a finger and then another as I ticked off a list of facts. "His favorite artist is Jodeci, and yes, that surprises the heck out of me, too. And his favorite song is 'Purple Rain' by Prince." After last night's cram session, I'd memorized all of those details.

Dr. Sparling looked up at me from over the rim of his glasses and then gave me a kind smile. "Not exactly what I asked, but it's nice that you know all of those particulars, Cassidy." Pen, paper. Uh-oh, busted. "Since you do, how about if you tell me what Shaw's favorite food is?"

"Abby's cookies!" I announced, plenty proud of myself.

"Hell yeah!" Shaw exclaimed. He rubbed his belly, and I could imagine his mouth watering by the way his eyes rolled back into his head. "Aw, man . . . they're the best in the world, Doc. Wish I had some now."

"Chocolate chip?" Jeremy asked.

Shaw nodded. "Melts in your mouth."

"Sounds delicious. And what is Cassidy's favorite food?"

"Umm . . ." Shaw looked toward the ceiling as if searching for the correct answer.

Come on, Shaw. We went over this. My brow crinkled as I mentally willed the right answer toward him, as if telepathy were a skill I possessed.

"Oh! Lobster!" He sported a childlike grin in expectation of approval.

Approval that would not come because that was the wrong answer. I shook my head in disappointment and withdrew my hand from his. "Nope. I don't even like seafood."

"But you're from a fishing village, and your pops is a fisherman, so I just assumed—"

My eyes narrowed, disappointment turning into aggravation. Even if we hadn't spent all night going over this crap, he'd never seen me eat any sort of seafood, so that showed me just how well he paid attention. "You assumed wrong."

"It's really not that big of a deal. Sometimes we miss these little details," Jeremy said, jotting away in his notebook. Strange that he should feel the need to jot down a "not that big of a deal."

"Now, Cassidy, please fill in these blanks: Shaw may be the world's best blank, but he may also be the world's worst blank."

"Shaw may be the world's best . . . lover," I said, watching his head grow about ten times its normal size, "*but* he may also be the world's worst . . . partner."

My lover/partner growled, and there was nothing sexy about it. "How'd I know *that* was eventually going to come up?"

Again, Jeremy leaned forward, intrigued by the response. "What do you mean, Shaw?"

Shaw reclined back, his demeanor oozing condescension. "I mean, she's still holding a grudge over my getting the partnership. A partnership she willingly gave up, I might add."

"Oh, don't flatter yourself," I barked. "I wasn't talking about that. I meant partner as in life partner. You didn't even know that I don't eat seafood, for crying out loud! How could you not know that?"

"Jesus Christ, Cass! My plate's been a little full, in case you haven't noticed. Cut me some slack."

"Oh, I've noticed, and you're right, it has been full. Full of yourself! My plate's been full, too, just *not* with lobster."

"*Pfft.* Whatever." He looked away with a dismissive wave of his hand. The same hand attached to the wrist with that stupid watch.

"Cassidy?"

"What?" I snapped at Dr. Sparling, my misplaced anger getting the best of me.

When my voice softened with an apology, Jeremy said, "It's quite all right. Can we keep going?"

I nodded, but still crossed my arms over my chest defensively and turned my head in the opposite direction of Shaw. I was sure we looked like quite the brooding pair.

"If you had a day off alone and could do whatever you wanted, what would it be?"

It was a good, safe question, which I was sure was the point. "Wow. A day off alone?"

Before I could answer, Shaw opened his big, fat mouth. "She has every day off."

I turned to look at him like he'd lost his damn mind, because it was apparent he had. "Excuse me?"

"What? It's true." And then the proverbial lightbulb went off above his head. "Wait, I didn't mean it like that. You have Abe all day. I'm sure running around the house playing superhero *is* hard work. So I take it back." Even without the sarcastic smirk, I would've known his poor excuse for an apology wasn't sincere.

"You know what?" Jeremy interjected. "That's not really an important question. Let's just move on from it."

"No. I want to answer it." I set my chin in defiance. "If I had a day off alone, I'd still want to spend it chasing my son around the house playing superhero. Because that's not only my *job*," I emphasized, "it's a privilege."

Shaw was quick on the retort. "Well, it must be nice to have that privilege."

"You could spend just as much time with him, but work always comes first," I challenged.

"Someone has to make the money to support us, Cass."

I sat up straight on that one, prepared to get down and dirty with him. "Maybe you've forgotten, but I happen to have plenty in my savings account, Matthews! No one asked you to take over the bills. But you've just gotta be in control of everything, don't you? You want me beholden to you."

"Beholden to me? Go fuck yourself, Cass."

"Ooookaaaayyy!" Dr. Sparling bolted forward. If he'd been a

referee on the field, I was sure he'd have thrown a flag on the play with a loud squawk of a whistle. "Let's just go back to our neutral corners and take a breather, all right?"

I was fuming mad. Teeth grinding, jaw clenched, nostrils likely flaring, and crossed leg nearly doing a can-can. Closing my eyes, I began a mental countdown from ten in an effort to get myself under control. I had no idea what Shaw was doing on the other end of the couch, but I could hear him breathing, so that was getting on my nerves.

"I'm a little leery about continuing at this stage," Jeremy said. "We can stop if you want."

The sound of that pen making long strokes amped up my determination not to let Shaw get to me. "No. Let's get this over with."

"Very well." Jeremy sighed. "Cassidy, a meteor is headed for your house. You and Shaw have saved your family, pets, and the family photos. You have time to save one more item. What do you think Shaw would choose to save?"

I spared him a sideways glance, my leg continuing the rhythmic bounce on my knee. "His watch."

Shaw turned on me. "You say that like it's a bad thing. It was a gift from your father, plus it's an antique. It's irreplaceable. Of course, I'd save it."

With a roll of my eyes and a bored huff, I said, "Next?"

"I think maybe we should stop." Clearly, our coach was throwing in the towel. Maybe he'd already determined we were hopeless.

"Keep going!" Shaw ordered him.

"Um . . ." A caged Dr. Sparling flipped the paper over to look at the page beneath it. "Shaw, complete the following sentence: 'A perfect mate is one who . . . ?' "

"A perfect mate is one who understands and accepts me for who I am."

"I accept you just fine for who you are." How dare he insinuate otherwise? I'd overlooked all of his flaws and had the patience of a saint. Saint Cassidy, that's what they should've named me.

"No, you don't. You're constantly trying to change me."

I could feel my blood pressure spiking. I'd had it! Sitting up to lean in to face off with Shaw, I called it like I saw it. "Well, I guess I'm not your perfect mate, then!"

Shaw mirrored my pose, his nose coming within inches of mine. "Guess not!"

"Whoa, whoa, whoa!" Dr. Sparling again sprang forward in his chair. "Boy, you two really do go from zero to a hundred at the snap of a finger, don't you?"

We both sat back, resuming our previous positions on the couch. Again, I got my can-can on, and again, Shaw sucked the oxygen out of the room.

"Would you look at that," Jeremy said, drawing my attention to see he was looking at his watch. "Saved by the bell!" He laughed, though I failed to see the humor.

"So we failed epically, huh?" Mad as I was, I still needed to know the results of his test.

He perused his notes, doing his best to maintain a positive air. "It's clear that you know all the facts about each other, that part was . . . well rehearsed. But when it came to the questions with a little more substance . . ." He canted his head.

Shaw raked his fingers through his messy locks. "We fumbled the ball."

Jeremy's smile was polite, not one of genuine satisfaction over our antics. "And do you know what that tells me?"

Much like a child being chastised, I looked down at the fidgeting fingers in my lap, unable to meet his eyes. "That we're a couple of head cases who should never be with anyone else, let alone each other, for the rest of our lives?"

This was it, the part where he'd recommend Shaw and I go our separate ways.

"Quite the opposite, actually." My head shot up in surprise at his statement. That faux smile finally turned into something genuine as he eased back into his chair, looking for all the world a thousand times more relaxed than any one person locked up in a room with the two of us should be. "While there are a few issues, at least we now know what they are and have a good starting point. The good news is that while you two can be your own worst enemies, you're also each other's closest allies. I've never seen couples be as opposing yet defensive of each other as you are. Plus you're a couple of cheaters. I'm guessing there was a cram session last night, wasn't there?"

I nodded, guilty as charged.

He laughed. "I figured as much. But all that I've observed today tells me that you care enough about staying together to go to the lengths you have to make sure you do. And that's a passing grade in my book." He looked down at his notepad and started scribbling on it again. "Not that you were being graded, but you two are the most ardently competitive couple I've ever met." He shook his head in amazement.

Tell us something we don't already know.

CHAPTER 11

Shaw

The meeting with Dr. Sparling hadn't exactly gone as well as we'd thought it would. But he hadn't given up hope on Cassidy and me as a couple, so that was encouraging. Even if he had told us it was time for us to go our separate ways, I wouldn't have listened. No one was going to tell me whom I should and should not love. Cassidy was it for me. Period. And I was going to make this shit work, even if it killed me.

The good news was that our next meeting was with Dr. Minkov, my new best friend. And that meant someone was going to get off. Maybe even the both of us. So it wasn't going to be anywhere near the train wreck our session with Jeremy had been.

In the meantime, Marcel and I had gotten in some one-on-one together while Camille and Vale were hitting up some sort of Mommy-and-me day spa that Cassidy had suggested. Of course, I'd insisted on taking care of the tab. The Ingrams would be heading back to Kentucky in the morning, and I wanted to give them a send-off they wouldn't soon forget.

Marcel continued to impress me every second I spent with him. The kid had a pretty solid head on his shoulders. He was in this for all the right reasons. Not for fame or glory, but for the genuine love of a game that had set him on the straight and narrow in life, while helping him grow into the man he wanted to be for his young family. I admired the hell out of him. And he taught me a few things I needed to see about myself, as well. If Marcel could overcome the odds that had been stacked against him from the day he was born, I could do the same. I didn't have to let my fucked-up past determine my future, as it would be whatever I made it. I was the master of my own destiny. I just needed to figure out how to overcome the one obstacle standing in my way: me.

Yeah, I had some shit, on a very personal level, to deal with. Hopefully, I wasn't already buried so deep in it that I couldn't tunnel my way out.

After giving him a tour of San Diego, we made one last pit stop, the illustrious home of the one and only Denver "Rocket Man" Rockford. As promised.

"You don't have any sort of homophobia, do you?" I asked as we pulled into Denver's neighborhood.

"Man, I've been getting naked in a locker room full of dudes since high school, and it's never bothered me. Besides, if Rocket were to hit on me, I'd probably take him up on it." He laughed. "That's one pretty motherfucker, pardon my language."

"Yeah, he is. And believe me, he knows it." I laughed along with him, not because I thought he was seriously crushing on my superstar quarterback but because I knew it was all about getting his fanboy on. Anyway, if Quinn was at home and sensed so much as an inkling of a flirt, he'd climb all over my next big thing, and I couldn't have that.

"He's not the only gay athlete out there," Marcel continued.

"What he did, the whole coming out publicly and all, it sort of led the way for others to do the same."

Marcel was right. Since Denver, four other pro football players had made a similar announcement.

"That took some giant balls. He's got my respect."

"Aw, man. Don't talk about his balls in front of him. Unless you want him to whip them out. 'Cause he'll do it, I swear."

"Noted." He chuckled as we got out.

Denver and Marcel took an instant shine to each other, and it made me feel like a proud papa. I didn't need to do much by way of getting them familiar with each other, as athletes tended to be aware of other athletes, particularly when the numbers they were putting up were also putting them in a spotlight they either coveted for themselves or had to share with one another. Denver never felt threatened, though. His confidence in himself surpassed even my own. He was all about the "welcome aboard"s as he passed Marcel a beer and showed him around, bragging with an "All of this could be yours someday, and Shaw Matthews is the man who can make it happen."

I really fucking loved that big lug.

We'd spent the next three hours with Denver—talking football, swapping tales about key players in the industry, and coming up with strategies—before Quinn came home, pleased to make Marcel's acquaintance.

With a not so subtle bomb drop, he said, "Uh, Shaw . . . I just talked to Cass a little while ago, and I'm pretty sure you're supposed to be somewhere *important* right now, but here ain't it."

"Oh, shit!" I said, jumping up. "Cassidy and I have an appointment."

With Katya, and I was perilously close to missing it. I hadn't even realized how late it had gotten, and that made me feel guilty as hell, seeing as how I'd always had an awareness of the time when I was with Cassidy and Abe. That was when every comment she'd made—about the watch, about my putting work before my family, about my inattention to her—smacked me upside the head. I finally got it.

Goddammit! I hated it when she was right.

"Man, you better get going, then." Denver had incurred the wrath of Cassidy Whalen a time or two himself, so he was very much aware of the consequences I faced if I got her ire up.

"Yeah, I know," I said, and then I realized I still needed to take Marcel back to his hotel. Shit. I looked down at my watch, knowing I wasn't going to make it in time. "You ready, man?" I asked him.

"Hey, don't worry about Casper, bro. I'll get him where he needs to be."

"Casper?" Marcel and I said at the same time.

"Yeah, Casper. Every pro football player needs a nickname, and I just figured out yours." Denver beamed, proud of himself.

"But why Casper?" I asked.

"Isn't it obvious? 'Cause every time our man here gets handed the ball, he disappears like a ghost and leaves 'em all standing around looking at each other like, 'Where the fuck did he go?'"

Marcel gave a slow, contemplative nod. "Yeah . . . I think I like it, man."

"That's very clever, babe." Quinn gave him a quick peck on the cheek and then patted his head. "Shaw, go!"

"It's okay with you if Denver gives you a ride?" I double-checked with Marcel.

"Oh, yeah, it's cool, it's cool," he said as he stood and the three of them closed in on me, practically pushing me out the door. "Go. Just be careful. I don't want to land back in Kentucky only to turn on ESPN and find out my agent bit it before we could make great things happen."

My agent. He called me his agent. Mental fist pumps were rocketing off inside me, the need to get my *Jerry Maguire* "In Rod We Trust" celebratory dance going on. I had no idea how I kept my cool about me when I would've loved nothing more than to bask in the glory of my epic win, to wrap him up in a big bear hug, or to even whip out a contract to get him to sign the bottom line, but I hadn't the time for any of that. Because Cassidy was waiting for me, and I'd be damned if I'd let her down again.

So I smiled and clapped him on the back as I shook his hand, told him to have a safe flight home and I'd be in touch. And then I ran out the door, hopped into my car, slammed it into reverse, and shot out of there like a bat out of hell to speed toward my woman.

I'd already scored one major win on the night. With any lucky, Katya would make sure I'd score again.

When we pulled into the parking lot of the abandoned warehouse, the reverse lights were illuminated on the rear of Katya's car. The driver, the same as the last time, had just been about to leave us. Whipping in beside him, Cassidy and I jumped out, locked things up, and went to greet him in the same fashion as we had before.

Once we'd reached Katya's, still in blackout conditions, our escort again stood by the door as we got out, and then turned to leave us.

"Hey!" I called after him, and he stopped. "You got a name?" After all, an introduction seemed in order if he was going to be our regular chauffeur during our visits.

He inclined his head with a clipped show of respect. "Nikola," he answered, offering no more than that.

"Cool. Thanks, Nick!" I said, offering my fist for a knuckle bump. Nick only grumbled in return, so he either wasn't into the nickname or the informal knuckle bump. Nevertheless, though his expression was still stoic, I could've sworn the twitch at the corner of his lips was what passed as a smile from that one. It was quite possible that this was the extent of any kind of friendliness the man ever exuded.

Teddy was the butler's name. Okay, so it was Teodor, but I liked Teddy better. Cassidy elbowed me for my apparent rudeness after he smiled with a respectful bow without commenting on the name and then led the way to Katya's office.

Where she was waiting for us.

A leopard-print body glove was her choice of apparel for the evening. Or so I assumed it was a body glove. Fit her like one, anyway. Her boobs were spilling out of the top, her waist was cinched, and there was zero imagination left as to the shape of her flawless body. She was trying too hard to fit the part, in my opinion, but Cassidy was seriously checking the woman out with a bit of drool threatening to dribble down her chin.

I tried not to be jealous—because, yeah, her attraction to another woman was hot—but I was a red-blooded man, so my girl checking out anyone other than me set the little green monster inside on edge.

And then Katya did that European thing where she pulled Cassidy in close to kiss her on each cheek. Really close. With little more than the thin material of her barely there clothing and Cassidy's tank top preventing nipple-to-nipple contact.

I did not receive the same greeting. Perhaps that was about maintaining a certain level of professionalism, which I appreciated, but any propriety to that end had been shot to hell the moment she pressed herself all over my woman like a cat seeking a rubdown.

Not that I was complaining. If it got my girl worked up, I'd be the one reaping the rewards. Maybe, just maybe, that was the point. Dr. Minkov was tricky that way.

"Tell me, did you accomplish the task?" Katya asked me after we'd taken our places in the sitting area. Cassidy and I were on the couch built for two—again, probably by design so we'd always be touching—with Katya getting comfy in the chair to Cassidy's left.

"Yes," I told her, slipping my hand between Cassidy's knees.

Dr. Minkov grinned knowingly at that claiming maneuver. "How did you manage it?"

"You told me I couldn't touch her, but you didn't say she couldn't touch herself, so I gave her direction while she masturbated."

Cassidy cleared her throat, her cheeks warming to a lovely shade of pink.

Katya, however, crossed her legs with a slight arch to her lower back and a noticeable squeeze of her thighs. My guess was that while Cassidy was embarrassed, Katya was well pleased. "Very good. Did you come *hard*, Cassidy?"

The exchange I witnessed next was nothing short of a thing born of fantasy. Cassidy met Katya's penetrating gaze, a silent seduction arcing between them. And then the mother of my child covered my hand with hers, moving it farther up her thigh ever so slightly. "We had to change the sheets afterward," Cassidy admitted with a boldness I hadn't ever seen from her outside the boardroom. "I'd never done anything like that before."

"It is my desire to get you to open up about your sexuality, to try things you might not have thought to do on your own. You will find my techniques reveal lessons within lessons and will also teach you things about yourself." Somehow, her Bulgarian accent made everything sound erotic. "To that end, why do you think I gave you this particular assignment?"

The answer was obvious, by my way of thinking. "You were torturing me, making me see what it felt like to know she was getting hers without any hope of getting mine."

Before Katya could say whether I was right, Cassidy weighed in. "I was thinking something along the same lines, only slightly different in that it was about Shaw needing to learn how to give without *expecting* anything in return."

"I like those answers, but both are wrong." Katya leaned forward, the soft scent of musk fanning through the air. "This was a lesson in control. Cassidy, you need to learn to give it up, and Shaw, you need to learn how to maintain and then influence it. Yield and wield. You understand?"

I could see her point with Cassidy but not myself. "I've never had an issue with control, Doc."

"Have you not?" she contested. "I do not doubt that you are able to take control, but maintaining it and then to be able to manipulate it to the benefit of someone other than yourself is not the same. If you had mastered that, perhaps there would not have been an issue with bringing Cassidy to orgasm and you would not be here with me now."

Touché.

"I do, however, find it curious that you saw the exercise as torture without realizing the gift being given to you. How could this have been about Cassidy's pleasure when you received two for the price of one?"

"I don't follow."

"How did it make you feel when you accomplished the task and brought Cassidy to orgasm without a single touch from you?"

Like a fucking stud in beast mode. "Pretty damn victorious."

"It pleased you when she came?"

"Very much."

"Her pleasure was yours, and then you were permitted to take pleasure for yourself. You see?"

I nodded because I got the afterschool-special moral of the story. Sometimes rewarding another was a reward to oneself. My masculinity was rebuilding with some crazy testosterone-fueled confidence. Mostly.

"Did you complete the questionnaires I sent home with you after our last session?"

"Oh, yes," Cassidy said, opening her purse to retrieve our separate envelopes.

We hadn't been allowed to know how the other had answered the rather naughty questions. They were all about either how we saw ourselves, our confidence level, or our secret fantasies—things we'd done before, things we had not, things we wanted to try, and things that were a hard no for exploration. There wasn't much I'd said no to, but I was surprised by how vanilla my experiences had actually been. It wasn't that I wasn't good in bed. On the contrary, I was very good at what I did. It just seemed like my reach into new territory hadn't been as broad as I'd thought.

One of the questions referred to whether we ever had been or would be curious about being with someone of the same sex. While my answer had been a negative, after witnessing the ongoing seductive interactions between my significant other and our sex therapist, I wondered if Cassidy had answered differently.

Katya opened the envelopes and read each of them over, a grin tugging at her lips. After a time, she put the documents together, folded in half, and then tucked them beside her. "You both seem eager to explore areas you have not before. This is good."

I tightened the grip I still held on Cassidy's leg, sending up a silent prayer that she wanted to try some of the same things I wanted. One in particular made my cock jerk in my excitement to learn what might be in store for us next.

Katya became contemplative when she sat back, her posture imperial as she considered her next move. With a graceful tilt of her chin, she finally spoke again. "I have decided what your next assignment must be."

Preparing herself to receive the new information, Cassidy aligned her own carriage to mimic Katya's. There was something about it that made me believe it was possible this woman possessed characteristics that Cassidy wished she had for herself. Which was absurd because my Cass was about as close to perfection as a woman could come.

"But I will only give the instructions to you, Shaw."

Sure I'd misheard her, I drew my head back. "Me?"

"Yes." The devilish grin that followed solidified one thought: she was setting me up for failure. Again. "And it must take place right away."

Cassidy

Everything about our next assignment was hush-hush. When Katya had said she would only give Shaw the instructions, that was exactly what she'd meant. With a quick dismissal, I had been promptly escorted from the room and out of the house by Teodor to where Nikola was waiting by the car with the door opened. It felt like I waited there forever, in total darkness, before Shaw joined me. And he wasn't the least bit interested in enlightening me as to what Katya had said.

What was it about secrets that could make life so sensational and dramatic? The mystery behind the puzzle needing to be solved, that human need to fill in the blanks made our existence exhilarating and gave us purpose. That was what Katya Minkov had done for me. I'd become settled, though not content, in my routine. There'd been no "what's next?" for me because I'd somehow reached the end and there'd been no other goals that I'd set for myself. Goals were what had driven me before, had kept my feet moving forward. Before I'd reached one, I'd already had the next in mind.

Now, I was just a mother who got up every day to follow the same routine, over and over again. That wasn't to say that being a mother wasn't of significant importance, but that importance had revolved around nurturing the development of someone else without any thought of furthering my own.

Time and time again, I'd accused Shaw of being selfish. Could I have been guilty of the opposite? An extreme selflessness that had actually been a flaw rather than a strength?

The mirror in the bathroom Shaw and I shared had begun to fog over, thanks to the steam from the hot shower I'd started. Standing naked before it, I forced myself to take a long, hard look at myself. I had many imperfections. Shadows beneath my eyes, crow's-feet, faint creases at the corners of my mouth, and "stress hair" that was graying at the roots with a lackluster coloring that had once been vibrant as a fresh-stamped copper penny. My breasts weren't as perky as they'd once been, nor were my waist and hips as trim. I turned this way and that, desperate to see something different, but as I blew a limp lock out of my eyes, I knew it was hopeless.

Maybe I should turn the idle time I had on my hands while Abe was away into something productive. Hit the gym, get my hair and nails done, possibly even do a little shopping for some new clothes that wouldn't make me look and feel so frumpy. Rejuvenate myself. Yeah, that's what I'd do.

Stepping into the shower, I pulled the door shut and closed my eyes to the sting of hot spray I pretended could rinse away the layers of yuck my body had been building up over the last few years. Blindly reaching for the shampoo, I squeezed a dollop into my palm and washed my hair, rinsing and then conditioning as I moved farther under the spray.

I nearly jumped out of my skin when I felt a pair of arms encircle my waist and then a very naked, distinctively male body being pressed to mine from behind.

"How long has it been since we've showered together?" a gravelly voice said at my ear. Two hands slid over my ribs to cup my breasts and gently roll my nipples between agile fingers as a warm tongue and firm lips sucked at my neck. Shaw . . .

Not since I'd been pregnant with our son. Back then the changes happening to my body had been a novelty, sexy to the man who'd been partly responsible for the life growing inside my very round belly. He'd been particularly fond of my overly swollen breasts, and the ass he'd been obsessed with before had given him more to love.

The swollen breasts were now gone and a flabby tummy had replaced the novelty belly, but the fat ass had remained. Gravity had had its fun with all three, and at my expense.

Self-consciously, I covered the pooch of my stomach, not wanting his wandering hands to venture anywhere near it. "What are you doing?"

"Perfecting my control." His teeth nipped at my shoulder,

distracting me as he took my wrists and forced my hands away from my body to plant the palms against the wall in front of me. "Stay."

"Shaw, I—"

"Shh. Stay," he ordered, cutting off my protest before the feel of his body against mine disappeared.

Thick strands of my own hair clung to my forehead and cheeks as the shower continued to pelt me. My eyes were closed to the deluge of water running down my face, so I couldn't see what he was doing, but I heard the sound of my body wash being opened and then closed. Though I didn't need further proof, the aroma of vanilla and lavender hung heavy in the confined space.

"Do you know how crazy it's made me that I've been forbidden to touch you?" The soft, spongy feel of my loofah made contact with my back as he began to wash me. Jesus, it felt good.

I arched my back, encouraging more of it. "About as crazy as it made me that no matter how badly I wanted you to, it was against the rules."

Shaw's husky chuckle returned to my ear, and the loofah had now moved to my front. "You're beautiful, you know."

I shook my head, not bothering to voice my disagreement and becoming even more self-conscious about him seeing me. All of me.

"Yes, you are." His empty hand joined the loofah, cupping one breast again while the texture of the loofah played havoc on the other nipple. Soft suds cascaded down my abdomen with a teasing caress. "Your breasts are full and heavy, capped off by those delicious nipples, which happen to be the same shade of peachy pink as your succulent lips. They make my mouth water to suck on them."

My breath hitched when his fingers and the loofah circled

both with a delicious sort of pressure, and then he tugged at the one beneath his hand to mimic the suck.

"You don't notice how often I watch you, how much I stare in awe of the woman I get to look at every day for the rest of my life. And I haven't done a very good job of reminding you just how sexy you really are. You've forgotten, haven't you?"

"Shaw, you really don't need to say these things."

"Yes, I do. Because I forget that unlike me, you aren't full of yourself and you need the reminder."

I shook my head again, though he was right. Hadn't I just been examining all of my flaws?

"Do you know that your ass, the way your hips move back and forth when you walk, is enough to bring me to my knees? I've seen men watching it, but you don't notice them. If I didn't know beyond a shadow of a doubt that you belonged to me, I'd rip their heads from their shoulders, Cass. I swear, I would."

Now he was just being silly. He was also moving lower down my belly and farther still, even as his hand continued to knead my breast and tweak its nipple.

"You're mine. All of you. And you are perfect, make no mistake about it."

I moaned when I felt the bunch of fluffy mesh dip between my legs and begin to methodically move up and down. Opening my eyes, my lashes batting away the drops of water, I watched as he worked me.

Shaw's breath was hot against my neck, his hand sure, and his cock rigid on the cleft of my ass. "Open wider for me, sweetness."

I took half a step to the side, granting him the room he sought, though I knew it might be a mistake.

"Is this the assignment?" I asked, taking a chance that maybe I was wrong.

Another chuckle that was just plain sexy. "You know how this works, Cass. If she'd wanted you to know, she wouldn't have sent you out of the room."

"Am I at least allowed to come?"

He nipped at my ear, sucking the lobe between his teeth and sending a shiver of pleasure down my spine before he released it. "Did she tell you that you could come?"

I shook my head, mentally chastising myself for setting up my own failure by agreeing to go along with this show and for lacking the restraint to end it now because I was already too far gone.

"Then I guess you have your answer." I could feel the pressure from three of his fingers behind the mesh, circling my clit with every intention of pushing me to the brink of the cliff and not allowing me to fall over.

Oh. So this was supposed to be my lesson in control. Shaw had been tortured and now the tables had been turned. Redundant, but I supposed Katya had felt it necessary.

When the long strokes back and forth over the apex between my legs started up again, I almost came undone. Shaw's teeth were on the back of my shoulder, nipping, before his lips kissed the same spot. His hips moved against my ass, his cock nuzzling between the cheeks.

"You're beautiful. I want to hear you say it."

"I'm not," I told him with another shake of my head.

"So you're saying I chose to spend the rest of my life with someone who isn't?" He sucked at the most sensitive part of my neck, rolling the loofah round and round.

I shrugged, and the pressure on my pussy intensified, causing me to bend forward more in an effort to back away. But Shaw was there to prevent my retreat, and he wasn't budging.

Crossing his free arm across my chest, he held me still even as he began to torture my other nipple, squeezing the mound beneath it and rolling the taut peak under his palm. "Say you're beautiful. Say it and mean it, and I'll think about letting you come."

"But Katya didn't tell me I could come," I reminded him as much as myself.

"Then I guess you better not break her rules. If you do, I'll tell her what you did. Every. Single. Detail of it."

There was something wholly erotic about Katya knowing I'd orgasmed and how. And Shaw seemed to know I'd be turned on by it because he continued to work the loofah in circles over my clit until my legs began to shake. Of their own accord, my hips started to rock in time with his movement, the momentum of something wicked building and building from deep inside me. "Shaw . . . You have to stop or I'm going to come."

"Don't you dare do it," he warned, though he made no show of stopping the thing in the driver's seat of my disobedience in the first place. "You're beautiful. I want to hear you say it."

But I wasn't, and I couldn't let the lie spill.

The tempo of his manipulations increased and his cock slid along the cleft of my ass with a sinful sort of pressure right where I wanted it most. And still Shaw was making demands. "Say it."

I couldn't take it anymore. My will was not greater than that of my body's, and definitely not greater than that of the selfish woman inside me yearning for release.

"I-I'm beautiful. . . ."

"Goddamn right, you are," he growled, and then the loofah . . . oh, God, the loofah did things to my pussy that inanimate objects just should not be able to do. The friction, the delicious pressure, the creamy glide of silky soap over the hypersensitive bundle of nerves shoved me headlong into oblivion. The orgasm that had been building surged forward and there was nothing I could do to stop it. I came, grinding against Shaw's hand unabashedly because I'd already failed.

I'd failed. Shaw had passed the test Katya had given him, but I had failed.

"That's my good girl." Shaw growled his approval, his movements slowing to ease the pressure against my swollen clit.

The loofah dropped to the floor of the shower with a wet thud, and I could do nothing but look at it lying there as my shame—my failure—washed down the drain.

Struggling to get my breathing under control, I straightened and turned to a very smug Shaw. "Why? Why didn't you stop?"

"Isn't it obvious? I wanted you to fail."

"But why?" Was he really that competitive?

He reached around me and shut off the water. "Because now I get to punish you." Whipping open the door, he stepped out and then grabbed me by the arm, saying, "Get out. Now."

Stunned by his sudden change in demeanor, and still hyperventilating from the astronomical orgasm and the failure he'd just forced upon me, I did as he said and remained standing on the bath mat awaiting further instruction. It was clear that whatever was about to go down next was Shaw's call, and I was expected to do as he said.

Now he'd get to punish me? I had no clue what that meant, but a kaleidoscope of emotions was merging inside my confusion. My body was still trembling, though not so much from the orgasm or the cold air hitting my wet skin. This quaking was all about fear of the unknown. I wasn't afraid of Shaw, per se—I knew he'd never hurt me—but punishment was something we were all groomed to dread from childhood.

Still holding my arm, he moved me in front of the mirror and stood behind me, pointing ahead. "Look at yourself and say it," he told me.

I focused on the reflection in the mirror. Not at mine, but at his and the hungry expression in those paralyzing blues as he looked back at me. There it was . . . the way he used to look at me, the way his proximity oozed a predator-like threat. And I knew I was about to be ravaged.

"Not at me. Look at yourself. See what I see and fucking *say it*," he ordered again, the gruffness of his voice threatening.

I averted my attention to my own reflection, the flush of my skin, the glow surrounding me—all courtesy of the way the man standing behind me had made me feel. Everything about the mother, the lover, the woman before me was just as he'd said. As I set my chin in newfound confidence, my voice was sure. "I am beautiful."

"Yes, you are." Pressing himself to my backside, he moved the hair off my shoulder so he could reach my ear. "You're also in very deep shit because you came and you weren't supposed to do that. Were you?"

I shook my head, and that was all the admission he needed. Before I realized what was happening, the top half of my body was flat against the counter of the sink and both arms were stretched out behind me, both wrists held captive by one of his big hands at the small of my back.

"What are you going to do?" I asked, unsure whether he'd actually answer.

He did, but not with words. Shaw moved his other hand forward so I could see what he held in it—his leather belt. I gasped, wriggling and trying to get my arms loose, but there was nothing doing with the grip he had.

"Be still," he said, the thickness of his cock wedging between my ass cheeks as he pinned me further. I fell in line, a surge of excitement jolting my body to awareness yet again. "Good girl." He backed off of me just a bit. "Spread your legs."

I did the best I could with my limited mobility, but that didn't seem to be good enough. "Wider," Shaw ordered, and I managed to eke out a little more.

He hummed his approval, the leather of that belt caressing my bare skin ever so gently. Tracing the curvature of my ass, he let it dip between my thighs to rub against the tender flesh of my pussy. I moaned, arching my back and trying to push against him for more.

"You like that?"

All I could do was nod.

"Well, you won't like this." I jumped as the belt lashed across my backside, leaving a slowly dissipating sting in its wake. Shaw's tongue followed up, the warmth of his mouth mixing with the sting to create an unbelievable mix of pleasure and pain.

The sound that came out of me couldn't have been human. It most certainly hadn't been premeditated.

Shaw and his mouth were gone as quickly as they'd come, and then another lash from the belt followed. Only this time, it was lower, across the place where my thighs met my ass. I arched again, moaned again, thought myself crazy for getting any sort of pleasure out of this. What the hell was wrong with me?

"Wider," Shaw ordered again. And, hell yeah, I complied. The next smack was reserved in force and centered only on my pussy. Tugging at Shaw's hold on my wrists was a fruitless attempt to free myself so I could throw the man against the wall and have my way with him. This was supposed to be punishment? Oh, yeah, I could see it.

Again he whipped at my pussy, and I was sure he'd left it dripping wet from the contact.

"Fuck, sweetness," he groaned and then pushed his cock between my legs, not entering me, but coating himself in my juices instead. He was thick and hard, the wide head rubbing against my clit and nearly making me come again.

Shaw noticed and pulled away. With a growl, he bound my wrists with a couple of wraps of the belt, and then he took a step back. I could only imagine him swiping his hands over his face, pulling at his hair, pacing to regain the control he must have lost. But it was short-lived because he resumed his place behind me, grabbed my ass with both hands, and then spread my cheeks wide. And there was nothing gentle about it.

Another groan was the last thing I heard before an intense sensation of warmth radiated from the place I'd least expected. Shaw's mouth—his lips and tongue—were all over the puckered skin at the forbidden entrance in the cleft of my ass. He was *rimming* me!

"Holy fuck!" I yelled, overtaken by the eroticism of it all. Not only did it feel amazing, but it was also so taboo, so naughty-naughty, and I couldn't help but wonder why in the world we'd never done this before.

Saliva made its way down my crevice, joining the wetness seeping from the opening of my pussy. The cool air kissed the sensitive flesh, setting all my nerve endings on edge, and I heard myself beg with a mewling sort of moan that was barely decipherable even to my own ears.

Shaw's tongue dipped lower, pushing inside me before quickly withdrawing so he could nip at the spot. And then he stood. I maneuvered my head so that my chin was propped on the counter and I could see him in the mirror. His attention was pinpointed on one place. He was watching with rapt fascination as his hands covered my cheeks, his thumbs keeping me spread for his viewing pleasure. And then I felt him at my entrance, the thick head of his cock pressing against my opening until it gave way to his quick thrust.

His head fell back as he pushed farther inside me, spreading the walls of my pussy to accommodate his girth.

I didn't care about how good he felt inside me. I didn't care that the pressure from my position was hurting my chin or that my tits would be sore or that my wrists would likely be bruised by morning. All I cared about right then was watching this beautiful man take pleasure from his beautiful woman.

Punishment? Not in this lifetime. This was a reward. And I might have fallen a little in love with Katya for dishing it out.

Shaw's head came forward again as he watched himself fuck me. His mouth had fallen open, his breaths were coming much quicker, and the wet sheen on his chest had more to do with the sweat that had broken out across it than anything left over from our shower together. In and out of me, he moved with long, deep strokes that increased in rhythm. I ignored the burning sensation coming from the harsh grip on my ass as he kept me spread for him because I knew the visual was driving him. Driving him into me and driving him mad.

I came again and again, the walls of my pussy pulling him deeper, squeezing his thick cock with gratitude. Finally, he thrust hard, his groin slamming into my backside as he replaced his hold on my ass to grab my hips instead. Shaw came. Hard. His jaw clenched tight and every tendon bulged until he'd spent all he had to give.

And then he collapsed on top of my still-bound arms.

Thank you, Katya.

CHAPTER 12

Shaw

During our private meeting, Dr. Minkov had expressed her concern that Cassidy didn't quite see herself the way the rest of the world did and had perhaps lost a bit of her sensuality as a result. I was confounded by her assessment at first, thinking it impossible for someone as beautiful as Cassidy, as confident as she'd always been since the day I'd met her, to not know she was made up of the stuff that could make grown men cry. But after we left, I'd really started to pay attention to the way she carried herself. Something had changed. Looking back over the years, I realized the change had come shortly after Abe had been born. Actually, I think maybe even before then, around the same time she'd taken an indefinite leave of absence from her position at Striker.

Jesus. Did being an agent really define the way Cassidy had seen herself that much?

I still hadn't been sold on the whole idea. That is, until the opportunity to carry out Katya's assignment had presented itself. And then I'd seen with my own eyes that it was true; Cassidy no longer thought herself beautiful, and that had, in large part, been my fault because I hadn't told her often enough, I hadn't shown her, I hadn't made her feel desirable, and I hadn't considered for a second that she might need me to do all of those things because I'd been too busy doing my own thing.

Though I'd enjoyed our assignment immensely, I was most satisfied that maybe it had gotten Cassidy back on the right footing in terms of her self-image and how I saw her.

I was also now convinced that Dr. Katya Minkov was an evil genius. Not only were her assignments orgasmic, but she'd also somehow figured out a way to effectively use sex as a tool to get people to realize things about themselves on a deeper, more personal level—a level that really didn't have a thing to do with sex in the first place. If I could find some way to market that shit, I'd be a very rich man, indeed.

But forget the money. My girl had been walking around naked with her chin held a little higher, her back a little straighter, and her eyes a lot more satisfied when she looked at herself in the mirror. Seeing her like that, glowing with self-confidence like she used to, made me damn happy.

We were finally getting somewhere with all this shit, and I could see the light at the end of the tunnel. So I didn't bitch one bit about our session with Dr. Sparling. In fact, I had been looking forward to it and had even shown up *before* Cassidy.

Dr. Sparling had cheesed it up over that, of course, patting me on the back and telling me how proud he was of me. I half-expected him to give me a gold star sticker to wear on my shirt for the rest of the day. Yeah, I guessed I was becoming the teacher's pet or some shit like that.

Today, his hair was pulled back into a stub of a ponytail on top of his head, and he was decked out in penny loafers with no socks, skinny jeans, and a Hawaiian button-up. For a second, I allowed myself to wonder what must go through his mind in the mornings when he picks out his attire for the day, but then I decided that was probably one cracked pot I didn't want to pour too much thought into.

When Cassidy showed up—looking well and properly sexed up, I might add—she had this air about her that made me nostalgic. She had a new hairdo, freshly painted nails, a makeup job, and somebody had obviously been shopping because I was sure I would've remembered those jeans on that ass if she'd ever worn them before. But more than her physical appearance, there was something familiar about the way she carried herself. She wasn't quite the frigid bitch of an ice queen from a few years back, but she was definitely wearing the ice queen's confidence. Yeah, my girl was Stella, and I was proud as fuck of her for getting her groove back.

So I gave her a greeting worthy of the woman before me. "Hey, beautiful!"

"Hey yourself, handsome," she said as she bent over to give me a quick kiss. I couldn't take my eyes off of her as she took up her spot on the couch, leaning into my side and linking her fingers through mine.

"Well, you two certainly look satisfied," Dr. Sparling said with that cheesy grin as he took a seat. "Might my colleague have had something to do with that?"

"She's doing her thing." I chuckled with a knowing wink.

"Excellent! Time for me to do mine, then," Dr. Sparling said, getting things under way as he pressed the button on the recorder. "Today, I want to talk about something we touched on in our last session. I don't think I'm far off the mark when I say it was a very sensitive subject between the two of you, one you both seemed happy to move on from, which tells me that it just might be at the core of your issues." He took a deep breath as if debating whether or not he should move forward and then deciding it was already too late to turn back. "This partnership you competed for—"

Every defensive mechanism I had slammed into place before he could finish what he was about to say. Gone was my stupid grin. Gone was that light at the end of the tunnel. Gone was Cassidy's hand, and there was now a gaping space between us on the couch.

I wanted to fire him on the spot.

"—seems to still be an unresolved issue for both of you."

My jaw tensed with grinding teeth. "I really don't see the point of reopening old wounds, Doc."

Goofy grin. "I think we have to, Shaw. Otherwise, all we're doing is putting a Band-Aid over the lesion without repairing the severed vein bleeding out beneath the surface."

Damn. This was not *Grey's Anatomy,* and Jeremy Sparling sure as hell wasn't Dr. McDreamy.

He pushed his glasses higher on the bridge of his nose, continuing. "So, it's a sore spot, yes?"

I sighed, and got comfy in my corner of the couch because this session was about to get really messy. "Yep."

Back when I'd first come to Striker, Cassidy had taken some potshots at me in this superior sort of voice that was meant to put me in my place before I'd ever ventured outside of it. That was the same voice she used now. "Sometimes, I think Shaw thinks we're still competing for it."

"Why is that?"

"Because I didn't win it fair and square," I told him, my knee beginning to bounce with my aggravation. "She did, and then she gave it up." All those old feelings of knowing I'd been second best came flooding back to me. It was safe to say I didn't do well with inferiority. A fact I was sure our host would've had a field day with if ever given the chance for a one-on-one.

"Tell me what happened."

Cassidy told the story, wrapping it up nicely with a big, puffy bow on top, while I sat back and rubbed the hell out of my chin, listening to her recount the details in that methodical way of hers. She didn't show any weakness with it, no sign that it had been as much of a bother to her as it had been for me, but I knew differently. Someone with the amount of tenacity Cassidy possessed did not give up the golden goose without feeling the loss on a fundamental level. The doc was right; it was definitely an unresolved issue, and it was a very big deal. Otherwise, we wouldn't have fought so hard over it.

Dr. Sparling looked up from his pad once he'd finished scribbling his notes from the tale. "So you gave the partnership to Shaw, and now you're not working at all. Do you miss it?"

"Miss what?" she asked.

"Working."

She nodded hesitantly. "Up until Abe came along, it had been the center point of my life, that thing that had defined who I was and where I was going."

"And where are you going now?"

She shrugged. "I don't really know. The partnership had been the end goal for me. Not getting it was a failure. Until then, I'd never failed at anything."

Her admission made me feel like a thief. But I hadn't taken it from her, dammit!

"And now Shaw has the partnership," Jeremy said, stating the obvious and really testing my restraint. "Is there some part of you that might be transferring some of the blame for the failure to him?"

"Some? Try all," I answered, figuring I'd stayed quiet for long enough.

Cassidy's eyes narrowed to slits, invisible death rays shooting out of them. I didn't give a shit. A man could only take so much of being cut down before he had to start defending himself.

So I did some chopping of my own. "It's cool, though. She just faked her orgasms and announced that to the world to get back at me. Isn't that right, Cass?"

It was like waving the red cape in front of a bull. "We're back to that now? Okay, fine. No, it wasn't to get back at you. I faked my orgasms to give you some sense of accomplishment that you did not earn. Yet again."

Like the smart-ass that I was, I turned toward Dr. Sparling and clapped my hands. "Congratulations, Doc! You were absolutely right in your assessment. Everything does come back around to that damn partnership."

Cassidy rolled her eyes. "Stop it, Shaw. You're acting like a child."

I got serious then, sitting forward to lay it all out on the table for her. "No, I'm not acting like a child, though you like to treat me like one. I'm a man who's doing everything he can to take care of his family. But that's not good enough for you, is it? Trust me, no one knows better than I do what you gave up when we had Abe. Don't you get it? All I'm trying to do is be worthy of the sacrifice you made."

The woman infuriated me to no end. I knew how much she'd sacrificed for me, for Abe. She'd worked damn hard to be the best sports agent in the country. Admittedly, even better than me.

She'd given up the partnership, not for my sake but so she could return to Stonington to care for her mother. And her giving up her career was so she could be the one to raise our son instead of some stranger. She gave up something she loved for someone she loved more. Not a day went by that I wasn't reminded of it, that I didn't see the resentment toward me because of my part in it, that I didn't feel the weight of the burden placed upon my shoulders to make it fucking be worth it.

She was full-on crying now, her face beet red with emotion. "Don't you dare do that, Shaw. Don't you make me a martyr, and don't label my being a mother to Abe a sacrifice. I love him, and I want to spend as much time with him as I can because I don't want to miss a *second* of his life. His first words, his first steps, the first time he donned that Superman cape . . . I was there for each one of those milestones. But you? You missed them all."

Yeah, I fucking knew that, too. "And why do you think that is, Cassidy? You think I didn't want to be there?"

"If you did, you would've been. All I can go on is what you show me, and what I know from that is you always put your work before your family. You care more about your clients and what's going on with them than you do your own son. I'm tired of making excuses for you when he cries, wanting his daddy to play with him. I'm tired of having to explain to him that his daddy can't come home to eat the lunch *he* made for you because Daddy is having lunch in some fancy restaurant with whichever famous athlete you're schmoozing that day. And I'm tired of apologizing to him because his daddy can't be there to read him the bedtime story he picked out because he thinks it's one *you* would enjoy. I'm just plain tired."

I raked my fingers through my hair, ready to pull it out by the roots. "What do you want me to do, Cassidy?"

"I don't know! Something! Anything!"

"I can't be at work and with you guys at the same time. Do you want me to give up everything I've worked so hard for? Is that it?"

"Oh, what you've worked so hard for," she repeated. "You're talking about the partnership I earned and then gave to you, right? Because if memory serves me correctly, I'm the one who clawed her way out of a town that no one leaves, studied her ass off to become an attorney just to get a shot at being an agent, and then worked my way up from an entry-level position to finally see all of my hard work pay off. No one gave me an internship simply because I was good at kissing ass! And now you're sitting in an office that should belong to me, with a title that should belong to me, and schmoozing clients that should belong to me while I raise our child by myself."

"Ho-ly shit. I finally get it," I said, having a *eureka* moment. "You're jealous, aren't you? That's what all of this is about."

Cassidy guffawed despite her tears. "Of course you'd think that. I'm not jealous, Shaw. I resent the hell out of you. It should've been me. You know it, and I know it."

"You didn't have to give that partnership to me."

"And you didn't have to accept it."

"Well, it's a good thing I did because then you went and got yourself pregnant." I regretted the words the second they came out of my mouth.

"Oh, I got *myself* pregnant, did I?" More incredulous laughter followed. "With what? A turkey baster? It takes two to make a child, Shaw. Sex Ed 101. Perhaps if you'd stayed in school long enough, you would have learned that."

And then I was fired up all over again. "Ah, there we go! Finally! You want to know what the core of the matter is, Doc? Well, *that's* it, right there. She sits up on her high and mighty pedestal, looking down her nose because she thinks she's better than me."

Cassidy's eyes shot wide. "I do not!"

I ignored her objection, calling it like I saw it. "How in the world did Stonington, Maine's favorite daughter end up with an uneducated, underprivileged inferior from the hard streets of Detroit? Right?"

"That's not what I think at all!"

I nodded like a madman. "Yes, it is. I may not have been formally educated, but I've done pretty damn well for myself despite the fact. It doesn't matter, though, because I'll never be good enough for you!" I stabbed my finger in the air toward her.

Cassidy did some finger stabbing of her own. "It's always all about you, you, you! This has nothing to do with where you came from or how educated you are. I don't love you despite that; I love you *because* of that, because it's what's made you the person you are. *I* don't think I'm too good for you. *You* do!"

Cassidy shot off the couch, snatched up her purse, and stormed out of the office without another word. The door slammed so hard behind her that it rattled the framed certificates hanging on the walls, one falling to the floor, and its glass cover cracking.

"Fuck!" I jumped to my feet, too, turning to pin Dr. Numbskull to his seat with a glaring dare. "Are you trying to help us stay together or break us apart? Because everything was just fine before you had to go and bring this shit up!"

Dr. Sparling's eyes were wide as saucers as he sat staring after Cassidy's hasty exit. His Adam's apple bobbed in his throat with a deep swallow when he slowly turned to me. "Was it?" he asked.

"Yes, it was," I answered through clenched teeth.

He cocked his head. "Then why did you come here to begin with?"

"Because *she* wanted to!" I was so tired of repeating myself.

"And you think *she* wanted to because everything was fine? Because *she* was happy?" He let that hang in the air for a moment. "Were *you*?"

I could've killed him in that moment. I could've snuffed out that know-it-all's existence in a nanosecond using nothing more than my bare hands. But I didn't. I didn't because I knew the point he was driving at was legit and I just wanted someone else to blame for it. So before my frustration with myself got the better of me and I took it out on the man we were paying to do the very thing he had done, I turned on my heel and followed Cassidy's lead.

"Shaw," he called after me, and I stopped without facing him. "Is it true what she said? *Do* you think she's too good for you?"

I turned my head to the side. "Of course, I do. Because she is," I grated, and then I was out of there.

Shit. Just . . . shit.

CHAPTER 13

Cassidy

Two steps forward, three steps back.

Shaw and I had come so far in our therapy, only to now find ourselves worse off than what we had been before we'd ever started. I supposed it was true what they said about it always getting darkest just before daylight. As it was, I was drinking, drowning myself in the deep, dark abyss of "I don't give a damn."

But that wasn't entirely true, the "I don't give a damn" part. I gave a damn. I gave a big damn. Sitting at my usual table at Monkey Business, I let the happenings of the past two weeks have their way with my gloom and regret.

Even after the massacre of a session we'd had with Dr. Sparling, Shaw and I still kept our appointment with Katya the next day. I was sure the animosity he and I had felt toward each other was palpable to her, but she didn't acknowledge it. Instead, she'd congratulated us on a job well done for the "I am beautiful" thing and had explained the second part of that lesson was that, sometimes, even failure had its own reward. I think the overall message was that I was too hard on myself. Maybe I would've heard it loud and clear if not for the Dr. Sparling debacle, but I was still feeling guilty as sin over my part in that.

Then Katya had given us the next assignment. Ha! That one was a joke.

Role-playing. Shaw was supposed to show up at our door, disguised as the pizza delivery guy while I played the lonely housewife whose husband was away on business. Only, Shaw had stayed over late at work, conferencing with Dallas's general manager to get Marcel the best deal he could, and I'd fallen asleep. When I'd heard the knock at our door, I'd been startled, nearly falling off the couch before taking a moment or two to remember what was supposed to go down. And then I'd finally opened the door to find Shaw standing there with a pizza in hand, still in his suit and tie from the day and looking nothing at all like a pizza guy.

"Special delivery for the lady of the house," he'd said, porno creep factor in full effect.

I'd frowned at his pathetic attempt, not at all trying to look the part of a sexy minx prepared to give him the tip of a lifetime. But Shaw had forged on ahead, propping himself against the doorjamb like the neighborhood pervert and saying, "Don't you want to unwrap your *package*?" with a Chippendale-esque thrust of his hips.

With an exaggerated huff of annoyance, I'd said, "Shaw, you're supposed to be the pizza boy, not the mailman," before turning and walking away, leaving him standing in the doorway.

Like I said, it was a joke, and not a funny one. Plus the pizza was cold.

When we'd gone to see Katya again after that, Shaw had wanted to lie to her, to tell her that we'd done exactly as she'd directed. But I knew she'd be able to see right through it, and lying wasn't going to do anything to help solve our issues, so I'd come clean with the truth.

Katya had merely given us that knowing smirk I'd become accustomed to and said, "You could not complete the task because you do not want to be with anyone but each other."

I thought she was reaching on that one since the reason was more likely that our newly opened wounds were still super-fresh. Though if I put all of that to the side, I knew we still would've failed because she was right. I didn't want to be with anyone other than Shaw, which was exactly the reason I was so stressed.

It always gets the darkest just before dawn? Yeah, well, it had been another long week since our last session, and I wasn't even seeing a sliver of the moon at this point.

Good God, I needed a beer. Or two. Or three. So when I'd gotten the phone call from Quinn to meet him and the girls at Monkey's, I'd practically run the couple of blocks to get here.

Apparently, Shaw had received a similar phone call to hang with the boys. Part of me wondered if this was our friends' idea of staging some sort of secret intervention, but there had been no way they could have known about what had been going down between Shaw and me. If I drank enough, the truth would likely spew out of me like vomit into a toilet after way too many beers. Yeah, I wanted to get that drunk.

When my three friends arrived all together, my suspicions about the intervention escalated and my defenses were at DEF-CON 4 in preparation for the possibility of an attack. I'd planned to plaster a smile on my face—the whole fake-it-till-you-make-it—but found it wasn't necessary because there was something infectious about my friends and their devil-may-care personalities that made everything else not matter.

I was simply going to enjoy this time I had with them while I had it.

It had been too long since Quinn, Demi, Sasha, and I had been able to all be together at the same time and in the same place. Demi and Sasha had remained the closest, but Quinn was off jet-setting with Denver and I was busy being a mommy. Child and Family Services sort of frowned upon a mother taking her baby to a bar so she could kick back a few with her gossip buddies.

Once we'd done the whole round of hugs and "Oh, my God, you look so great!"s, we settled down into our normal spots around our regular table. It was luck that had kept it clear for us, seeing as how Chaz was out with the boys and not on shift to reserve it for us this time. Sandy, the server, came over to take our orders—another weird thing I hadn't been used to since Chaz always had our drinks prepared and slid down to the end of the bar.

Another beer for me, one for Quinn, two for Demi, and . . . an iced water for Sasha?

Quinn and I both pulled up short, drawing our heads back in unison with matching expressions of WTF.

"What's going on?" I asked, unknowingly calling the "meeting" to order.

Sasha crossed her legs and then sat forward, leaning on the table as she looked all around us to be sure no one else was listening in. I was 99 percent sure she was about to tell us the location of Jimmy Hoffa's body or maybe where we could find D. B. Cooper and all that money.

Boy, was I wrong.

"I'm pregnant," she said, her nose bunching up, shoulders lifting to her ears, and eyes squinting with a smile that was so wide, I swear I could see all of her teeth.

Chaos erupted after that with a slew of squeaks, claps, hugs, and congratulations. And then Quinn plopped back, eyes narrowing with an expression of resentment preempting his "You just had to steal my thunder, didn't you?"

Sasha's smile faded with confusion. "What are you talking about?"

Quinn sighed and sat his beer back on the table. "Fine. I might as well tell you anyway. Denver and I are adopting."

"What!?!" we all shrieked.

"Holy crap, Quinn!" I was shocked, stunned speechless because I'd had no idea that he and Denver even wanted children, let alone that they'd gone through the grueling process and had been approved for adoption. And he was my best friend, for crying out loud.

Instantly, I turned to Demi. "And what about you? Are you preggers, too?"

Jesus, did *I* need to go take a pregnancy test? I picked up Sasha's water and sniffed it, sure I'd find proof of the secret string of pregnancy virus that everyone had always said was in the water.

Demi's shoulders slumped as she stuck out her bottom lip. "I wish."

"Well, just to be safe, don't drink the water," I grumbled.

My besties looked at me like I was the Antichrist.

"What's gotten into you, Debbie Downer?" Sasha asked. "I always thought Abe was the best thing that ever happened to you?"

"He is! It's just . . . You know what? Never mind," I waved them off, grabbing my beer up because I definitely needed more of that. "Just forget I said anything. Really. Congratulations! I'm so happy for you both! Do you already have a baby in mind,

Quinn, or are you still looking? I mean, like, they don't exactly make a catalog for that sort of thing. Or do they?"

No answer.

"Oh, Sasha! Are you hoping for a boy or girl? Hey, you know what? At least you won't be having yours out of wedlock." I stopped to gasp. "I bet Landon is on cloud nine! He's going to be *such* a great dad! That's what the guys are doing now, right? He's telling them?"

No response.

There came a moment when I finally realized how quiet it had gotten and that I was doing all the rambling while my friends sat there staring a hole right through me. Smiling, happy faces gradually turned into sad puppy-dog eyes as they regarded me with pity, like someone had just died and I hadn't quite gotten the memo yet because I was stuck in the denial stage.

And that was when I felt the first tear streak down my face. I averted my eyes, fascinated with picking the label off the bottle of beer that had become my focal point. As I slumped low into my chair, hoping to simply melt into the polished wood, a voice as small as a traumatized child's said, *Everything is going to change now,* and I realized it had come from somewhere deep inside me.

Sasha reached over and took my hand, stopping me from completing the removal of the label. "Cass? What's wrong?"

The label thing bothered me more than I could admit out loud, simply because it was just hanging there with clumps of paper still stuck to the glue on the bottle. Messy, messy. I hated leaving things undone.

"Cass?" Sasha's persistence demanded my full attention.

I looked up, my eyes meeting hers, then Quinn's, and finally Demi's. A waterfall of tears gushed from me then, as did all the miserable details of my life as of late. I let it all spill—the issues Shaw and I had been having, that we'd been seeing a relationship coach, that we'd been seeing a *sex* therapist, that Abe was in Stonington until we could get our acts together, that I was terrified that I was on the verge of losing the man I loved because I wasn't sure if we would or *could* ever work things out completely, and that I knew but didn't want to admit that I knew what that might mean not only for me but for Shaw and Abe as well. I told them everything. And my friends . . . my friends sat there, letting me get it all out, absorbing every single detail even as they kept handing me tissues and beer because that was such a healthy combination.

"Aww, sweetie." Sasha handed me yet another tissue from her purse. "Why didn't you talk to us about this?"

I shrugged and sniffled. "Because you guys are busy living your perfect lives with your perfect men."

Demi guffawed. "Ha! Perfect? Not hardly. Honey, every couple has issues. Look at how long it took for Chaz and me to hook up in the first place. And now, not only are we not married, but we've also been trying to get pregnant. Out of wedlock and without success." Since her beer was empty, she took mine, gulping it down. Taking a deep breath afterward, she continued, "Truth is, we don't know if the issue is just with the timing, or his sperm count, or my girlie bits. And both of us are too chicken to go see a professional to find out because what if they tell us we'll never be able to have children of our own?"

She took another deep breath and then finished off the beer.

Sandy brought over another fresh one, and Quinn grabbed it the second she sat it on the table in front of me, taking a swig for himself before adding his own two cents. "And Denver and I are constantly battling the rumors of infidelity, thanks to his fame.

I'm not just talking about from female fans either. Since he came out, all kinds of mister-sisters have made allegations that my Rocket Man has been blasting off into every planet in the universe. I know it might look like I'm living the dream, but, honey, loving a superstar ain't easy. Just yesterday, I found a gray hair. Can you believe it? I'm twenty-nine!" He shook his head, disgusted, and then chugged the beer again.

"Where?" Demi asked, invading his personal space to find it for herself.

Quinn shoved her shoulder, pushing her away. "Stop it! I yanked the fucker out!"

"Oooh," Demi drawled out like a child telling a sibling he was going to be in trouble. "You shouldn't have done that. You're going to get three more in its place now."

Ignoring them, I turned to the only one of us who hadn't said anything. "What about you, Sasha?"

"Um, okay, so Landon and I are sort of the perfect couple," she admitted, looking guilty as hell when the rest of us grumbled. "*Buuut* . . . you remember how long it took me to see what was right in front of my face, right? Landon went through all of those horrible relationships with me, even did the cleanup after the shit hit the fan with each one of them. He never brings that up, but I know it's got to weigh on him from time to time, and that kind of messes with me, you know? Like, I'm always wondering when he's going to finally realize that he's too good for me. I bet Shaw wonders the same thing about you."

Clearly, she'd forgotten who the man was. "*Pfft!* Shaw Matthews holds himself in high enough regard to never think anything of the sort," I said, despite the fact I'd accused him of thinking I was too good for him during our meeting with Dr. Sparling. He'd never denied it, but he'd never admitted it either.

Sasha furrowed her brow in contemplation. "Hmm. You definitely know him better than I do, but I think I'm going to have to disagree with you on that point." She reminded me so much of Landon in that moment. While Sasha had been the somewhat flaky one of us, Landon had been the quiet observer, wise and insightful, with a knack for seeing and hearing things the rest of us might have missed.

"Oh, really? And why's that?"

"Because I think maybe his egotism is his way of overcompensating for the positive reinforcement he never got from anyone else. I mean, look at his childhood, Cass. Isn't it possible that he's still trying to prove himself *to* himself? The mold that contains our perception of self-worth is forged during adolescent years. What do you think his mold might look like? The man never had anyone to tell him they were proud of him. Maybe he's just trying to make himself someone his son can be proud of, that *you* can be proud of."

The bottle I was about to drink from was forgotten, suspended in midair, as her hypothesis sank in.

Freaking. Lightbulb. Moment.

I set the bottle down, allowing my slightly inebriated mind to sober in order to process the clicking of the puzzle pieces.

Baggage. Shaw had plenty of it. And though he didn't acknowledge its existence, though he'd figuratively replaced his own parents with a surrogate in Abby along with the rest of *my* family, that didn't mean *his* baggage had magically disappeared. It was still there, an invisible weight around his shoulders that kept him fighting just to be able to keep his head above water while the rest of us without the stuff were buoyant enough to simply float along the current of life.

Dr. Sparling had been trying to help us get to the root of our issues so we could repair and rebuild from the ground up. Maybe, just maybe, those roots ran deeper than our relationship alone. Maybe our roots were being entangled and smothered by those attached to his past.

I jumped up and lunged across the table, taking all of my friends by surprise when I grabbed Sasha's face and laid a big, fat smackaroo on her lips. "Sasha, I love you! And P.S., I'm calling Mulder and Scully because I'm pretty sure you and Landon are the same person."

She laughed. "Nah. He just completes me."

Balance . . . she and Landon had it, I wanted it. So it was time I helped my other half help me help us.

It was time we both came clean.

CHAPTER 14

Shaw

"A career is wonderful, but you can't curl up with it on a cold night."

That was what Landon had told me last night when Chaz and I had gotten together with him for dinner. The meal was so he could tell us he was going to be a daddy. The advice was a direct result of me spilling my guts to my two best friends about what had been going down between Cassidy and me as of late. Better out than in, right?

The man was a guru, an elder of wisdom, and, apparently, he was also the number one fan of Marilyn Monroe because that had been her quote, not his. Either way, it was spot-on.

Cassidy and I hadn't spoken much since the *War of the Roses* incident that had gone down in Dr. Sparling's office. Neither of us had brought that shit up again because nothing good was going to come of it until we had the time to simmer the fuck down and process it. A lot of stuff had been said. Hurtful stuff. Hurtful stuff that was now out there and no longer capable of being put back into Pandora's box and hidden out of sight in a dusty attic as if it didn't exist. It did. And the only way to exorcise it was to acknowledge its existence, admit my fault in every part, and simply beg Cassidy for forgiveness. But I knew I couldn't go to her with a bunch of empty promises. Cassidy was all about "show, don't tell," so I'd been busy working behind the scenes to do just that.

"Hey."

I looked up from the stack of getting nowhere fast on my desk to see Cassidy standing in the doorway to my office. Something about seeing her there made me feel equal parts relief and trepidation. She hadn't been back at Striker since she'd taken her maternity leave, but there she was, not looking the least bit out of place.

"Hey," I echoed, not really sure what else to say.

"Are you busy? I thought maybe we could talk, but if now isn't a good time—"

"Please don't go," I blurted out when she turned to leave. It occurred to me that I wasn't only trying to keep her from leaving the office, but me, as well. Wow. Was that where we were? Had it come down to a possibility of Splitsville for us?

"Come in," I told her. "I've actually been wanting to talk to you, too."

Finally, she crossed the threshold, closing the door behind her. I stood, motioning toward the couch, and then called Ben to tell him to hold all my calls before I went to join her.

I felt awkward as hell when I sat on the edge of the cushion, leaning forward with my elbows on my knees and popping my knuckles. The cold leather made a sound beneath our weight that was too loud in the uneasy quietness of the room.

"I'm sorry," we both said at the same time.

Whirling around in her direction, I scooted across the couch until my knees were touching Cassidy's and took her hands. "You don't have anything to be sorry about, sweetness. It was all me.

It's always been all me. I just keep fucking up and I didn't know how to stop, but I do now."

"Shaw, wait," she said, squeezing my hands. "I need you to let me say what I came here to say."

Closing my eyes shut to the onslaught of all the negative things I knew she could and might tell me, I ducked my head and nodded for her to continue. If she railed on me, if she left me in a heaving lump of fucked-up-ness on the floor by the time she was done, it would be what I deserved. So I sucked it up and made the choice to take it like a man.

"I'm proud of you," she said, shocking the ever-loving shit out of me.

I popped my eyes open, my voice jumping an octave or two when I said, "You're proud of me? For what?"

"For everything you do," she said. "I get so mad at you sometimes because it's easier for a person to complain about the things a person isn't doing instead of acknowledging what they are doing. You've been an amazing provider for Abe and me, Shaw, and you're right, you work so hard every day to make sure we have all the things we need and want . . . all the things you didn't have when you were growing up. You work so hard to not be like your parents. But I haven't done my job very well because if I had, you'd know that you aren't *anything* like your parents."

I inhaled a deep breath because it was the only way to stave off the pussified tears threatening to emasculate me. Cassidy wiggled her fingers beneath mine, and I eased my grip, not aware that I'd been squeezing the shit out of them. My reaction wasn't about being angry or ashamed; it was about feeling like a kid, buried under years of shit upon shit with nothing more than his fingertips breaking the surface, suddenly being taken by the hand and pulled out to emerge as a man.

This woman had done that for me. So, yeah, she had done her job very well.

"Cass." I ducked my head again as I sniffled, not wanting her to see me lose composure. *I was not a pussy. I was not a pussy. I was not a fucking pussy.*

"I'm not done," she said, giving me more time to get my shit together. The next deep inhale came from her. I listened intently, my ears perking with every word and my skin feeling too tight for my body. "Technically, I might have won the partnership, but you deserved it every bit as much as I did. And no one, not even me, could've made of it what you did. It isn't fair of me to resent you over it because I was the one who gave it up. And it isn't fair of me to hold a grudge against you just because you're still working while I'm at home with Abe because that was a choice *I* made. The break in my career was by my doing, not yours, so I apologize for the hell I've put you through over that as well."

The battle with the pussy factor was lost. I knew it the second I saw a tear go cliff diving from my face and splash into the carpet between my feet. Her hand was on my shoulder then, rubbing in that tender sort of way that only a person who loved another could do. She'd just assumed complete responsibility for our issues, and she was comforting me. I couldn't let her do it. I couldn't let her blame herself when I had plenty to be sorry for myself.

"Thank you for saying that."

"You don't have to thank me, Shaw."

I turned my head toward her from my huddled position, fully aware that she'd be able to see the likely redness of my eyes and maybe even some residual wetness there. "Yes, I do. And I owe you an apology or two, myself."

Pushing off my knees with my elbows, I stood and began to

pace, trying so damn hard to formulate into words all the messages my heart and my brain wanted to deliver. "I know I haven't been there for you and Abe like I should've been."

She started to interrupt me, but I cut her off. "Let me finish. Please."

Cassidy nodded once, and I continued.

"When you said I put work before my son, it nearly crushed me. But that was because it was true. I hadn't seen it that way, and it hadn't been my intention, but it happened. I was so intent on making sure I could give him everything, I forgot all that little boy wants is his daddy. He doesn't give a shit about the money or the material things. And, God"—I rubbed my hands over my face, tilting my head back to look up at the ceiling—"when I think of how I made you feel—that you'd lost your self-worth because *I* didn't make you feel important or beautiful or loved," I said, smacking my chest even as my face twisted up in disgust, "it makes me sick to my stomach."

My girl was crying now, but I had to keep going because I had to get out every single bit of this admission. "All those things my parents did to me, Cass . . . neglecting me and treating me worse than shit . . . I've done the same exact thing to you and Abe. So while I might have bested them in the provider category, I failed you in that."

I moved from the couch, bending at the knees into a squat in front of her. Cupping Cassidy's face in my hand, my thumb wiped the wet track from her cheek. "I rarely ever admit when I'm wrong, a fact you well know. So believe me when I say I'm so fucking sorry, sweetness. No one means more to me than you and our son. I'll spend every day of the rest of my life proving that to you and doing my damnedest to make sure you're happy. Because all of this," I said, waving around the room, "means nothing if I don't have you."

She held my wrist, nuzzling her face into my hand to kiss the palm. A shiver of warmth ran down my spine from the tenderness of it, making my flesh pebble.

"I love you," she told me.

"Not nearly as much as I love you," I said back. Because it was the truth.

Cassidy

I felt weightless as a joyful sprite in a field of spring buds when I left Shaw to finish his work for the day. A page had been turned, a corner rounded, and a new day begun. Shaw and I were well on our way to our happily-ever-after. Now, more than ever, I felt confident of that. No, things were not perfect between us, and, yes, we still had a lot of work to do, but those core issues that Dr. Sparling had been trying to root out were now aboveground and withering in the light of our mutual forgiveness. We were on to bigger and better things, and we had a session with Katya this evening to look forward to, to boot.

After our last failed assignment, Katya hadn't given us another, and I'd been worried that she might be dropping us as clients. However, while I'd been in Shaw's office, he'd received a cryptic text from her simply saying, *Dessert will be served tonight. Come prepared to be seen.* Neither of us knew what that meant, since everything about our arrangement with Dr. Minkov was supposed to be handled with an insane amount of confidentiality. But the "come prepared to be seen" part made us think maybe we should be dressed up, just to be safe. I had zip by way of anything fancy, so I was going to get to spend the afternoon shopping. Yay, me!

Standing at the end of the hall waiting for the elevator, I bit my lip, still feeling the warmth of Shaw's breath on my neck when he'd leaned in to give me his only request for my attire for the evening. "No panties, sweetness," he'd said just before he'd nipped my lobe and smacked me on the ass to send me on my way. God, I loved that man.

"Hold the elevator!" a loud, booming voice echoed down the corridor as the doors parted. I'd know that voice anywhere.

I turned, smile already in place as I greeted my onetime mentor and favorite boss ever. "Wade . . ." Instant warmth filled me when he pulled me in for a big bear hug and then released me, keeping his hand on my shoulder.

"How have you been, kiddo?" he asked, stepping onto the elevator with me.

"Good," I told him with a bob of my head. "How about you? Shaw tells me you're retiring. Say it isn't so. You're too young for retirement!"

"Young enough to *enjoy* retirement," he qualified with a chuckle. "We miss you around here, kid. I hear Ingram signed with Shaw because of you."

Well, that came from out of left field. "What? No, I had nothing at all to do with that deal." I laughed. "That was all Shaw."

"Hmm . . . well, that's not what I heard." He lifted the arm attached to his attaché case to look at his watch and then back to me. "Hey, have you eaten yet?"

"No, I haven't, actually." I hadn't been eating very well at all since that meeting with Dr. Sparling. Or sleeping, for that matter.

"I was just about to go grab a late lunch. You wanna join this old man so we can get caught up?"

"I'd love to," I told him, suddenly feeling like I could eat a horse. Besides, I had nowhere else to be and I really did want to catch up with the man who'd been like a second father to me. Plus, with any luck, I might even be able to get something out of him regarding his replacement as partner to report back to Shaw, which would give him one less thing to worry about.

Lunch with Wade had been very enlightening. Ginormously so. In fact, I almost wished I hadn't agreed to go.

I knew who the new partner of Striker was going to be, though I wasn't sure how Shaw was going to feel about it. I was sworn to secrecy, of course. Wade was adamant that springing the surprise on Shaw would be one of those opportunities that only came around once in a lifetime. Respectfully, I disagreed. This would be a second in his lifetime, at the very least. Revealing my pregnancy to him had been the first, but he'd taken that pretty well.

Reluctantly, I had a hand in the decision Wade had made. A decision that would have a direct effect on the future of the life Shaw and I shared, the plans we'd made for our future, the end goal, as it were—and I hadn't given Shaw any say in the matter. If it backfired, everything Shaw and I had worked so hard for of late would be the casualty.

So naturally, I was nervous about keeping the secret from Shaw. Nail-biting nervous. It was a pretty epic secret, after all. But after much consideration, I'd decided the most honest response from a person was usually his initial reaction to a situation. I was anxious enough for Shaw, so I figured that left either rage or elation as his choices.

Metaphorically, I was crossing every body part imaginable in hopes it was the latter, but that would be dealt with tomorrow. The more pressing matter was the agenda for the night: Katya.

And that was awesome because it meant I'd get a mind-numbing orgasm to quell the worries, which meant if I got to reciprocate, it might soften the sting of betrayal and/or rage Shaw might or might not feel in less than twenty-four hours from now. Come on, elation!

Not wanting to embarrass myself by showing up overdressed for our session with Katya, I settled on a simple royal blue cocktail dress with modest heels. My shoulders were bare, thanks to the halter-style bust, which made my boobs look way more bodacious than they actually were, and the dress was cinched at the waist with a flowing tea-length round skirt that helped hide my pooching belly while showing off my legs.

Shaw checked to be sure I'd honored his no panties request, and I allowed his fingers no more than a graze of the tender flesh between my legs, smacking his hand away before he could take further liberties. The groan that came out of that man when he touched me made me juiced in all the right places, which was the reason it was absolutely necessary that we get out of our apartment and into public before I gave him more than just a sampling of what I hoped Katya would allow us both before the night was over.

To our relief, there was no dinner party at Katya's, which was confusing, to say the least. And Nikola didn't escort us to her office. This time, he took us to a different room, upstairs and to the far right corner of the back of the house. Super-duper weird. This room was lit by the soft glow of a fire and candlelight—lots of candles—but the décor was the same deep red as the rest of the house. There was no desk in this room and no couch. The only furniture was a dressing screen and a single, plush chair at one end of a high table that had a set of black steps at the center of one side. Or so I supposed it was a table, since I'd never seen one that stood that high and with a cushioned leather top, to boot. Nor had I ever seen leather the color of blood. There was something innately sexy about it.

"Was there a special occasion tonight?" Katya walked into the room, her eyes sweeping over me in my dress and Shaw in his black suit and tie.

"Your text said come prepared to be seen," Shaw told her.

"It did, though I think you translated its meaning incorrectly."

"How so?"

"As I was devising the . . . how do you say . . . *curriculum* for our sessions, I was very happy to see that on your questionnaires, you both had the same overlap in terms of things you have never done but would like to try. One of those things was the desire to be watched."

A flushed heat warmed my skin, and I could only imagine the color of pink I must have turned. That heat wasn't anything about being embarrassed; it was about arousal in its most concentrated form.

"I'm going to need you to spell it out for me, Doc." Shaw was pulling at his collar, a dead giveaway to the fact he knew very well what she meant. He just wanted her to say it.

That flushing thing happened to me again because, God help me, so did I.

Katya leaned back against the end of the table or bed or whatever it was, her long, elegant arms stretched out behind her. "Your lover will be bared naked, Shaw, lying on this bed for only you and I to see. And then I am going to watch you pleasure her."

Shaw's hands went to his hips and he stepped closer, as if that would allow him to hear better. "You're going to *what?*"

Exactly. She was going to *what?*

Even the exasperated sigh that left Katya and the smooth way in which she rolled her eyes oozed sex. "Must I really repeat myself? You know how I detest doing so."

"No. I think I got the gist of it," Shaw told her, stepping back into place and half-hiding me. "You want to watch me as I pleasure Cassidy."

She tilted her head to the side, giving herself a better angle from which to see me. "Not quite. I want to watch Cassidy as she is being pleasured by you."

The way she regarded me, that look, made me feel as if she were undressing me on the spot to get the show on the road. My hand went to my bare neck, slowly slipping down to my throat and then my chest. Without realizing it, I bit my lip. Was it getting hot in here?

The corner of her mouth turned up into the sort of grin a crossroads demon might wear right before claiming a promised soul. This woman was fully aware of the effect she was having on me. Then she pulled a piece of silk cloth from her pocket. "You can wear a blindfold, if you like."

"You're pressuring her."

"Darling, I think we both know that Cassidy will not be pressured into doing anything she does not want to do." They were talking about me as if I weren't even in the room. "She wants this. Do you? You did mark exhibitionism as an experience you would like to have, did you not?"

"Yes, but—"

Katya didn't let his protest go any further. "You do trust me, do you not?"

I got the point she was trying to emphasize. The agreement we signed would protect all three of us, from a confidentiality standpoint, so this was actually the safest way to experience the fantasy without the intrusion of perverted strangers or law enforcement. Because, jeez, how would we explain that to Abe?

"Yes, but—" Shaw's reservations were apparently still in full effect.

"But, but, but," Katya said, waving her hand. "Why must you follow a positive response with hesitation? Do you not know what you want?"

"Yes, I do," he answered assertively.

"Well then, tell me what is making you uncomfortable. Are you worried I will see your lover naked, or that I will judge your skills?"

"Neither." Shaw's confident smirk was in place. He knew he was crazy good at what he did.

"Then I am confused. I do not like being confused." Katya straightened, walking toward the door. "If you no longer wish to experience this thing, we do not have to move forward."

"No!" I blurted, taking them both by surprise.

Katya stopped, facing me. That grin was back in place. She wasn't the least bit surprised by my reaction. In fact, I could hear the *Well done* in her expression, though she didn't speak it.

We'd already failed two assignments in a row. Well, Shaw had only failed once while I'd failed twice, but I wasn't ready to get my third strike. Plus, yeah, I really did want to do this. YOLO and all, right? The thought of someone watching, the thought of Katya watching, did very naughty things to me. It was hard to ignore the exhibitionist that apparently resided not only in my fantasies but also in some perverse reality.

I turned my attention to the man at my side, needing him to see how important this was to me even though I could barely understand it, myself. "Shaw, I want to do this. Please."

The backs of his fingers stroked my cheek. "Sweetness, I will take you anytime, anywhere, and no matter who's watching . . . because you're *mine*," he told me. It was entirely possible that he threw in that last part for Katya's benefit, but whatever. "I just need to be sure this is what you want to do."

Boldly—damn boldly—I held his gaze as I reached behind my neck and undid the clasp there. The bodice of the dress fell forward to expose my bare breasts.

"Exquisite," Katya whispered.

Of two things I was sure. One, I was definitely overdressed. Two, I couldn't get out of my clothes fast enough.

Shaw smirked. "You ain't seen nothing yet, Doc." He nodded toward the dressing screen in the corner, silently telling me to finish the job.

I did. And I did it slowly, knowing my shadow was likely playing across the thin, white dressing screen, thanks to the light of the fire behind me courteously keeping my naked body warm. Draping my dress over the screen, I took a deep breath to steady my nerves. Confidence was a thing the other two people in the room had in spades. Too bad I couldn't borrow some of it. If I were going to keep up with them, I'd have to dig down deep into my reserves. This was a test that needed to be aced; not unlike finals in college or the bar exam or packing up to leave my family and home behind to venture into the unknown; not unlike having to prove myself in the realm of sports agents, dominated by men. I'd succeeded in all those things. I would succeed in this, too. So with my head held high and my shoulders back, I took the first step forward. And then another and another until I was facing the man I loved and the woman who confounded my natural instincts.

Shaw's jacket and tie had been removed, the first two buttons of his shirt unfastened, and his sleeves rolled up. He'd been pacing the floor but became frozen in his tracks when he registered my appearance. That hungry look was in his piercing blue eyes as his gaze raked me over. He was ready, anxious, even.

Katya crossed the room, circling me with her slow perusal. Goosebumps spread out over my exposed skin, gone as quickly as they'd come. "You are so beautiful, Cassidy," she said, stopping before me.

"I've told her the same thing." Shaw's voice was deep and filled with pride.

"Thank you," I said, because what else was I supposed to say to that? "Um, what do you want me to do now?"

She took my hand—hers, warm and soft—and the contact sent a bit of something-wicked-this-way-comes rolling through my veins. Guiding me toward the table, she swept her arm over it like Vanna White showcasing a prize to be won. There was a pillow at the head now, draped in white silk that matched the sheet covering the red leather. And then Katya stopped once I was in front of the steps.

"I don't understand," I said, watching Shaw as he went to stand at the foot of the table.

I could feel the satiny smoothness of her blouse on my naked back when she pressed against me to whisper into my ear, "You are the dessert, darling girl. Positively scrumptious," she drew out.

Shiver, shiver, shiiiiver . . .

"Come now. Step up. Carefully." I took my cue, gingerly placing one foot at a time on the steps as I climbed to the top like a virgin sacrifice being guided to lie on an altar.

Once I got comfortable with my head on the pillow, Katya smoothed my hair against the silk, and then she went to my feet. "Excuse me," she said, edging past Shaw.

After a series of movements later, the bottom part of the table dropped out from under my legs, and my heart soared into my throat. I snapped my head up to see what was going on. What happened next was far too familiar in an unfamiliar sort of way. Stirrups appeared from the table, and then my feet were lifted one at a time and placed in them.

My breath hitched and the already erratic thumping of my heart intensified with the knowledge that my very private parts were on display, just hanging out there in the open in the most vulnerable state they could be. My knees slammed shut.

Shaw cleared his throat, watching me for any sign of distress, so I relaxed, giving him nothing to find.

I could feel the heat of Katya's gaze on my core, her rapt fascination with everything female about me nerve-racking and arousing at the same time. "Such a pretty little pussy," she said, still admiring the view. "So pink and juicy. I envy you."

She envied me? Katya was sex and sex was Katya. I appreciated her kind words, but—

"You *should* envy me," Shaw said. "Now, if *you* will excuse *me* . . ."

Oh. She'd been talking to him.

"Ah, ah, ah," she told him, going to the side and pulling open a drawer. "Not before you don these." She held up the blindfold in one hand and what looked to be earplugs in the other.

Shaw took the earplugs, turning them over in his hands. "Why do I need these?"

"I have no doubt that you are quite skilled, Mr. Matthews, but imagine with me for a moment the sort of pride that would be had knowing that you brought your lover to orgasm with no other cue than her body. With the absence of sight and sound, imagine how sweet your reward would taste."

With no further argument, he plugged his ears and nodded in her direction to do the honors with the blindfold.

Katya gave me a conspiratorial wink and then covered his eyes, taking care to also cover his ears and the plugs before securing it behind his head. When she was done, she guided him to stand between the stirrups with his hands placed on my legs. Coming back around to my head and taking her seat, she leaned in to whisper, "Anything we say now will only be between us. I have but one final touch to add," she said with a bit of sin in her voice as she dangled yet another blindfold for me to see. It would be the last thing I saw before this session was through. I think I was relieved by the notion. "Lift your head for me, darling."

I did as she asked, relishing the darkness that followed when the blindfold found its place and was secured.

"Did you know that when one sense is removed, the others become intensified?" She was so close I could feel the heat of her body warming mine.

I swallowed thickly, knowing the sensation was proof of what she'd said. "Yes."

"Your taste on his tongue, the smell of your arousal will be heady, rich, and dark. He will never forget it." She inhaled deeply as if scenting me for herself. I felt the release of her breath on my neck, and my breasts drew tight. Katya noticed. "Your nipples are so pert, Cassidy. I believe they, like you, are eager to please me, no?"

Shaw's hands were on my knees then, and with a quick snap, they were pushed open. I gasped another "Yes . . ."

"Bon appétit, Mr. Matthews," she said in a low voice, though he couldn't hear her. He also couldn't hear the grin in her voice, but I could.

A warm, wet sensation centered on my core with a firmness that caused me to cry out. Actually cry out, which was something I never did. My back arched off the table, but Katya was still at my ear with an apparent intention to stay there and talk me through the rest of the session.

"Very good, beautiful girl. Your senses react well to your lover. I do not believe this will take long at all. You have a body made for coming."

Shaw's tongue swirled my clit again and again as he gave a ravenous groan before he sucked it between his lips to torture me with rapid lashes. Oh, holy hell, she was right: it wasn't going to take long at all.

He was feasting on my flesh, a man starved and deciding to forgo all decorum to eat straight from the plate in order to capture every morsel and drip of gravy on his tongue. My head slammed back when two fingers slid inside me, leaving me moaning and writhing on the table.

"Mmm, a good finger fuck will make you come so hard you will squirt," Katya said. "I can only imagine how tight," she enunciated the *T*'s, "that pretty little cunt is, how the walls must be milking his fingers even as his tongue laves your clit."

I moaned again, reaching for his head but stopped short when Katya put her hands on my shoulders to still me. "No. Do not give him direction. Let him do this on his own."

Shaw's knuckles pounded against my pussy over and over again, his fingers reaching as deep as he could get them and the tips provoking the patch of ultra-sensitive nerves at my deepest core. His full mouth was on me—lips, tongue, and teeth—and he was showing no mercy with the nip, lick, and suck. Jesus, I was going to break apart at the seams. My back arched off the table, all sense of shame gone in the wake of the pleasure that succumbing served up. Back and forth, I undulated, riding Shaw's fingers and face to a rhythm he'd set.

"Oh, how you move," Katya said, coming so close that her lips grazed my ear. "I see you. Your beautiful breasts are begging for attention, and that glorious bundle of nerves is swollen, ready to burst in his mouth. You make me squirm in my seat, Cassidy. I am so well pleased by you that I believe I will have to let Nikola fuck me on this very table once you leave. I wonder what image I will see when I close my eyes. I wonder"—she paused, her voice growing more seductive with her next words—"can you imagine him fucking me now?"

As if her words had been a spell she'd conjured—or more likely I was simply highly open to suggestion from this woman— I could see it as clearly as if it were happening right in front of me. Katya lying naked where I now lay, her full breasts on display with what I imagined to be large, tan nipples, a natural arc to her back courtesy of the firm, round ass holding it aloft, and her legs spread with her feet in the stirrups, still wearing those fuck-me heels. And Nikola, broad and muscular, a gentle giant now pounding into his boss with every tendon taut, every vein bulging with his surging blood.

Her words and the implanted image started a chain reaction that I would likely feel guilty about later, but I didn't have the presence of mind to feel anything other than *every*thing in that moment. Because I was coming, and, Jesus Christ, it was the most intense sensation I'd ever felt. I'd come hundreds, maybe even thousands of times in my life—Shaw was an orgasm specialist— but this? This was different. The warmth that surged from that mysterious place in my body wasn't merely a sensation attached to a bit of natural lubrication. This time it was a gush of liquid that spilled from my nether region, soaking the silk sheet beneath me.

"Oh, my God!" I called out at the top of my lungs as the pressure kept shoving the wetness forward.

Shaw was still there, drinking me down with a moan like that of a man who'd never eaten pussy before and had just found out it was his absolute most favorite thing in the world. My orgasm compounded over and over again to the point that it was too much to be contained and I wasn't sure if my body, mind, or soul could or would survive it.

"Feel it," Katya urged me. "Let it consume you. Let it become you."

As if the lid had suddenly blown off a container under pressure, the most euphoric sensation I'd ever experienced exploded and radiated from my center and through my limbs, obliterating every molecule of my makeup like a supersonic blast wave. It was quite plausible that light shot out of my fingertips, but with the blindfold still blocking my sight, I'd never be certain.

"Fuck this," I heard Shaw growl. Not angry. More desperate.

In my blindfolded, post-orgasmic state, I had no idea what was going on. That was until I heard the distinct sound of metal against metal as a zipper was ripped down. And then he was inside me, that thick, hard cock penetrating me deeply and fully.

I panicked. What was a sure win had just turned into yet another fail. My shoulders left the table and I yanked at the silk over my eyes. "Shaw, no! Katya didn't say—"

The force of Katya's hands pushing me back down to the table was followed by a calm voice. "No, darling girl. You must let him enjoy you as I only wish I could."

How would I ever be able to describe what I saw next? Shaw's head fell back, his silk-covered eyes raised toward the ceiling, his pristine white teeth threatening to break the skin of his lip, his large hands gripping my hips roughly . . . and his own hips pistoning so hard, he'd likely have bruises there in the morning from the way they were slamming against the table, slamming into me. He was every bit a ruthless beast grunting with each thrust as he claimed his mate, and all I could do was stare in awe of the man.

"Yes," Katya hissed. "Show that tight cunt no mercy."

Sweat soaked Shaw's shirt and dripped from his face, but his momentum never wavered. My whole body jarred with the force of his thrusts, my teeth clinking, my breasts bouncing in an almost painful measure, and if I hadn't been in stirrups, I was sure I would've been pounded right off the table, thanks to the silk sheet. But Katya held my shoulders in place with her head next to mine and her attention focused on the hardcore fucking going down at the end of the table.

Though I wouldn't have thought it possible, I came again, feeling rather victorious about the way the walls of my pussy pulsated around his cock. He would've felt it, that milking draw as my body stimulated his own release. A release he would claim.

Shaw did not make a liar out of me. Harder, faster, shallower, his thrusts came. A drawn-out growl building higher and higher with each thrust and retreat until it burst from his chest and he slammed home. With a roar, his hot semen shot into me. Shaw's movements became erratic, stuttered with three quick, one slow, two quick and deep, and then four slow, deep, and grinding until he pushed all the way inside and stopped.

His chest heaved right along with mine as he stood there, both of us unmoving and without words to be said.

Katya broke the silence with a laugh that startled me into a slight jump. Removing her hands from my shoulders, she sat back and then stood, clapping. Shaw pulled the blindfold down and the earplugs out of his ears. Though his eyes were adjusting to the sudden appearance of light, he captured mine and held them. There were all kinds of messages that transpired between us with that look, none of which I could put into words. But it was all good. And hot. And sexy. And we wanted to do it again, right away.

"Well done," Katya said, slowing her clap. "Well done, indeed."

The corner of Shaw's mouth lifted up once again into that smirk he'd made famous, and then he pulled out of me, quickly tucking himself back into his pants before Katya got an eyeful. And then he returned his attention to me, gently lifting my feet from the stirrups. Yep, my thighs were already sore. I sat up, taking the sheet with me and wrapping it around my body.

"I am so utterly proud of you both," Katya said, coming to stand to the side of where I was sitting. "Tell me, did you enjoy yourself?"

I nodded. "It was an experience I will never forget."

"Good. And the lesson to be learned?"

Shaw answered first. "That no one is going to tell me when I can and can't have my woman."

"Yes!" she squeaked with more glee than she'd ever displayed. "You have mastered your control, Shaw. Well done, you." Turning to me, she said, "And . . . ?"

Luckily, she was standing to the side, which allowed me to look at her without Shaw seeing my face. I gave her what I hoped was a sultry grin and wink, knowing she'd get the gist of it. Katya had allowed me to satisfy my curiosity about being with a member of the same sex without my having to cross the line, just as I'd requested on the questionnaire I'd completed for her. But I knew it was more than that. "I should worry less about how others see me because I am far more judgmental of myself than anyone else is."

"And?" she prompted again.

"Confidence is what makes an already beautiful woman sexy."

Katya took my head in both hands and looked down at me with a proud grin, her catlike eyes hinting at the depths of her wisdom. "Yes, and you are *very* sexy, my darling girl. I recommend that you practice on depriving your other senses so you can become as attuned to your body as you are with your glorious mind."

"I will. So does that mean we can keep this?" I asked, holding up the piece of white silk dangling from my finger.

"Of course." She laughed and kissed me on the cheek before stepping away to allow me room to attempt the steps with my still wobbly legs.

"Now, I will give you one last assignment," she told us as I went to the dressing screen to clean myself up. "This lesson will be based on trust. Complete it successfully and the intimacy issues between the two of you will be no more. Then you may bring your child home."

Well, that certainly got my attention. I peeked around the screen just as Katya reached into her pocket, pulling out a thick, plastic card and tucking it into Shaw's hand.

My brow furrowed. "Last assignment? You're leaving?"

"Yes. I have been called away. This is merely my vacation home, darling. I do not know when I might return."

Vacation home. That explained the less than clinical environment, though nothing about Katya and her methods was clinical. Still, I had to know. . . . "Did we do something wrong?"

"Oh, no, darling. On the contrary. You have pleased me very well. I have been called back to where I am needed. You will see me no more." She went to leave.

Called back to where she was needed? For only a moment, I allowed the silly, dreamlike part of me to imagine her as a Mary Poppins or Nanny McPhee for adults and with a naughty twist, showing up where couples needed her most before moving on to the next. But that was silly, right?

"But what if we fail the assignment?"

Katya stopped, turning in my direction with a silent pause before those to-die-for lips curled up into a smile that reached all the way to the fathomless depths of her eyes. Her confidence in me, in us, didn't need to be spoken. Needed or not, it was. "You will not fail. In our short time together, the two of you have shown more progress than any of my very long list of clients. But these sessions were not meant to be a miracle cure. You will still need to work on the areas we have identified as problematic. Have fun with it, use your imagination, explore the possibilities and the limits of your bodies, and do not ever relax the grip on control and confidence that you have both recaptured with a firm hand. However, if you should find yourselves in need of a . . . how do you say . . . a *tune-up* of sorts, the card I gave you has a direct line to me. An invitation, if you will." She turned back toward the door, adding, "Do not hesitate to use it."

Cryptic was Katya's middle name.

"Katya?" I stepped from the dressing screen, going no farther. She hesitated, but I didn't really know what to say next. We should thank her, beg her to continue seeing us, tell her she would be missed. Something.

Nothing came out.

As she turned her face to the side with a mysterious smile in place, I knew all of that was understood. "The pleasure was not only yours" were her final words, and then she walked away without looking back.

Shaw flipped the card over in his hand and grinned.

"What does it say?" I asked, going to look over his shoulder.

Before I could see it for myself, Shaw shoved it into his pocket. With a sexy wink he said, "You'll see."

CHAPTER 15

Shaw

Something had gone down between Cassidy and Katya during our session with her last night. Though I couldn't hear or see anything, once the blindfold and earplugs had been removed, I certainly noticed the difference in the way they interacted. But I wasn't going to obsess over it or pry into something I was sure had nothing to do with me. Cassidy and I both had our own issues to deal with, and Katya had been a mastermind at bringing them all to the forefront by using sex as a tool. Fucking genius; that's what it was. Besides, I was probably better off not knowing anyway.

After the heart-to-heart we'd had—without Doc Sparling, I might add—I felt good about where we were in our relationship. I'd owned my fuckups, and Cassidy had let go of the grudge she'd been holding over the partnership. I was still worried about her, still felt the guilt of the career she'd loved and lost on a personal level. She'd said it wasn't my fault, that being a stay-at-home mom was a decision she had made, but it didn't make me feel any less responsible. I was the one who'd gotten her pregnant, after all. Jesus, had I really said she'd gotten herself knocked up? Yep.

I'd been such an ass, true to my bastardized reality. But that was all behind us now. Things were looking up, up, up for us, and victories abounded as we soared to new heights.

So why didn't I feel the weightlessness of a bird in flight? Quite the opposite; some small part of me felt like I was still choking on saltwater, with my lungs unable to fill with the breath they needed. And instead of breaking the surface of the ocean and finding land in sight, I was steadily sinking deeper and deeper into the dark abyss that had once tried to claim me.

I tried to shake off the negativity, focusing all of my energy on the positive.

Like how we'd graduated from Katya's course. Well, almost. There was still the matter of the last assignment that needed to be completed before we could bring our son home, and I knew Cassidy had been missing him like crazy, we both had, so I wanted to do that right away. Not only for the sake of bringing my little man home, but because what Katya had written on the back of that card she'd handed off to me had made my cock punch inside my pants, and that was after I'd already blown my load inside Cassidy like an eruption from Mount Vesuvius. Damn straight, I wanted to get on with that.

As soon as I could get the emergency Striker-wide meeting Wade had called out of the way. An emergency meeting I knew nothing about. I was a partner, for Christ's sake. You'd think he'd run these things by me first. Mulling over the list of possibilities of topics that might be discussed, I settled on the obvious. Wade was going to make some grand announcement about his replacement; specifically, *who* that person was going to be. Yeah, that pissed me off even more because, again, I was his partner. Shouldn't I have a say in the choice, be given some kind of final approval or something? I trusted him to make the selection, but the least he could do was tell me who that person was before announcing it to our employees. I was blind, and I didn't like being blind . . . unless Cassidy was going to be lying on a table with her feet in stirrups and her pussy served up for my dining pleasure.

"Hey, boss man! It's time for the meeting. You ready?" Ben ripped me from my thoughts before I could get too carried away.

"Yeah," I told him, grabbing my cell and standing to button my suit jacket. "What's the word around the office on this one?"

"What do you mean?"

Joining him, we walked side by side out into the corridor, making our way toward the boardroom. "You usually know before me what's going on. I figured you'd already know who Wade's replacement is going to be."

"I was going to ask you the same thing. If anyone knows, they've kept their lips sealed on this one."

I noticed then that Ben was dressed impeccably, his suit pressed and fresh as if he were prepared to make a standout first impression. Could Ben be the chosen one and he just wasn't spilling the beans under orders from Wade?

Glancing at my watch, I noticed the time. Determined to keep my word, I pulled up my cellphone and pressed the speed dial to Cassidy's. When she answered, her voice sounded off, like maybe I'd just interrupted some personal time she'd been having with herself. I mentally chastised my cock for getting carried away with the thought, and powered through. "Hey, sweetness. What are you doing?" Okay, so maybe I wasn't powering through it as well as I'd intended.

"Um, nothing," she said, but I wasn't buying it. She was definitely doing something. Plus, I could hear an echo in the background, like she was in our bathroom, so what I already suspected became even more obvious.

"Yeah, okay." I laughed, deciding to not call her out on it, while making a mental note to have her give me all the details later. "I just wanted to let you know that we're about to go into the meeting, and I don't know if it'll run long, so I might be a little late getting home."

Look at me being a grown-up and checking in with the little missus. Just like all responsible adults in a committed relationship.

"Oh. Yeah. That's fine. No worries." Shaky words equaled "Let me the hell off the phone so I can come already."

A fat grin spread across my face, but I played nice, ending the call to let her get back to it. Putting the ringer on mute, I tucked the phone into the inside pocket of my jacket and stepped into the boardroom.

The place was crowded, every seat around the table taken except for two—mine and Wade's at the head—while the rest of the employees lined the walls. I took my place, greeting those around me and making small talk as best I could to hide my curiosity over Cassidy's naughty biz going down right at that moment back at home, and that staved off my frustration with Wade over blindsiding me like this.

Swiveling around in my chair, I looked out at the city through the floor-to-ceiling windows that lined the far wall. Yet another grin pushed at my cheeks as I got lost in the memory of the night, not so long ago, that I'd played a game of hide-and-seek in the dark with Cassidy in this very room. A game that had ended with two winners, if I recalled correctly.

"Is everyone here?" The booming sound of Wade's voice as he made his grand entrance pulled me back to the present, and I turned to level him with a "What gives?" expression that he ignored. Instead, he made a quick sweep of the room and then clapped his hands together. "Good, let's get started. As you all know, I am retiring." Right to the point. There were a series of *aww*'s from a few of the employees, which were without a doubt heartfelt. Wade could be a no-nonsense sort of hardass, but he took care of his employees, and everyone really loved the guy for it. "I know, I know," he continued, "but every voyage must come to an end, and every captain must have his final docking, but that doesn't mean the ship will never sail again."

I half-expected Wade to fall into a dramatic recital of "O Captain! My Captain!"

"Matthews will be at the helm," he said, acknowledging my presence with a nod, to which I gave a wave. "So I know the Striker crew will be in good hands, but he needs a first mate."

A pregnant pause followed, during which time everyone got quiet, looking around the room at their co-workers and undoubtedly speculating who that might be. Whoever it was, they weren't giving themselves up before Wade gave the formal announcement.

"Having said that, please join me in welcoming someone who is not a stranger among you, someone who I know you will all follow without question, one of the most successful agents to have ever made a name for herself in the industry—"

Her*self*? *A woman?*

"—my very good friend and the new co-partner of Striker Sports Entertainment. Elizabeth, show her in," he said to his assistant, whom I just realized wasn't only standing by the door, she'd been guarding it.

Those who'd been sitting with their backs to the entrance turned in their seats, every pair of eyes in the place glued to that door as it swung open. Elizabeth stepped out, telling someone to come in, and then went back to her place.

In walked a woman dressed in a gray pencil skirt and a matching, form-fitting vest over a white silk collar shirt underneath that had the first couple of buttons unfastened to show the skin—and the cleavage—beneath. I'd know that form, that skin, and that cleavage anywhere.

Cassidy.

I nearly fell out of my seat at the sight of her and that confident smirk she wore. Her ginger hair was done up in a bun, Wayfarer glasses sat on the bridge of her nose, and she strolled in with those signature red fuck-me peep-toe heels I'd nearly lost my mind over back when we'd been adversaries. We were no longer adversaries. Now, it seemed, we were fucking partners.

The room erupted in conversation while she made her way toward the front of the room, joining Wade.

He beamed like a proud papa as he put his hand on her shoulder. "I'm sure my onetime protégée needs no introduction, but just in case . . . Ladies and gentlemen, Cassidy Whalen."

Agents, receptionists, accountants, and assistants—employees of every rank and file—stood and clapped. I stood as well, not really feeling my legs as I walked to the front of the room. Wade roared with laughter when I looked at her like I couldn't believe what I was seeing, then at him, and then back at her again.

"Told you I had it covered," Wade said, clapping me on the back. "The dynamic duo . . . back together again. Damn, I'm good."

Cassidy leaned into me, smelling damn amazing as she spoke low so that no one else would hear. "Shaw, are you okay with this? You haven't said anything."

Shit. I hadn't, had I? Then again, neither had she . . . this whole damn time. How long had she known? Those two, Cassidy and Wade, had both duped me on this one. Duped me good. I waited to feel my blood pressure blow, for some type of angry outburst to find a raucous way to cause a scene.

And it never came.

Shaking off the dreamlike haze of the surprise, I got my wits about me because I wouldn't be able to stand it if this woman thought I was unhappy with this decision in the least bit. "I am *more* than okay with this, sweetness. Um, I mean, Whalen," I corrected myself, catching the slip a little too late.

"It's okay," Wade whispered. "You're the bosses. Which means, you can pretty much get away with anything now. And I do mean *any*thing." He elbowed me, following it up with a conspiratorial wink.

Cassidy drew her head back. "He most certainly can*not*. There will be no hanky-panky at the office. Striker will not be run into the ground under my watch." Her hand went to her hip as she wagged a finger at the two of us with an expression that was stern, serious, and so familiar.

Yeah, Cassidy Whalen was back. The woman I loved, the mother of my child, was now my partner. The career she had worked so hard for and lost was hers again. And that made me pretty damn happy. One thing I knew for sure was that I wasn't going to let anything take it from her again.

"Settle down," Wade called out, bringing the meeting back to order. "I'm turning over the reins now, so you need to listen up."

Once everyone was quiet again, Wade melted into the background, giving Cassidy the floor. I wasn't sure what was expected of me, so I turned to take my seat again, but Cassidy stopped me with her hand on my arm. "Where are you going?" she asked. "This is a united front, Matthews."

"Oh. Right. Okay," I said, adjusting my tie before putting my hands in my pockets to let her take the lead. It wasn't like I knew what she was going to say.

She gave a quick wave to Ally, her former assistant, before starting. "First, I want to thank you all for the warm welcome. I know a few of you were hoping to be named partner, but hopefully there won't be any hard feelings." Quiet laughter followed and then she continued.

I stood there, proud as the day was long, and listened as my woman gave her background with Striker and all of her qualifications. Cassidy talked about her love for the company, her vision for its future, and she assured everyone that I had the lead with her full support. I didn't correct her because undermining her in front of our staff wouldn't be cool, but I'd make sure she knew we were going to be as equal in this partnership as we were in life.

And then she snuck a little something in on me. "Though I see some new faces, I know most everyone here by face and name. Before I left, I also knew what was going on in most of your personal lives. That's because we've always been a family here at Striker. How could we not be when we spend so many hours out of the day together? But those are hours that are being taken away from your families at home. So Shaw and I have decided that the first change that will take effect right away is that Striker will be opening an on-site daycare so you can have your family here with you."

Eyes shot open, accompanied by some surprised gasps from the women present, and then deafening applause from every single employee.

My fucking partner just did that. God, I loved this woman.

I took a step back, bowing as I faced her with applause of my own. There was no "Shaw and I" in her first order of business. That had been all Cassidy. Because she had the foresight to take care of our employees even better than Striker had done in the past, because she was a career woman who had felt the loss of her sense of self when she'd become a mother, and because she was a mother who would feel that loss, too, if forced to choose.

She could have it all, and she could give it all to our employees, as well.

Wade couldn't have made a better choice. As I stood back watching and listening to her, I couldn't help but think how funny it was how things just sort of worked themselves out. Cassidy and I had competed hard-core to be named a Striker partner. Though there could only be one winner, we'd both deserved it, and we'd both earned it. Hell, because of it, we'd fallen for each other and had even been blessed with a child and a family of our own. And now? Now we both held the title.

Destiny, fate, karma . . . whatever you wanted to call it . . . Yeah, I believed in it.

Cassidy

God, I felt so alive, so much more like my old self!

I'd had no idea when I'd agreed to have lunch with Wade that my career would be served up with my end goal as a side dish. At first, I'd hesitated because of Abe—I hadn't planned to go back to work until he'd started school—but then Wade had indirectly suggested I make changes at Striker that would solve that issue, not only for myself but also for the rest of the staff. Free rein to make whatever decisions that served the best interests of our employees and Striker were the result.

My second hesitation had been over how Shaw might feel about us working side by side. Wade had explained the dynamics of the partnership, that Shaw would have the majority say with Wade, Monty, and me balancing out the other half. And you know what? I was truly okay with it.

So I'd given him an apprehensive yes because my being okay with the whole deal didn't necessarily mean that Shaw would be. Add to that the fact that Shaw hadn't been included in the decision-making process and that not even I, his partner in life, had discussed this major game changer with him, and it had been a recipe for all-out nuclear war in the making. But I'd done it. I'd made the leap and I'd taken back my life, putting myself and the goals I'd made for my career back into the driver's seat. Whatever fallout might come of it would just have to come. But I had confidence in Shaw, in us, in the indestructible team we'd make.

When I'd left Wade to shop for the cocktail dress I'd worn to what I'd thought was going to be a dinner party at Katya's, I'd also shopped for new office attire. Putting on that suit, those glasses, and those heels again . . . it was like Diana Prince spinning her way out of uniform to transform into Wonder Woman. I'd turned this way and that as I'd looked in the mirror, loving what I saw and eager to show it off in front of Shaw.

But once I'd made it to the parking garage to wait for all of the employees to pile into the boardroom in order to not be seen before the big reveal—Wade's idea, not mine—the nerves had begun to sink in. What if Shaw got pissed that I hadn't discussed this with him first? What if he didn't want to share the control of Striker with me? What if he thought my taking the offer was somehow taking something away from him?

By the time all of those last-minute reservations had come into play, it had been too late to back out. This announcement was going to be the true measure of how far we'd come. If Shaw and I survived it, we could survive anything.

So I forged ahead, putting our relationship to the test. Shaw, there wasn't even a hint of anything negative when the big reveal had been made, not even a suspicion that he was hiding his true feelings. No, that look on his face, in his eyes, had said it all. Pride, speechless pride that didn't need to be spoken. Love, adoration, awe; they were all there as well. And there'd even been a bit of something naughty present in the way he looked me over. So I'd strutted my stuff for his benefit and the staff's, not mine. Because I was feeling myself and owning it.

After the meeting, we'd called up the gang and met them for dinner to celebrate, and then we'd headed to Monkey's afterward for drinks. It hadn't escaped my notice that Shaw was trying ultra-hard to booze me up. When I'd given him the single-eyebrow raise in question at the fourth beer he'd placed in front of me before I'd ever finished my third, he'd leaned over and said into my ear, "Drink up. You're going to need to be numb for what I'm about to do to you when we get home."

The way he'd said it had oozed so much with a sensual promise of "you won't regret it" that I'd barely taken a breath while downing the beer. Whatever assignment Katya had written on the back of that card, it was about to be accomplished.

So there we were in the elevator on the ride up to our condo, making out like a couple of teenagers. Me, leaning against the back wall for support and definitely feeling numb, and Shaw, kissing my neck and nuzzling my ear, slowly releasing the zipper at the side of my skirt while his other hand popped the buttons on my vest. His cock was hard at my hip as he grinded against me, and though the sensible part of my brain told me the doors could open to give any one of our neighbors a sight they wouldn't soon forget, the wanton hussy in me didn't give a good goddamn.

Edging a slight retreat, I palmed my lover fully on the outside of his pants, rubbing and basking in the vibration of the sexiest man on earth's moans against my skin. When Shaw gave up the nuzzling to take my mouth in a kiss that promised unspeakable things would be done to my body before the night was through, I worked his belt and the button of his pants loose.

By the time the bell dinged, signaling we'd reached our floor, and the doors parted, we were already well on our way to being undressed. Shaw growled, and the heat of his body left mine as he took my hand, yanking me out of the lift and toward our door. A fury of impatience accompanied his hurried unlocking of our place, and then we were inside with everything shut and locked behind us.

I was spun around with my back pressed against the door, but the room didn't stop spinning just because I had. A whoosh of euphoria washed over me when Shaw's mouth came back down on mine with a kiss that was much more demanding, insistent.

Suddenly, the prop was gone from my back and we were rushing toward our bedroom. Once we'd stopped inside, I was whirled around again, left standing surprisingly stable as Shaw took a step back and looked me over.

"Finish," his gravelly voice ordered, indicating my partially undressed state. "And leave the fucking shoes on."

Jesus, I loved a domineering Shaw. When we'd first started our affair, I'd been confounded by how a woman like me who was so much in control of every aspect of her life could be aroused by a man who robbed her of that control in the bedroom. I wasn't any less confounded by it now, but I was still every bit as aroused.

Shaw disappeared into the bathroom while I carried out his order, stripping naked for him, except for the shoes, of course.

Once I was done, I stood there with my hands on my hips, damn proud of what he'd see when he reemerged. No, it wasn't liquid courage; it was confidence.

When Shaw came out, he was naked as well. Gloriously naked. His cock jutted, proud and hard and thick and just plain yummy. The rest of him was every bit as yummy, but I found it hard to look away from the appendage that demanded I give it my full attention. Mine. All mine.

Though I really wanted to fall to my knees and crook my finger to beckon it closer, I kept my composure.

"I'll never get tired of telling you how beautiful you are," Shaw said, stopping at the opposite corner of the bed. "Come here."

With one heeled foot placed in front of the other, I was sure to let my hips sway seductively as I crossed the space between us. Shaw noticed. So did his cock.

When I stopped in front of him, he took my chin between his fingers, giving me a sweet kiss. The look in his eyes was tender when he pulled back, his voice soft as he said, "Do you know I love you?"

"Yes."

"Good." Another sweet kiss, and then he released me. Gruffer, much different this time, he continued, "It occurs to me that you might need to be reminded who actually wears the pants in this relationship, Whalen. We might be partners at the office, but at home, I am the man and you are my woman. Do you understand?"

Comprehension at the direction he was taking dawned on me, and I barely kept myself from jumping up and down, clapping, because this was some role-playing we could both really get into. "Yes."

Before I knew what was happening, Shaw had spun me around with my back against his front and had grabbed my hair to pull my head back, craning my neck. "I don't believe you do, so I'm going to show you."

He yanked me impossibly closer to his body, using the arm around my waist to force me to bend forward. In this new position, I was straddling the corner of the bed with my legs spread out on either side, my bare pussy coming into contact with the rounded edge of the mattress. Though it might have been kinky as hell, I couldn't deny the delicious sensation of the friction to my clit.

The heat of Shaw's bare chest was pressed against my back once more, his mouth at my ear and his gruff voice issuing yet another order. "Tell me."

I tried to lift my head, but he held me still. With a grunt, I told him what he wanted to hear. "I—I love you."

A sound of approval followed, and then a nip at my shoulder that sent shivers down my spine despite his warmth. "Do you trust me?"

I nodded, but that wasn't enough for Shaw. He yanked back on my hair. "Say it."

A thrill shot through me at the mystery of where this was going. "I trust you."

A bottle of lubrication and the plastic card I'd seen Katya give to Shaw landed on the bed just within my line of sight, the mystery revealed. Katya's final assignment was written in elegant script on the back of the card. One word: *Anal.*

The gasp of breath that left my lungs was one part trepidation and one part exhilaration, and both of those were wrapped up in a cocoon of *God, yes!*

"Now," his lips brushed my ear, his cock nestling into the valley of my ass, "say it again."

Shaw's cock wasn't *Guinness World Records* long; however, it was thick. If I had to guess, I'd say that was where the pain factor was going to come in. Thank God, he'd had the forethought to numb me up ahead of time. Besides, this was Shaw—the man I loved and who I knew loved me—and this *adventure* was one we'd both wanted to experience for years. It would be the final step in being claimed—fully and completely—by the only man I'd ever trust enough to go there.

Pushing back into him as best as I could due to the limited amount of space he had afforded me to work with, I moaned at the pressure given by his cock's presence against my entrance. "I do, Shaw. I trust you."

Shaw

Jesus, the cheeks of Cassidy's ass closed in around my cock like they had no intention of letting it get away.

With little guidance, she'd figured out I was doing my damnedest to correct our previous failure at the role-playing attempt, and she was playing along with my quote/unquote need to establish my dominance in this relationship. Because my girl was an undercover freak, and I wasn't complaining one bit about that. But I had to be sure she was okay with this assignment. Anal sex was the most intimate act one person could have with another, and I was sure it was going to hurt like a son of a bitch at first. Not that I wanted to hurt her. So I got my Cassidy Whalen on and researched the hell out of the topic because if we were going to do this, I wanted to do it the right way, inflicting as little pain as I could manage on the woman I really fucking adored.

My game plan was to balance the pain with pleasure, and I'd figured out how to do that through her penchant for kinky shit—which she'd never admit to. Hence, the corner of the mattress massaging that pretty little clit.

"Yeah? Well then, lift your hips for me," I told her.

When she did, I wedged my cock between her pussy and the mattress. Fuck! I groaned, not expecting how good it would feel to me as well. Dwelling on it was only going to make me come, so I got to work with the lube, squeezing a small amount onto the fingers of my free hand and then slipping them between those two glorious globes of her ass to prep her asshole.

Down below, Cassidy was soaked, grinding against my length with a slight roll of her hips that was making me lose my ever-loving mind.

I bit the nape of her neck with a growl that made her pause. "Fucking be still, woman. You're not in control here," I reminded her.

"Anything you can do, I can do better," she sassed.

Tightening my grip on her hair, I reveled in the gasp of surprise that came next. She'd be gasping more than that by the time I was done. My fingers pushed on her opening, not entering but making the threat very fucking real. And then I pulled my cock free, denying her that sensation any longer and opting instead to thrust it into her pussy.

"Ahh," she cried out with a buck that went nowhere real quick. Yeah, I liked this vocal side of my woman.

"You were saying?" I goaded.

Nothing. She was saying nothing now. Point proven.

With a quick retreat and none too gentle resurgence, my cock was buried deep inside her again. Pushing against her backside, I bump-and-grinded her clit against the mattress. Cassidy bit down on her lip, her eyes closing to the feel-good I'd just served up. And that was all part of the plan because I was still massaging her other opening with the pads of my fingers and pressing forward even more.

"That's my good girl."

Settling into a rhythm, I fucked her pussy. "God damn, Cassidy. I swear to everything I am or ever will be, you have the most amazing pussy in the world. So tight, so wet, so eager."

She moaned, moving against me, greedily taking the triple pleasure being dealt. The puckered skin of her asshole was slick, squeezing and then relaxing with each of her undulations against the bed. So I timed it out, slamming my cock into her hard while penetrating her ass with two fingers.

She sucked in a breath and I hushed her with tender kisses along her shoulders until her taut body eased back into a relaxed state. To my utter shock, Cassidy started moving against my fingers, drawing away and then taking them deeper.

"Yeah, sweetness? You like that?"

A wanton moan and even more deliberate motions were my response. Fucking A, this was going to happen. My cock swelled thicker, moving in and out of her to the beat of the song she'd written. I'd give her that much control, but no more.

"Look at you," I said, resuming my role, ready to accept my Oscar. "You want to be top dog at the office, but who's mounting who in our fucking bedroom? Tell me, Cassidy, whose fingers are fucking your ass right now?"

A moaned "Yours."

"Damn right, they are." I pushed farther, taking more liberty with in and out, deeper and faster, rotating my fingers to open my woman up for me. All the while, my cock was getting busy with the power drive into her pussy, the momentum rocking her clit back and forth over the corner of the bed.

"I'm going to fuck this tight little ass, Cassidy. I'm going to fuck it because it's mine and I can. I'm going to fuck it to remind you that when it comes to you and me, I will always be the alpha dog."

She didn't get sassy with her mouth this time. But oh, God, the walls of her pussy clamped down, putting my cock in a rear naked choke to rival any MMA superstar's. Riding my cock, my fingers in her ass, and the corner of the bed, Cassidy came. Her body got really animated then, trying to rise off the bed and being denied, trying to crawl forward and being denied, trying to scramble off and being denied. It was like trying to stay on a bull's back at a rodeo. And I really goddamn liked it. I gritted my teeth, batting down the orgasm climbing its way up my shaft.

"If you fucking make me come, I won't be able to put my cock in your ass, Cassidy. Is that what you want?"

Just like that, she settled back into place and the pulsing grip of her orgasm waned to a whimper.

I was well pleased, and anxious to give her what she truly wanted, but not before I gave her another one of those. Removing my fingers, I hooked her under the arms to hold on to her shoulders. Bending low at the knee, I got a good footing with a wide-open stance, lifting her chest only slightly off the bed so that her sensitive nipples could get a little friction of their own. And then I used my legs, my thighs, and my hips to fuck the ever-loving shit out of her.

Smack! Smack! Smack! My pelvis slapped against her ass, the push and shove of that swollen knot at the apex of her pussy folds no doubt getting a good workout on the mattress. Cassidy held on to the duvet for dear life, chanting, "Oh, God! Oh, God! Oh, God!" and sounding breathless as hell. I didn't stop, just kept thrusting and thrusting and thrusting until she came all over my cock, the juices spilling down over me to coat my balls.

Because that's how it is fucking done, people.

Once she'd gone completely limp, I released my hold and allowed her to collapse back on the bed. Though no reprieve would be given because this situation with her well sated, limp as a noodle, and completely relaxed was exactly what I'd planned.

Not missing a beat, I lubed her up again, pushing two fingers inside her ass and finding no resistance and even earning another moan. Perfect. My woman was ready.

I growled low at her ear, nipping and sucking along her shoulder as I positioned my cock at her ass. "I'm the man," I said. Pushing forward, I penetrated her.

JesusfuckingChrist! It felt amazing!

Cassidy sucked in a sharp breath and held it, her whole body going stiff. *Shit, shit, shit!*

"Relax, sweetness," I told her softly. "You have to relax. Don't move. Just breathe."

It was a tense moment before she inhaled and exhaled, slowly but surely uncoiling her muscles and easing back down onto the bed.

"Do you want to stop?" I asked, linking my fingers through hers on the bed.

She shook her head, holding on to me. "No. Just give me a minute."

I'd give her as long as she goddamn needed. Continuing to kiss her shoulder, her neck, her back, while straining like a motherfucker, I refused to budge even though, yeah, the squeeze around my cock was about the best feeling I had ever experienced. The hot recess of the canal, the whole taboo of the forbidden deed, the grip . . . Oh, God, the grip. And then she shifted under me, pulling forward and then pushing back to take me deeper. Bit by motherfucking bit.

"Does that feel good, sweetness?" I asked her, though the way she'd begun to moan and rub herself on the corner of the mattress was more than answer enough.

"Yes." Her whisper was about the sexiest thing I'd ever heard. The way she hissed the *S* and drawled it out, rolling her body beneath mine as if mimicking the letter's curvy shape. And then . . . "Dominate me. Fuck my ass, Shaw."

Hell yeah, that was a go.

I took it slow at first, still peppering those kisses while retreating and pushing forward, sinking my cock deeper and deeper. Cassidy was completely relaxed, tightening her hold on my fingers and moaning her pleasure. Again, she closed her eyes and her teeth scraped over the tender flesh of her bottom lip.

"More," she told me. "Feels so good."

"Mmm, yeah. Tight little ass," I grunted, moving more freely now. "I wish I had two dicks so I could fuck you in your ass and your pussy at the same time."

Yes, I knew they made adult toys for that kind of thing, but we didn't have one at the moment. And yes, I'd be investing in one the next time I made it out of this apartment.

Dislodging one of my hands, I moved all of my weight to the opposite side and grabbed her hip, angling my cock for deeper penetration. Cassidy moaned again, liking the new position, so I gave her more of what she wanted. Careful not to get too overzealous, I read the body language she was putting out, steadily increasing the pace and force of my thrusts until I found what worked for both of us. And then it was on.

I fucked my woman's ass. Thoroughly. Grunting and growling all the ways she belonged to me, how she would forever belong to me, how I owned her pussy, her ass, her fucking soul. Truth was, my soul was the one that had been owned so much more completely by this woman . . . because she was the one who'd found it in the first place.

And everybody knows finders are keepers.

CHAPTER 16

Cassidy

I wasn't as sore as I thought I would be. And the feeling of being violated wasn't really there either. Shaw and I had shared something very personal, something very intimate, and neither of us felt the need to talk about it. As I lay there in his arms with my head on his chest, the sound of his heartbeat beneath my ear was all the comfort I'd needed as we'd fallen asleep.

We were happy, but I still felt like there was something else lurking in the shadows that remained a threat to our happiness. Sort of like a stain beneath a fresh coat of paint that somehow manages to find a way to seep through no matter how many times you cover it. Until it was thoroughly removed, it would always stalk us.

The next morning was hectic. We had a session scheduled with Dr. Sparling later in the afternoon, but until then, we each had plenty on our plates. Shaw had a couple of his athletes in town that he needed to meet with, and I had the business of choosing an assistant to attend to. Though I'd love to have Ally back, no way was I going to take her agent title from her when she'd worked so hard to quickly become one of the best we had. Like

Shaw, I still planned on recruiting clients, though I'd keep my load on the lighter side so that at least one of us would always be available to handle the day-to-day operations of Striker. Wade's official retirement date wasn't for another month, so that freed me up to handle getting the employee daycare set up.

In the meantime, the item at the top of my list was making arrangements to get our Abey Baby home.

Oh, my God, I couldn't wait to see his chubby cheeks and teeny-tiny baby teeth when he smiled upon seeing us. I'd missed the little stinker; the crystal blue of his father's eyes as he eventually lost the battle with Mr. Sandman and they shuttered closed, the messy ginger of his mother's hair when he woke with way too much energy for that early in the morning, all his little piggies and that cute tushy when he streaked naked through the house before bath time, the sound effects he made with the production of the ultimate Batman and Superman battle, and the scrunch of his angelic face as he contemplated how they were going to save the world. I even missed stepping on, and cursing under my breath at, the cluttering of superhero figurines scattered throughout the house.

Oh, man, I hoped he wouldn't put up much of a fuss about my not sleeping with him anymore. I'd come up with a plan for that, though. Well, Shaw had. I was relieved he was taking the lead on that one. Katya was right; I belonged in the bed I shared with Shaw.

As we got ourselves ready for the day, Shaw and I worked together like a well-oiled piece of machinery, despite all of the inappropriate touching that was threatening to make us late. We showered together, brushed our teeth together, he handed me the jewelry he thought would complement my suit, and I picked out the tie that I thought would complement his. Breakfast worked much the same way, with Shaw getting the bowls and divvying out the cereal while I got the spoons and poured the milk. It was exactly how I'd always wished it would be.

I didn't even get upset when his cell rang, interrupting my time with him. He'd looked at the caller ID, mumbled something about not recognizing the number, and then sent the call to voicemail. It rang again, almost immediately, and Shaw repeated the action, tucking the phone into his pocket afterward with no intention of answering it. The next time it rang, he cursed.

"Shaw, it's really sweet that you don't want to take a call while having breakfast with me, but no one is that persistent unless it's an emergency. Answer it."

Peeved by the annoyance, he fished it back out of his pocket and stabbed at the green button on the screen. "Matthews," he barked into the receiver. And then, "Yes, Shaw Matthews. Who is this and why are you interrupting my breakfast?"

I grinned because grumpy Shaw was still a sexy Shaw.

"When?" he asked the unknown caller. After a pause, "Where? . . . How bad? . . . What's that got to do with me? . . . Just do it. . . . Why not?" And then a frustrated growl before, "I don't know what you expect me to do about it. I'm in San Diego. Can't somebody else handle it? . . . Nobody? . . . Typical . . . No. Figure it out on your own." And then he disconnected the call, abruptly getting up to take his bowl to the sink for a rinse.

"What was that about?" I normally didn't ask about his business calls because they didn't concern me. Now, however, they did.

His back was still to me when he answered. "Seems Jerry and Clarice have gone and gotten themselves into a car accident. If I had to guess, I'd say an extremely drunk Clarice was behind the wheel."

I nearly choked on my cereal. "Oh, my God! Are they okay?"

He moved around the kitchen, drying his hands on the towel and then going to retrieve his jacket from its place over the back of the couch as he filled me in. "Jerry didn't make it. Clarice isn't far behind. Apparently, she's on life support. They need the next of kin to come in and sign a bunch of paperwork so they can pull the plug. Apparently, that's me."

What was it about news like this that made something inside of us put ourselves into the other person's shoes, to experience his grief when it wasn't ours? For just a moment, I did that. I imagined the loss of my own parents, how devastated I would've been, how I would've crumpled to the floor in a heaving mess of tears if I'd been the one to get that call instead of Shaw. But it wasn't my parents; it was Shaw's, and he wasn't devastated or crying or showing any emotion whatsoever.

"When do you leave?" My voice was small when I asked the question, as if I was already paying my respects to the recently departed. I supposed in some way I was.

Shaw's eyes still didn't meet mine, though I didn't know what I expected to find there if they did. "I'm not going."

"What do you mean, you're not going? Shaw, you have to go."

"No, I don't."

"But they're your parents."

Finally, he stopped and faced me. Full-on rage that I didn't take personally rolled through his chiseled features and behind blue eyes that turned a stormy gray when he was this upset. "They were never my parents. Where were they when I watched a man get murdered right in front of me? Where were they when I came home drenched in brain matter and blood? Where were they when I was hungry, scared, cold, and practically living on the streets? Where were they any of the times I needed them? I'll tell you where they were. My alcoholic mother was passed out drunk and my con father was plotting his next scheme. So I'm not going. They can rot in hell for all I care."

"But Shaw, your mother isn't—" I stopped, trying to think of the appropriate way to say the next word.

"Dead?" Shaw provided for me. He propped himself against the back of the couch, crossing his arms over his chest. "You can say the word, sweetness. It's not going to hurt my feelings. And maybe she isn't dead yet, but she's as good as. Someone else can figure out the legal part of it. I'm sure there's a plan in place to take care of these things once the government gets tired of paying the bill."

"Shaw, you can't . . . You can't just leave her there like that."

"Why not? She'd do it to me. Christ, those two have left me for dead all my life."

This was so not a healthy way for him to process this. "Two wrongs don't make a right."

He straightened, standing tall and defensive. "And what about the countless number of wrongs they've done? Do they add up to a right? Because I've gotta tell ya, I'm having a hard time following the math you're doing here."

I went to him and took his face in my hands. My heart was utterly shattering for him, for all the ways he'd been made to feel like he didn't matter because to the two people he should've mattered the most to in this whole world, he simply didn't. None of that was going to change now, but how Shaw handled this situation would make all the difference in the world. "You're not that person, Shaw. You're not them. But if you don't do this, if you don't go to Detroit and face this, you'll never have closure and it will haunt you for the rest of your life."

Taking my wrist, he pulled my hand free, turning to kiss the palm so I'd know his caged anger had nothing to do with me.

"No offense, sweetness, but I don't need closure, and I certainly don't owe them a damn thing." Stepping away, he picked up his attaché, coming back to give me a chaste kiss. "I love you. See you at the office?"

"Yeah. I love you, too." Throwing in the towel on the battle in order to win the war, I let him leave.

This was it, that thing lurking in the shadows of our happiness. Shaw's past with his parents was like a plague on his soul, the spot on the proverbial wall. And if he didn't exorcise that plague, if he didn't scour that spot, the walls we'd built to keep our family happy and safe would never come clean.

As soon as he left, I pulled out my cellphone and dialed a soldier whom I knew fought on the side of good, a specialist in this field of battle.

Shaw

Fucking Jerry and Clarice dying on me like that. I had way too much to do to deal with their shit. I meant what I told Cassidy. I wasn't going. She'd tried to bring it back up at lunch, but I'd shut that topic down. My only concern was her, Abe, and making Striker the best sports agency it could be. Likewise, the phone call I'd gotten this morning was all but forgotten as I threw myself into my work and took care of business in plenty of time to make a prompt appearance at Dr. Sparling's office for our appointment.

When I'd entered his office, Jeremy was alone, customary cheesy smile in place. Today, he was all business in the front and party in the back with his mullet hairstyle. He was wearing canvas deck shoes without socks, a pair of white linen pants rolled up to bare his ankles, a matching sports coat with the sleeves pushed up past the elbows, and a baby-pink T-shirt underneath.

"Hey, Doc. Crockett and Tubbs called. They want their wardrobe back," I told him with a chuckle.

He looked down at himself, taking a minute to get the *Miami Vice* reference before returning the laugh. "Huh, I never even noticed. I'll just call it retro chic," he said with a wink.

Or about thirty years too late, I thought to myself. "Where's Cass?" I asked, surprised I'd beaten Miss Punctuality to our session.

"She won't be joining us today." He sat in his normal chair, smiling up at me.

"What do you mean, she won't be joining us? Is she okay?" I started to pull out my phone to call her, but Doc Sparling stopped me.

"No, no, no, she's fine," he assured me. "This was her idea. Please, take a seat."

I was confused as all get-out, but I found my spot on the couch and waited for him to get down to explaining what was up.

At my questioning look, he said, "Cassidy thought you might benefit from a little one-on-one with me today."

"Why's that?" I asked, though didn't I already know the answer to that one?

"Well," he began, crossing his legs. "She's filled me in on the dynamics of the relationship you have with your parents, and she's concerned about how it might be negatively impacting you as a whole."

I rolled my eyes because of course she was. Before the strides she and I had made lately, I might have been pissed about her telling my business like that. But I'd gotten used to being exposed as of late. Her intentions were good, although unnecessary. "It's not," I said, simply.

Jeremy leaned forward in that way he did that made me feel like he was getting into my space. "Shaw, you just got a phone call regarding your parents' well-being. Your father has passed away and your mother isn't far behind, yet you don't want to attend to the matter. It's a classic case of avoidance."

A short burst of humorless laughter came out of me. "So the therapist who's gone out of his way to *not* fit the stereotype is now getting clinical on me, huh?"

It occurred to me that I'd probably just proven his point by addressing the fact that he was changing his M.O. rather than calling bullshit on what he'd said. It must have occurred to him, too, because he frowned in this pity-filled way, choosing not to defend himself and instead charging forward with his analysis.

"You're avoiding dealing with this issue because it brings back unpleasant memories."

With one leg stretched out and an elbow on the armrest, I propped my head up with two fingers at my temple and my chin resting on my thumb. "No, I'm avoiding dealing with it because I give as much of a damn about them as they gave about me."

He wasn't going to be dissuaded. "Shaw, your past is affecting your present and will continue to affect your future until you face it. The relationship issues between you and Cassidy are due, in large part, to your issues with your parents. And they will persist until you gain some sort of closure."

How the hell did my parents kicking the bucket have anything to do with Cassidy and me? Besides, he was way off base. Cassidy and I were fine and dandy now.

"See, that's where you're wrong, Doc. Because Cassidy and I have resolved all of our issues."

"No, you haven't, not all of them. You've simply put a Band-Aid over the wound. But this isn't some knee scrape, Shaw. This is a severed artery. *Your* severed artery. And whether you realize it or not, it's affecting your relationship with Cassidy. Right now, you're bleeding out under the skin. If you don't stop it, if you don't repair the artery and restore the flow, you're going to have to keep putting Band-Aid after Band-Aid over that wound until eventually, you won't need Band-Aids anymore at all because your relationship will be dead."

"What the hell are you talking about, man? Fucking severed arteries, bleeding out, Band-Aids? I'm starting to think maybe I need to make a trip to the emergency room. You wanna call nine-one-one or should I?" I patted down my body, looking for the crimson pool that should've been staining my clothes and found none.

Talk about your graphic metaphors . . .

Dr. Sparling looked as frustrated as I'd ever seen him before. "Abandonment issues, *Shaw*." More clinical bullshit.

"I don't have abandonment issues, *Doc*," I said, mocking him, "because my parents were never there to abandon me in the first place."

"By not being there, they were abandoning you," he said, qualifying his assessment. "And you may not realize it, but you were doing the same thing to Cassidy and Abe."

"The apple doesn't fall far from the tree. That's what you're telling me?" My leg started to bounce and I could feel my blood pressure rise.

"No, I'm saying it's learned behavior. You weren't taught any differently."

I shrugged. "So I'll unlearn it."

"I wish it were that simple." He shook his head, saying, "Shaw, you're going to have to fix your issues with your parents or you're going to keep having issues with Cassidy. That's the bottom line."

"And the only way to do that is to go to Detroit and pull the fucking plug?"

"In a sense, yes," he said, sitting forward with urgency. "If you're angry with your mother and father, tell them you are. Tell them what you've become, who you've become, without their help or their love. Brag about yourself, about how you overcame the crappy hand you were dealt and won the jackpot with a woman and son who love you unconditionally."

"Kind of hard to do when they're dead, don't ya think?"

Jeremy chilled, relaxing once again. "Maybe the fact that they can't talk back is better. At least then, you won't have to listen to them giving you one bullshit excuse after another for why they weren't there for you."

Well, that threw me for a loop. The doc never used swear words in our sessions. In fact, he had always oozed wholesomeness— like a Boy-Scout-helping-an-old-lady-across-the-street kind of wholesomeness. But he was wrong again. With a shake of my head, I gave him the sad truth. "Bullshit excuses would take too much effort on their parts anyway. I don't think you understand how much of a shit they just don't give."

His shoulders sagged. "And that's sad. Very sad. But be that as it may, you still need to confront them."

"Why? It won't make a difference. Besides, even if I did decide to go to Detroit, Jerry is fucking dead and Clarice is on life support, so not only will they not be able to say anything back, but they won't be able to hear me either."

"And that's okay, too," Jeremy said, assuming he'd gained some ground. "Because this isn't for them, Shaw." He sat forward to look me in the eye. "It's for *you*. I know it sounds cliché, but the sooner you can get Jerry and Clarice's skeletons out of your closet and into the ground, the sooner you can fill the space they occupied with happier memories of the people in your life who do love you."

I sat there, quietly contemplating what he'd said. Maybe he and Cassidy were right. I'd gone through my life believing that chapter had been closed—hell, never even begun, for that matter. Now, I supposed, it might be possible that I'd just left it unfinished and skipped ahead, thinking it unimportant, only to find out it held the missing piece to a puzzle I couldn't solve without it.

"Shaw?"

"Hmm? Yeah," I told him, and then with an annoyed huff of defeat, "Fine. I'll go."

Jeremy sighed in relief. Evidently, he hadn't believed he'd succeed. I wouldn't have thought it either.

"But I'm only doing it because you and Cassidy will stay on my case, otherwise, and probably make me have to keep coming to see you every week."

"I'll try not to take that personally." He laughed. "Whatever helps me help you, I'll use it."

I had zero doubt about it. Jeremy Sparling, Katya Minkov, and Cassidy Whalen—masters of manipulation, those three. They knew how to get what they wanted, and it seemed at least Jeremy and Cassidy wanted me to confront the two people who'd brought me into this world and then fucked it up from the start. I was going to do it. For Cassidy and Abe, and maybe even myself. Whether it helped or hurt or had no effect at all on my current situation remained to be seen, but at least no one would be able to say I wasn't putting in my 110 percent toward this relationship.

CHAPTER 17

Shaw

The first-class flight from San Diego into Detroit was fine. The luxury limousine ride from the airport was comfortable. And the grand suite at the Westin Book Cadillac was, well, grand. But none of that mattered because I didn't feel fine, or comfortable, or even grand. I felt numb, cold, and like an entirely different person from an entirely different world, like while the skin I was wearing belonged to me, neither it nor I belonged here. Nonetheless, I was here, and I just wanted to get my "obligation" over with so I could get back to where I belonged.

When I arrived at the hospital, the hallways were crowded with people of various walks of life with their own reasons for being there. Wading through them as best I could, I stopped at the information desk to get directions to the morgue to identify the body of my sperm donor. The thirtysomething female behind the computer was sweet and beyond helpful, despite the chaos surrounding her. I supposed it was like this every day and she'd grown immune to it.

Deep into the belly of the hospital, I went, where it was freezing and in desperate need of more lighting, something a little softer than the harsh glare of the fluorescents they were using. Seeing the dead body the attendant had pulled out of the freaking wall gave me a case of the heebie-jeebies, but once the sheet was pulled back, I did my duty with a curt nod. It was definitely Jerry Matthews.

Looking down at his corpse was too much like looking into a mirror. This man couldn't have denied I was his son, no matter how much he'd probably wanted to. He was me, only gray and stiff with hard lines, too much scruff, unkempt hair, and deep wrinkles forged by his chosen lifestyle. Cause of death: a broken neck when he'd been ejected from the car after hitting a lamppost. He should've worn his seatbelt.

The next order of business was dealing with Clarice's situation. The hospital staff had blown my fucking phone up to make sure I was on my way. So much so that I was on the verge of blocking their number. They either needed the bed or the government medical benefits had refused to pay for another day.

Cassidy had placed her fair share of phone calls to my cell, as well, offering words of encouragement. Her concern was legit, but I also suspected she was making sure I hadn't chickened out.

While I was forced to deal with this bullshit, she was on her way to Maine to get our son. I should've been there with her. I should've been in Stonington, grabbing my little man up to toss him into the air and making myself sick on Abby's cookies instead of playing the Grim Reaper for two wayward souls. I wasn't even sure there was a God, but if he existed, I had to think he wasn't going to be very happy with those two.

An elevator ride and a couple of turns later, I was stepping through the threshold to Clarice Matthews's room. There were no vases of flowers—withered or alive—with cards wishing a speedy recovery on the designated shelves, no friends or relatives

pacing outside the door wringing their hands and anxiously awaiting word from the staff. There was nothing. Because my parents
had nothing and nobody. There was only me.

Moments after my arrival, a tall, lanky man dressed in tan kha-
kis and a blue button-up with a long white lab coat over it came
into the room. The blue stitching on the pen pocket gave him a
label, much like what a mother would stitch into her son's underwear. Not that my own mother had ever done any such thing.

"My name is Dr. Steven Kirschner, Mrs. Matthews's attending
physician," he said, tucking a clipboard under his arm to offer his
hand. "And you are?"

I shook his hand. "Shaw Matthews. Her son."

"Ah." He undocked the clipboard, clasping the edge of the
thing with both hands and holding it with his arms stretched
down his center, rocking back and then forward on his heels. "We
weren't sure whether you'd come."

"Neither was I," I answered honestly. "Tell me what I need to
know. And don't bother with all the medical jargon I'm not going
to understand."

He inhaled and exhaled a long breath as if preparing to say a
mouthful. "She suffered blunt force trauma to her chest, causing
irreparable damage to her heart and collapsing both lungs. There's
also a lot of swelling on the brain. Given her age, medical history,
and other injuries sustained during the accident, it's a miracle she
survived at all."

Yep, a mouthful. "So she's basically dead. Is that what you're
telling me?"

I couldn't tell if Dr. Kirschner was disturbed or relieved that I
wasn't tiptoeing around the bottom line. "What I'm telling you is
that the only thing keeping her alive is the machine. We need your
permission before we can end her suffering."

"She's suffering?" That caused something of a pang inside me. Though there was no love lost between my parents and me, I wouldn't wish suffering on any human being.

The doctor shifted on his feet again, no doubt struggling to find the right words to ease what he thought would be a loving son's emotional distress. "Perhaps that was the wrong choice of words. She can't exactly suffer if she isn't feeling anything at all. There is no chance of recovery. Leaving her on the machine is doing nothing but prolonging the inevitable."

"Is that the paperwork?" I asked with a nod toward his clip-board.

"Yes," he said with a grim nod. "But we can wait until—"

I grabbed it out of his hand, took the pen clipped to his pocket, and signed the damn thing on the dotted line. Handing it back to him, I didn't look him in the eye. I was sure he was confused as to why it had been so easy for me, but he didn't know me any better than the woman whose last, artificial breath I'd just signed away.

The doctor tucked the clipboard back under his arm. "I'm sorry for your loss, Mr. Matthews. I'll give you some time to say your goodbyes." And then he was gone, leaving me alone in a cold room with essentially the corpse of a woman who'd barely even acknowledged my existence.

Clarice Matthews. The woman who had birthed me. My mother. So why did I feel nothing at all as I looked down at her nearly lifeless body?

Her eyes were shut and there was a patch of gauze at her tem-ple, no doubt covering the stitches from her head wound. Her normally gaunt cheeks were swollen and bruised, and her bleached-blond hair—dark mixed with gray at the roots—obviously hadn't been dyed in a while. There were nicotine stains between the index and middle fingers of her left hand, and what part of her natural nail that showed through the pink chipped polish was a dingy yellow. She'd still been smoking. A mask was over her mouth with a tube attached to it that ran over her chest, off the bed, and connected to what I assumed was a respirator. If her lifeless appearance hadn't proven the doctor's fatal prognosis, the steady *beep, beep, beep* of the machines and the rhythmic rise and fall of her chest as oxygen was pumped into her lungs did.

Taking a seat in the chair placed by her bedside, I rested my arms on the bed rails and just looked at her. Perhaps I was searching for the words I was supposed to say to her that would set me free or give me closure or whatever. Either way, I hadn't a clue where to start. God, I was glad Abe would never have to go through this.

Reaching into my back pocket, I pulled out my wallet and opened it to retrieve the photo of Abe and Cassidy from between the plastic sleeve. "I had a little boy. His name is Abraham. Abe," I told her, tracing the outline of his chubby cheek. "Did you hear me? I said I'm a father. A real father, unlike Jerry."

I paused, suddenly realizing what Cassidy had been trying to tell me all along, what Dr. Sparling had just pointed out in our last session. There was more to my likeness to Jerry than just looks. "Well, maybe I don't spend as much time with Abe as I should, but I'm going to change that. Because he's the most precious thing to me on this earth."

I studied the picture, the tiny teeth that made his smile, the freckles that dotted his nose like his mother's, the haphazard way that red cape hung from his shoulders.

"He's into Superman and Batman and all those other superheroes. Most grandparents would know that about their grandchild, but you didn't even know he existed. Care to guess who his favorite hero is?" Of course I didn't get a response, didn't expect one. "Me. He thinks I can do anything. You thought I could do nothing."

I turned the picture toward Clarice's unresponsive face. "See this woman here?" I asked, pointing to Cassidy's image. "She's his mother. Her name is Cassidy, and she's the one who insisted I come here. I wasn't going to, you know, but she always somehow manages to get me to do things I don't want to do. She's strong that way. Strong enough to keep my ass in line, that's for sure. You've gotta respect a woman like that, right?"

Still no response. Not even an eye twitch.

"Yeah, well, you damn well better. She's a far better mother to our son than you ever were to me. She's amazing. And she loves me, though I don't really deserve her. You know, she was the first person in my entire life to ever love me. *You* were supposed to be that person. Did you ever? When the doctor pulled me from your womb and laid me in your arms, did you love me then? Because I know when Abe was born . . . God, I thought my heart was going to explode because no way in hell was my chest big enough to contain the kind of love I felt when I first saw that kid. Still today, I think I should probably be wearing some med-alert bracelet or whatever, just in case. Did you look down at me the same way?"

No response.

"Did you ever feel *anything* at all for me?"

Still nothing but silence. This woman who'd given birth to me would never respond to my questions. But she didn't need to because I already knew the answers. No, to all of the above.

I sat upright and returned the picture to my wallet before putting it back into my pocket. "You missed out," I told her. "I'm a good man and a great father, despite your absence in my life. Hell, maybe even because of it. And I will never be anything like you and Jerry. Not for one second will I take for granted the gift I've been given in Cassidy and Abe. Not like you did. Not ever again."

I stood, looking down at her weary face. "So goodbye, Mom. May God have more mercy on your soul than you had on your only child's."

I said nothing to the staff when I left, didn't even spare them a glance, though I could feel their stares on my back. My feet still felt heavy as I traversed my way through the labyrinth of halls, and I wasn't entirely sure that added heaviness wasn't causing an exceeding of the weight limit for the elevator when I rode it down to the first floor in silence.

The limousine pulled into the pickup zone when I reached the doors. Good. The driver would definitely earn a tip for not making me have to wait. So I didn't make him wait either. Waving off his offer to get the door for me, I jumped inside and slammed the thing shut. "Get me out of here," I told him.

"Where to, sir?" he asked, pulling away from the curb.

Home would've been ideal. Back to my real family. But that couldn't happen just yet, so I had some time to kill. "I want to go shopping," I told the driver.

The phone call from the hospital came just a short while after I'd gotten back inside my room. Clarice had passed, peacefully. Roger that. So then I spent the rest of the afternoon and into the evening making the arrangements for a quick double burial—because apparently, that was my responsibility, too—which would take place the next day. All the sooner for me to get the hell out of this shithole and back where I belonged.

I'd also hired a company to do something about all the crap my folks had hoarded in their humble abode because I was sure their slumlord would want to rent out the decrepit space as soon as possible. The moving company could keep it, auction it off, give it away—I didn't care so long as I didn't have to deal with it. There certainly weren't any cherished memories among the shit.

Nightfall came, and after scarfing down some room service, I scoured away the scum of the day, texted Cassidy an update, and then crashed, hard-core, before I even got a response from her.

A knock on my door the next morning was what woke me. I sat up, bleary-eyed, and stumbled toward the damn thing to go off on whatever cleaning person had ignored the *Do Not Disturb* sign I'd left hanging on the knob. But when I opened it, I was startled into the bright-eyed-bushy-tailed zone.

"Su'pwise!" my little man yelled from his mommy's hip with a huge smile and the excited clapping of splayed hands. A chubby ball of excitement launched into my arms to hug my neck tight.

Half asleep, I managed to catch it, hugging my son back to make up for all the ones I'd missed while he was away. "Oh, my God, what are you doing here?"

Abe giggled at my shocked expression, saying, "Your hair wooks funny, Daddy!"

I was sure it did, seeing as how I'd fallen asleep with it wet, though I normally wore it in a messy style anyway. Still, I smoothed it.

Cassidy popped up on her tiptoes and kissed me. "Sorry we woke you," she said, breezing past me and into the room. Had I been more awake, I would've taken the carry-on she was lugging over her shoulder.

"No, it's okay," I told her, croaky voice and all, as I shut us in and shuffled across the floor with my little boy in tow. "What are you doing here?" Abe was doing his best to wiggle out of my arms, so I sat him on his feet.

Before he could go tearing off into the other room of the suite, his mother grabbed him by the back of his shirt. "Hey, where do you think you're going, mister?"

"To pway," he said, like that should've been obvious.

"Mmm-hmm. More like going to find something to get into. Here." Sitting on the sofa, she reached into the bag and pulled out a couple of superheroes. "Take your dolls with you."

I hated it when she called them dolls. Boys didn't play with dolls; they played with action figures. Dolls, action figures, didn't matter. Abe still snatched them up and took off running.

"Cass, what are you doing here?" I asked again. Cozying up next to her on the couch, I seriously contemplated putting my head in her lap to fall back to sleep.

She drew her head back. "What kind of question is that? Your parents just died. Where else would I be?"

"I told you that you didn't have to come."

"I know you did, but Abe and I took a vote, and we won, so here we are," she said with a quick shrug and victorious smile.

I gave her a scornful look. "You should've spent more time with your family. I can handle this on my own."

She turned my head to face her, running her elegant fingers through my messy locks. "Shaw, *you* are our family, and families stick together through the good times and the bad. What you endure, so shall we. Because of that, because we have each other, we'll all be stronger as a unit and as individuals. You don't have to be on your own anymore. And you won't be . . . ever again."

I fucking loved my woman.

"Now," she said, shoving me toward the other end of the sofa and pushing up her sleeves. "What do you want me to do?"

Face planted against the sofa's arm, I groaned and then mumbled, "Nothing. It's all been handled."

"All of it?"

I nodded, my nose scrunching against the couch. "All of it. They'll be buried this afternoon, and then I'm off the hook."

"Funeral service?" she asked.

"No need."

"Graveside service?"

"Nope."

"Are you sure you're okay with that?"

With a disgruntled huff, I sat up. "I'm positive, sweetness."

"Okay. Well then, what are you going to wear to the cemetery?"

"Sweetness, no burial service," I said, emphasizing each syllable since she clearly hadn't heard me the first time.

She wasn't amused. "And that's fine, but we're still going to the grave site to make sure they've been laid to rest properly, Shaw. So stop your whining and get dressed."

Fine. I knew there was no use arguing with her. The woman was as persistent as a kid with a small bladder after guzzling a Super Gulp on a road trip. What I didn't tell her was that I had to be there anyway to sign the paperwork for the cemetery.

Golden Pond Cemetery wasn't anything special. In fact, there wasn't even a pond. But it was cheap and clean, and the business manager was easy to deal with. And they were fast. I'd sent Cassidy and Abe to grab some lunch while I got the paperwork done, and by the time they'd gotten back, Jerry and Clarice were already in the ground.

I'd insisted upon Cassidy and Abe waiting at the car as I went over to the plots to lay the flowers my tenacious woman had picked up while they were out. Abe didn't need to see the whole grave thing, and he was too young for me to explain who these people were in the first place. Perhaps I'd tell him when he got older and started asking questions. I didn't know what I'd say about them, but I still had some time to figure that out.

Jerry and Clarice were buried next to each other, pinned to each other's side in death as they had been in life. Placing the white lilies on their grave markers, I picked up a handful of dirt left over from the dig and tossed it on top of each mound. Of course it was wet, thanks to the burst of rain that had made a brief appearance, so now I was muddy. And that's when it occurred to me: though there was soil beneath my fingernails, my hands were clean.

I'd given them a better home in death than they'd given me in life. They didn't deserve it, but Cassidy was right: I wasn't anything like them. My conscience was clear and I'd paid respect where respect hadn't been earned. Suddenly, I felt weightless and everything became clearer, like a film of muck had been cleaned from my eyes. I supposed this was what closure felt like.

Relief. And a huge gasp of breath as the weight that had been pulling me under released its hold and I broke the surface of the water. The threat of drowning I'd been feeling despite the strides Cassidy and I had made was now gone.

There was nothing further left to say or do. So I turned my back on Jerry and Clarice Matthews and simply walked away.

Cassidy was standing next to Abe, who was sitting on the hood of the car. I couldn't take my eyes off them as I watched them play. Cassidy had this glow about her, something angelic that I supposed every mother should have. A glow that Clarice never did. And Abe was happy. Truly happy. He would never feel like a burden. He would never feel like he was on his own. And he would never doubt what it feels like to love and be loved.

A grin I couldn't help tugged at the corner of my mouth when

Cassidy tickled our son's ribs and I heard him laugh from somewhere deep inside his belly. Closer and closer they got, faster than they should have. It was then that I felt the first clue that my breaths were coming quick and hard, my arms and legs pumping, the horizon before me jumping up and down with a jarring motion. I couldn't take my eyes off my family to verify what I already knew: I was running. I'd walked away from my past to run toward my future.

I slowed by the time I reached the car, coming to a stop before them and smiling even though Cassidy looked somber, as you'd expect one to be for another who'd just left his parents' grave site. She picked up our son and settled him on her hip. "Hey. Are you okay?"

I kissed Abe on the forehead with a loud *smack*. "Yep! I just had a thought," I told her.

"Uh-oh," she said, wary.

But that didn't stop me from forging ahead, wagging a finger at her as I said, "I think it's time you made an honest man out of me."

She hiked Abe up farther on her hip with a confused chortle. "What are you talking about?"

"I'm talking about you getting the milk for free for long enough. It's time you bought the cow."

She laughed, shaking her head. "You're not making any sense."

"Yeah? You need me to be clearer?" I leaned in, whispering into her ear so that Abe couldn't hear me. "You . . . fucking my brains out without any sort of commitment. It's gotta stop. If you like it, then you better put a ring on it."

Cassidy drew back, an amused sort of confusion about her. "Are you saying what I think you're saying?"

"Excuse me, little man. Daddy's got something to do." I slipped my hands under Abe's arms, removing him from his mommy's hip and then sitting him on the hood of the car beside her.

When I dropped to one knee, Cassidy's hands flew to her mouth, and then I pulled the little black box I'd picked up the afternoon before from my pocket. Opening it, I gave her a moment to inspect the antique diamond ring inside. Big, fat teardrops welled in her eyes as she looked down at my token of forever.

With shaking hands, a trembling voice, and no clue what I'd say, I let go and gave my heart the lead. "I don't think it comes as much of a surprise when I say that with the exception of our son, I have never loved anyone in my entire life. Maybe that's because no one had ever loved me. Until you. You were my first, you are my only, and you will be my always . . . till death do us motherfucking part."

She laughed through her tears, not even bothering to scold me for using foul language in front of Abe.

"You are my partner in business, you are my partner in parenting, and you are my partner in the bedroom, so it only makes sense for you to be my partner in every other way. What do you say, sweetness? Will you marry me?"

She shrugged. "Yeah, sure. I guess I can do that."

Abe giggled and then started clapping. "Yay!"

"Well, don't do me any favors," I told her, getting off my knee to square off with the woman I'd poured out my heart to, just to get a "Yeah, sure, whatever" in return.

Before I could really let her have it, Cassidy fisted my shirt and yanked me forward. "Shut up, Shaw. . . . You had me at 'till death do us motherfucking part.'"

Her lips crashed into mine with a kiss that was far too hot for a giggling Abe to witness, but I wasn't about to stop her. Wrapping her up, I crushed her against me with an intensity that matched our kiss, desperate to hold on to her and never let go. Because without Cassidy Whalen, there was nothing left to hold on to anyway.

She was the one who finally had to break the kiss, but I still clutched her to me, not ready just yet to let anything more than her sweet breaths come between us and this moment. Her forehead rested against mine, so that all I could see was the sexy little smirk she wore on those delicious lips. "I knew I'd eventually wear you down, Matthews."

"Oh, you did, did you?" My cheeks hurt and my heart was about to burst out of my chest, but I wasn't about to let her half-ass this any more than she'd ever let me half-ass anything I'd done since the day we'd met. "So, was that supposed to pass as a yes, Whalen?"

"Hmm," Cassidy hummed in contemplation, and then turned toward Abe. "What do you think, Abey Baby? Should Mommy marry Daddy?"

The smile on my little man's face was big enough to split the heavens and break my heart in two at the same time. He nodded emphatically, his little head practically bouncing off his shoulders with his joyful giggle.

"Well, there you have it," Cassidy said when she turned back to me. Her expression grew serious, her eyes full of every wonder in the world as she gazed into mine. Time stood still for the long moment she regarded me, her fingers lovingly playing with the hair at the back of my neck in contemplation. And then she sighed. "I would love nothing more than to be your wife, Shaw Matthews. Of course I'll marry you."

The birds in the trees chirped a little louder, the breeze across my skin felt a little warmer, the sun grew a little brighter, and the colors of the world around us became a little richer. All of that cliché stuff happened in the span of the five seconds it had taken Cassidy to make me the happiest man on earth, and I realized that was because until this moment, I'd been walking around with a veil over my eyes, seeing nothing more than a blurred version of a reality that was mine for the taking if only I'd reach out and grab ahold of it. So I did. And I was never letting it go.

EPILOGUE

Cassidy

Stonington, Maine, was not only my hometown, but it was also the place where Shaw and I had finally realized our feelings for each other ventured beyond the realm of lust and into the mystical kingdom of love. We'd conceived our first child there, weathered a hurricane of epic proportions, and Shaw had found his surrogate family, my family. So it only made sense that it was where we should make it all official with a fairy-tale wedding. Our fairy-tale wedding, which meant it was every bit as conventional as our relationship had been from the beginning, in that it wasn't conventional in the least.

About a year after the likewise-unconventional proposal of marriage from Shaw, our knot had been tied. It had been a beautiful wedding out on the lawn of the Whalen House at night, with twinkling lights strung up in the trees, antique lanterns dangling from iron rods, and floating paper candles littering the calm water of the bay. A mild ocean breeze kept the summer night light and airy, only adding to the ambience of the most perfect day of my life.

I'd walked the aisle to the tune of Bruno Mars's "Marry You," against Ma's wish for the traditional wedding march, and more comfortable with my body now, I'd worn a simple strapless beach dress with a sweetheart neckline that showed off my bust and a breezy gauze skirt that ended above the knee. And yes, it was white, also against Ma's wishes. Abe had been the ring bearer, wearing a cute little suspender-shorts suit set of khaki seersucker with a hat and tie to match and his Superman cape proudly blowing in the wind. Da had walked me down the aisle, looking dapper in his cream-colored suit and tie, the first time I'd ever seen him in one. And Shaw had been waiting for me at the end in a white linen shirt—unbuttoned at the top to show off a glimpse of his toned chest—and matching pants. But all I'd seen was his smile, and the brief darting of his tongue across his bottom lip and the adjustment of the front of his pants when he saw me, which our guests seemed to have missed because they were looking at me.

Everyone we loved and cared for was present, friends and colleagues alike. The whole town of Stonington was booked solid, with our nearest and dearest staying at the Whalen House with us, of course. It was all hands on deck. Ma was a busy bee, and that was exactly how she liked it. Abby, when she wasn't spoiling Shaw and Abe rotten, had been a tremendous help as usual. Casey and Mia had pitched in to help keep everyone comfortable, and many of the townspeople had lent a helping hand to get all of the preparations in place.

The *I do*'s were said, because he did and I did, and the whole legal part of our binding had gone off without a hitch or even a misfire from Da's shotgun. Moments after the wedding—and a toe-curling kiss to seal the deal—we were introduced to the world as Mr. and Mrs. Shaw Matthews. Well, I was going to keep my last name since I was the only remaining Whalen to carry it on, but Shaw was okay with that.

Sitting at the bride and groom's table with our closest friends, I looked around at all our loved ones and smiled. I couldn't help but feel an amazing sense of pride and completion, like we'd all come full circle.

The Ingrams—Marcel, Camille, and Vale—had even made the long trek from their new home in Texas to share in our happiness. Marcel had become Shaw's number one. Fitting, since he'd also gone number one in the draft, signing a very generous contract with Dallas, thanks to Shaw.

Sasha had given birth to a beautiful little girl, whom they'd named Holly. Landon was wrapped so tight around his little princess's finger, even though she was only four months old, that it melted my heart every time I saw the quiet soldier of war with her. Though he was never ostentatious about it, everyone within a mile of the two most important females in his world could feel Landon's protectiveness. No one would ever get within distance to cause them any harm, and if someone did, I could imagine a quick snap of the neck, Liam Neeson–style.

Denver and Quinn had adopted a little girl from Guatemala, Rocklynn, who had just reached the terrible threes. Though it had been a tradition in Denver's family to name their children after a city in their home state of Colorado, Rocklynn had been a compromise. Quinn had refused to name her Rock Ford Rockford. Denver had still given her the nickname he'd wanted, Rocky, which was fitting because she was a little rambunctious tomboy, always climbing her quarterback father for a rough-and-tumble wrestling match.

And then there were Chaz and Demi. God, I felt horrible for them. They'd wanted a baby of their own so bad, but month after month, the tests had come up negative. The stress levels had been high, and all of that getting their hopes up only to have them dashed had taken a toll on their relationship. So they'd given up, because having a child isn't worth losing the one you love in the process.

It had to have been especially hard for them to see Mia's belly, swollen with child, and the way Casey rubbed on it every chance he got, cooing to his unborn baby. Casey and Mia were a match made in heaven, and it warmed my heart to see my best friend so happy and in love. Casey had never been mine and I had never been his, we'd simply been keeping each other company until our soulmates arrived.

Wade and Monty were living out their dream retirements without a care in the world now that Shaw and I had taken over things with Striker Sports Entertainment. He and I worked together like a well-oiled piece of machinery, juggling the business end of things with clients and employees while also being the best parents we could be.

Abe had been sleeping on his own every single night since the day we'd returned from Detroit. I was so incredibly proud of him. Always eager to please his parents, he'd taken the change with ease. Especially after Shaw had explained to him that it was his duty to help him transition from a little boy into a little man, and little men did not sleep with their mommies. Abe had this whole hero-worship thing for his daddy, so whatever he said was like martial law. I was sure it had helped that Daddy was now reading to him every night.

Yes, Shaw was an outstanding father, always attentive, always present. His family came before anything and everything now. In fact, if I really added things up, I bet he spent more time with Abe than even I did.

Things weren't perfect between us. Every couple has their issues, and given the amount of passion Shaw and I put into every-thing we did, there was no way to avoid a scuffle here and there. We were still seeing our relationship coach, Dr. Jeremy Sparling, to keep things on an even keel, though we'd cut back the appoint-ments to once a month.

As for our sex life . . . I smirked to myself. Yeah, no issues in that department. Shaw always, *always* made sure I was well satis-fied, which wasn't to say there weren't times when he got his and I didn't, or that I got mine and he didn't. It was a game we liked to play. Being denied was a torture well worth getting even for in the end, and the buildup to taking what had been denied was a form of foreplay we'd come to really enjoy.

Dr. Katya Minkov had done her duty in reigniting the fizzling flame into an all-out inferno. We owed her a lot. In fact, in the morning, we were going to visit her for a long overdue vacation/honeymoon. I could hardly wait to see what she'd have in store for us. Even if everything about Katya, including the location of her establishment, hadn't been so hush-hush, we'd still continue to lie to our friends and family about where we were honeymoon-ing. Some things were better kept between couples, and this was our own dirty little secret.

"Ouch! You little stinker!" Sasha laughed down at a nursing Holly nuzzling her breast.

The ever-protective daddy jumped to attention, not that he'd ever relaxed his guard. "What's wrong?"

"Nothing. She just has a tight suction," Sasha said, easing his worry.

"I'm glad I didn't have to breast-feed," Quinn commented, as if that were ever a possibility. "Rocky! Stop that!" His voice was low so as not to alert the whole list of guests to his tomboy daughter's social faux pas of lifting the skirt of her pretty pink dress over her head. Rocky only giggled in response, dancing around in a circle to show off the cute bloomers she wore beneath. Denver whirled in to save the day, sweeping his baby girl off her feet to place them on his own for a daddy-daughter dance.

Mia's hand flew to her chest as she looked on at them. "Oh, my God! That's adorable! I wish we were having a little girl." Casey and Mia had learned they were having a boy, news that Casey was very happy to hear because now he'd have a son of his own to pass down his family's legacy.

Quinn exhaled a frazzled breath and sunk into his chair. "Take that one."

"Quinn!" Demi yelled at him because of course she'd be sensitive to someone offering to give his child away when she couldn't have one.

"What? Oh, I don't *mean* it. I'm just saying she's a handful, is all. I need some R-and-R from my little R-and-R." He laughed at his own play on Rocklynn's initials. "I'm constantly chasing her around, and she always wants to wrestle, thanks to my big brute of a husband," he said, waving toward Denver. "I blame him. He gets her all riled up, and then I'm the one who has to play the bad guy. She's going to hate me."

"No, she isn't." I patted his hand, doing my best to reassure him. "They call it the terrible twos for a reason."

"She's three," he corrected.

"And it'll last until she's four or five, but she will grow out of it. And if she doesn't, put her in jujitsu classes or something. Mixed martial arts as a sport is growing in popularity more and more every day. We've even signed a few of those athletes at Striker."

"Oh, hell. Look at me complaining about my baby and being

insensitive," he said, frowning across the way at Demi. "I'm sorry, Demi."

"Huh?" Demi's head popped up, her concentration on fiddling with the stem of her champagne flute broken.

Her very full champagne flute. I furrowed my brow in contemplation. Demi could keep up with even my da when it came to kicking them back, but I couldn't recall her asking for any refills.

Chaz leaned over her shoulder, his hand disappearing beneath the table and moving back and forth. "You good, little mama?" he said under his breath, but she was beside me, so I heard him loud and clear.

With a loud gasp, I sat back. "Say it right now, Demi Renée!"

"Say what?" she asked, looking around when she saw we'd drawn the attention of all our friends.

"You know what!"

"Cass, you're making a scene," she said under her breath.

"And it's going to get even bigger if you don't spill! You haven't touched that champagne, and I heard and saw what Chaz just said and did."

Quinn sat forward, eyes wide with excitement though he didn't know what was happening. "What? What?"

Sasha popped Holly off her boob and handed her over to Landon. "Demi, what aren't you telling us?"

"Just tell 'em," Chaz prodded her.

"No! It's Cassidy and Shaw's big day," she said out the corner of her mouth to him. Yep, I could still hear them.

"Say it, or I will," I warned her.

"Okay, fine! I'm pregnant!"

Sasha and Quinn gasped much like I had when I'd figured it out. "Why didn't you tell me!" Sasha yelled at her.

"Because we wanted to make sure everything was going to go

okay with the pregnancy first, and by the time we were sure, it was time for Cass and Shaw's wedding, so I didn't want it to seem like I was trying to trample all over that."

"Shut up!" I screeched. "This is the best wedding gift ever!"

I hugged her, hard, and then backed off, worried that I might somehow cause something to go wrong if I didn't.

"How far along are you?" Quinn asked.

"Twelve weeks, and everything looks very normal and healthy. I twisted the doc's arm until he agreed to give us two ultrasounds to be sure."

Knowing Demi, she probably meant that literally.

"Well, congratulations!" I squealed, excited for two of our very best friends. After all the heartache they'd endured they were finally going to get to have their little bundle of joy.

I scanned the room, finding my Abey Baby at his mimi and pop-pop's table, while the woman he was named after, Abby, was feeding him full of cake and cookies. Laughing to myself, I shook my head because, hey, all that sugar-induced hyperactivity was going to be her problem for the night.

"Ladies and gentlemen, may I have your attention?" the MC boomed. "Please clear the floor for the bride and groom's first dance."

I was caught off guard when Michael Jackson's duet with Justin Timberlake, "Love Never Felt So Good," began. Where I had been in charge of choosing our wedding song, Shaw had been in charge of the one for our first dance.

I shook my head at him when he stood and offered his hand. "I can't dance to this, Shaw." I laughed.

"You can with me in the lead. You still haven't learned that sometimes it's okay to follow, woman?" A playful smirk of challenge graced his gorgeous lips.

Challenge accepted, I stood, allowing him to guide me out onto the dance floor. Once we'd found our place with one of my hands in his, another on his shoulder, and his other on my waist, I told him, "I will follow you anywhere." And then, *whoosh,* I was swept off my feet.

Shaw twirled me round and round in long strides, his maneuvers so graceful that I felt as if my feet never touched the ground until finally we stopped, and I was forced to lift one foot into the air when he took me in for a deep dip. The town of Stonington erupted into applause, and if I hadn't been holding so tight to him while dangling so precariously close to the ground beneath me, I might have done some clapping of my own.

The man of the hour brought me back upright, and before I had the chance to regain my bearings, his lips were on mine for a scorching kiss that left nothing to the imagination as to how we'd be spending our honeymoon night. Many *aww*'s and wolf whistles later, I was laughing up at him, my cheeks frozen from the enormous smile I couldn't quite get under control. But who needed control when a man like Shaw Matthews was holding you with strong arms and twirling you around and around so much that everything else became a blur?

Standing there with him, quite drunk on love, the rest of the world whizzed by in an attempt to catch up with us. Eventually, it did, but though my equilibrium had returned, Shaw still held me tight. Swaying back and forth to a slow dance despite the upbeat tempo, we looked into each other's eyes.

"Are you happy, husband?"

"Very happy and extremely anxious to get you back to our room and out of that dress. How about you, wife?"

I would've blushed and maybe even looked around to be sure my da or our son hadn't overheard him, but I'd stopped worrying about that sort of thing a year ago, thanks to the man before me and a naughty therapist, who wasn't a therapist at all, named Katya Minkov. "I don't ever want to be anywhere other than in your arms . . . *naked*," I tacked on.

"Let's go now." He pulled away to drag me along behind him.

Luckily, I was able to stop him with a hard tug on his arm. "No! Ma would kill us!"

Shaw took me into his arms again, looking down at me with a mischievous grin. "Then I would die a happy, very *satisfied* man." He did this sexy wink thing that made me go weak in the knees.

Canting my head to the side, I was serious when I asked, "If you die first, promise you'll come back to haunt me? Because if you don't, I know I won't be far behind you."

"Sweetness . . ." He paused, seemingly not able to speak as he swallowed thickly and then shook his head. "Even if I'm not here in the flesh, my soul will forever be tethered to yours. Because that's where my home is. *You* are my home."

I might have swooned a little bit with that, but Shaw was there to catch me. Just like he always would be because he was my hero.

The kiss that followed his declaration made me feel like Shaw had sprouted wings to whisk me away to a place that was high above the noise and commotion of the party. Behind my closed eyes, we were floating among a sea of stars where we were the moon, the Earth was our world, and the sun was the love we shared that kept it all moving in perfect synchronicity. When his lips pulled away, I opened my eyes to see our feet were firmly planted on the ground, but all those stars were still present in the deep blue galaxy staring back at me.

This was what happiness and contentment felt like, and Shaw felt it, too.

"Tell me," I told him.

Shaw smiled down at me and my heart skipped a beat. He was such a beautiful man. "I am so in love with you," he said, and I felt and saw the truth of his words.

I sighed, full of contentment. "And yet, it's still not as much as I'm in love with you."

"Respectfully, Mrs. Matthews, I disagree. You forget you rescued me," he countered.

"And you, Mr. Matthews, forget you rescued me from myself."

"Draw?" he offered, and I accepted with a nod.

The whole world melted away again when he pulled me in closer. Resting my cheek on his chest, I let him guide me along with no thought as to my next move. His heartbeat was the music I danced to, his scent was my comfort, and his arms were the cocoon of my everything because, right here and right now, nothing else mattered.

We were where we needed to be. Our son was where he needed to be. Our friends and family were where they needed to be.

And so there was nothing left for us to do, but to live happily ever after.

ACKNOWLEDGMENTS

I have never written a book as fast as I wrote *Coming Clean*. I believe that's because the inferno of this fictional tale began with a spark of reality. Every great love story must not only be forged in white-hot fire, it must somehow keep feeding oxygen to the flame, or else burn out completely. I had lots of inspiration to draw from while spinning this yarn, but the contributions from various people still had a huge impact. This is where I get to thank them.

First, to my person, Patricia Dechant. My best friend and yet she still hasn't read any of the books in this series. What gives? I'll tell ya. She hasn't read any of the books in this series because every single morning, as I sit on my front porch with my first cup of coffee of the day, she's on the phone with me, listening to me ramble on and on about what I wrote the day before, what I plan to write that day, and every twist and turn this story has taken and will take before all is said and done. There's no need to read a book when you've been force-fed all the details, and then some. Thank you, Trish, for enduring my crazy, for all the *mm-hmm*'s and *uh-uh*'s, and for blocking off that part of your day for all me, all the time. You're a real trouper, and I'd do it for you. You know, when we're finished with "all me, all the time." *wink*

Huge thanks to Maureen Morgan, Melanie Edwards, and Janell Ramos! Each of you has things going on in your own world, yet you always take the time to be invested in not only my writing but also my personal life. You are my anchors, my sounding boards, my biggest cheerleaders, and my very best friends. Love you. Mean it.

I still can't believe how lucky I am to have scored my very remarkable agent, Alexandra Machinist, and my extraordinary editor, Shauna Summers. Though *agent* and *editor* seem like such blasé words to describe what you do because you truly make dreams come true. Thank you for believing in the Monkey Business Trio and me.

And last, but nowhere near least, I want to thank *you*, the reader. I've said it before, and I'll say it until the cows come home . . . your support makes all the difference in the world. A writer can put pen to paper, but without anyone to read the words, the tale does not truly exist. Thank you for giving my characters life, for granting them access to your imagination, and for indulging their need for their story to be told.

ABOUT THE AUTHOR

C. L. PARKER is a romance author who writes stories that sizzle. She's a small-town girl with big-city dreams and enough tenacity to see them come to fruition.

Since she's been the outgoing sort all her life—which translates to "she just wouldn't shut the hell up"—it's no wonder Parker eventually turned to writing as a way to let her voice, and those of the people living inside her head, be heard. She loves hard, laughs until it hurts, and lives like there's no tomorrow. In her world, everything truly does happen for a reason.

clparkerofficial.com
Facebook.com/CLParkerOfficial
@theclparker

ABOUT THE TYPE

This book was set in Galliard, a typeface designed in 1978 by Matthew Carter (b. 1937) for the Mergenthaler Linotype Company. Galliard is based on the sixteenth-century typefaces of Robert Granjon (1513–89).